NEVER GO BACK

Robert Goddard

BANTAM PRESS

LONDON · TORONTO · SYDNEY · AUCKLAND · JOHANNESBURG

TRANSWORLD PUBLISHERS
61–63 Uxbridge Road, London W5 5SA
a division of The Random House Group Ltd

RANDOM HOUSE AUSTRALIA (PTY) LTD
20 Alfred Street, Milsons Point, Sydney,
New South Wales 2061, Australia

RANDOM HOUSE NEW ZEALAND LTD
18 Poland Road, Glenfield, Auckland 10, New Zealand

RANDOM HOUSE SOUTH AFRICA (PTY) LTD
Isle of Houghton, Corner of Boundary Road & Carse O'Gowrie,
Houghton 2198, South Africa

Published 2006 by Bantam Press
a division of Transworld Publishers

A catalogue record for this book is available from the British Library.
ISBN 9780593053652 (cased) (from Jan 2007)
ISBN 0593053656 (cased)
ISBN 9780593053669 (tpb) (from Jan 2007)
ISBN 0593053664 (tpb)

Typeset in 11½/14pt Times by
Kestrel Data, Exeter, Devon.

Printed in Great Britain by
Clays Ltd, St Ives plc.

1 3 5 7 9 10 8 6 4 2

Papers used by Transworld Publishers are natural, recyclable products made
from wood grown in sustainable forests. The manufacturing processes
conform to the environmental regulations of the country of origin.

In memory of Daisy Taylor,
a dear and kind friend

ONE

If he had flown back with Donna, of course, it would have been all right. If her flight had been delayed by a couple of hours, it would have been enough. If he had simply turned right instead of left coming out of the cemetery, he would probably have got away with it.

But it was not all right; it was not enough: he did not get away with it. In the end, the ifs and therefores amounted to nothing. Fate had set a trap for him that day. And he walked obligingly and unwittingly straight into it.

Thus did a decade of good fortune for Harry Barnett come to an end without him even realizing it. Marriage and fatherhood had proved during those years to be the sweetest of surprises. He regretted coming to them so late, but the circumstances that had brought Donna and hence their daughter Daisy into his life made the delay inevitable. He had never been one to dwell on missed opportunities. The present – and their future as a family – were his to enjoy.

The recent death of his mother had failed to puncture his contentment. A swift and gentle exit at the age of ninety-three was no cause for anguish. Her race had been run to a dignified finish.

Harry's links with his birthplace had effectively died with her. He had returned to Swindon to arrange her funeral and to clear out the house she had lived in for more than seventy years. The Council would want to put another tenant in as soon as possible. The fact that 37 Falmouth Street held so much of Harry's past could not stand in their way. Nor would he have wanted it to. It was time to move on.

That morning, Donna had flown back to Seattle, where Daisy had been staying with her grandparents. Mother and daughter would drive home to Vancouver tomorrow. Harry planned to join them in a week or so, when he had disposed of his mother's clothes, crockery and furniture. It was not a task he was looking forward to. But it had to be done. And there was no-one to do it but him. Such was the lot of an only child.

Seeing off Donna at Heathrow and travelling back alone to Swindon had left Harry feeling sorry for himself, however. He was in no mood to begin emptying cupboards and filling bin-bags. He walked away from the station past the boundary wall of the former Great Western Railway works, then crossed the park and made his way up to Radnor Street, where his old primary school, now converted into offices, stood opposite the entrance to the cemetery.

For the first time in Harry's memory, the gravestone commemorating his father, Stanley Barnett, killed in an accident in the GWR locomotive-erecting shop when Harry was three, no longer stood in its familiar place near the highest point of the cemetery. It had been removed to have the name Ivy Barnett added at long last to the inscription. Harry stood for a few minutes by the flower-strewn mound of earth that marked the spot where his mother's coffin had been lowered in on top of his father's two days ago. He breathed the clear spring air and gazed towards the flat horizon. Then he turned and slowly walked away.

Leaving the cemetery on the far side, he seriously considered making for the Beehive, his local in those distant days when he had been a Swindon householder in his own right and co-proprietor of Barnchase Motors. But he reckoned a descent into beery nostalgia would not be a good start to a week of solitude and toil, so he headed downhill instead to

8

the market hall, where he bought a couple of lamb chops for his supper before returning to Falmouth Street.

It was a mild April afternoon of watery sunshine and warbling birdsong. Even the office blocks of downtown Swindon contrived to appear, if not attractive, then at least inoffensive in the restful light. The Railway Village was quiet and tranquil, a condition the average age of its residents generally guaranteed. Turning his back nobly on the beckoningly bright yellow frontage of the Glue Pot – or at any rate deciding he should put the lamb chops in the fridge before allowing himself a swift one – Harry crossed Emlyn Square and started along Falmouth Street.

He saw the two men ahead of him before he realized it was his mother's door they were standing at. They were about his own age, which he would once have described as old, but, now he had attained it, seemed merely a bemusingly high number. One was short and tubby, anoraked, tracksuited and baseball-capped. The other, though scarcely much taller, was thinner, his clothes shabby and old-fashioned – beltless raincoat, crumpled trousers, laced shoes in need of a polish. He had a full head of white, tousled hair, a beak-nosed, bony face and a put-upon stoop. His companion looked contrastingly at ease with himself, staring at the unanswered door of number 37 with his hands thrust idly into his anorak pockets, sunlight flashing on his glasses in time to the gum-chewing motion of his well-padded jaw. They were debating something in a desultory fashion, or so a shrug of his shoulders suggested. A battered leather suitcase and a smarter, newer holdall stood beside them on the path. Harry did not recognize them, nor could he guess what they wanted. Whatever it was, though, he felt certain they had not come to see him.

Then the thinner of the two spotted him and touched the other's arm. A word passed between them. They turned and looked at Harry. As they did so, he stopped. And everything else stopped too, even the chewing of the gum.

9

'Ossie?' the fat one said after a moment of silence and immobility. 'That's you, isn't it?'

No-one had called Harry Ossie since his National Service days, which had ended fifty years ago and been largely forgotten by him for almost as long. While his brain sent a none too nimble search party off in quest of memories that might explain this turn of events, he opened his mouth to speak – but found nothing to say.

'It's Jabber. And Crooked.'

The words lassoed Harry's scrambling thoughts and wound them in. Jabber; and Crooked: the nicknames of two of his comrades from the strangest and most memorable episode of his spell in uniform. Mervyn Lloyd, dubbed 'Jabber' on account of his talkative nature; and Peter Askew, whose sobriquet 'Crooked' counted as a salutary example of National Service wit. For Harry's part, 'Ossie' was a reference to his middle name, Mosley, inflicted on him by his father in tribute to none other than Oswald Mosley himself, much to Harry's lifelong chagrin.

'Don't you recognize us?'

Technically, the answer was 'Just about'. The years had wrought their changes with a heavy hand. Lloyd's Welsh lilt survived, but his spry figure had not. If he had denied being Mervyn Lloyd, Harry would not have argued. Askew meanwhile had been bleached and bent by time, like some potted plant left outdoors through too many winters.

'Bloody hell,' said Harry at last. 'It really is you two.'

'Good to see you, Harry,' said Askew, who had never been one of the most assiduous deployers of nicknames, perhaps because he resented his own.

'Well, it's . . . good to see you.' Harry shook them both by the hand. 'But . . .'

'You look surprised,' said Lloyd.

'I am.'

'Didn't you get Danger's letter?'

Johnny Dangerfield was evidently a party to whatever was going on as well. It had to be some kind of reunion to mark

10

the fiftieth anniversary of their demob. Harry could think of no other explanation, though left to him the anniversary would have been allowed to pass unmarked. 'I've had no letter,' he said, frowning in puzzlement.

'You must have. This is the address Danger gave us.'

'I haven't lived here in years, lads. Decades, actually. It's my mother's house. She died recently. I'm only over to clear the place out.'

'We struck lucky, then, didn't we, Crooked?' Lloyd grinned. 'Danger asked us to drop by on the off chance, Ossie, seeing as we were both coming this way.'

'Sorry to hear about your mother, Harry,' said Askew.

'Thanks, Peter.'

'Where are you over from, then?' asked Lloyd.

'Canada.'

'All right for some. How'd you end up there?'

'It's a long story.'

'I'll bet. When d'you go back, then?'

'A week or so.'

'Perfect. How d'you fancy a couple of days north of the border?'

'The border?'

'Scotland, Ossie. Johnny's arranged for us to get together at Kilveen Castle this very weekend.'

'You're joking.'

'No. All the old crew. Well, those who are still in the land of the living. Those he's been able to track down. We'd given up on you.'

'My mother must have forgotten to forward the letter,' Harry mused. 'Or else it went astray.'

'Well, you know what the post is like these days. But never mind.' Lloyd clapped Harry heavily on the shoulder. 'We've found you now.'

TWO

The road that led young Harry Barnett to Kilveen Castle in March 1955 began at Swindon Labour Exchange two years previously, when he passed a perfunctory National Service medical and asked to enlist in the RAF, commonly believed to be a softer option than either the Army or the Navy. The half a dozen weekends he had spent gooning around in the RAF Reserves out at Wroughton swung it for him and six weeks later his third-class rail warrant to RAF Padgate dropped through the letterbox of 37 Falmouth Street.

After the trauma of basic training, he was despatched to Stafford, where his suspended career as a filing clerk in Swindon Borough Council was regarded as suitable grounding for work in the stores. There was to be no soaring across the sky for Aircraftman Barnett, for all his boyhood fantasies of Battle of Britain derring-do. His unit had its feet firmly on the ground.

It was amidst RAF Stafford's cavernous repositories of the equipment and effects of disbanded wartime squadrons that Harry met his future business partner, Barry Chipchase. Though the same age as Harry, Chipchase had acquired from somewhere a maturity beyond his years, one feature of which was his unerring eye for the main chance. The moment when Barnchase Motors collapsed under the strain of his wheeler-dealing and Harry finally saw his friend for what he was lay nearly twenty years ahead of them. For the present, Harry

12

was happy to follow Chipchase's lead where the pursuit of female company and a fast buck were concerned. What could have been a tedious sojourn in the Midlands became under Chipchase's tutelage an education for Harry in the wilier ways of the world.

At first Chipchase funded his activities through straight-forward black marketeering, but the demise of rationing forced him to resort to other methods of turning a profit. During 1954, he reigned supreme as the station's fixer, trading everything from weekend passes to cushy postings and, beyond the gate, more or less anything that had not been bolted down. Harry was his trusted assistant at the outset and, by the end, his loyal partner.

That end came early in 1955, when, with only a few months left to serve, Chipchase overreached himself. Siphoning off fuel from the station tank to sell to local farmers and smuggling out surplus mess furniture to flog round the pubs of Stafford was not enough for him. He wanted to go one better – and bigger. The stores held several collections of silver belonging to squadrons unlikely to be re-formed short of a Third World War. Much of it, Chipchase calculated, would never be missed and could be put to better use providing him and Harry with what he called 'demob dosh' – a nest egg for a fast and loose future on civvy street.

The plan foundered, as such plans often do, on bad luck. When Air Chief Marshal Bradshaw saw a silver salver bearing the insignia of a squadron he had once commanded for sale in a shop in Birmingham, he initiated an inquiry that led the RAF Police by a winding route to the barrack-door in Stafford of Aircraftmen Barnett and Chipchase. The game was up.

It was useless for Chipchase to protest to Harry that the deal he had struck with a certain nameless individual had been based on melting down the silver, not selling on items intact. He should have realized he was doing business with people he could not trust. It was a point Harry had ample opportunity to expand upon during the weeks spent in the guardroom cells awaiting court martial. The prospect, as the witless flight lieutenant appointed to defend them explained, was bleak. For such an outrageous offence against the honour as well as the property of the Air Force a sentence of six months or more in detention could be anticipated. And those months would then be added to their service. With a conviction for theft round his neck, Harry would probably find he had no job to return to in Swindon. His future suddenly looked far from rosy. And Chipchase's stubborn insistence that he would somehow contrive to get them off the hook failed to improve the view.

Then, *mirabile dictu*, came salvation. Chipchase tried to claim credit for it, but Harry was more inclined to thank his guardian angel. The station CO, Group Captain Wyatt, summoned them under close guard to his office a few days before the court martial was due to be held and offered them, much to Harry's incredulity, a way out. Volunteers were needed for a special project of three months' duration. No details were forthcoming beyond Wyatt's dry assurance that it would not involve being parachuted into Russia. If they signed up for it, did as they were told unquestioningly throughout and generally kept their noses clean, the charges would be dropped. If not . . .

But refusal was scarcely an option, as Wyatt must have anticipated, since he had already arranged for their kitbags to be packed. He wanted them off his hands. And they were happy to go. Chipchase theorized later that retired air aces might have cut up rough if they had discovered how little care was being taken of their old squadrons' silverware. A court martial would have attracted unwelcome publicity. The top brass had probably sent a message down the line that it was to be avoided at all costs. He and Harry should have held out for a better deal.

The one they had got was still pretty good, though. Forty-eight hours later, they arrived at Kilveen Castle, an outstation of RAF Dyce, near Aberdeen, and met their fellow volunteers for special duties of an unknown nature.

*　　*　　*

There had been fifteen of them in all, three of whom were drinking tea and taking their ease fifty years later in the kitchen at 37 Falmouth Street, Swindon. Ease was of course a relative term in Peter Askew's case. It occurred to Harry that he was one of those people who had never quite got the knack of life, which was a pity, given how much of it had now passed him by. Mervyn Lloyd, on the other hand, was a stranger to inhibition. And to silence. He was currently living up to his nickname by summarizing for Harry the contents of the letter from Johnny Dangerfield he had never received.

'Seems Danger made a packet in the oil business, which took him back to Aberdeen. The castle's been turned into a hotel. That's what made him think about staging a fiftieth anniversary reunion of our little band of brigands. Got the University to approach the MoD for our discharge addresses and started writing round. There was a good bit of forwarding and phoning after that. One or two have fallen off the twig. Well, you have to expect that at our age. And one or two – like you, Ossie – were hard to track down. But Danger's done a bloody good job, all things considered. I'll leave you his latest round robin to take a shufti at. The long and the short of it is he's booked the castle for this weekend. Just us. And it's a freebie. Danger's paying. His treat. Well, he's probably got a bargain price this early in the season, but it's still bloody generous of him. Seven of us are going up on the train from London tomorrow. I'm staying with my daughter in Neasden overnight. She doesn't know it yet, but she's putting up Crooked as well. Turned out he and I both live in Cardiff, so it made sense for the two of us to travel up today. Plus it meant we could stop off here and see if you really were a lost cause. Which I'm happy to say you aren't.'

'You'll come along, won't you, Harry?' Askew asked plaintively. 'It wouldn't be the same without you.'

'No more it would,' said Lloyd. 'The invitation's too good to refuse.'

15

'Is Barry going to be there?' Harry asked, guessing as he spoke that Chipchase would have proved peculiarly elusive.

'Who?' Lloyd looked confused, wedded as he was to the nicknames of fifty years ago.

'Fission,' said Harry, recalling with a mental turn of speed that surprised him the punning handle that had attached itself to his friend early in their Aberdeenshire exile. (Nuclear fission had been much in the news at the time, though fish and chips had been more often in their thoughts.) 'Barry Chipchase.'

'Yes,' said Askew. 'He'll be there.'

'Right. Your best mate. I remember.' Lloyd levelled a podgy forefinger at Harry, apparently considering this clinched the matter. 'Wouldn't want to miss out on the chance of catching up on old times with Fission, would you?'

'He's already up there, actually,' said Askew.

'He is?'

'All covered in the round robin, Ossie,' said Lloyd. 'No stone unturned.'

'Well, I—'

'Can't say no?' Lloyd cocked one eyebrow expectantly. 'That's it, isn't it? Same as us. You just can't turn down old Danger when he wants to throw his money around.'

Harry had more or less promised to join the expedition by the time he saw Lloyd and Askew off on the train to London later that afternoon. An all-expenses-paid jaunt to a Scottish castle of which he had mixed but by no means harrowing memories won out over a weekend of house-clearing in Swindon every time. He was confident Donna would not begrudge him a brief amble down memory lane. He could never be accused of living in the past. But a fleeting visit to its poignant purlieus could surely do no harm.

THREE

Operation Tabula Rasa – or Clean Sheet, as its participants
more commonly referred to it – was the brainchild of Professor Alexander McIntyre of Aberdeen University. He
wanted to test his theory that anyone could be taught any
academic subject to a reasonable level of proficiency, given
the right environment and the right methods. Kilveen Castle,
thirty miles inland from Aberdeen and available at a bargain
rent, was deemed by him to be an ideally secluded location for
such an experiment. And a group of National Servicemen who
had kicked over the traces of Forces discipline constituted
appropriately unpromising material. Through the good offices
of a cousin of his, an Assistant Under-Secretary of State at the
Air Ministry, the RAF agreed to provide fifteen such bad
boys, hoiked from punishment units, detention centres and
guardroom cells at short notice in March 1955, for a three-
month trial. If Professor Mac wanted them, it was implied, he
was welcome to them.

Professor Mac was afterwards heard to complain that three
months was not enough. Six was the minimum necessary. But
the University, who were paying the rent and supplying
the teaching staff, would not go beyond three. Nor would the
RAF, who reluctantly seconded a flight lieutenant and a
warrant officer from 612 Squadron at Dyce to ensure the
fifteen recalcitrants did not run amok.

Thus, in a sense, the experiment was doomed to failure

from the outset. From the point of view of the participants, however – the students, as Professor Mac called them – it was a resounding success. Three months lounging around a classroom in a Scottish castle studying art, literature, history, algebra, geometry, psychology, philosophy and suchlike with less than determined zeal involved a modicum of mental effort and occasional bouts of cataleptic boredom, but was so vastly preferable to the alternatives that not a single voice was raised in protest. Nor did anyone abscond, disrupt the proceedings or steal so much as a teaspoon. In disciplinary terms if in no other, they were model students. The three months passed uneventfully and ended with few signs of startling intellectual progress, at least as far as Aircraftman Harry Barnett was concerned, although one or two of his fellow students succeeded in developing scholarly habits if not attainments. It was, nonetheless, not what Professor Mac had been hoping for. He went back to the drawing board. While Harry and the other Clean Sheeters went their separate ways.

Harry found himself posted to RAF Records, Gloucester, for the remainder of his service. Chipchase was despatched to a battery-charging station on the south coast. They did not meet again for several years. And they did not even dream of meeting the thirteen men with whom they had shared a Nissen hut in the grounds of Kilveen Castle, Aberdeenshire, for the three months in the spring of 1955.

The Nissen hut was happily long gone. Accommodation for the Clean Sheet reunion was going to be in the Kilveen Castle Hotel's luxury guestrooms. This was just one of the nuggets of information contained in Johnny Dangerfield's latest round robin, which Harry perused over a pint in the Glue Pot on his way back from the station. Dangerfield had clearly done extremely well in the oil business to judge by the lavishness of the entertainment he was laying on. But he had always been a generous soul, quick to offer the loan of a quid or a drag on his cigarette. It was, to that extent, in character.

The e-mailed photographs of Kilveen Castle suggested it

had hardly altered outwardly. The original sixteenth-century building was a stocky, mean-windowed tower sporting turrets at the corners and battlements between, to which had been added, a couple of hundred years later, like a smart new growth from a gnarled tree stump, a plain but well-proportioned Georgian gentleman's residence. The interior in Harry's day had been more than a little dilapidated, especially in the tower. The rooms had had a bang-up-to-date designer makeover since then, however, with rich-toned fabrics and fine-lined furniture much in evidence. The dining room where they had eaten frugal meals in draughty gloom had been transformed into an elegant restaurant, while the classroom where they had blunted their wits on cubism and calculus was now a stylish conference centre equipped with every technological aid known to corporate man.

If Kilveen Castle was wearing its years lightly, the same could not be said of all the veterans of Operation Clean Sheet. Dangerfield had supplied notes on their careers and accomplishments since, though in some cases these were distinctly sparse. He described himself as 'pensioned off by an oil giant and divorced by a man-eater', but his address – Sweet Gale Lodge, Pitfodels, Aberdeen – did not sound like a hovel and Harry saw no reason to doubt Lloyd's assertion that 'Danger's rolling in it'.

Lloyd himself had spent forty years shuffling paper for the Cardiff Port Authority and boasted a wife and three grown children. It was not a life story to set the pulse racing. Nor was Askew's. Crooked had apparently worked with animals in assorted zoos and vets' practices. His relations with humans were a blank.

A blank was nonetheless preferable to a full stop. Mike 'Three Foot' Yardley had written himself off in a motorbike accident in 1964. Les 'Smudger' Smith, double-glazing salesman, had succumbed to a heart attack while explaining his employer's unique beading system to a client in Chatham in 1993. Leroy 'Coker' Nixon had drowned (circumstances unknown) in 1983. And Lester 'Piggott' Maynard, after making something of a name for himself as a radio comedy script-writer, had died of AIDS in 1987, which some – not including Harry – had already realized on account of a couple of newspaper obituaries at the time. In addition, Ernie 'Babber' Babcock, long emigrated to Australia, was reported to be gaga following a stroke. Thus the original fifteen had been shorn to ten for the reunion Dangerfield had taken it into his head to arrange.

Some of them had clearly done better than others. Gilbert 'Tapper' Tancred never had been a dullard. Harry could remember him surprising the tutors at Kilveen on several occasions with the breadth of his knowledge. And he had been responsible for the more ingenious of the nicknames conferred on every one of the Clean Sheeters. It was no surprise to learn that he had finessed his way into the City, prospered in the pinstripe-suited world of merchant banking and retired to suburban leisure in Carshalton Beeches. His intellectual equal, Neville 'Magister' Wiseman, had likewise done well and was now a semi-retired art dealer living in London SW1. Bill 'Judder' Judd had risen from hod-carrier to house-builder courtesy of several property booms and still had a hand in what had become a family business in Essex – Judd & Sons. Those three plus Dangerfield counted as definite success stories.

The story was less happy where Owen 'Gregger' Gregson was concerned. He had taken early retirement from Colman's Mustard of Norwich to care for a disabled wife and keep pigeons. It did not sound as if his fifty years since Clean Sheet had been fun-packed. Nor did those of Milton 'Paradise' Fripp, bookkeeper for a laundry in Derby prior to uneventful, unmarried retirement.

It was perhaps as well that Harry remained for the purposes of the round robin a question mark. He could only assume his mother had thrown away Dangerfield's initial letter, mistaking it for junk mail, which she had often complained about. What if she *had* sent it on to him: would he have volunteered about himself anyway? Ten years filing memos for Swindon Borough Council; seven running a garage business that ended in Chipchase-induced bankruptcy; six holding down a desk job with Mallender Marine in Weymouth; nine lotus-eating in Rhodes; six going to seed in London; and ten married to a beautiful, brainy American academic: it was hardly an arrow-straight progression and an explanation of every turn it had taken was best not attempted for a number of very good reasons.

Chipchase could have supplied some of this information, of course, but he seemed to have been as reticent concerning Harry as he had been concerning himself. Dangerfield said that he had 'contacted Fission just as he was about to relocate to South Africa, a move he's magnanimously put on hold so that he can join us at Kilveen, pending which he's shacking up at my humble abode'. There was no mention of anything Chipchase had done in the intervening years, but he was surely going to have to come up with some sort of account of himself when he met his old comrades face to face.

Among those comrades he presumably did not expect Harry to figure. Dangerfield would get a phone call from Lloyd tonight reporting that they had struck lucky in Swindon. Only then would Chipchase realize that Harry was going to reappear in his life. They had last met, entirely by chance, in Washington DC more than ten years ago. At that time, Chipchase had been romancing the wealthy widow of a Yorkshire undertaker. Somehow, Harry suspected little had come of that in view of the old reprobate's imminent relocation to South Africa – assuming such relocation was not a cover story in itself. All in all, he was looking forward to subjecting Chipchase to some gentle grilling.

And if he did not do it, others might. Professor Mac was dead and gone, so was in no position to be curious about whether his experiment had had any long-term effects. But his gloomy young research assistant, Donald Starkie, now Dr Starkie and far from young but probably still gloomy, was going to join them and might be expected to pursue the question. The fact that he would be accompanied by an old student of his from the University, Erica Rawson, certainly suggested that something more than a simple knees-up was planned. Dangerfield had not quibbled over her attendance, apparently. 'I'm sure I speak for all of us in welcoming some young, intelligent – and, more to the point, pretty – female company. Just don't mention her to your wives/partners/ girlfriends/live-in lovers!'

Harry did indeed fail to mention Erica Rawson when he telephoned Donna late that night. But that was because there were so many other things to say rather than because he had taken Dangerfield's sexist sentiments on board. Donna, as he had expected, was all in favour of him making the trip to Aberdeenshire.

'You've got to go, hon. I remember you telling me about the place. You absolutely have to find out what these guys have been up to since.'

'Not a lot's my bet. It could be a dire weekend.'

'But Barry will be there, right?'

'Apparently.'

'Well, you'll enjoy seeing him again, won't you?'

'I'm not sure enjoy's the word, but—'

'Go for it. What have you got to lose?'

'A couple of days out of my house-clearing schedule.'

'You'll just have to work harder when you get back.'

'OK, but—'

'Daisy and I'll expect a postcard. And take a camera. I'll want to see how these reprobates have aged compared with my craggily handsome husband.'

'You think it's a good idea, then?'

'A good idea?' Donna laughed. 'Why not?'

FOUR

Slumped bleary-eyed and woolly-headed aboard the 8.30 train to Paddington the following morning, his thoughts as blurred as the passing landscape, Harry winced at a scalding sip of plastic-cupped coffee and wondered if a cigarette would sharpen his mental processes. The answer was almost certainly, but he had forsworn smoking when Daisy was born and his lungs worked the better for it even if his brain did not. Besides, First Great Western in their corporate wisdom did not permit smoking.

That was just one of the ways in which life had changed since he had last travelled to Kilveen Castle, with Chipchase, in a succession of fug-filled third-class carriages, back in the early spring of 1955. They had probably puffed their way through fifty or sixty cigarettes in the course of their tortuous journey, which had begun at Stafford before dawn and had ended, well after dark, at Lumphanan, the closest station to the castle, thirty miles west of Aberdeen on the Deeside branch line. Harry shivered at the memory of stumbling off the train into the bone-numbing chill of an Aberdeenshire night. 'Bloody hell,' he remembered Chipchase gasping. 'There've sent us to Siberia.'

But Siberian their exile had not turned out to be. Far from it. Their three months at Kilveen had been cushier than even they would have claimed to deserve. 'Never mind Clean Sheet,' Chipchase had remarked after only a few days of

Professor Mac's gentle regime. 'We've got ourselves a bloody feather bed here, Harry.'

There had in truth been much to be thankful for. 'You've all been given a second chance,' the CO from Dyce had told them during his one and only visit to the castle. 'Be sure you make the most of it.' And so they had, though not necessarily in the way the CO had envisaged. As to whether their second chance had had any lasting effect . . . time was about to tell.

Harry headed straight into the ticket office when he reached King's Cross and felt grateful for the twenty minutes he still had in hand before the Aberdeen train was due to leave. The queue was long enough to remind him of the days of rationing. He was not destined to make much progress towards the front of it, however.

'Ossie.' A gravelly voice sounded in Harry's ear. He turned to confront a tall, broad-shouldered, big-bellied man wearing a loose and expensive-looking overcoat over jeans and a sweatshirt. His large, smiling face was familiar, though only faintly so in its current condition of broken-veined puffiness. His hair was even shorter than the day after an RAF short-back-and-sides and Persil white into the bargain. The stud gleaming in his left earlobe was likewise no aid to recognition. But there had been a cockney twang to the one word he had so far spoken, which was as much of a clue as Harry needed.

'Judder.'

'Good to see you, mate.' Bill Judd bestowed on Harry a crushing handshake and a pat to the shoulder that felt more like a clout. 'Come and meet the others. They're out on the concourse.'

'I haven't got my ticket yet.'

'We've got it for you, in case you left it till the last moment to turn up. You always were a tardy bugger. Come on.'

Lloyd had said seven were travelling up on the train. Harry therefore expected to see a sizeable huddle of half-remembered figures ahead of them as Judd piloted him out of the ticket office. What he actually saw, however, was Lloyd and Askew standing together in front of the information screens – and no sign of anyone else.

'Expect you're wondering where they've all got to,' was Lloyd's prescient greeting.

'Well . . .'

'Tapper's already on board. Seems he preferred resting his arse on some first-class upholstery to waiting for you on these hard-as-nails benches out here.'

'They've just called the train, Harry,' said Askew, nodding up at the screens.

'Yeah. We'd better get a wiggle on, boys,' said Judd. 'Some of us don't move as fast as we used to.'

'Did you say first-class, Jabber?' Harry asked as they hefted their bags and joined the general rush towards platform six, where the 10.30 to Aberdeen awaited. 'Isn't Tapper travelling with us, then?'

'We're all in first, mate,' Judd shouted over his shoulder. 'I bumped us up when Tapper showed his hand. I think he was hoping for a quiet journey. We'll knock that idea on the head, hey?'

'But—'

'Don't worry about it. My treat.'

'I can't—'

'Don't argue, Ossie,' said Lloyd in an undertone. 'You'll queer the pitch for the rest of us.' He nodded ahead at the lurching figure of Judd. 'I reckon bricks and mortar have served him well. Just look at the cut of that overcoat.'

'All right. I won't argue. But where *are* the others? You mentioned seven.'

'Didn't you read Danger's notes?'

'Yes, but—'

'Gregger and Paradise live up the line. Gregger's joining us at Peterborough, Paradise at York.'

'That still only makes six.'

'Not if we count you.'

'But you *weren't* counting me. Were you?'

'No. Bit of a change of plan where Magister's concerned, actually. I'll fill you in when we're on board. You'll have to get over the shock of meeting Tapper first.'

'Shock? Why should it be—'

'Just you wait and see.'

Harry followed the others onto the train mentally preparing himself for his first sight of Gilbert 'Tapper' Tancred's time-ravaged features. Perhaps, it occurred to him, there was worse to be faced than the imprint of the years. Disability; disfigurement: who knew what?

Then he saw Judd move ahead of him down the aisle between the seats and touch the shoulder of one of the passengers already aboard. The passenger looked up at Judd, then rose and turned towards Harry.

The shock, it turned out, lay in the ease of recognition. Tancred was as slim and erect as he had been at twenty. His black hair had been lightened by no more than a few strands of grey. There were more lines about his pale, high-cheeked face, but fewer than might have been expected. All in all, he was quite astonishingly unaltered. If he had swapped his smartly tailored jacket and rumple-free trousers for his old RAF uniform, the effect would have been positively uncanny.

'Ah. You found him, then.' Tancred's voice *had* altered. A career in merchant banking had given him a syrupy drawl that Harry did not recall. 'Well met, Ossie.'

Harry advanced to shake his hand. 'Life treating you well, Tapper?'

'Can't complain, old boy. Yourself?'

'Oh, fair to middling.'

'Are you, er, staying here?' Tancred frowned at Lloyd's hoisting of his bag onto the rack.

'Thought we'd join you in first, Tapper,' said Judd, grinning broadly. 'Keep you company, like.'

'Really?' Tancred smiled. 'Excellent. *I'd* have joined *you*, of course, once we were under way. But this . . . is better all round.'

'Supercilious sod,' Lloyd whispered to Harry as Judd's manhandling of his bag briefly shielded them from Tancred.

'What were you going to tell me about Magister, Jabber?' Harry asked, loudly enough to be heard by everyone.

'Oh, he's flying up. That's all. Meeting us there.'

'That's not quite all, Ossie,' said Tancred as they sat down. Harry joined Lloyd, Askew and Judd in occupation of the quartet of seats on the other side of the aisle from Tancred. 'Magister, we're told, has to attend an auction this afternoon in Geneva, so he's flying from there to Aberdeen tonight. Such is the life of the international art dealer.'

'He's not . . . retired, then?' asked Askew.

'Doesn't wish to be thought retired, at all events,' said Tancred. 'There's a spot of one-upmanship in this breathless announcement of his hectic schedule, I suspect.'

'One-upmanship's not something you'd know anything about, though, is it, Tapper?' Lloyd enquired sarcastically.

'Sniping before the train's even pulled out of the station,' said Judd, pressing several podgy fingers to his brow. 'Blimey, we've gone straight back to how it was in that Nissen hut.'

'Pax,' said Tancred, holding up a hand and bowing his head in a gesture of humility. 'We're the lucky ones, gentlemen, for being alive and well enough to undertake this journey. Yes, we often used to irritate one another and may do so again before the weekend's out. But to meet again is nonetheless cause for celebration. Shall we try to put half-remembered petty grievances aside and concentrate on the task in hand?'

'I'm all for that,' said Judd.

Lloyd shrugged. 'So am I.'

'Me too,' said Harry.

'But . . .' Askew looked thoughtful. 'What task would that be . . . exactly?'

'Why, enjoying ourselves, of course.' Tancred beamed benignly at Askew. 'What else?'

FIVE

Tancred was as good as his word. It was clear to Harry that he felt little real kinship with his fellow survivors of Operation Clean Sheet. But then the same was true of Harry himself. They were not the veterans of some arduous campaign in foreign parts, after all. They had simply been thrown together for three months fifty years ago in strange but scarcely hazardous circumstances. There were many humorous recollections of those months to be shared, however, and Tancred did his best to encourage the flow of them as the train headed north, much to the obvious exasperation of the several businessmen seated nearby, who had been hoping for guffaw-free quietude in which to concentrate on their *FT*s and laptops.

The opening of the buffet was the signal for Tancred to order a bottle of champagne, swiftly followed by a second and a third when Owen 'Gregger' Gregson joined them at Peterborough. Alerted by a mobile-phone call from Lloyd to their presence in coach L, Gregson was meeker and milder spoken than Harry recalled, a shrunken, vague-eyed man with a faint tremor in his hands, who took one sip of champagne, then ordered tea, and insisted on writing Judd a cheque for the supplement on his fare, which Judd had settled smartly in cash with the ticket inspector. Askew asked after Gregson's wife and the pitiful account that followed of their domestic routine took the fizz out of everyone until Judd called to mind an incident in the pub in Lumphanan one Saturday night involving a barmaid and a yard of ale that set them all laughing.

GNER provided smoking accommodation in coach M, which Judd and Lloyd repaired to for periodic fags, while Tancred shared with Harry the responsibility for anecdotalizing. Gregson smiled stiffly at their embroidered recollections, as if uncertain whether he had truly participated in such antics or not. Carefree youth was for him more remote than the most distant of memories. Askew, nervous and distracted though he often seemed, contrived nonetheless to make one or two telling contributions to the badinage, recalling the rules of a word-game they had played to pass an idle hour or four in the hut more accurately than Tancred, its inventor.

Askew had also hunted down an obituary of Professor Mac in the *Daily Telegraph* from twenty years ago and had brought along copies to distribute. There was, as he pointed out, no mention in it of Operation Clean Sheet. Most agreed with Tancred's assessment that academics were no keener than politicians on trumpeting their failures. A fuzzily reproduced photograph of 'Professor Alexander Stuart McIntyre, died 24 October 1985, aged 87' showed him much as he had been in the spring of 1955, bald and beaming in half-moon spectacles, one hand clasping a fat-bowled pipe, the other the lapel of a heavy tweed jacket.

By the time the train reached York, where Milton 'Paradise' Fripp joined them, the champagne was wreaking havoc with Harry's thought processes. Fripp, lean, stooped, balding and taciturn, consequently made little impression, accepting Judd's generosity and that of whoever was paying for the next bottle without demur. Alcohol rapidly loosened his tongue, however, though what he actually said Harry could not have even vaguely summarized more than a minute after he had said it.

This was soon true of everyone. Drinking sessions at the Macbeth Arms; kick-about football matches on the lawn behind the castle; half-hearted square-bashing on a patch of tarmac adjoining the hut at the bawling behest of Warrant Officer Trench; the idiosyncrasies of the teaching staff brought in by Professor Mac; the inadequacies of their reluctant students: all these and more floated in and out of the conversation as the champagne flowed and the North of England slid past the window.

As the train neared Newcastle, the decision was taken to adjourn to the restaurant car for a lunch that had the potential to last until Aberdeen. Gregson, who had drunk virtually nothing, said he would stay where he was and eat the sandwiches he had brought, cueing much eye-rolling by Judd and a faintly patronizing smile from Tancred.

Gregson's withdrawal had the advantage that the six remaining could occupy a table for four and an adjacent table for two at one end of the restaurant car, where a bibulous time ensued, although Harry found himself sharing the table for two with Askew and was consequently at one remove from the centre of quippery and merriment. At some point, however, Chipchase's name cropped up and Harry was obliged to admit to a brief business association with him some years after they had left Kilveen. This aroused an unhealthy amount of curiosity, which he deflected as best he could, though not very effectively in Tancred's case.

'A garage, you say, Ossie?'

'Yes. Barnchase Motors. In Swindon.'

'Well, Fission always did have a way with a spanner and a greasy rag,' put in Lloyd.

'True,' Tancred agreed. 'But I'm not sure I'd have cared to have him as a business partner.'

'That's because of your distrustful nature, Tapper,' Fripp observed drily.

'Perhaps. But let's ask Ossie to adjudicate on the point. Was Fission an entirely reliable man to work with?'

'Well . . .'

'I sense the answer's no.'

Harry shrugged. 'We all have our flaws.'

'What became of Barnchase Motors?'

30

'It folded up.'

'And whose fault was that?'

Harry managed a smile. 'I always put it down to decimalization myself.'

The joke raised a laugh and set Judd off on a cheery diatribe against all manner of modern reforms.

At some point in the ensuing discussion, Askew leaned across the table towards Harry and said, quietly but distinctly, 'Are you sure Professor Mac's obituary didn't mention Clean Sheet because it was a failure?'

'Sorry?'

'Are you? Really?'

Tancred and Judd were by now locked in an argument about the European Union. Harry could clearly sense that none of their companions was aware of Askew's question – or of Harry's faltering attempts to answer it. 'What do you . . . What are you getting at, Peter?'

'Looking back on our time at Kilveen, what do you remember best?'

'Well, the . . . kind of stuff we've been laughing about, I suppose. Booze-ups. Cock-ups. The usual.'

'What about the lessons?'

'Not much stuck, as I recall. I don't think we were exactly model pupils.'

'Because not much stuck?'

'Well, it didn't, did it?'

'Perhaps it wasn't intended to.'

'How d'you mean?'

'I don't know.' Askew laughed. 'Sorry. Let's forget it.'

'OK, but—'

'Excuse me.' Askew rose suddenly from his seat. 'I'll be right back.'

It was only as Askew slipped through the sliding door into the vestibule that Harry realized he was answering a mobile-phone call. He heard Askew say 'Hello?' as the door slid shut behind him, and noticed the phone held to his ear. It must, Harry supposed, have been set to vibrate rather

31

than ring. He was mildly surprised Askew should sufficiently have kept pace with technology to possess such a thing, let alone master its greater intricacies. Harry himself was technically the owner of a mobile, but never switched it on other than to make a call and that rarely. When he did, he usually found the battery had run down. Today, he had left it in Swindon.

Tancred had commenced his own musings on Professor Mac's achievements by the time Askew made a low-key return to the carriage. The minor puzzle of Askew's questions about the purpose of Operation Clean Sheet was thus jettisoned from Harry's mind.

'We all qualified for Professor Mac's residential tutorial by rebelling against RAF discipline in one way or another,' Tancred reasoned. 'It seems those of us here stopped rebelling at that point, however, so you could say the old boy achieved something, even if it wasn't exactly what he had in mind. Of course—'

'Some of the others might have taken to a life of crime without us hearing about it,' said Fripp.

'Or some of us might be hiding our rebellious light under a bushel,' said Lloyd.

'Danger's researches have turned up nothing out of the ordinary,' Tancred responded. 'We all seem to be desperately respectable.'

'Who are you calling respectable?' growled Judd.

'Three Foot might have been making a getaway from a burglary when he died in that motorbike crash,' said Lloyd.

'And someone could have been holding poor old Coker's head under the water when he drowned, for all we know,' said Harry. 'I was sorry to hear he'd gone. After everything he told us he'd had to put up with in Germany.' (Leroy Nixon had cracked under the strain of racist abuse at RAF Gütersloh and broken a warrant officer's nose, thus earning his passage to Kilveen and the grudging respect of WO Trench. His was the first black face most of them had ever seen, back in the monocultural days of their youth, when

32

a Jamaican in Aberdeenshire counted as a contradiction in terms.) 'I'd like to have met him again and shaken him by the hand.'

'You're not serious, are you, Harry?' asked Askew suddenly.

Harry frowned. 'Certainly.'

'I mean about how he drowned. You don't think . . . he was murdered, do you?'

'Murdered? No. Of course not. I just meant—'

'Ossie was speaking metaphorically, Crooked,' Tancred mellifluously intervened.

Askew looked around at his companions in evident bemusement. Then he shaped an uneasy smile. 'Sorry. You're right. Obviously. Not sure I'm used to drinking so much. I . . . think I'll leave you to it. Maybe take a nap. Yes. A nap.' He stood up. 'That's what I need.'

'Are you OK, mate?' Judd called as Askew headed along the aisle towards coach L.

'I'll be fine,' Askew replied, with a wave of the hand. And on he went.

'Think someone should go and see if he's all right?' Harry asked as the door at the end of the carriage slid shut behind him.

'Gregger'll look after him,' said Lloyd. 'Crooked probably needs one of his sandwiches to sober him up.'

There was general laughter at that. And an observation by Fripp that the next bottle would now stretch further prompted more laughter. It was not long, indeed, before the bottle was duly ordered.

'You're going to drink us dry, gents,' the steward said with a wink as he pulled the cork. And it was instantly agreed that this was a challenge they could not let pass.

During the train's ten-minute lay-up at Waverley station in Edinburgh, Harry stepped out onto the platform for a breath of air. He badly needed to clear his head, having drunk too much and sat too long. It was an imprudent start to the weekend and he foresaw some crippling hangovers among his companions, none of whom was young enough to be setting such a pace.

Askew was on the platform ahead of him, walking up and down, frowning pensively and breathing heavily, like a man psyching himself up for an important speech.

'Did you ever get that nap, Peter?' Harry called to him.

Askew started and looked round. 'What? Oh, Harry. The nap? No. Not yet.'

'You seem a little . . . on edge.'

'Do I?' Askew's eyes widened. He grimaced. 'Well, I suppose I am. To be honest, I'm having second thoughts about this whole reunion idea.'

'Really? Why?'

'Not sure. It's just . . .' Askew stepped closer and lowered his voice. 'Meeting people you haven't met in fifty years makes you realize how quickly those years have passed – and how little you have to show for them.'

'We're all in the same boat, Peter.'

'No, we're not. Believe me, we're not.'

'OK.' Harry smiled appeasingly. 'Depends on your point of view, I suppose.'

'It depends on how you remember things, actually. And how you forget them.'

'I don't . . .'

'Understand? No. You wouldn't.' Askew shook his head. 'Sorry. I'm not making any sense.'

Harry laughed. 'Neither are that lot.' He gestured with his thumb towards the restaurant car.

Askew rubbed his eyes. 'I think maybe I will try and get my head down.'

'Good idea. I reckon I'll join you.'

They found Gregson dozing in his seat in coach L. Harry sat down next to him. As the train eased out of the station, he felt his eyelids grow heavy. Askew was sitting across from him on the other side of the aisle. Whether he was nodding off too

Harry could not have said for certain. Fuzzy shafts of sunlight misted his vision. Askew became a silhouette, then a shadow. Harry closed his eyes.

He was never to see Peter Askew again.

SIX

It was difficult, looking back, to say exactly when Askew had gone missing. Harry slept as solidly as only a man who has drunk too much can until roused by the noisy return of Judd, Tancred, Lloyd and Fripp from the restaurant car. This was as the train was nearing Stonehaven, with half an hour to go till it reached Aberdeen. Two hours of oblivion had passed for Harry since its departure from Edinburgh. Gregson, who had slept less heavily, recalled registering the train's arrival in Dundee and was more or less certain that Askew had still been there then. He also recalled registering Askew's absence some time later, but was vague about when that would have been.

Harry and his companions did not actually take seriously the idea that Askew was missing until the train entered the outskirts of Aberdeen and the guard announced their imminent arrival at 'our last and final station stop'. A hasty check of the nearest loos began, but Askew was in none of them. They did find his bag, however, left where he had stowed it on the rack, and duly took it along with theirs when they stumbled off the train into the grey chill of an Aberdeen afternoon.

They followed the ruck of passengers off the platform assuming Askew had for some reason gone to the front of the train and would soon be sighted. But he was not. They lingered on the concourse, expecting him to appear from one direction or another. But he did not. Harry accompanied Lloyd and Judd back to the train, where the cleaners were already at work and the guard assured them that all the passengers had left. He surmised that their friend had simply got off earlier. Why Askew would have left his bag behind was a puzzle the guard neither needed nor wished to dwell on.

Back on the concourse, Johnny Dangerfield had arrived to collect them. A weather-beaten but still handsome figure in Barbour, guernsey, corduroys and brogues, he had kept the trimmed moustache and Brylcreemed hairstyle of his youth, but the moustache had lost most of its colour, while his face had reddened with age and whisky. The twinkle in his eyes, that had once been like Venus in the night sky, was now more akin to a distant star in an unnamed galaxy. But there was still enough dash about him to suggest he had left an E-Type in the car park, rather than the minibus he had actually hired to transport them to the castle.

Harry had expected to see Chipchase at Dangerfield's elbow, but there was as little sign of him as of Askew. The mystery of Askew's whereabouts took priority, however, and it was not until a deputation, which he and Dangerfield were both part of, had been despatched to the railway police office, that Harry had the chance to ask after his old friend.

'Did you leave Barry in the van, Danger?'

'Fission? No. Actually, this is a bit of a double whammy, chaps. Fission's sister died last night. Her husband's in a godawful state, apparently. Fission's had to fly down to Manchester. He's not going to be able to join us.'

'Sister, did you say?' It was the first Harry had ever heard of Chipchase having siblings, dead *or* alive.

'Yes. Know her, did you, Ossie?'

'No. Actually, I didn't.'

'Well, there it is. Can't be helped. At least we know where Fission's gone. Unlike Crooked, blast the fellow.'

The railway police were not a lot more helpful than the train guard. The officer on duty took a note of their friend's apparent disappearance, but emphasized that much the likeliest explanation was that he had got off the train at an earlier stop or had disembarked at the front on arrival at Aberdeen and left the station, forgetting to take his bag with him.

It was only then that Harry remembered Askew's mobile. Why not simply ring him and ask where the blue blazes he was and what he thought he was playing at? But no-one had the number. Lloyd, indeed, did not even know Askew possessed a phone.

'He never made or took a call while I was with him yesterday. Or while we were at my daughter's.'

'He took a call on the train,' said Harry. 'While we were having lunch.'

But no-one else had noticed. And some suggested Harry was confused.

'Your powers of observation while under the influence were always close to zero, Ossie,' said Tancred. 'I can't think age has improved them.'

Harry could not find the energy to be riled by this and it was generally agreed that none of them could claim more than partial recall of the events of the journey anyway. They adjourned to the station buffet for much-needed coffee, which completed the sobering-up Askew's vanishment had kick-started without inducing much in the way of inspired thoughts.

But Harry's memory was slowly booting up, distracted though he was by the parallel mystery of Chipchase's sudden flying of the coop. (He did not think this was the moment to voice his certainty that Chipchase had never had a sister.) 'I spoke to Peter on the platform at Waverley station. He said he was having second thoughts about the whole idea of the reunion.'

'Why?' snapped Tancred.

'Something about it reminding him of how little he'd achieved in life.'

'He's hardly alone in that,' said Fripp.

'Well, it seemed to be preying on his mind,' said Harry.

'That's it, then,' said Lloyd. 'He's baled out. He always was chicken.'

'It's possible, I suppose,' said Dangerfield. 'Let's see.' He flourished a GNER pocket timetable and leafed through it. 'We know from Gregger he was still on at Dundee. But if he got off after that, at Arbroath, say, or Montrose . . .' He recited various train times under his breath. 'Mmm. Montrose would've been too late. It has to have been Arbroath.'

'Can you spell it out for us, Danger?' pleaded Judd. 'You might be firing on all cylinders, but I can assure you the rest of us aren't.'

'It's simply that if he'd got off at Arbroath and caught the next southbound train . . . he could connect with the seven o'clock from Edinburgh to London . . . and get into King's Cross just after midnight.'

'You mean he's bolted back to London?'

'I don't know. What do *you* think, Ossie? Based on his state of mind during your chat at Edinburgh.'

Put on the spot, Harry had to admit it was a distinct possibility. 'I reckon he must have done.'

'Charming,' said Lloyd. 'I go to all the bother of arranging for my daughter to put him up and he goes and does this.'

'He obviously wasn't thinking straight,' said Dangerfield. 'Otherwise he'd have taken his bag. No doubt he'll be in touch with us about that – and to apologize. Sorry, gents, but we're two down and we'll just have to make the best of it. That's all there is to it.'

Harry did not share Dangerfield's complacency. He knew Chipchase was lying about a dead sister and a distraught brother-in-law in Manchester. He also knew Askew had a mobile and had been using it on the train. If Askew had been capable of working out the logistics of getting back to London from Arbroath, he would surely not have been so forgetful as to leave his bag behind. What all this meant Harry had no idea, but the coincidence of Chipchase *and* Askew going missing was too much to swallow. Something was going on. And Chipchase was up to his neck in it.

Still Harry said nothing about the non-existence of Chipchase's sister. Some loyalty to his old friend that he could not shake off, despite the many occasions on which that friend had let him down, bound him to silence. Denied this information, his companions naturally made no connection between the two turns of events. Chipchase had been called away. And Askew was AWOL. There was no more to be said.

They piled into the minibus and began the final leg of their journey. The Deeside railway line was long gone, a victim of the Beeching cuts of the mid-sixties. Their arrival at the castle would not be a re-creation of how they had arrived fifty years previously, in ones and twos, on different days, by slow, labouring steam train. It was the road for them this time, with Dangerfield at the wheel, cursing and swearing his way through the rush-hour traffic as a pallid sun cast a sickly hue across the grey city. Conversation was subdued, thanks to encroaching hangovers, incipient indigestion and a general feeling that the absences of Chipchase and Askew had taken some of the gloss off the proceedings. Some even wondered if Wiseman had deserted them as well, though Dangerfield seemed certain he would join them before the evening was out.

Their spirits revived somewhat when they left the straggling suburbs of Aberdeen behind and headed on towards the sun-gilded hills of Deeside. They had a first encounter with Erica Rawson to look forward to – and a weekend of carousing. As Lloyd put it: 'Bugger Crooked. And bad luck, Fission. They're going to miss a right royal piss-up.'

SEVEN

For the last few miles of their route to Lumphanan, the road ran alongside the disused cuttings and embankments of the railway line. The countryside was bare and empty, stands of silver birch and pine giving it a vaguely Nordic look. Spring had been in spate in Wiltshire, but was still feeling its way in Aberdeenshire. Harry had forgotten just how bleak and alien the surroundings of the castle had initially looked to him. Some of the gloom they had plunged him into washed back over him as he gazed through the minibus window at the twilit hills and fields and patches of scrub.

The village of Lumphanan had not changed much in its essentials. The disappearance of the railway station and the humpback bridge over the line was disorientating at first glance. Bungalows had been built in the old goods yard and the station building itself converted into a private house. The footbridge which Harry and Chipchase had trudged over with their kitbags that cold March evening in 1955 was now just a memory in thin air. But the post office, the Macbeth Arms, the main street of the village and the narrow-steepled parish church on its hillock at the far end were instantly familiar.

'See the spire, chaps?' said Tancred. 'An admonitory finger of a Calvinist God raised over the cowering villagers.'

'They didn't do a lot of cowering, as I recall,' Judd laughed.

'That's because you never went to church.'

'We wouldn't have been welcome if we had,' said Lloyd. 'They didn't want us here.'

'So we should have hit it off straight away,' said Judd. 'We didn't want us here either.'

Kilveen Castle stood half a mile out of the village, on the southern flank of Glenshalg Hill. The estate's boundary wall, so tumbledown and overgrown in 1955 as to be barely distinguishable from the rock-strewn woods screening the castle from the lane, appeared on their left, solid and well maintained. Daffodil-sown glades had been opened up in the woods, affording glimpses of the castle as they climbed. They turned in between stout granite pillars, past the swag-lettered hotel sign and up the no longer potholed drive.

The photographs had not lied. The damp and draughty hybrid of medieval stronghold and Georgian villa where Harry and his fellow Clean Sheeters had passed their unproductive days was now an elegant retreat for well-heeled tourists. The lawns were trimmed, the paths neatly gravelled, the harling of the tower honey-tinged by the setting sun. The very appearance of the place promised ease and indulgence. And most of Harry's companions seemed in the mood for both.

They pulled into the yew-hedged car park and clambered out. A couple of porters appeared with trolleys to take their bags. Dangerfield led the way into the reception area on the ground floor of the tower, where a massive fire blazed and tartan-uniformed staff flitted around them. The manager, a small, trim, sleek-haired fellow called Matthews, introduced himself and welcomed them to Kilveen. Dr Starkie and Erica Rawson had arrived, he reported, but Mr Wiseman was still awaited. Dangerfield broke the bad news about Askew and Chipchase. Matthews took it in his modest stride. The register was signed. Keys were distributed.

Harry followed a bright-eyed young woman identified by her lapel badge as Bridget to his room, high up in the tower. A lift had been installed in place of one of the two spiral

42

staircases he remembered stumbling up and down. Bridget praised the view, which was panoramic, and rattled through detailed advice about heating controls, meal times and telephone extension numbers. Then she was gone. To his relief, Harry found himself alone. But not for long. The porter arrived with his bag. Soon, however, bag delivered and tip dispensed, Harry's solitude was restored.

He sat down on the four-poster bed and looked about him. Every comfort was on hand. But he did not feel comfortable. He did not feel relaxed in any way. And neither a satellite television nor a Jacuzzi bath was going to change that. Where was Chipchase? What was he up to? What in God's name was going on?

Harry took a shower and dressed for dinner, which meant donning the dark-grey suit he had worn at his mother's funeral, paired with a rainbow-striped tie Donna had given him for Christmas a few years ago. Then, after casting a wary eye over the telephone tariff, he put a call through to Seattle.

Donna and Daisy were having brunch, prior to their drive back to Vancouver. It was good to hear their calm, cheerful voices. He reported Chipchase's no-show, but not Askew's disappearance. He did not want Donna to worry, especially when there was, obviously, nothing to worry about. She promised to give him a wake-up call in the morning. He promised not to drink too much.

When he put the phone down, Harry realized how much he missed his wife and daughter. He wanted to be with them, not carousing with half-forgotten comrades from fifty years ago. He wished profoundly that he had not come to Scotland. But he had. And if he did not head down to the bar soon, they would probably send up a search party. With a sigh, he grabbed his key and set off.

Halfway down the stairs, he literally bumped into another guest, who was emerging from his room. They stepped back to examine each other and Harry's brain scrambled to deduce

43

who the fellow might be. Tall and fleshy, with thinning, white, curly hair, an eagle's-beak nose, a broad but not altogether warm smile and an intense, faintly sceptical gaze, he was wearing an expertly cut suit of some shimmering dark-blue material, a blue shirt with a white collar and bright-red tie that matched the hue of a flamboyantly disarranged breast-pocket handkerchief.

'Magister.'

'That's right. And you must be . . . Ossie Barnett.' They shook hands, the band of a signet ring grinding into the knuckle on Harry's little finger.

'You made it, then.'

'Got here half an hour ago. Checked in with Danger. He seemed relieved to hear from me. I gather Crooked and Fission have dropped out.'

'Looks like it.'

'On your way to the bar?'

'Yes.'

'Let's go, then.'

They carried on down. 'Buy anything at the auction?' Harry asked as they went.

'*That.*' Wiseman's laugh echoed in the stairwell. 'No. Complete and utter waste of time. Telephone bidders are taking all the fun out of the auction business.'

'But you're still active in it.'

'You've got to stay active, Ossie. You must know that. The brain as well as the body. They have to be kept in trim.'

'Oh, absolutely.'

'And what this brain and this body need at the moment . . . is a stiff drink.'

The bar was next to the dining room on the ground floor of the Georgian wing. There was a stag's head over the mantelpiece, but otherwise little in the way of Caledonian kitsch, just a welcoming fire and lots of soft leather armchairs. Harry and Wiseman were evidently the last to arrive, for Dangerfield and the rest were all there, along with Dr Starkie and Erica

44

Rawson, who seemed to be coping well with being the only woman in a gathering of men too old to have absorbed many feminist principles.

Short and slender, with boyishly cropped black hair, the young woman's large, teak-brown eyes had a sharpness of focus that made Harry feel, albeit briefly, the undivided object of her attention as they shook hands and exchanged pleasantries. She was plainly but elegantly dressed in a dark top and palazzo pants, prompting Judd to mutter in Harry's ear, 'It'd be nice to know what she'd look like in something a bit more figure-hugging, don't you reckon, Ossie?' as Dangerfield piloted her away to meet Wiseman.

Donald Starkie, who had stooped slightly, even as a young man, stooped even more fifty years later. His mop of black hair had turned wire-wool grey and his spectacles had acquired alarmingly thick lenses, but otherwise he had changed little, remaining beanpole thin, scruffily dressed (even with an Aberdeen University tie on) and unsmilingly lugubrious.

'You heard of Professor McIntyre's death, Barnett?' he husked to Harry.

'Not at the time. But he'd be over a hundred now, so . . . it was no surprise.'

'He achieved a lot, let me tell you. More than his obituarists could comprehend.'

'But not with us, hey? We must have been a sore disappointment to him.'

'Oh, I wouldn't say that.'

'No?'

'What I mean . . .' Starkie took a sip from his glass of mineral water. 'What I mean is that Professor McIntyre regarded failure . . . as no less instructive than success.'

'So, at least we were instructive.'

'Aye.' Starkie looked thoughtful. 'So you were.'

EIGHT

The table of twelve planned for dinner had become a table of ten, with the advantage, according to Dangerfield, of more elbow room all round. He had devised a seating plan based on the alphabetical order of the Clean Sheeters' surnames, from which he had exempted only himself. He was seated at the head of the table, with Dr Starkie and Erica Rawson to his left and right. In Askew's absence, Harry found himself sitting next to Erica, with Fripp on his other side and Wiseman opposite. Judd, at the far end of the table, looked disappointed by his distance from Erica and shot Harry an envious glance as they sat down.

It was the same room where they had eaten their plain and not always wholesome meals during Operation Clean Sheet, but barely recognizable as such. Silver service, fine napery and haute cuisine heightened the contrast. 'Danger's doing us proud,' Harry murmured to Fripp. But the response hardly came freighted with gratitude. 'I wish I'd gone into oil instead of bookkeeping. My God, I do.'

It was no hardship for Harry to concentrate his conversational attentions on Erica Rawson. To his surprise, she spoke to him more than anyone. Dangerfield and Starkie became immersed in a discussion of the effects of the oil boom on Aberdeen, while Tancred and Wiseman began trading points in delicately barbed arguments ranging from politics to poetry.

'It's a pity only eight of you made it in the end,' Erica said, as she toyed with her starter. 'Eight out of fifteen isn't very representative.'

'Representative?' Harry responded. 'Are you *studying* us?'

'In a sense, yes.' She turned to smile at him. 'I hope you're not shocked.'

'Depends why, I suppose.'

'Oh, to see whether Professor McIntyre's experiment really was as futile as his colleagues maintained. Ever since Dr Starkie told me about it, it's interested me. This reunion gave me a chance to meet some of the people I've only previously known by name.'

'What exactly do you do at the University, Erica?'

'Teaching and research. In the Psychology Department. My specialism's the effect of extreme environments on mental states, short- and long-term. Aberdeen's a good base for it, what with the offshore oil and gas industries and the fishing fleet.'

Harry suspected the rig workers and fishermen would be duly grateful for her ministrations. But all he said was, 'There was nothing extreme about the environment here, I can tell you.'

'No. But it was unusual, wasn't it? Very unusual, I'd say.' She laughed. 'That counts as extreme for my purposes.'

'I'm afraid we didn't learn much, despite Professor Mac's best endeavours.'

'Are you sure?'

'I think so. Well, I'm sure *I* didn't.'

'What about Barry Chipchase? Johnny tells me you and he stayed friends over the years. Do you mind me calling you Harry, by the way? I can't get the hang of these nicknames you've all been throwing around.'

'Harry's fine.'

'Great. So, Harry, do you think your friend Barry Chipchase got much out of his time here?'

'Same as me, I'd say.'

'Zilch?'

'More or less.'

'You see, I don't buy that. I've checked the facts as best I can. A surprisingly large proportion of you have gone on to achieve success in your own field. You may not have learned much that was tangible or examinable, but what you may have acquired . . . is a certain way of thinking.'

'Kind of you to say so, Erica, but—'

'Did life seem clearer after you left here? More manageable? Did you feel, however slightly, different?'

Harry thought for a moment, but the instinctive reply did not change. He felt obliged, though, to dress it up a little. 'I knew a few more Shakespearean quotes. And I thought I understood relativity. That was about it. Mind you, I've forgotten most of the quotes since. And I've had second thoughts about understanding relativity.'

Erica laughed. 'I get the feeling you're underselling yourself, Harry.'

'Impossible.'

She laughed again. 'Come on. Johnny said you were over from Canada, right?'

'Right.'

'Whereabouts?'

'Vancouver.'

'What took you there?'

'Er, my wife . . . works at the University of British Columbia.'

'Really? So she's an academic – like me?'

'Well, yes.'

'Small world, hey? But hold on. Barnett. She's not Donna Trangam-Barnett, is she?'

Harry could not have looked more surprised than he felt. 'Yes. How did—'

'I read her piece on disconnection syndromes in one of the neuroscience journals a few months back. Impressive stuff. You're married to her?'

Harry shrugged. 'I am.'

'Amazing. And it rather proves my point, doesn't it?'

48

'Does it?'

'Well, we've Johnny here, the affluent oilman. Plus a merchant banker and an art dealer across the table. Then there's you, husband of an eminent neuroscientist. Given the position you were all in before coming here, isn't that quite something?'

'I don't—'

'And mightn't it be partly because of what you learned while you *were* here?'

'Maybe. Maybe not.' Harry was confused. There was something about Erica's line of reasoning he did not trust. He was not sure, in fact, that he trusted her at all. He had the disquieting impression that she knew more about him than she logically should. 'I got lucky. Several of us did. But several of us didn't. That's life.'

'Exactly,' Wiseman cut in. Harry looked up, unaware till then that anyone had been listening to their conversation. Clearly Wiseman had for one, though for how long was hard to guess. His hooded gaze was fixed on Erica. 'Harry's quite right, my dear.' He had dropped Harry's nickname, as if some contexts were too important for its use. 'I'm afraid the idea that the three months we spent here fifty years ago had a significant effect – or any effect at all – on our lives is, well, I won't say absurd, but . . .'

'Wide of the mark?' suggested Erica, with a self-deprecating smile.

Wiseman returned the smile. 'I'm afraid so. Ask any of us. It really didn't amount to anything.'

'That you're aware of.'

'Well, obviously.' Wiseman sighed and sat back in his chair. He sipped some wine. 'That goes without saying.'

'Not planning to psychoanalyse us this weekend, are you, Erica?' Harry asked, seeking to lighten the mood.

'Absolutely not.' She turned to look at him. 'Unless you want me to.'

*   *   *

49

Their conversation drifted onto other, blander topics as the meal progressed. Mellowing with each glass of wine, Wiseman reeled off a few entertaining anecdotes about the art world. Dangerfield chipped in with some less rarefied recollections of the oil business. Starkie said little, as had always been his wont, but watched Erica closely throughout. Harry tried not to wonder why. His own attempts to draw Erica out on the subject of her career were deftly deflected and he was too fuddled by alcohol and fatigue to sustain them. He kept reminding himself to drink plenty of water, as Donna was forever encouraging him to do, but somehow found himself picking up the wineglass more often than not. The evening took a woozy turn. Dangerfield made an impromptu speech. There was a lot of laughter, then an adjournment to the bar, where Harry was persuaded to sample one of the hotel's malts. He was going to regret drinking it, he knew. Dawn was going to be a painful experience. But it tasted very, very good.

Halfway through his second whisky, Harry became aware of Dangerfield waving to him through the doorway from the corridor leading to reception. He managed a quizzical gesture of raised eyebrows and hands, but Dangerfield went on waving, if anything more frantically. Harry had thought he was on the other side of the bar, puffing at a cigar, and so he had been at one point. But no longer. There was no sign of Lloyd either, who had surely been with him. Harry registered this much during his unsteady progress across the room.

'What's up, Danger?' he asked on reaching the corridor.

'Jabber and I are in the conference room,' Dangerfield replied in a whisper. 'With the police.'

'The . . . what?'

'The police. They want to talk to you.'

'What about?'

'Not what. *Who*. Peter Askew. He's dead.'

NINE

Shock sobered Harry up faster than any amount of strong black coffee. His brain might not have snapped into top gear at Dangerfield's words, but it was at least a forward gear. He listened hard as Dangerfield gave him the few facts he knew on their way to the conference room.

'Crooked's body was found on the railway line near Carnoustie late this afternoon. That's about halfway between Dundee and Arbroath. They traced him here from the copy of my letter he had in his pocket. We've got an inspector and a sergeant here from the Tayside Police. Jabber mentioned you were the last to speak to Crooked, so they insisted I wheel you in. Be careful what you say, Ossie. I'm not sure exactly what they're after.'

'Are you telling me Peter killed himself, Danger?'

'Sounds like it.'

'I can't believe it.'

'Neither can I. But he's dead all right. We have no choice about believing that.'

The conference room was a bare, starkly lit space, the chairs that normally filled it stacked at one end. At the other end, by a broad-topped table positioned in front of a projector screen, stood the inspector and sergeant, who introduced themselves as Geddes and Crawford. Lloyd, who had been supplied with a chair, looked up at Harry with

51

wide-eyed bemusement and stroked his chin fretfully.

Geddes was a short, barrel-chested, shaven-headed man in early middle age, with a stubbly beard and a darting gaze. Crawford was a taller, younger man running to fat, with greasy hair and a conspicuous plaster over one eyebrow. They looked tired and bored and faintly hostile.

'Take a seat, Mr Barnett,' said Crawford, pushing a chair into position alongside Lloyd's. 'Sorry to be the bearers of bad news about your old comrade. You want to sit down yourself, Mr Dangerfield?'

'I'll stand, thanks.'

Harry might have preferred to stand as well, but he could not be sure if further shocks were on the way, so he lowered himself cautiously onto the proffered chair.

'We gather you had a conversation with Mr Askew at Waverley station, Mr Barnett,' said Geddes, stifling a smoker's cough. 'The last conversation anyone seems to have had with him.'

'It was a brief chat. Nothing more.'

'What about?'

'The reunion. Has Danger—'

'Aye, aye. We're in the picture about your fiftieth anniversary get-together. Did Mr Askew say he was looking forward to it?'

'Not entirely. He told me he was, well, beginning to regret agreeing to come.'

'That's really why we assumed he'd got off the train and gone back to London,' said Dangerfield.

'Oh, he got off the train, sir,' said Crawford. 'No doubt about that.'

'Do you know . . . what exactly happened, Inspector?' Harry asked.

'Not *exactly*, no, sir. That's what we're trying to establish. Mr Askew's body was spotted a mile or so north-east of Carnoustie station, lying between the tracks, by the driver of an Aberdeen to Glasgow train a little after half past four this afternoon. There'd been no report of a previous train

52

hitting a pedestrian and his injuries were more consistent with falling from one, rather than walking into it.'

'What . . . sort of injuries were they?'

'Oh, the fatal sort. Mostly to the head. Mr Lloyd's generously agreed to come down to Dundee tomorrow morning to identify the body, but judging by the photograph in his passport . . .'

'He had his passport on him?'

'You'd be surprised how many Englishmen think they need one to travel to Scotland. Not that we're complaining. It makes our job a lot easier. No next of kin, you tell me, Mr Lloyd?'

Lloyd shook his head. 'He said all his family were gone.'

'So, we come back to his state of mind. Did he seem depressed while you were with him?'

'Crooked – Peter – was never what you'd call a barrel of laughs, Inspector. But depressed? No. I don't think so.'

'Mr Barnett?'

'He was a bit down. Probably a bit drunk. We all were. It could have turned him maudlin. You know how it takes some people that way.'

'Aye, I do,' said Geddes with feeling.

'But that's a long way from being . . . suicidal.'

'Oh, a very long way indeed.' Geddes pushed himself away from the desk, against which he had been leaning, and paced out a slow, deliberative circle. 'And there are other problems with the suicide theory. *Practical* problems. Throwing yourself from a high-speed train is no easy matter these days. The doors are centrally locked. They can't be opened when the train's moving. That leaves us with the windows. The only ones that open are in the doors. But it'd be quite a scramble to climb out. You'd need to be determined as well as desperate. Is that how Mr Askew seemed to you this afternoon, Mr Barnett?'

'No. He didn't. But I suppose . . .' Harry shrugged. 'He must have been.'

'Aye. Him . . . or someone else.'

53

'Someone else?'

'The inspector means he might have had help,' said Crawford.

'You're not serious?'

'We'll know more after the post mortem,' said Geddes. 'For the present, I'm just turning possibilities over in my mind. Aside from getting cold feet about your carry-on here, did he . . . do anything strange during the journey?'

'He got het up at one point,' Lloyd responded. 'For the life of me, I can't remember what about. Oh, and, er, didn't you say he seemed out of sorts after taking a phone call during lunch, Ossie?'

Harry nodded. 'A little, yes.'

'He had a mobile?' put in Crawford.

'Yes. He did.'

'Interesting,' murmured Geddes.

'What is?' asked Dangerfield.

'None found on the body, sir,' said Crawford.

'Perhaps it dropped out of his pocket while he was, er . . .' Dangerfield's line of reasoning petered out. Then he said, 'Or he could have left it in his bag. I forgot to tell you, Inspector. We took his bag with us when we left the train. We expected to hear from him, you see, and—'

'Where is it?' snapped Geddes.

'Er, in the minibus.'

Geddes smiled tolerantly. 'Well, perhaps we could go and take a look at it.'

They took the rear exit to the car park. The night was cold and still, though Harry suspected he was shivering for other reasons than the temperature. Dangerfield opened the minibus, turned on the internal light and pulled Askew's bag out from under the seat where he had left it.

It was a small and clearly very old leather suitcase, much scuffed and scratched around the edges. And it was not locked. Dangerfield released the catches and raised the lid. Inside was a humdrum assortment of clothes and toiletries, including the neatly folded suit Askew had presumably been planning to wear that evening. But no mobile phone.

'It doesn't seem to be here, does it?' growled Geddes.

'Perhaps it did fall out of his pocket after all,' said Dangerfield. 'Like you said, it must have been a struggle to climb out of the window.'

Geddes gave a sceptical grunt. 'Or it could have been taken. From his pocket. Or, later, from this *unlocked* case.'

'Now, hold on,' Dangerfield bridled. 'If you're suggesting—'

'I'm suggesting nothing.' Geddes sighed and flicked the lid of the case shut. 'I must thank you all for your co-operation. I may need you to make formal statements about what you know of the circumstances leading up to Mr Askew's death, but that can wait. First things first. I'll send a car for you at eight o'clock tomorrow morning, Mr Lloyd. Is that too early for you?'

'Well . . .' Lloyd shrugged. 'I suppose not.'

'Good. Let's go, Sergeant. Give Mr Dangerfield a receipt for the bag. Then we can leave these gentlemen to get some sleep. I'm sure they need it.'

They watched Geddes and Crawford climb into their car and drive away. The noise of the engine receded into the night and was swallowed by the prevailing silence. None of them said a word for a minute or more. Then Lloyd coughed, his breath pluming in the still, cold air.

'Bloody hell, Danger. What do we do now?'

'Go in and tell the others.'

'Tell them what, exactly? That Crooked's topped himself?'

'Well, he has, hasn't he?'

'Geddes isn't sure,' said Harry with bleak conviction.

Lloyd stared at him incredulously. 'What are you saying?'

'I'm saying Geddes doesn't buy the idea of Peter Askew crawling through a window and jumping to his death from the train. And the missing phone's made him doubly suspicious. It would have revealed where that call Peter took came from. There might have been messages on it as well. Who knows?'

'No-one,' said Dangerfield. 'Now.'

'Exactly.'

'You're the only one who saw the bloody thing, Ossie,' Lloyd said irritably.

'Think I imagined it?'

'No. 'Course not. But . . . it's bloody odd he never used it while he was with me all yesterday and this morning.'

'You can't have been with him the whole time.'

'No. Obviously. But most of it. Apart from when he was asleep. And, er . . . a few hours yesterday afternoon and evening.'

Despite lingering shock and the onset of bone-deep fatigue, Harry's curiosity was aroused. 'How'd that come about?'

'Oh, well, when we got to Paddington, after leaving you in Swindon, Crooked said he was going to meet a friend and would join me at my daughter's in Neasden later. He got to her house . . . about eight o'clock.'

'What friend was this?'

'Somebody he'd worked with at London Zoo, he said.'

'Name?'

'If he told me, I don't remember.'

'And where were they meeting?'

'Somewhere in the centre. I don't know.'

'Did you mention this to Geddes, Jabber?' asked Dangerfield.

'No. I . . . never thought to.'

'Perhaps that's just as well. Some reunion, hey? This is going to knock them all for six. Do you think I should let Barry know what's happened?' (Chipchase's nickname had evidently deserted Dangerfield at this time of stress.)

'Have you got a number for him?' Harry was more than slightly interested in the answer to that question.

'No. He left in such a rush. I . . . forgot to ask. But I thought you might . . .'

''Fraid not.'

A few wordless seconds expanded in the darkness around them. Then Lloyd said, 'He did have a sister in Manchester, didn't he, Ossie?'

Harry weighed his answer as carefully as he could. 'I don't know. For sure.'

'A sister anywhere?'

'If you'd asked me before today . . . I'd have said no.'

'Oh, great. Bloody great.'

Dangerfield cleared his throat. 'Let's go in.'

And in they went.

TEN

Donna's wake-up call the following morning was literally that, rousing Harry from seldom-plumbed depths of unconsciousness. No-one had hurried to bed after Dangerfield's announcement of Askew's death. Reactions had varied from the numb to the disbelieving, but all had taken time to be articulated. Harry had finally reached his room around two o'clock and had been unable to sleep for another hour or so after that.

For reasons he did not completely understand, he failed to pass the news on to Donna. Sparing her unnecessary worry was no longer the point. Now it was *necessary* worry he was determined not to inflict. She seemed to blame his lack of obvious jollity on a hangover, which strangely he did not have. But he was happy to let her believe he did.

'You didn't drink enough water, did you?'

'Guilty as charged.'

'Promise me you won't spend the whole weekend in a dehydrated haze of alcohol.'

'I promise.'

And somehow he suspected this was a promise he could be confident of keeping.

He made himself some coffee, then took a bath and, skipping the communal breakfast, headed out on foot. He needed to think and hoped some bracing lungfuls of Deeside air would

58

aid his efforts. He left the hotel, walked downhill towards the village, then struck out along the footpath behind the church. It had formed part of the cross-country route WO Trench had insisted they flog round twice a week, 'to stop you going any softer than you already are'. But there was no question of Harry breaking into a commemorative trot. A steady walk would serve his purpose.

The path curved round the hillside ahead of him as he went, the pale trunks and branches of the still leafless silver birches casting an illusion of frost across the surrounding woodland. He tried to recall what Askew had said to him on the platform at Edinburgh and earlier on the train, but could retrieve only snatches of disconnected phrases. He had been anxious about something. That at least was clear. And it concerned Operation Clean Sheet. 'It depends on how you remember things,' he had said. Yes. Those had been his very words. 'And how you forget them.' What had he meant? What *could* he have meant?

A figure appeared suddenly on the path ahead, a dark shape moving fast. Harry pulled up in surprise, then recognized Erica Rawson, running lithely towards him in tracksuit and trainers. She smiled and waved, slowing to a halt beside him, where she jogged on the spot, breathing hard, her face flushed, her hair damp with sweat despite the chill of the morning.

'I'm running off last night's food and drink,' she panted. 'How are you feeling?'

'OK. I . . . needed some air myself.'

'Plenty of it out here.'

'We used to . . .' He smiled ruefully. 'Never mind.'

'Thinking about Peter Askew?'

'Hard not to.'

'Especially as the last person to speak to him.'

'Thanks for reminding me.'

'Sorry. I didn't mean . . .' She stopped jogging. 'Really. I'm sorry. It was a terrible thing.'

'We never know what's going on in someone else's head, do

we? I mean, why come all the way to Scotland just to . . .' He looked past her into the ghostly grey depths of the wood. 'It doesn't make sense.'

'Everything makes sense, Harry. It's just that sometimes it takes a while to figure out what the sense is.'

'Very profound.'

'No. Just true.'

'Yeah. I suppose so. Well, you'd better get on. I don't want you catching cold on my account.'

'I'll see you later, then.'

'OK. 'Bye.'

She turned and ran on down the slope towards the church. Harry watched her go, then set off slowly in the opposite direction.

Erica was right, of course. Everything did make sense. But Harry was a long way from deducing how. When he got back to Kilveen Castle, he found Dangerfield gathering the Clean Sheeters together for the excursion he had planned for them. 'The show must go on,' he declared optimistically.

But the cast for the show was undeniably reduced. With Askew dead, Chipchase absent, Lloyd performing his civic duty at a mortuary in Dundee, Dr Starkie opting out for reasons of his own and Erica sending a message to the effect that she did not wish to cramp the boys' style, just seven were left to embark on Dangerfield's mystery minibus tour of Deeside.

They had scarcely strayed beyond Lumphanan during Operation Clean Sheet apart from fortnightly excursions into Aberdeen on the train. Their knowledge of Kilveen's wider surroundings was thus zero. Dangerfield took them on a scenic drive west, up the valley into the foothills of the Cairngorms as far as Braemar, where they sought out the hair-of-the-dog drink that several of them badly needed and Harry bought a postcard to send to Donna and Daisy. On the way back, Tancred specially requested a stop at Crathie, so that he could satisfy his royalist sentiments by gazing at the turret-tops of Balmoral Castle, which was all of the castle he *could* gaze at above its screen of trees. Dangerfield switched to the south bank of the Dee at Ballater so that he could show them one of his favourite salmon-fishing spots. Then it was on to Aboyne – and lunch at the Boat Inn.

So far, no-one had mentioned what must have been at the forefront of all their thoughts. That changed as they started on the beer, however, and soon theories were being swapped as to how Askew's suicide could be explained. Since Dangerfield and Wiseman had not actually met him, they had to rely on the others for insights into his state of mind at the time. Judd gave it as his opinion that Askew was exactly as he had always been – subdued, introspective, unpredictable. Tancred, on the other hand, said he was surprised and yet not surprised by what Askew had done. 'If I'd had to nominate one among us as a suicide risk, it would have been Crooked. There was always something slightly unstable about him.'

Harry sought to avoid putting forward a theory himself. The truth was that he did not have one. He kept trying to imagine Askew pushing down the window in the train door as far as it would go, then heaving himself out into the battering rush of air. But the image would not stick. Another, more macabre yet oddly more plausible version of events intruded. In this, Askew was already unconscious from a blow to the head as an unknown figure pushed the window down and propelled him through the gap to his death on the track below. Put on the spot by Wiseman, however, Harry said nothing of this. 'I don't know what happened to him,' he maintained. 'I simply don't know.'

Dangerfield's choice of afternoon destination was Craigievar, the pink-hued masterpiece of Deeside castle-building on which the architects of Kilveen had clearly based their work. Tancred and Wiseman derived more pleasure from a tour of the apartments than the rest, for whom details of Scottish baronial plasterwork held limited appeal. All in all, Harry and the others gave a poor impersonation of historically sensitive tourists, but put away a National Trust tea with gusto.

Nobody mentioned Lloyd, but Harry assumed he was not alone in wondering how poor old Jabber's trip to Dundee had gone. It was only a matter of time before they found out. Back at Kilveen they established that he had returned an hour or so previously, but no-one felt inclined to call up to his room. Harry indeed was glad to retire to his own, in the hope of catching up on some of the sleep he had missed the night before.

He had barely lain down on the bed, however, when there was a knock at the door. Given that he had put out the DO NOT DISTURB sign, this was either exceptionally inconsiderate housekeeping or some kind of emergency. His sleepiness was instantly banished.

'Yes?'

'It's Jabber, Ossie. I spotted the minibus coming up the drive. Can I come in?'

Harry got up and opened the door. Lloyd made a heavy-footed, downcast entrance and sank into one of the armchairs flanking the mullioned window.

'Christ, what a day it's been.' He rubbed one hand across his forehead. 'You see these . . . drawers they use to store corpses . . . in cop shows on the telly . . . but you never think some day you're going to find yourself watching a real one sliding open . . . and an old chum's face staring up at you.'

'It must have been grim.'

'And then some.'

'What sort of injuries . . .'

'Nothing too gruesome. They'd cleaned him up quite a bit, I think. Here' – Lloyd tapped an area above his left eyebrow – 'was still a mess, though. Must have smacked it on a rail or something. What a way to go, hey?'

'You said it.'

'How was your day?'

'OK. A drive along the valley. Pub lunch. A National Trust

castle. Tea and scones. It was fine. Like a regular OAPs' outing. I'm sorry you couldn't join us. We all were.'

'Yeah, well . . .' Lloyd coughed. 'I didn't come to make you feel guilty for having a nice day, Ossie. After the horror show at the morgue, Geddes had some more questions for me.'

'Oh yeah?'

'Mostly about this.' Lloyd pulled a sheet of paper from his pocket. 'It's a photocopy of something they found on Crooked. Geddes wants me to pass it round. See if it rings a bell with anyone. Take a look.'

It was an official notification of some kind; originally enclosed perhaps with a letter. The name that appeared in capitals at the head of the page seized Harry's attention at once.

CHIPCHASE SHELTERED HOLDINGS LTD
Creditors of and investors in the above-named company, now in receivership, are invited to attend a meeting at the Thistle Hotel, Fry Street, Middlesbrough, at 2.30 p.m. on Saturday 22 February 2003, at which a representative of the officially appointed receivers, Grey & Williamson, chartered accountants, of Marston House, Bright Street, Middlesbrough, will be available to answer questions concerning the company's remaining assets and outstanding liabilities.

'I had to tell them Fission was one of us, Ossie,' said Lloyd, when he had given Harry more than enough time to read and digest the contents. 'There was no way round it.'

'Of course not.'

'I had to tell them he'd high-tailed it off to attend the funeral of his sister as well.'

'A sister I told you I'd never heard of.'

'Yeah. Well, I didn't mention that. Or your garage business. Geddes never asked the right questions. I didn't want to make trouble for you by volunteering anything.'

'Thanks. Though where the trouble for me is in this . . .'

'Geddes didn't buy the sister story, Ossie. He assumed Fission vamoosed to avoid meeting Crooked because he was one of his creditors. Matter of fact, that's what I reckon too.'

'It certainly looks like it.'

'Question is, did Fission drag any of us apart from Crooked into . . . whatever Chipchase Sheltered Holdings was?'

'Who knows? And what if he did? It's not the first time one of Barry's little enterprises has gone bust owing people money. And this was . . . two years ago. Why was Peter carrying it around with him? What was he planning to do when he met Barry?'

'Search me.'

'Did Geddes have any suggestions?'

'No. None he gave me the benefit of, anyway. But he did ask me a strange question as I was leaving. Bloody strange. It's been bugging me ever since. I can't figure out what he was getting at.'

Harry waited for Lloyd to continue, but there was only silence. For several long, slow seconds. Then Harry's patience snapped. 'And the question was?'

'What?' Lloyd jumped in his seat. 'Oh, sorry. Of course. Yes. The question. Well, he asked me . . . how I could be sure Fission wasn't on the train when it left Dundee.'

ELEVEN

The strictly logical answer to Geddes's question was that no-one could be sure. Chipchase had told Dangerfield he was flying to Manchester. But he could have travelled south by train instead and boarded the London to Aberdeen train at Dundee – or Edinburgh, come to that. Almost anything was possible. But where was Geddes's speculation leading? He surely did not suspect Chipchase of murdering Askew. The very idea was absurd. Except that Geddes did not know Chipchase as well as Harry did, so perhaps the absurdity was not apparent to him. He reckoned he was onto something. Or someone. And the obvious candidate was the former proprietor of Chipchase Sheltered Holdings Ltd – long since in receivership.

The true explanation for his old friend's daylight flit from Aberdeen seemed clear to Harry. It was what Geddes had grudgingly suggested himself. Chipchase had persuaded Askew to invest in one of his dodgy enterprises, with predictable results he had no wish to discuss during the weekend at Kilveen Castle that had loomed ahead of him. Cue dead sister and grieving dash to Manchester. It was as simple as that.

Ironically, as things turned out, he would never have had to discuss the matter with Askew. But Askew, of course, might not have been the only veteran of Operation Clean Sheet duped into trusting Chipchase with his money, which Harry could have told them from personal experience was an act of folly. It would be interesting to find out how many had fallen for the silver-tongued old rogue's patter – assuming anyone was prepared to admit it.

The clouds thinned as the afternoon turned towards evening. Mellow sunlight bathed the castle. A call from the reception desk alerted Harry to a change of venue for pre-dinner drinks. They were to be held on the roof. The upper reaches of the tower had been out of bounds to Professor Mac's students during Operation Clean Sheet and the door leading to the roof permanently locked. This was actually their first chance to sample its panoramic views. Dangerfield, it was revealed, had planned that they should do so all along, on a 'weather permitting' basis. And the weather had happily permitted.

Harry phoned Donna before leaving his room and came clean about Askew's death. He presented it as a complete mystery, which it was, of course, while failing to mention the connection with Chipchase Sheltered Holdings Ltd. 'I didn't want to worry you,' he explained lamely, only for her to retort, as well she might, 'But now I'm worried about what else you mightn't be telling me.' He assured her there was nothing, by which he really meant nothing he judged she needed to know. A weekend of domestic normality was about to unfold in Vancouver. Daisy would be going back to school on Monday after the Easter break. Donna would be preparing to stretch her students' minds at UBC. Fretting over what might be happening to him in Scotland would not be good for them. Accordingly, Harry struck a jaunty tone throughout the conversation – and hoped it was more convincing over a long-distance telephone line than it would have been face to face.

He spent longer talking to Donna and Daisy than he had anticipated and was consequently the last to make it to the roof party.

It was strange to have spent three months at Kilveen Castle

without ever stepping out onto the flagged and balustraded platform at the top of the tower. The gilded weathercock on the next turret was shimmering in the sun, the flag of St Andrew above them stirring lazily in the slightest of breezes. A golden hue had been cast over the ruckled carpet of farmland around the castle, while the mountains to the north and west and the undersides of the clouds were purpling in the evening light.

Waitresses were on hand with champagne and canapés. Matthews, the hotel manager, was schmoozing with his guests. There was laughter amid the burble of conversation and the popping of corks. A phrase drifted into Harry's ear as he accepted a glass of bubbly and took a first sip. 'Crooked would have wanted us to carry on, I'll bet.' The words were Judd's, but there were nods and murmurs of endorsement all round.

'Do you think it's true?'

Harry turned to find Erica standing close beside him, looking intently at him as she rotated her nearly empty glass back and forth by the stem. Judd for one, Harry sensed, would approve of the closer fitting outfit she was wearing this evening – and its lower neckline. 'Hello,' he said, smiling. 'Isn't it lovely up here?'

She smiled back at him. 'It is.'

'As for Peter, I don't know. It's the sort of thing people say, isn't it?'

'Yes. So, here's another platitude. Tell me about your day. Braemar, Balmoral, Craigievar and a pub somewhere in the middle, according to Johnny. Is that right?'

'Spot-on.'

'All new territory for you?'

'Absolutely. Professor Mac and your boss kept us chained to our desks. There were no jaunts into the countryside during Operation Clean Sheet.'

'And getting out onto this roof with its unforgettable views is a first too?'

'Not according to some,' Tancred cut in, rounding a corner of the balustrade to join them and flashing Erica a raffish smile. 'Jabber's just been telling Magister and me that he's been up here before.'

'Really?' Harry watched Erica's gaze slide past Tancred towards Lloyd and Wiseman. 'How did that come about?'

'He was more than somewhat vague as to specifics. Indeed, it may be no more than stress-induced déjà vu. He hasn't had the carefree day the rest of us have enjoyed, after all. I certainly don't envy him his visit to the mortuary in Dundee. Are you familiar with the city of jam, jute and journalism, Erica?'

'Not at all. Actually, excuse me, will you? Dr Starkie's looking lost.' And with that she was gone, threading a path through the Clean Sheeters and waitresses towards Dr Starkie, who was standing alone near the flagpole.

'I think you frightened her off, Tapper,' said Harry.

'Nonsense. More likely my arrival on the scene was the excuse she was waiting for to shake you off.'

'If you say so.'

'What she sees in that bloodless creep Starkie I can't imagine.'

'A mentor, I should think.'

'Should you? Well, your judgement isn't exactly flawless, is it, Ossie? Choosing Fission as a business partner doesn't say much for your powers of discrimination. From what Jabber's been telling us, he's still up to his old tricks. What was it? Chipchase Sheltered Holdings Ltd? Were you involved in that?'

'No. I wasn't. Were you?'

'Certainly not.'

'No reason to be so tetchy, then, is there?'

'What?'

'You'd be more of an expert than me on the etiquette of occasions like this, Tapper, but isn't the idea to have a pleasant little chat over a glass of champoo and admire the view?'

'Yes.' Tancred smiled through clenched teeth. 'Isn't that what we're doing?'

*   *   *

68

They were joined by Judd, Gregson and Fripp, sparing Harry further verbal fencing with Tancred. He swiftly drifted to the margins of the group and, noticing that Wiseman had left Lloyd to join Dangerfield and Matthews, walked across to where the Welshman was leaning heavily against the wall flanking the door at the top of the spiral staircase. His face was flushed, sweat sheening his upper lip. His gaze was skittering and unfocused.

'This stuff goes straight to your head, doesn't it?' said Harry, raising his glass.

'It's not that,' said Lloyd huskily. 'Bloody vertigo. Came over me while I was standing by the parapet. And not just vertigo either. Something . . . weird.'

'Tapper said you'd . . . been up here before.'

'Feels like it.' Lloyd shook his head. 'God, this is . . . the strangest bloody thing.'

'Are you sure you're all right?'

'No. Matter of fact, I'm . . . sure I'm not.'

'You've had a long hard day, Jabber. You're probably just tired. We're not as young as we were.'

'Have you been up here before, Ossie?'

'No.'

'Sure?'

'Absolutely. It was always kept locked.'

'Yeah. It was, wasn't it? So, how did I get up here?'

'Maybe you didn't. We've all experienced déjà vu. It doesn't mean—'

'*This* means something.' Lloyd drained his glass. 'You can take my word for that.' He pushed himself away from the wall and clasped Harry by the elbow, swaying slightly as he did so. 'Do me a favour, will you, Ossie?'

'Sure.'

'Apologize to the others for me. I'm going down to my room. I need a lie-down. Might skip dinner. Ask them to send me up a sandwich later. I'd be sorry to, er, miss out on the . . . grand supper, but . . . I just can't . . . at the moment . . .' Lloyd's hand fell back to his side. 'I just can't. OK?'

69

'OK, Jabber. They'll understand. You take it easy.'

'Thanks. Don't worry. I'll be fine. I just need to rest.'

'Of course.'

'Yeah. A rest. OK. Thanks. I'll, er, see you, Ossie.'

Lloyd turned and started down the stairs, taking each step with exaggerated care, his hand grasping the rail tightly, like a man negotiating a ship's companionway in a storm. But there was no storm. Unless it was inside his head.

Harry was never to speak to him again.

TWELVE

Dinner that night, planned by Dangerfield as the high spot of the weekend, never quite lived up to its billing. The quality and quantity of the food and drink could not be faulted and Dangerfield did his best to jolly them along. But Lloyd's absence – and the shadow cast by Askew's death – took a perceptible toll. There was also the question of their stamina, both mental and physical. Harry suspected he was not alone in running short of amusing recollections of life at Kilveen in 1955, nor in yearning for a beer and a light snack followed by an early night, instead of fine wine, haute cuisine and a soak in the bar until the small hours.

His suspicion was confirmed when Gregson headed for bed as soon as dinner was over. Dr Starkie soon followed. Then Erica made her excuses and left them to it. Harry felt he had done his duty when the longcase clock in the lounge adjoining the bar struck midnight. Judd had just proposed a few rounds of a game called Cardinal Puff they had sometimes played at the Macbeth Arms to decide who would buy the next round. Harry could not recall the rules, but was certain it was a bad idea. With slurred accusations of cowardice ringing in his ears, he took himself off.

He woke late next morning, no more than mildly hung over and relieved to realize that the reunion had nearly run its course. He would stay until Monday and travel back to

London on the train with the others because that was the easy option. The truth was, however, as he explained in a phone call to Donna, that he would rather clear out straight away.

'I guess Barry was the biggest draw. I'd have enjoyed seeing him again, despite all the bad turns he's done me. If I'd known he wasn't going to show up, well, I'm not sure I'd have bothered.'

'You'll be glad you went in the end, hon. You know you will. There'll be the pics to laugh at for a start. Taken many?'

'Pics?'

'You did buy a camera, didn't you?'

'Well, er . . . no, I . . .'

'Oh, *Harry*. I told you to. A cheap disposable. Come on. There's still time.'

'It's Sunday. All the shops will be closed.'

'Rubbish.'

'Well, most of them. This is Scotland.'

'Yeah. And this is your wife speaking. Buy camera. Take pictures. That's an order.'

After a bath and room-service breakfast, Harry headed out into the grey, still morning. He doubted if the post office and general store in Lumphanan would sell cameras, but the receptionist reckoned the shop would at least be open, so he had little choice but to make the effort.

The village had grown in fifty years. The view through the trees as he descended the hill from the castle revealed a lobe of modern housing east of the main street, which had been farmland back in 1955. The gaps between the old cottages in the centre had been filled in as well. Strangely, this did not make it a busier place. Sunday morning in Lumphanan was as quiet as it had ever been.

There was a modest queue at the post office, however. Newspapers, cigarettes and milk were much in demand. Harry toured the shelves in vain search of a camera, but decided he had better double-check before giving up. He joined the queue.

The man in front of Harry turned round and squinted oddly at him, then did so again. He looked local, flat-capped and dressed in ancient tweed. He was a short, lean, tanned old fellow, with an unshaven chin and watery but sharply focused eyes. There was a smell about him of damp dog and stale tobacco. Harry suspected the venerable Jack Russell terrier tethered outside was his. They made a natural pairing.

'Morning,' said Harry in response to the second squint.

The man held the squint, then said, 'Good morning to you.'

'Nice one, for the time of year.'

'Aye. We get such mild springs now. Not what I'm used to. And not what you got last time you were here, I seem to recall.'

'Sorry?'

'You're staying up at the castle?'

'Yes.'

'So, you're here for the reunion?'

'I am. Yes.'

'Then you'll understand what I mean.' He turned away as he reached the head of the queue and handed over the money for a newspaper already folded for him to take. Then he was gone. Leaving Harry to confirm the shop's stock of necessities did not extend to cameras before making his own exit.

The old fellow was waiting for him outside, Jack Russell untethered. 'Which one are you, then?' he enquired with a cock of the head.

'Which *one*?'

'I remember most of your names. Let me see.' He nodded. 'Aye. You're Barnett, I reckon.'

'Good God. How did you—'

'It's Stronach, man. Do you not know me?'

'Stronach.' Of course. The gardener-handyman kept on when the University acquired the castle, whose wife had been responsible for cooking their meals – if cooking was the right word to describe what she had done with food. But the couple had surely been middle-aged. Stronach had to be ninety if he was a day. 'Is it really you?'

'It is.'

'How are you?'

'As you see me.'

'Mrs Stronach?'

'Dead and gone.'

'Sorry to hear that.'

'I've had a good few years to get over it.' He smiled crookedly. 'You'll not be surprised to know I eat better now I'm cooking for myself.'

'I'm amazed you remember me.'

'Well, fifty year ago is sharper in my mind than last week. And you've not changed so very much. White hair and a beer belly aren't so hard to imagine away.'

Harry laughed despite himself. 'It's good to know you still tell it like it is.'

'Are you going back to the castle?'

'Yes.'

'I'll walk with you as far as my cottage.'

They set off, rounding the corner by the Macbeth Arms at a faster pace than Harry would have expected a nonagenarian to set.

'What were you after in the shop?'

'A camera.'

'For some snapshots to remember your old comrades by?'

'Something like that.'

'It's too late to snap Askew, though, isn't it?'

'What?' Harry could not disguise his surprise at the question. How did Stronach know about Askew?

'They named him on the local news last night. Travelling to Aberdeen for an RAF reunion, so they said he was. And the police are keeping an open mind about the circumstances of his death. They said that as well.'

'Did they?'

'That'll have blown some of the froth off your get-together, I shouldn't wonder.'

'You could say that.'

74

'He was a nervy one, as I recall. Jump at his own shadow, would Askew.'

'Not any more.'

'Who else have you got up there, then?'

'Johnny Dangerfield's organized the do. Then there's, er, Milton Fripp, Owen Gregson, Bill Judd, Mervyn Lloyd, Gilbert Tancred . . . and Neville Wiseman.'

'What about the rest?'

'Most of them are dead, I'm afraid.'

'Aye, well, fifty years is a long time. You'd expect that, I suppose.'

'Why don't you come up and say hello?'

'I don't think so.' Stronach pulled up by the gate of his cottage, a hotchpotch of brick, timber, slate and corrugated iron camouflaged by an overgrown garden. There was a well-tilled vegetable patch off to one side, but otherwise little sign of active cultivation. Picture-postcard countryman's dwelling it was not. 'I was surprised when I heard about the reunion.' He slipped the latch, stepped through with the dog and closed the gate behind him. Harry was clearly not being invited in. 'A mite risky, that kind of thing.'

'Risky?'

'You never know what'll come of it, man. Simple as that.'

But it did not seem simple to Harry. And then a thought struck him that made it even less so. 'When we were here, in 'fifty-five, the upper floors of the tower and the roof were kept locked, weren't they?'

Stronach frowned. 'Aye. They would have been.'

'Why?'

'The Urquharts, my original employers, left behind a good deal of their furniture when they moved out. It was stored in the tower. They'd not have wanted you lot clodhopping around up there.'

'So, none of us could ever have gone up to the roof?'

'Not in the ordinary way of things, no.'

'Was there an *un*ordinary way of things?'

'I wouldn't know.'

'Wouldn't you?'

Stronach's only answer was a half-smile and a faint nod of the head. 'I'm away in to read my paper, so I'll say goodbye.' He turned towards the shrub-shrouded door of his cottage. 'Enjoy the rest of your reunion.'

Harry wandered off along the street, puzzling over Stronach's remarks. It was hard to judge whether they meant anything, or were just an old man's deliberate attempts at mystification. There was no reason why Stronach should know more of events at Kilveen than the Clean Sheeters themselves – no reason, at any rate, that Harry was aware of.

As he approached the sharp bend below the church, a car nosed into view, descending the hill from the castle. It was a silver-grey Peugeot saloon, identical to one Harry had seen parked at the hotel. As it rounded the bend, he recognized the driver as Wiseman. Lloyd was sitting next to him in the passenger seat.

Harry raised his hand, but Wiseman drove straight on, his gaze fixed firmly ahead, apparently oblivious to Harry's presence on the verge. Lloyd did see him, however. Their eyes met as the car passed him.

Whether Lloyd said anything to Wiseman there was no way to tell. The car cruised on along the village street at a steady pace, turned onto the main road at the end and vanished from Harry's sight.

He was never to see Mervyn Lloyd again.

THIRTEEN

Back at Kilveen Castle, Harry met Dangerfield in reception, looking far from happy. He was cross-questioning Bridget about something – or rather someone.

'Is that all he said?'

'I'm afraid so, Mr Dangerfield. Back as soon as possible. Those were his words.'

'But we're— Oh, Harry.' Now, just like Barry's, Harry's nickname had deserted him. 'Thank God *you* haven't run out on us.'

'I walked into the village. Magister passed me in his hire car on my way back. Jabber was with him.'

'Jabber too? This is bloody ridiculous. I told everyone yesterday we'd start at eleven. Well, I'm not waiting on that pair. They'll just have to catch up with us at the pub if they're not back by the time we leave. Can you tell them where we'll be, Bridget? The Lairhillock Inn.'

'Certainly, Mr Dangerfield.'

Harry stepped back outside with Dangerfield, whom he judged to be in need of a calming breath of fresh air. Wiseman's unexplained jaunt with Lloyd had clearly stretched his patience. He tried to raise Lloyd on his mobile, but got no answer. And he had no number to try for Wiseman.

'I'm beginning to wonder if organizing this reunion was a

good idea,' he complained as he snapped his phone shut. 'Nothing seems to be going the way I'd planned.'

'Perhaps Magister just wanted to show Jabber some of the sights he missed yesterday.'

'You'd think he might at least have consulted me in that case.'

'That would have been rather out of character, wouldn't it?'

'You can say that again.'

'I went to the post office to try and buy a camera,' Harry remarked in an effort to brighten Dangerfield's mood. 'Thought we ought to take a few commemorative photographs.'

'Before there's no-one left to photograph, you mean?'

'I'm sure it's—'

'No, no. It's a good idea. I should have thought of it myself. Get one?'

'No such luck.'

'Never mind. We'll stop in Banchory. Should be able to buy a camera there. Smith's will be open.'

'Great. Oh, and I, er, bumped into Stronach.'

'Stronach? You're having me on. He must be older than Methuselah.'

'Looked well on it.'

'You should have asked him to join us.'

'I did.'

'And is he going to?'

'No. But then he always was a miserable so-and-so.'

Dangerfield sighed. 'We don't seem to be too popular, do we, Harry?' Then he summoned a smile. 'Well, we'll just have to put a brave face on it.'

Dangerfield's plan for the day comprised a visit to another well-preserved old castle, Crathes, near Banchory, a leisurely lunch at a country inn, followed by tea back at Kilveen. In the event, he delayed their departure by more than half an hour in the hope that Wiseman and Lloyd would return. But they did not. The subsequent stop in Banchory to buy a camera ate further into their schedule and a decision was taken to proceed straight to the Lairhillock Inn, several of the party freely admitting to having had their fill of castles.

Much of the conversation over lunch naturally concerned the absence of Wiseman and Lloyd. Erica, who had joined them today, while Dr Starkie rested up at Kilveen – 'He's not as fit as he pretends,' she explained – wondered if their sudden departure, destination unknown, might be connected with Lloyd's strange turn on the castle roof the evening before. He had, after all, been talking to Wiseman at the time.

'And to me, my dear,' said Tancred. 'But, as you see, I was not invited along. I suppose it's possible Magister suggested a drive to Jabber in an effort to jolly him out of his fit of the blues.'

'That would explain why he left you out of it, Tapper,' laughed Judd, who was putting away the Lairhillock's beer at an impressive rate. 'Probably reckoned a succession of snide cracks by you wasn't what Jabber needed.'

'This weekend's been a positive revelation to me, Judder,' Tancred responded. 'I'd quite forgotten how side-splittingly funny you could be.'

Harry attempted to head off an exchange of insults between the two by describing his encounter with Stronach. Astonishment that the gruff old gardener was still alive and well was the general reaction. But Erica took a more probing and disturbingly perceptive line.

'Did you think of asking him about how easy it was to get onto the roof back then, Harry?'

'Yes. As a matter of fact . . . I did.'

'And?'

'He said the Urquhart family furniture was stored on the upper floors. That's why they were strictly off limits to the likes of us.'

'No exceptions?'

'None.'

'He was positive about that?'

'Yes. He was.'

Harry had shied away instinctively from admitting just how ambiguous an answer Stronach had given. But he instantly regretted misrepresenting the old man, not least because the expression on Erica's face suggested she did not quite believe him. Dissembling never had been his forte.

Dangerfield tried Lloyd's mobile several times during lunch without success. It was not even ringing now, a circumstance which bred a number of wild theories about where he and Wiseman could be that was blocking the signal. They were evidently not en route to the Lairhillock Inn. A phone call to the hotel confirmed nothing had been seen or heard of them.

This was still the case when they returned to Kilveen in mid-afternoon. Dangerfield's exasperation had run its course by then. He suggested it was now or never where group photographs were concerned, so Matthews was drummed into service as cameraman, Dr Starkie was lured down from his room and they all assembled in grinning formation on the castle's front lawn. Gregson, it transpired, had brought his own camera, which he had been too diffident to mention. That too was put to use. It was agreed more photographs could be taken later when Wiseman and Lloyd condescended to rejoin them – assuming they did so before nightfall.

Sarcasm about the pair's mystery jaunt camouflaged an underlying anxiety. Harry felt sure everyone was thinking what he was thinking. It began like this with Askew. Would it end the same way? There was more going on over this week-end at Kilveen – far more – than the simple, light-hearted reunion Dangerfield had proposed. But Harry for one had not the remotest idea what it was.

The photographic session over, the party dispersed, some to their rooms, others to tea in the lounge. Harry took himself off for a walk around the grounds, transformed from the wilderness Stronach had presided over into artfully land-scaped lawns, hedges, shrubberies and rockeries, with a winding path beyond tracing a circular route through the surrounding woodland, which Harry followed for a quarter of an hour or so.

Returning via the extensive kitchen gardens, he heard the clink of mallet on ball from the croquet lawn as he was climbing the steps leading to it. At the top, he saw, to his surprise, Dr Starkie lining up a shot – and looking fit enough while he was about it – with Erica Rawson watching from the sidelines, leaning on her mallet. A less likely pair of croquet players he would have been hard pressed to imagine.

Erica saw him a second before Starkie, who was stooped in concentration over the ball, talking as he squinted towards the targeted hoop. 'We should beware of connecting events simply because they coincide,' he said. 'It's a classic—'

'Harry!' Erica shouted, cutting the doctor short.

'Barnett,' said Starkie in muted surprise, unravelling him-self stiffly from his stoop.

'Hi,' said Harry. 'Who's winning?'

'No clear leader so far.'

'He is,' said Erica, with a rueful smile. 'It's just that one of his tactics is not to admit it.'

'Aye, well, I have to try everything to compensate for the age gap.' Starkie ventured a rare smile of his own.

'I should have thought this was one sport where age wasn't much of a factor,' said Harry.

'It's always a factor,' Starkie responded. 'Surely you've—'

'*Erica*!' The voice slicing through their conversation was Dangerfield's. They looked up to see him hurrying along the flagstoned path from the castle towards them, his face clouded with concern.

'What's the matter?' Erica called.

'Is there any chance you could drive me into Aberdeen in your car? I honestly don't feel up to taking the minibus.' He arrived breathlessly at the edge of the lawn. 'It's . . . an emergency.'

'What's happened?' asked Harry.

'What? Oh, Harry. I didn't . . . see you there.' Dangerfield wiped some sweat from his brow. 'Sorry. I ought to . . . It's . . . bad news. There's been an accident. Magister's in Aberdeen Royal Infirmary. They've just phoned. I, er, think I ought to go and see him. The thing is, er . . .'

'What about Jabber?'

Dangerfield did not answer. His mouth shaped words he seemed unable to speak. His gaze met Harry's grimly across the lawn. Then, slowly and decisively, he shook his head.

FOURTEEN

Dangerfield told Harry and Erica the little he knew as soon as they had started for Aberdeen. Wiseman's car had run off the B road somewhere between Aboyne and Ballater around midday and had plunged into the river Dee. Wiseman had scrambled free, but Lloyd had been trapped inside, unconscious, and had drowned.

'It sounds like that stretch I showed you yesterday, Harry, where I sometimes fish. The road runs right along the riverbank. If you lost control travelling in either direction, you could easily end up in the river. There's simply nothing to stop you. You'd have to be gunning it, though.'

'I don't see Magister as a careful driver,' said Harry.

'No. Neither do I.'

'And which direction *was* he travelling in?' asked Erica.

'They didn't say. We can ask him. He's not in bad shape, apparently. Basically just cuts and bruises. But shaken up, of course. And shocked. He was too confused at first to get a message to us.' Dangerfield rubbed his eyes. 'What a bloody awful thing to happen.'

'At least this time we can be sure it was an accident,' said Harry. But, even as he said it, he realized they could not be sure. Of that or anything else.

At the Royal Infirmary, Erica suggested she wait in the car, reasoning that three visitors – one of them a woman he hardly knew – might be too much of a strain for Wiseman. So Harry and Dangerfield went in without her, following the signs through a warren of stairways and corridors to the ward where he was being kept under observation.

'The doctor thinks there may have been some concussion,' the sister explained, 'so we're keeping a careful eye on him. It'd be best if you didn't go straight in. The police are with him.'

There was a small seating area halfway back along the corridor leading to the ward. There Harry and Dangerfield perched on plastic chairs and toyed listlessly with dog-eared magazines while the late afternoon ticked slowly by.

It had not in fact ticked very far when an unpleasant surprise materialized in the form of Inspector Geddes. Harry had assumed the sister meant a local constable was noting down Wiseman's recollections of the crash. Instead, here was Geddes, all the way from Dundee, this time *sans* Sergeant Crawford.

'Mr Barnett and Mr Dangerfield. That's handy.'

'We've come to see how our friend's doing, Inspector,' said Dangerfield levelly.

'Not so bad, considering. Why don't you go on in and see for yourself, Mr Dangerfield? I'd like a wee word with Mr Barnett in private, if that's all right with him.'

'Fine,' said Harry, as casually as he could manage. 'Send Magister my best wishes, Danger.'

'Will do.' Dangerfield headed for the ward. He cast Harry a cautioning, sympathetic glance over Geddes's shoulder as he went.

'There's a room down here the sister said we could use,' said Geddes, leading the way along the corridor.

It occurred to Harry that he and Dangerfield had not given their names to the sister, so there was no way Geddes could have known he would have the opportunity of a 'private word'. Yet he had already arranged a venue for it. He must have been more or less certain Harry would be one of Wiseman's visitors, though in reality that had been largely a matter of chance. Vindicating the inspector's guesswork was a good way to attract suspicion, however – whether inadvertently or not.

The room was small and cheerlessly furnished, with a window looking out onto a loading bay. This, Harry surmised, might be where relatives of a patient were brought to receive bad news. And bad news, he already felt certain, was coming his way.

'I'm liaising with the Grampian force on this, Mr Barnett,' Geddes began. 'In view of the obvious connection with Mr Askew's death, they're happy for me to take an interest in what happened today.'

'Is there an obvious connection, Inspector?'

'It's obvious to me. How much do you know about the crash?'

'Not much. We were hoping Magister – Mr Wiseman – could tell us more.'

'Aye, well, he's told me as much as he seems able to, so I'll sum it up for you. Apparently, he left his fountain pen at the hotel bar in Braemar you all visited yesterday. The Fife Arms. Remember it?'

'Yes. That is, I couldn't swear to the name, but—'

'He phoned them this morning. They said they'd found the pen. So, he decided to drive over there in his hire car. He met Mr Lloyd on his way out and invited him along, Mr Lloyd having missed the trip yesterday. They got to Braemar, collected the pen and started back. He took the B road from Ballater to Aboyne, on the southern side of the Dee. He began to notice some play in the steering. Nothing too serious at first. Then it got worse. He should have stopped. He should certainly have slowed down. But he wanted to catch up with the rest of you, so . . . he didn't slow down. Just where the road runs close to the river, as he was approaching a bend, the steering failed completely. They went straight into the river. At some speed. Mr Lloyd wasn't wearing his seatbelt. He probably knocked himself out on the windscreen when they hit the water. Plus the car keeled over onto his side in the current. Mr Wiseman got out. He's not exactly sure how. He reached the bank and flagged down the next car. The driver helped him pull Mr Lloyd out, but it took a lot of doing. And by then it was too late.'

'Terrible,' Harry murmured.

'You said it. Especially for Mr Lloyd. He had a wife and grown children, I'm told. There'll be a lot of grief going around.'

'So there will.'

'Your reunion's beginning to look jinxed, isn't it?'

'Yes. It is.'

'But I don't believe in jinxes, Mr Barnett.'

'No?'

'Absolutely not. Our pathologist couldn't establish whether some of Mr Askew's head injuries were inflicted *before* he fell out of the train. But he couldn't rule out the possibility either. It'd be as easy to shove an unconscious man through an HST window as for a conscious man to crawl through, don't you reckon?'

'I'm not sure.'

'Well, *I'm* sure. And that's what matters. It's only a theory. I grant you that. But if we find evidence that the steering on Mr Wiseman's car was tampered with, it'll turn into a betting certainty.'

'Really?'

'Take my word for it. Now, whoever sabotaged the car was obviously out to get Mr Wiseman. They couldn't have known Mr Lloyd would be along for the ride. And they got lucky in a sense, with Mr Wiseman taking that riverside route and the Dee being in spate after all the rain we've had. Of course, they also got *un*lucky, because he survived. Maybe they were just chancing their arm. Making use of their . . . expertise . . . and seeing what might happen. You see the variables in all this, don't you?'

'Yes. I suppose so. But why—'

'*Why*? I don't know, Mr Barnett. Why should one of you old airmen – if that's who the culprit is – take it into his head to start murdering people he hasn't seen for fifty years? It's a good question. But it assumes you *haven't* seen each other for fifty years. And that isn't strictly true, is it? You and the absent Mr Chipchase, for instance. Close friends and business partners throughout that period, I gather.'

'You gather wrong.'

'Do I?'

'I haven't seen Barry in ten years. And our business association ended more than thirty years ago.'

'What kind of business was that?'

'A garage. Car sales and repairs.'

'Repairs? So, you know all about . . . steering mechanisms, for example.'

'Since you ask, no. I don't know anything about them.'

'Perhaps Mr Chipchase handled that side of things.'

'As a matter of fact, he did.'

'But he's attending his sister's funeral in Manchester, so we can rule him out. Or can we? Where *exactly* did his sister live, Mr Barnett?'

'I don't know.'

'But he did have a sister?'

'I . . . don't know.'

'You're going to tell me you don't know anything about Chipchase Sheltered Holdings Ltd as well, aren't you?'

'It's true. I don't.'

'A nasty little scam. Investors thought they were buying into a chain of exclusive nursing homes, with guaranteed rights to see out their days in one free of charge if they needed to. But it was Mr Chipchase's old age they were subsidizing, not their own. It looks like he suckered Mr Askew into investing. Maybe other old RAF chums as well. Maybe some of them were hoping to settle a score with him this weekend. Him and his . . . partner.'

'*Ex*-partner.'

'Aye. Of course. Ex.' Geddes moved his face closer to Harry's. The suspicion that the inspector had been eating pickled onions earlier in the day became a stomach-turning certainty. But Harry's stomach was turning for other reasons as well. 'A lot of the money was never recovered. Salted away with a trusted friend for safekeeping while Chipchase served his all too brief prison sentence. That'd be my bet.'

'Barry went to prison?'

'You didn't know that either, of course.'

'No. I didn't.'

'Eighteen months. He got out last autumn.'

'I had no idea.'

'Just like you had no idea Mr Wiseman and Mr Askew were investors in Chipchase Sheltered Holdings.'

'Magister's confirmed that?'

'He was too embarrassed to admit being taken for a ride when Mr Lloyd handed round the notice I gave him. But a dip in the Dee's cured him of that. Yes, he's confirmed it. How many others are there, Mr Barnett? You may as well tell me.'

'I don't know. I had nothing to do with it. I don't even live in this country any more. I was thousands of miles away when Barry was setting up his nursing home fraud. He'd have known better than try to involve me, anyway.'

'So you say.'

'It happens to be true.'

'Looking forward to flying home to . . . Vancouver, is it?'

'It is. And, yes, I am.'

'Pity. I'm going to have to ask you to put that on hold.'

'What?'

'In fact, I'd like you to stay in the Aberdeen area, at least for a few days. Until we can draw all the forensics together and see where they lead. Perhaps Mr Dangerfield could put you up. I gather he has a guestroom going begging.'

Harry took a long, deep breath. 'Is that really necessary, Inspector?'

'It's purely precautionary, Mr Barnett.' Geddes smiled. 'But I find precautions are *very* necessary in my line of work.'

FIFTEEN

Harry never got the chance to ask Dangerfield if he would be prepared to put him up. Geddes did the asking for him, before leaving the hospital. In the circumstances, Dangerfield had little choice but to agree. He was also obliged to pass on a message from Wiseman to the effect that he was too tired to see anyone else. Harry found himself turned away by one fellow Clean Sheeter and foisted on another. For this last he could only apologize, which he attempted to do as he and Dangerfield stood outside the main entrance to the hospital, watching Geddes hurry away towards his car.

'The bloody man's got it into his head that Barry and I are involved in some sort of murderous conspiracy. I'm sorry you've ended up with me as a house guest because of it, Danger. But it won't be for long. I'm sure of that. Once they establish the car crash really was an accident, he'll have to drop it.'

'What if they establish it *wasn't* an accident, Harry?'

'You surely don't believe Magister's car was sabotaged.'

'Magister believes it.'

'What? And that I was responsible?'

'He didn't come out and say so. But when I told him you were waiting to see him, he pleaded with me to stop you going in. He seemed . . . frightened.'

'Frightened? Of me?'

'I know. It's crazy. But what with Jabber dying in front of

89

him and Geddes banging on about Chipchase Sheltered Holdings . . .'

'You didn't invest in that, did you, Danger?'

'No. I'd never heard of it before yesterday. Besides, Barry's been staying with me. Do you think I'd have put him up if I'd been one of the punters he ripped off?'

'Point taken.'

'Personally, I don't think either of you has what it takes to kill anyone.'

'Thank God for that.'

'Unfortunately for you, my opinion doesn't count for much.'

'Perhaps I should go back in and try to make Magister understand how—'

'Leave it for now, Harry. He'll probably be thinking more rationally after a night's sleep. We probably all will.'

They agreed to say nothing to the others about Harry's status as a suspect, at least for the moment. The atmosphere at Kilveen Castle for the rest of their stay promised to be strained enough without that information being added to the mix. It meant Erica had to be kept in the dark as well, which obliged both men to guard their tongues during the drive back. But when she suggested diverting to see the site of the crash, Harry did not object. He welcomed a postponement of their arrival at the castle – and the torrent of unanswerable questions it would set in motion. He was also curious to see the stretch of river where his alleged plot against Wiseman was supposed to have reached its climax – and where poor old Jabber had stopped jabbering for all time.

Blue and white police tape fastened to stakes marked out a cordon round a set of wheel ruts cutting across the narrow grass verge between the road and the riverbank. It was the only sign of the earlier accident. Otherwise all was much as it had been during the brief stop Dangerfield had made there during his minibus tour the previous day. The Dee was a cold, grey, speeding mass of water, with dull green fields on its other side and dark, whale-backed mountains forming the western horizon. The road hugged the line of the river, hemmed in by a wooded hillside. There was a fishermen's hut tucked away under the trees and a pull-in for cars, where they stopped and gazed at the empty scene in silence for a minute or more before climbing out.

'You'd never know, would you?' murmured Dangerfield.

'It looks so . . . peaceful,' said Erica. 'I can understand why you fish here.'

'I don't think I ever will again.'

'That's a pity.'

'It's all a—' Dangerfield was interrupted by the trill of his mobile. He yanked it out of his pocket and answered. 'Hello? . . . Oh . . . Yes, hello.' Then he waved an apology to Harry and Erica and walked away out of earshot.

'Is it my imagination, Harry, or does Johnny hold himself in some irrational way responsible for everything that's gone wrong this weekend?'

'I guess that's inevitable. The reunion *was* his idea, after all. But none of this is his fault.'

'He'll be left to cope with the aftermath, though, won't he, when you all go your separate ways tomorrow.'

'Actually, I'm not leaving the area. Not tomorrow, anyway. Danger's putting me up for a few days.'

'Good. That'll be a help. It was kind of you to suggest it.'

'I didn't. It was Inspector Geddes's idea.'

'Geddes?'

'I'm his prime suspect.' Pretence on the point seemed suddenly futile. 'Me and my supposed co-conspirator Barry Chipchase.'

'You're joking.'

'I wish I was.'

'But that's ridiculous. Co-conspirators in what? A man kills himself. Another dies in a car crash. The police surely don't think . . .'

'I'm afraid they do.'

'Christ.' Erica frowned. 'I'd no idea.'

'It's not true, by the way.' Harry smiled gamely. 'I didn't do it. I didn't do anything. Nor did Barry. You can trust me on that. I'd be grateful if you didn't mention this to the others just yet, though. I don't want them petitioning to have me turned out of the hotel.'

'Now you *are* joking, right? Anyway, don't worry. I won't breathe a word.'

'Thanks.'

'You haven't got a cigarette, have you?'

'I don't smoke.'

'Neither do I. Usually.'

'I stopped when my daughter was born. *Before* she was born, actually.'

'What about pen and paper? Got either of those? I want to write something down for you.'

'Here.' Harry produced a Kilveen Castle ballpoint and the copy of Dangerfield's letter about the reunion Lloyd had given him. 'Use the back of that.'

'My mobile number. Call me if you need any help.' Erica smiled. 'I'm sure you won't. The police will soon come to their senses. But just in—'

She broke off and handed the letter and ballpoint back to Harry as Dangerfield headed towards them, grim-faced.

'That was Jabber's daughter,' he announced. 'The hotel put her onto me. I should have phoned her earlier. She was . . . pretty cut up. She's travelling up with her mother tomorrow. There'll be a lot to arrange. I said I'd give them as much help as I could, of course, but . . .' He gestured helplessly. 'That'll amount to sod all, won't it? I can't bring him back.'

'No-one can,' said Erica softly.

'No.' Dangerfield's gaze drifted to the river. 'But if I could only turn back the clock . . .'

'No-one can do that either.'

'That's a shame.' He kicked a pebble off the bank into the water. 'A crying bloody shame.'

SIXTEEN

News of Lloyd's death and Wiseman's hospitalization killed off what little remained of the celebratory nature of the Operation Clean Sheet reunion. Toasting the memory of absent friends who had died young years in the past was one thing. Drinking in remembrance of two people who had been alive and well only a couple of days ago was an infinitely more sombre and dispiriting experience. It was possible to believe Askew had killed himself for reasons unconnected with the reunion and that Wiseman's car crash was a pure and simple accident, albeit a tragic one. But coincidence preys on the mind, whether rationally or not. Tancred summed up the feeling of all in his own Wildean style. 'To lose one old comrade may be regarded as a misfortune; to lose two looks like carelessness.'

Initial resolve to visit Wiseman in hospital before leaving diminished when Dangerfield pointed out that they would not be able to do so until Monday afternoon and would therefore miss the direct train to London they were booked on. They would also be in danger of meeting Lloyd's wife and daughter, a prospect none of them relished. With Harry volunteering to stay on and give Dangerfield what support he could, the others rapidly came round to the idea that there was no sense in delaying their departure. They had families to return to, lives to resume. They were, in truth, though no-one said so, eager to be gone. They might even have wished that they had never come in the first place. The reunion had been ill-fated. They wanted no more to do with it.

Dangerfield did not mention he had provided the police with all their names and addresses and, oddly, no-one asked if he had, perhaps because doing so would imply they believed Wiseman's crash might not have been an accident, Askew's death perhaps not suicide. Those were doors no-one wished to open. Accordingly, by unspoken mutual consent, they remained closed.

Nor did anyone question Harry's selflessness in staying on the scene to lend Dangerfield a helping hand, though Tancred came close. After they had adjourned to the bar following a dinner nobody had shown much of a stomach for, he eyed Harry over the rim of his whisky glass and remarked, 'You're an example to us all, Ossie, you really are.'

'Just doing my bit, Tapper,' was Harry's lame response.

'Unlike Fission. If only your partnership had endured, perhaps then he wouldn't have ended up fleecing the likes of poor old Crooked.'

'I doubt it. He never took much notice of me.'

'Ah. Do I take it that Barnchase Motors might not have had a whiter than white reputation even before its lamentable collapse?'

'Put a sock in it, Tapper, for God's sake,' Judd interrupted. 'Ossie's doing us a good turn.'

'Isn't that exactly what I was saying?'

'Didn't sound like it.'

'Then you should listen more carefully.'

'Oh Gawd.' Judd rolled his eyes. 'I've got seven bloody hours of this kind of malarkey to look forward to on the train. No wonder you've opted out, Ossie. Smart move.'

'It certainly won't be a happy journey,' said Gregson mournfully.

And no-one disputed that.

Harry had peddled the same line to Donna: that he was staying on for Dangerfield's sake. It was almost true. He might even have suggested it, if he had been left any choice in the matter. It would certainly do Donna no good to be told he was a suspect in a double murder inquiry, particularly since he fully expected the crash to be confirmed as an accident and Askew's death accepted as suicide in short order. All he had to do was hold his nerve and bide his time. There had been no murders. The inquiry would soon be abandoned. And he would be free to go.

So he told himself, anyway. His subconscious remained unconvinced. He slept poorly, falling into and out of dreams that swiftly became nightmares. In one, something dark and menacing and vaguely familiar pursued him up the spiral stairs of the tower, across the roof and over the battlement. In another, he was in the back of Wiseman's car as it plunged into the river. Chipchase was sitting beside him. They started arguing about 'alterations' to the steering – 'You altered it.' 'No, you did.' – as it sank, down and down, into the ever darker water. Then they were sitting opposite each other on a train, speeding through the night. As Chipchase dozed, Harry pulled his friend's bag from the rack, eager to see what it contained. It was an old leather suitcase, just like Askew's. He slipped the latches silently and raised the lid. And there, inside—

But he could not remember, when he woke, with a jolt and a cry in the greyness of dawn, what he had seen – and why it had terrified him.

They left Kilveen Castle straight after breakfast, seen off by Erica Rawson and Dr Starkie, who could afford to make a more leisurely departure later in the morning. It was a stilted farewell, a thick, chilling drizzle encouraging no-one to linger on the driveway. 'I'm sorry this hasn't worked out as you men must have hoped,' Starkie told them. 'Try not to let it prey on your minds.'

*   *   *

95

'I think he means he isn't going to let it prey on his,' said Fripp, as they loaded themselves into the minibus.

'It's good advice, nonetheless,' said Tancred. 'I for one intend to follow it.'

'Yeah, but you've always been a cold-hearted bastard, Tapper,' said Judd. 'That makes it easier for you than for the rest of us.'

Before Tancred could respond with more than an icy smile, Dangerfield turned to them and said, 'You can spend the whole train journey taking digs at each other if you want. I don't care. But do you think you could lay off until we get to the station? I'm not sure I can take much more.' Then he started the engine and pulled away. And no-one said a word.

Their departure at the end of Operation Clean Sheet, on a June morning in 1955, had been very different. All fifteen of them had squeezed into the back of an RAF lorry driven by WO Trench and been ferried to Lumphanan station in time for the first train of the day to Aberdeen. A mood of 'school's out' jollity had prevailed. Their laughter had filled the carriage. They were young and carefree, their futures alluringly uncertain. The only thing they could probably have agreed did not lie ahead of them, under any circumstances, was a return to Kilveen Castle. Yet now, fifty years later, six of them were leaving it again, its turreted bulk a receding image in the minibus's rear window. The mood was subdued. There was no laughter. But surely this time it had to be true. They would never go back.

The Northern Lights express pulled out of Aberdeen station on the dot of 9.55 that morning. Fripp, Gregson and Tancred were already in their seats, but Judd was still leaning out of the window, arm raised in farewell, as the train cleared the platform and picked up speed.

'You were on the London train with most of the others fifty years ago,' said Dangerfield to Harry as they turned and walked away. 'Bet you wish you were today as well.'

96

'*Most* of the others, Danger? Weren't we all on it?'

'No. I was heading further north. To Kinloss. And somebody – Babber, I think – was on his way to the Shetlands. They had some radar station way up there. Saxa Vord. That was it.'

'You're right. I'd forgotten.'

'No reason why you should have remembered.'

'I was bound for Gloucester. Barry was for Tangmere. Several were going to Germany. Nobody to the same place, though. They seemed determined to split us up.'

'Yes.' Dangerfield nodded thoughtfully. 'Maybe they knew best.'

SEVENTEEN

Sweet Gale Lodge was, by Dangerfield's own admission, absurdly large for one man to live in. A terracotta-tiled, snow-white-rendered villa with a domed conservatory attached to one side and a triple garage big enough to accommodate the local Fire Brigade to the other, it sat starkly in an avenue of older, mellower, more discreet residences on the south-western fringe of the city. A career in the oil industry, Harry concluded, had left Dangerfield well provided for.

The presence of a decrepit old Renault out front indicated that the cleaning lady was on the premises. Dangerfield led Harry through the vast, open-plan lounge, half of which was double-height, overlooked by a gallery landing, to the modernistic kitchen. There they found a broad-hipped, bustling woman of about fifty, with short, grey-streaked hair and apple-red cheeks, dressed in jeans and a Fair Isle sweater, heaving a load of shirts and underwear into the washing machine.

'This is Harry, Shona,' said Dangerfield. 'He'll be here for a few days.'

'You never said you were having another of your old soldiers to stay,' Shona good-naturedly complained.

'We were airmen, Shona, not soldiers,' Dangerfield retorted. 'And Harry'll cause you no problem. He can take Barry's room.'

'What about when Barry comes back?'

'*If* he comes back, we'll both be happy to stall him with a host of questions while you make up another room.'

'Och well, I suppose . . .'

'Good. I'll leave Shona to show you where everything is, Harry, while I drop the minibus back. I won't be long.'

Barry's room was as generously proportioned as the rest of the house and as minimally furnished, with a king-size bed, a pair of bedside cabinets, and a walk-in wardrobe ready to swallow Harry and his few belongings.

After dumping his bag and stowing his toothbrush and shaving kit in the equally oversized en-suite bathroom, Harry made his way down through the parqueted wastes of the lounge back to the kitchen, where Shona had promised him coffee.

She was talking on the telephone when he entered, explaining that Dangerfield was out. Then she mentioned Harry's name, which surprised him more than a little. And then she crowned his surprise by offering him the receiver.

'It's the polis,' she said, telegraphing her irritation that no-one had warned her she might have to field calls from the boys in blue.

Reluctantly, Harry took the receiver. 'Harry Barnett here.'

'Ah, Mr Barnett. Excellent. Detective Sergeant McBride here, Grampian Police.' He sounded brisk and businesslike. 'Detective Inspector Geddes of the Tayside force gave us to understand you'd be staying with Mr Dangerfield on this number.'

'Well, so I am.'

'Indeed. Now, would you be willing to call in at the station here in Aberdeen later today? This afternoon, perhaps.'

'What for?'

'We were hoping you'd agree to be fingerprinted.'

Fingerprinted? This sounded ominous. 'Why, Sergeant?'

'For the purposes of elimination, sir. We may be able to lift some prints from Mr Wiseman's car, you see.'

'I never went near his car.'

'Then you've nothing to worry about.'

'I know,' Harry said, trying to drain the terseness out of his voice.

'Good. So, you'll come in?'

'Well, I—'

'Oh, our colleagues in Tayside would appreciate a DNA sample as well. Likewise for elimination purposes. It's a very straightforward procedure.'

'That may be, but—'

'Inspector Geddes said you were keen to help in any way you could.'

'Yes. Of course. But—'

'So, shall we say about three o'clock?'

Harry's mind raced. He really did have nothing to worry about. He had not touched Wiseman's hire car. He had not laid a finger on Askew. Why, then, did he feel he was being lured into doing something he would come to regret?

'Sir?'

'OK, Sergeant.' Harry sighed. 'About three.'

As he put the phone down, Shona plonked a steaming mug of coffee on the marble-topped breakfast bar beside him. 'There you go.'

'Thanks.' Harry sat on one of the stools spaced around the bar and took a sip from the mug.

'This all about the car crash near Aboyne – and the fellow who fell out of the train down Carnoustie way?'

'You heard about them, then?' Harry was not surprised. Everyone seemed to have heard.

'It was all on the local news.'

'Yes. Of course it was.'

'Your reunion didna' exactly go to plan.'

'Far from it.'

'Heard from Barry?'

'No. Has he phoned here?'

'It's no for me to check Mr Dangerfield's answering machine. He'll likely do it himself later.'

Mr Dangerfield, then, but not *Mr Chipchase*. To Shona he was Barry. 'Barry and I . . .'

'Are old friends. Aye. He said so.'

'Did he?'

'"It'll be good to see my old mate Harry again." Those were his very words. Sat where you're sat now, drinking coffee, just the same. Then he got a message about his sister, so Mr Dangerfield tells me, and had to rush off to Manchester.'

'Yeah.'

'Must have been a shock. Did you know the woman?'

'Far as I know, Shona, Barry's an only child.'

Shona frowned. 'An only child?'

'Both his grandmothers died at least twice while we were in the RAF. Looks like he's still pulling the same stunts.'

'But . . . why?'

'That's what the police want to know.'

'They surely don't think . . . he had anything to do with . . .'

'They do. And they've roped me in as a suspect as well, on account of Barry and me being old friends and former business partners.' Harry shaped a mock-courageous smile. 'But don't worry about it.'

'I shan't.' Her frown deepened. 'Maybe you should, though.'

Dangerfield evidently agreed with Shona. He suggested Harry should consult a solicitor before pitching up at Aberdeen Police HQ and offered to put him in touch with one. Harry demurred. The best way to demonstrate his innocence was to arrive *sans* legal adviser, co-operate fully and keep smiling throughout.

'Innocence isn't far from naïvety,' Dangerfield counselled as he leafed through a copy of that morning's *Press and Journal: the Voice of the North*, then swivelled the paper round on the breakfast bar for Harry to see and pointed to an article on page 7. 'Read that. I'll be straight back.'

101

MYSTERY OF FATAL DEESIDE CAR CRASH

Police are investigating the circumstances that led to a car crashing off the B976 near Aboyne yesterday into the river Dee, killing one of its two occupants. The dead man was named as Mervyn Lloyd, 69, from Cardiff, who was attending a RAF reunion at Kilveen Castle Hotel, near Lumphanan, along with the driver of the car, Neville Wiseman, 71, from London. Mr Wiseman survived and is reported to be in a satisfactory condition in Aberdeen Royal Infirmary.

Detective Chief Inspector Graeme Ferguson of Grampian Police said he was not ruling out a connection with the unexplained death of another participant in the reunion, Peter Askew, 69, also from Cardiff, whose body was found beside the main East Coast railway line near Carnoustie on Friday. He went on to pay tribute to a passing motorist who came to Mr Wiseman's aid and appealed for anyone who had information relating to either of the deaths to contact him in confidence.

'Spot the missing words?' Dangerfield asked as he returned to the kitchen.

'What d'you mean?'

'They don't say it was an accident, do they? Or that Crooked's death was suicide. That's because they don't believe they were.'

'They'll have to, in the end.'

'Maybe. Meanwhile, you ought to watch your back, Harry. I don't like how this is panning out. I've just checked the answerphone, by the way.'

'Anything from Barry?'

Dangerfield rolled his eyes. 'What do you think?'

EIGHTEEN

Dangerfield drove Harry into the city centre in his Mercedes that afternoon, parked as close to Police Headquarters as he could and walked him the rest of the way. They had agreed to meet back at the car in an hour, before driving out to the hospital to visit Wiseman. An hour, Harry assumed, would be ample. But Dangerfield seemed less confident.

'You don't need to tell them anything, you know. You don't even have to give them your fingerprints if you don't want to. Here's my solicitor's card. Divorce and probate's his speciality, but one of his partners must handle criminal stuff. Give them a call if things turn hairy.'

'They won't.'

'For your sake, I hope not.'

'You're overreacting.'

'Am I really? Well, it's better than *under*reacting.'

At first, Harry sensed he had judged it right. Sergeant McBride, as cheerfully efficient in the flesh as he had sounded over the telephone, whisked him through the finger-printing and DNA sampling procedures, dodged his questions about the examination of Wiseman's car that Geddes had mentioned was going to be carried out and implied there really was nothing else they required of him.

Only when Harry emerged from the loo after washing the fingerprinting ink off his fingers did he find that McBride

103

had been joined by the Chief Inspector quoted in the *Press and Journal*. Ferguson was a youthful, snappily dressed, dark-haired man with film-starry looks and the featheriest of Scottish accents. He seemed altogether *too* young for such a senior rank and somehow the drive and ambition that hinted at worried Harry more than the challenging directness of his gaze.

'Thanks for coming in, Mr Barnett,' he said, with a geniality that lacked conviction.

'No problem.'

'I wonder if I could ask you to come in again tomorrow to answer a few questions.'

'You can ask me them now if you like.' The delay, Harry suspected, was designed to prey on his mind – as he was certain it would.

'No can do, I'm afraid. This would be a formal interview. It needs setting up. Inspector Geddes will want to be included, you see, so that we can . . . cover both inquiries.'

'What time?'

'Shall we say . . . eleven o'clock?'

'Suits me.'

Ferguson smiled. 'Splendid.'

'Formal means you'll be under caution, sir,' said McBride. 'You may wish to be accompanied by a solicitor.'

'Another reason for giving you notice,' said Ferguson.

'Thanks. I'll, er . . . think about it.'

Harry exited the station, turning over in his mind the ever-multiplying complexities of the situation in which he found himself. Ferguson and McBride must already have received some kind of report on Wiseman's car, but they did not propose to tell Harry what it contained. That, he supposed, would be sprung on him at tomorrow's interview. They were presumably hoping to match his fingerprints with some they had already found, though where he could not imagine. As for the DNA sample he had supplied, what did they hope to match *that* with? Blood discovered under

Askew's fingernails perhaps? They would not find any match, of course. But somehow that failed to reassure him.

'Bloody hell,' he murmured to himself. 'This is getting serious.'

The afternoon had turned grey and what Aberdonians would call cool but felt plain cold to Harry. The city's stonework absorbed the greyness of the weather and amplified it. There was nothing in his surroundings to lessen his sense of isolation – and an ever sharper sense of homesickness. He wondered if there was time for a stiff drink – or two – before meeting Dangerfield. Glancing up at the Town House clock ahead of him, he saw there was, but doubted if presenting himself at Wiseman's bedside reeking of beer was a smart move.

He was tempted, nonetheless. The Town House was preserved in his fifty-year-old memories of the city and gave him his bearings. Old Blackfriars, the pub where he and the other Clean Sheeters had done most of their drinking during their fortnightly forays into Aberdeen, lay to his left, near the Mercat Cross. He headed towards it.

Within minutes he would have been at the bar, pint in hand, but he was diverted from his course at the last moment by the red and yellow post-office sign hanging from the frontage of the newsagent's shop a few doors further along. He had promised to send Donna and Daisy a postcard and so far had done nothing about it beyond buying the card. An airmail stamp for Canada was what he needed. He hurried in, joined the queue at the post-office counter at the back of the shop and began composing a suitably anodyne message in his head.

He had made as little progress with the message as he had in the queue when he heard a familiar voice. Glancing round, he saw Shona at the front of the shop, buying a newspaper and a packet of cigarettes. But the newspaper and cigarettes were not all she was buying. The phrase that caught his ear was 'and a pack of Villiger's cigars, please'.

The choice of brand was such a shock that he instantly

lowered the hand he had half-raised to greet her. He stepped out of the queue – and out of her line of sight. She paid, dropped her purchases into her bag and left. And Harry went after her.

He did not know what he was going to do. He did not really know whether the coincidence was meaningful or not. But he had to find out. Emerging from the shop, he spotted her hurrying ahead. Hanging back a little, he followed.

Then, almost before it had begun, the game was up. A figure crossed the road from the Clydesdale Bank on the opposite corner and stepped smilingly into Shona's path. It was Dangerfield. And, a second later, glancing over Shona's shoulder, he saw Harry. He waved, obliging Harry to wave back. Then Shona turned and smiled at him.

'There you are, Harry,' said Dangerfield. 'I was just telling Shona I was worried they might have clapped you in irons.'

'I talked them out of it.'

'Have you just come from the polis now?' Shona asked.

'Yes. But I . . . took a wrong turning. Came the long way round.'

'We're off to the hospital next,' said Dangerfield. 'See how Magister's doing.'

'I'll leave you to it, then,' said Shona. 'I've some more shopping to do. I'll see you on Wednesday, Mr Dangerfield. You too, Harry?'

'Probably.'

''Bye, then.'

''Bye.'

'Is Shona married, Danger?' Harry oh-so-casually enquired as they made their way to the car park.

'Widowed. Her husband was killed in an accident on one of our rigs. Bernie McMullen. Nice guy. It was a real tragedy.'

'A good-looking woman like her doesn't need to stay a widow, though, surely.'

'Her druggie son could be the reason. I don't know.'

'Does she have to travel far to clean for you?'

106

'No. She lives in Torry, just over the river. Why are you so interested?'

'Oh, just curious.'

'You should concentrate on getting the police off your case. How did it go?'

'Fine. But I'm not exactly out of the woods. They want to see me again tomorrow. For a formal interview.'

'You need a solicitor, Harry. You really do.'

'I know.'

'I've had a call from Jabber's daughter, by the way. She's on the train with her mother. They'll be staying at the Caledonian. I've agreed to meet them there this evening for dinner. I didn't mention you. It didn't seem . . . a good idea.'

'It's OK, Danger. I get the message.'

'I'm trying to be fair to everyone, Harry. You know that, don't you?'

'Of course.'

'Now, are you going to phone my solicitor?' Dangerfield flourished his mobile. 'Or am I going to do it for you?'

It was in fact Dangerfield who did the phoning. Harry sat in the Merc, gazing vacantly at the blank wall of the car park and listening to him as he sought help from his friend and senior partner in Legg, Stevenson, MacLean. In the event, Harry did not have to say a word.

'All fixed,' Dangerfield announced as he rang off. 'One of his juniors, Kylie Sinclair, will—'

'*Kylie*?'

'She's good, Harry, OK? Try not to hold it against her that she's young enough to be your granddaughter. She'll be expecting to see you at ten o'clock, so you can cover the ground with her before you report to the police station. Their practice is in Bon Accord Square. You've got the address on the card. There's a street map in the pocket next to you. Borrow it if you like. We don't want you keeping her *or* the police waiting tomorrow, do we?'

'We do not. Thanks, Danger.'

'Don't mention it. One thing, though.'

'What?'

Dangerfield turned to look at him. 'You are playing a straight bat on this, aren't you, Harry? I mean . . .'

'I haven't a clue what's going on, Danger. All I know for sure is that I know nothing about it. Fair enough?'

'Fair enough.' Dangerfield started the car. 'I won't ask again.'

NINETEEN

At the hospital, Dangerfield left Harry in the same drab seating area where they had waited the day before while he went in to see how Wiseman was – and to find out if Harry was still *persona non grata.*

Ten minutes later, he was back, the expression on his face hinting at the answer before he even opened his mouth. 'He's looking a lot better. Reckons they'll discharge him tomorrow. Refuses to see you, though, Harry. Says the police obviously suspect you sabotaged his car and, until they rule you in or out, he doesn't want to have anything to do with you.'

'Great.'

'Advised me to kick you out of my house, as a matter of fact.'

'Even better.'

Dangerfield smiled. 'Magister always was too quick to believe the worst of people.'

'So, what do we do now?'

'I'll go back and try to talk some sense into him. I have to arrange for him to meet Jabber's wife and daughter, anyway. Widow and daughter, I should say. Why don't you wait in the car? Sit here long enough and there's no telling what you might catch.'

Harry wandered off glumly towards the exit. Wiseman's readiness to believe he had tried to kill him would have been risible had it not been so depressing. He was an intelligent man. Could he not grasp the absurdity of the idea? Apparently not.

Which only made it more obvious that the sooner Harry was off the hook the better. The day had yielded one tantalizingly frail lead. And he was determined to follow it.

At the hospital's main reception area, he sweet-talked the woman on duty into letting him consult a copy of the Aberdeen telephone directory. There was only one S. McMullen listed. He jotted down the address and headed for Dangerfield's car.

Sure enough, the street map located S. McMullen in the Torry district of the city. He had her. And therefore . . .

'Gotcha,' he announced, for no-one's benefit but his own.

Dangerfield was out within half an hour. He drove Harry away, heading straight for Sweet Gale Lodge, where he proposed to spruce himself up before heading back into the city to meet Mrs Lloyd and her daughter. Harry, of course, was not invited.

'There's plenty to eat in the fridge. Help yourself. That goes for the wine rack too. And I've got Sky on the television. Watch a film. Or a football match. There's always one on. Take it easy. I won't be back late. I wish I was having a quiet night in myself.'

'This relaxing evening you're sketching out for me sounds great, Danger, but contemplating my appointment with the local constabulary tomorrow and knowing how they've convinced Magister I'm party to some crazy plot to do him in isn't likely to put me in the ideal frame of mind for slurping your claret and surfing the satellite channels.'

'Miss Sinclair will force the police to put up or shut up. In the end, it'll be the latter. Once they've admitted defeat, Magister will have to fall into line. I still think it was an accident. These hire cars get some seriously rough treatment. Magister was just unlucky.'

'But not as unlucky as Jabber.'

110

'Too bloody true.' Dangerfield tut-tutted. 'Poor old Jabber.'

'We'll never know now whether his memory of being on the castle roof fifty years ago was genuine or not.'

'No.' Dangerfield looked round at him. 'We won't, will we?'

'*Watch out*!' Harry saw the van braking in front of them before Dangerfield did. By the time their own brakes were on, they were closing fast. But, thanks to Mercedes technology and a tiny margin for error, they stopped a couple of feet short of the Transit's bumper.

'Christ almighty,' said Dangerfield, slapping his forehead. 'Nearly another bloody accident.' He grinned crookedly. 'At least this one definitely wouldn't have been your fault, Harry.'

At Sweet Gale Lodge, while Dangerfield took a bath, Harry phoned Donna. He did not mention the police's doubts about the crash being an accident, far less their suspicion that he was somehow responsible for it. And he did not even hint at what he intended to do that evening. As far as Donna was concerned, he and Dangerfield were dining with Lloyd's grieving relatives and giving them as much help as they could.

'I should be able to leave tomorrow. Wednesday at the latest. And you'll be pleased to know I *did* buy a camera yesterday. So, I'll have pictures to remember this weekend by – whether I want to or not.'

Dangerfield set off shortly after seven o'clock, leaving Harry on the sofa, supposedly watching a Test Match in the West Indies on Sky Sports Xtra.

'I guess you don't see a lot of cricket in Canada,' said Dangerfield as he hurried out.

'None at all,' Harry responded, adding 'Thank God' under his breath.

'See you later.'

''Bye.'

Harry waited a minute or so after the front door had closed before he prodded at the remote, silencing the commentary.

111

He listened for the sound of the Mercedes starting, followed by the crunch of its tyres on the gravel of the drive. Then he jumped up, stabbed the off switch on the television and went to fetch his coat.

Harry had to wait twenty minutes for a bus into the centre, but he was in no particular hurry. In some ways, the later he left it the better.

He would have travelled by tram back in 1955. He remembered the streets of Aberdeen as mostly cobbled, lit by gas, traversed by grim-faced people in belted overcoats, old before their time. It was a different world, as so much of his past seemed to him, despite the fact that he had lived in it.

Old Blackfriars had altered little in its essentials, but the barmaids were younger and prettier – and that went for most of the customers as well. Harry ordered a toasted sandwich and took his beer off to the non-smoking area to await its delivery, smiling at the thought of what he would have said fifty years ago were the chances of living to see any part of an Aberdonian pub unobscured by a blue-grey haze.

He took out the postcard he had bought in Braemar, still lacking an appropriate stamp, and made a start at filling it in. *Darlings D and D, Having a grotty time. Wish I wasn't here.* Well, that was undeniably true. As far as it went.

It had not, in fact, gone any further at all when his sandwich arrived. He washed it down with a second pint, restrained himself from ordering a third and concluded, at half past nine by the Town House clock visible through the pub window, that the time was ripe.

The number 12 bus took Harry out past the ferry terminal and the fish market, over the Dee and into Torry, an area of the city he had never previously explored. Nothing he saw as the bus trundled past down-at-heel shops and Victorian terraces suggested he had missed much. He traced his progress on Dangerfield's map and hopped out when the bus got as close to his destination as he judged it was ever going to.

He headed downhill towards the docks, a large oil storage tank squatting floodlit beyond fencing at the bottom of the street. Halfway to it, he hung a right into a short cul-de-sac of two-up-two-downs and walked slowly along towards its end, before stopping in the darkest midway point between a pair of street lamps and gazing across at the house opposite.

There was a light visible at the ground-floor window, but the curtains were closed. The window above was unlit, as was the dormer above that. The house was in fact only one of two on that side with a dormer. An extra bedroom perhaps. Converted by Bernie McMullen before his untimely death, making it more plausible still that his widow had taken in a lodger recently.

But how to prove it? Harry hesitated to march across and ring the bell. He could not force Shona to let him in, far less insist on searching the house. If she brazened it out, what was he to do? He had no Plan B to fall back on. And Plan A was hardly distinguished by its subtlety.

Then, quite suddenly, in the form of leather-shod foot-falls approaching from the corner, providence intervened. A hatted, raincoated figure was steering a direct course for the very door Harry was watching, moving fast, at a faintly pigeon-toed gait that was instantly familiar.

The man was on the point of sliding a Yale key into the door lock when Harry tapped him on the shoulder.

'Hello, Barry. Long time no see.'

113

TWENTY

'Harry,' said Chipchase in a hoarse whisper. 'Christ Al-bloody-mighty, you nearly gave me a heart attack.'

'Sorry about that, Barry. I know how it feels. I've had one or two nasty shocks myself recently.'

'What the bloody hell are you doing here?'

'I could ask you the same question.'

'Will you keep your voice down, for God's sake. I don't want Shona knowing you've rumbled us.'

'Hard to see how we can avoid that. Aren't you going to show me in?'

'No, I'm bloody not.'

'We have to talk, Barry. Seriously.'

'All right, all right.' Chipchase considered the problem, then proposed a solution that, given the many hours they had spent together on licensed premises over the years, hardly counted as original. 'There's a pub round the corner. We can talk there.'

Cameron's Bar was a comfortless harbourside den dedicated to the consumption of strong lager, high-tar cigarettes and deep-fried snacks. Custom was slack, the atmosphere chill. Chipchase bought a couple of large Scotches, then steered Harry to a window table, as far as possible from eaves-dropping bar-proppers.

The ten years and a bit that had passed since their last

encounter had left their mark on Harry's old partner. He looked grey and weary. The luxuriant hair of his youth had grown thin and lank. His shoulders had acquired a despondent slump. Even his clothes were cheaper and shabbier than they would once have been. The hat and rain-coat dated from happier, wealthier days, but were overdue for replacement. And the cracked leather of his shoes told its own sad story.

'How did you find me?' growled Chipchase, dispensing with a toast as he started on his Scotch.

'Spotted Shona buying your favourite cigars.'

'Bugger. It's always your vices that trip you up in the end.'

'How did you persuade her to take you in?'

'She's a sucker for a hard-luck story. Especially the kind that's true. Thanks to all the scrapes her worthless junkie of a son's got into, she's quite sympathetic to, er . . . what you might call . . .'

'Ex-cons?'

Chipchase scowled. 'Go on. Rub salt into the wound. I suppose Plod were bound to slip that juicy little morsel your way. Chokey's where you'd have predicted poor old Chipchase would end up eventually, anyway, isn't it? Does Danger know about this?'

'Everyone knows, as far as I can tell. It's just that some knew sooner than others. I was one of the last.'

'Sorry about that.' An expression close to genuine regret flickered across Chipchase's face. 'Look, Harry, if I'd had any idea Plod were going to come up with the crazy notion that we'd become partners in crime just because one of our old Clean Sheet buddies does himself in and another dies in a car crash, I'd . . . well, I'd have . . .'

'Yeah? What *would* you have done, Barry? I'd really like to know.'

'I'd have warned you off, wouldn't I? What do you take me for?'

'You didn't give me any warning when you and Jackie ran

off to Spain and left me to face the music at Barnchase Motors.'

'Christ, Harry, that was more than thirty years ago. Can't we forgive and forget?'

'I'd like to. But leopards don't change their spots. As your recent foray into the nursing-home business clearly shows.'

'That wasn't my fault. It could have worked if I'd been given more time. I was badly let down.'

'Not as badly as your investors. And the jury were convinced it *was* your fault.'

'Bleeding-heart liberals, the lot of them. They call anything fraud these days. Let me tell you, Harry, we'd never have had an Industrial Revolution – we'd never have had an *Empire* – if we'd dragged all those thrusting entrepreneurs into court every time they cut the odd corner.'

Chipchase leaned back in his chair, took the telltale pack of Villiger's cigars from his pocket and lit one, his self-esteem briefly boosted by the belief that he was somehow making common cause with legendary titans of Britain's imperial past.

Harry allowed him one long, savoured puff, then asked, 'How was prison?'

The next puff was more of a sigh – and a heartfelt one at that. 'Bloody awful,' he murmured. Then he added, 'I can't go back inside, Harry. I just can't.' And it was quite clearly the truest thing he had so far said.

'That bad?'

'I'm a free spirit. You know me. I can't be . . . confined. I still catch the smell of the place in my nostrils. This godawful, sour reek. It's just a memory, of course. A rotten bloody memory. But I can't forget it.' He summoned a grin. 'The cigars help.'

'Going to ground when the police want to speak to you isn't the smartest way to avoid another spell inside, Barry. Surely you realize that.'

'I didn't go to ground to avoid *them*, did I?'

'Who, then? Peter Askew and Neville Wiseman? Them and

however many other of our old buddies you swindled in the nursing-home racket.'

'I didn't swindle them. It wasn't a racket.' Chipchase propped the cigar in the ashtray and slouched forward, elbows on the table. 'OK. Yes, I did a runner to avoid a face-to-face with some of my aggrieved investors. My *unjustifiably* aggrieved investors. What else was I supposed to do?'

'Why did you accept Danger's invitation in the first place? You must have known they were likely to turn up.'

'Why? Because I was down on my bloody uppers, Harry, that's why. I'd never even have got the invitation otherwise. My half-brother lives in the house I grew up in. That's where the MoD sent the—'

'Hold on. Half-brother? You always said you were an only child.'

'I thought I was. But it seems my mother had an illegitimate child before she married my father. Gave him up for adoption. He tracked her down about twenty years ago and weeviled his way into her affections. A real snake. An out-and-out bloody schemer. Managed to persuade her to leave the house and everything to him. I was . . . abroad at the time. Out of touch. Only heard my mother had died and he'd cheated me out of my inheritance when it was too late to do anything about it.'

'Of course, if you'd been a more attentive—'

'Don't start, Harry. Just don't start. OK? The point is I went to see him a month or so back, hoping I could talk him into buying me out of the half-share of the house I'm morally entitled to. No such luck. He's a stone-hearted bastard. And I choose my words carefully. Anyway, he'd just received Danger's letter. That's all I got out of the visit and it wasn't much. But I was desperate. Down to my last few rolls of the dice. So, I spun Danger the story that I'd sold my house and was about to quit these shores for good, but could stay on for the reunion if only I had somewhere to rest my weary bones in the meantime. Generous sod that he is, he asked me up here. Well, Sweet Gale Lodge is a cushy billet, as you know. I wasn't complaining. I knew I'd have to do a vanishing act if Judd, Tancred and Wiseman came to the reunion, but what the hell? The state my finances are in, I don't look much further ahead than—'

'Just a minute. Judd, Tancred and Wiseman. They all invested in Chipchase Sheltered Holdings?'

'Only Judd and Wiseman, actually. Tancred turned me down. But all three knew about it, so—'

'Plus Peter Askew?'

'No, no. Askew had nothing to do with it. I hadn't a clue where he was, anyway, even if I'd wanted to try and sell the idea to him. I only went after those I knew I could find and who might have some spare cash I could separate them from. I'd seen Judd's name on builders' hoardings around London and I'd come across Wiseman during my brief but lucrative phase as middleman for a dealer in Middle Eastern antiquities. He put me onto Tancred, much good that it did me. I tried Maynard as well, but he turned out to be dead. As for Askew, no. Absolutely one hundred per cent not.'

'That doesn't make sense. The police found an ad for a meeting of your creditors in his pocket. That's what pointed them towards . . .' Harry's words faltered as his thoughts raced ahead. 'It was planted on him. Which means he *was* murdered. And Wiseman's car *was* sabotaged. With you and me lined up to take the blame.'

'Bloody hell.'

'The police think I hid some of the proceeds of the nursing-home scam for you. They think we knocked off Askew – and tried to knock off Wiseman – to stop them finding out about it. They've taken my fingerprints and a DNA sample. I suppose they've already got yours. They're trying to tie us to two murders, Barry. And an attempted murder.'

'*Bloody hell.*'

'Can Shona supply you with an alibi for Friday afternoon?'

'No. She was out cleaning most of the day. Danger's not her only client. I was lying low. Not much choice, really. I didn't want to risk bumping into Danger after telling him I had to fly

118

to Manchester. Benjy saw me. That's the son. But I doubt he'd remember. Especially if he knew it'd help me if he did.'

'And Saturday night, which is probably when Wiseman's car was got at?'

'Shona was out with her sister till late. I can't prove I didn't borrow her motor and drive to Kilveen under cover of darkness, if that's what you mean.'

'I suppose it is.'

'So, where does that leave us?'

'Well, it leaves me reporting to Police HQ at eleven o'clock tomorrow morning, accompanied by a solicitor.'

'For your sake, I hope he's a good one.'

'It's a she, actually. And it's *our* sake you should be concerned about, Barry. Yours and mine. Because you'll be coming with me.'

TWENTY-ONE

In the end, Harry left Chipchase no choice in the matter. His hideout with Shona was going to be made known to the police next morning for the simple reason that Harry had no other way to prove they were not partners in crime. Words like treachery and blackmail were briefly bandied, but Chipchase soon ran out of bluster. He had the theoretical option of leaving Aberdeen before the police came looking for him, but he had nowhere to go and, as he admitted over his third double Scotch, he was too old to go on the run.

'Don't worry,' Harry consoled him. 'It's not as bad as it looks.'

'I don't rightly see how it could be.'

'I mean they have no evidence against us. They won't find our fingerprints on Wiseman's car for the simple reason that neither of us has been near it. And you can prove Askew wasn't one of your investors. They'll give us the third degree, but in the end they'll have to face it. We didn't do it. Danger will back us up. We'll go and see him tonight. Together. Explain why you went into hiding. He'll understand.'

'Yeah. All too bloody well.'

'It'll be OK, Barry. Trust me.'

Chipchase looked at Harry with barely concealed astonishment. Trust was perhaps a strange concept to introduce at this late and unexpected stage of their long acquaintance, but ultimately it was all Harry had to offer.

'Are we agreed, then?'

'No.' Chipchase stared lugubriously into his whisky. And gave a heavy sigh. 'But I'll do it anyway.'

They caught the bus back into the centre, a recourse that moved Chipchase to cast a leery eye over their fellow passengers and confide to Harry: 'I never thought I'd end up travelling on corporation omnibuses with the dregs and dross of humanity, you know. We used to sell sports cars, let me remind you. Leather-upholstered bloody limousines. And I've hobnobbed with the great and good on five continents. How's it come down to this, I should like to know. Poor old Chipchase on public bloody transport.'

'Between cars at the moment, are you, Barry?'

'Between bloody everything. Since getting out of clink, I've gone from bad to worse. Every time I've hit bottom, it's turned out there's a basement under it I've yet to visit.'

'What happened to that wealthy undertaker's widow you were sizing up for matrimony when we last met?'

'Some lounge lizard in New Orleans stole her from under my nose.'

'Bad luck.'

'Yeah. I've had more than my share of that over the past decade, Harry old cock, let me tell you.'

'Sorry to hear that.'

'It's been a different story for you, though, hasn't it? Marriage to some curvaceous Canadian blue stocking, so a little bird told me, with a young daughter to dandle on your arthritic knee.'

'Who was this little bird?'

'Jackie.'

'Ah. I might have guessed.'

Jackie Fleetwood, their not so dizzy blonde secretary at Barnchase Motors, later Jackie Chipchase and later still Jackie Oliver, owned Jacaranda Styling, a hairdressing salon in Swindon where Harry's mother had been given free perms in recent years for old times' sake – and where, no doubt, news of Harry had occasionally been dispensed. 'Oh yes,' a voice sounded in his mind's ear. 'That boy of mine's finally settled down, I'm glad to say.'

'Why were you in touch with her, Barry? Or is that a stupid question? Offering her an investment opportunity, were you?'

'She turned me down flat.'

'Surprise, surprise.'

'But not before telling me how your slice of life had landed butter side up again.'

'For the record, Donna's American. So's Daisy. We just live in Canada. And my knees are working perfectly.'

'I hope that's not all that's working perfectly. Must be quite a strain for an old fellow like you, keeping a young wife happy. How much younger is she, exactly?'

'Why don't we change the subject?'

'Have you got one to offer that'll take my mind off the fix we're in?'

Harry considered the point for a few moments – to no avail.

Then Chipchase sighed. 'I thought not,' he said gloomily.

They soon reverted to subjects very much related to the fix they were in. Upon arrival in the city centre, Chipchase insisted he needed another drink before facing Dangerfield. He took Harry into his current Aberdonian watering hole of choice, the Prince of Wales, and ordered a couple of pints. His debatable contention that it was Harry's round again led back to a question he had so far dodged.

'The police seem to think you squirrelled away some Chipchase Sheltered Holdings money they never found.'

'Pure bloody fantasy. The receiver cleaned me out. There was nothing left. Not a bean.'

'What makes them think there was, then?'

'Their suspicious bloody natures, that's what. If I had a nest egg somewhere, do you seriously suppose I'd be kipping in Shona's attic?'

'No, I suppose—'

'If you ask me, your murder theory's fantasy as well.'

122

'How do you account for that notice about Chipchase Sheltered Holdings finding its way into Peter Askew's pocket, then?'

'I don't. But unlike you, Harry old cock, I don't feel the need to account for anything. I'll leave that to the so-called professionals. Tell you what, though. You'd better hope I'm right and you're wrong and that there isn't someone systematically knocking off members of Operation Clean Sheet, just in case *we're* next on the list.'

It had not occurred to Harry until then that the murder plot, if there was one, might not have run its course. It was a disquieting thought, which he pretended to dismiss but in truth could not. It niggled away at the back of his mind as they left the pub, walked down to the railway station and jumped into a cab.

There were lights blazing at Sweet Gale Lodge, reassuring Harry that Dangerfield was back from his dinner with Lloyd's widow and daughter. He paid off the taxi driver and led the way to the door, Chipchase trailing a few yards behind and clearly not relishing the encounter that was shortly to follow.

Harry took a few stabs at the bell and stepped back. 'Come on, Barry. Best foot forward.'

'I'm not good at apologies.'

'Only because of lack of practice. Get up here.'

Chipchase joined him on the doorstep as he prodded the bell another few times and peered through the frosted porch window into the hall. There was no sign of movement.

'Where is he?'

'Asleep in front of the telly, like as not.'

'It's freezing out here.'

'Welcome to Aberdeen.'

'Surely he can hear the bell.' Harry left his finger on the button for several seconds. But still there was no response.

'Try this,' said Chipchase.

Turning, Harry saw a key nestling in his palm. '*Thank you.*'

He opened the door, calling Dangerfield's name as they advanced along the hall. The lounge to their left was filled with light. But the television was silent. And there was no recumbent figure on the sofa.

'Danger? It's Harry. I've—'

He saw the blood first, a spotlight shimmering on its dark-red surface. One further step into the lounge revealed the rest.

Dangerfield was sprawled face down on the parquet floor directly beneath the balustrade of the galleried landing. His head, round which the blood had pooled, was twisted, like a broken doll's, his eyes wide, staring . . . and sightless.

TWENTY-TWO

'Are you sure he's dead?' Chipchase asked as Harry stretched a shaking hand across the pool of blood to feel for a pulse beneath Dangerfield's ear. But Harry already knew he was not going to find one. The angle of Dangerfield's head to his body told its own story. A broken neck and a smashed skull were a fatal combination.

'I'm sure.' Harry stood up and retreated to where Chipchase was standing in the doorway.

'Bloody hell. How . . .'

'From up there.' Harry pointed to the landing. 'Straight down. Smack onto the floor.'

'Christ Almighty.'

'Somebody did this to him. It was no accident.'

'But . . .'

'I'm going to phone the police.'

'Hold on.' Chipchase clasped Harry by the elbow. 'This looks bad for us, Harry. They'll try to pin it on us.'

'What do you want to do, then? Scarper?'

'It's an idea.'

'A bloody stupid one. That would clinch it in their eyes. We have to phone them, Barry. Now.'

The phone call made, they retreated to the road and waited there. Neither wanted to remain indoors. The horror of what had happened in the house held them in an ever strengthening grip. Dangerfield dead; Dangerfield murdered: a killer on the loose somewhere, identity, motive and intentions . . . unknown.

'He could be watching us right now, Harry. You realize that, don't you? He could be sizing us up right this bloody minute.'

'No. He's long gone. Danger was . . . cold to the touch. He must have died . . . a while ago.'

'You're an expert, are you?'

'No. I'm just saying—'

'Who's doing this, Harry? Who the bloody hell is it?'

'I don't know.'

'And *why*?'

'*I don't know.*'

'Danger was one of the good guys. Salt of the earth. He didn't deserve . . . *that*.'

'There isn't something you're not telling me, is there, Barry?'

'What the hell do you mean?'

'I mean . . . something that might explain what's going on.'

'I haven't the first bloody clue what's going on.'

'No?'

'*No.*'

'Well, that's a relief.'

'Why?'

'Because neither have I.'

The police came in waves. First one squad car. Then two more. Then several white vans and unmarked cars. Lights were set up. Radios crackled into life. Men in disposable boiler suits padded in and out of the house. A photographer arrived. Then a pathologist. And, last but by no means least, Detective Chief Inspector Ferguson and Detective Sergeant McBride.

Harry and Chipchase had not been allowed back into the house. Left under the wordless supervision of a PC in one of the squad cars to await Ferguson's convenience, they

126

exchanged apprehensive glances, shrugs and shakes of the head as the elaborate but orderly response to violent death took shape around them.

Then, eventually, the PC was ordered out. McBride took his place and Ferguson slid into the front passenger seat.

'Mr Barnett and Mr Chipchase,' he said, turning to look at them. 'Together at last.'

'We didn't move anything, Chief Inspector,' said Harry emolliently. 'It's all exactly—'

'I've heard what you've had to say for yourselves so far. You may as well know it won't wash.'

'It happens to be the truth.'

'Bullshit. A few hours ago, Mr Barnett, you claimed to have no idea where your friend was. Now I'm to understand you've had an impromptu boys' night out together. At the end of which Mr Dangerfield winds up dead. You'll forgive me if I make a connection between those events, won't you?'

'The only connection is that we came back here and found the body.'

'And we phoned you lot straight away,' said Chipchase.

'Can anyone vouch for what you were doing earlier?'

'Well . . .' Harry began.

'Not sure,' Chipchase finished.

'Thought so.' Ferguson drummed his fingers on the seat-back for a moment, then turned to McBride and said, 'Have them taken to the station, Sandy.'

'Are you arresting us?' Harry asked, hoping fervently that he had somehow misunderstood.

'Are we arresting them, Sandy?'

'Aye, sir,' said McBride. 'I think we are.'

The ironic and remorseless circularity of life presented itself with bleak force to Harry during the largely sleepless remainder of the night. His confinement with Chipchase in the guardroom cells at RAF Stafford had led them to Kilveen Castle and the apparent salvation of Operation Clean Sheet. Now, fifty years later, their connection with Kilveen unexpectedly re-established, they were confined once more, this time to the cells of Aberdeen Central Police Station.

He had not seen Askew's body after they had scraped it off the railway line, nor Lloyd's after it had been pulled from the wreck of Wiseman's hire car. Until he had stepped into the lounge of Sweet Gale Lodge and caught his first, indelibly memorable sight of Dangerfield, lying where he had fallen, the deaths were at one remove from him, reported, imagined – but not experienced. All that had changed now. The possibility that Askew committed suicide or the car crash was an accident had been replaced by the sickening certainty of murder.

'Who's doing this?' Chipchase had asked him despairingly. 'And why?' There was no answer that came close to making sense. Yet there was an answer. There had to be.

Who? And why?

In the end, one way or another, by hook or by crook, Harry was going to have to find out.

Who. And why.

TWENTY-THREE

The interview room was bare, stuffy and windowless. Harry sat on one side of the central table, opposite a flint-faced triumvirate of Ferguson, Geddes and McBride. To his left sat Kylie Sinclair, petite, crop-haired, bushbaby-eyed and, Harry had to assume, quite a few years older than she looked. The fact that the victim of one of the murders about to be discussed was a client of Legg, Stevenson, MacLean had not prevented her turning up to act as legal adviser to Harry and, at his instigation, to Chipchase as well.

Chipchase was still languishing in his cell. Ferguson and Geddes had decided to start with Harry. Perhaps they reckoned him the easier nut to crack. His thoughts scrambled by lack of sleep and general anxiety, his stomach churning after a breakfast of brackish tea and soggy toast, he felt unable to fault their reasoning.

A tape recorder stood in the middle of the table. McBride loaded the machine, started it running, announced the date, location and names of those present, then sped through the caution he had recited to Harry the previous night. 'You do not have to say anything, but it may harm your defence if . . .'

Harry barely listened. Silence, he knew, would avail him little.

'Done this kind of thing before, Mr Barnett?' Ferguson asked when McBride had finished.

'Sorry?' Harry was instantly wrong-footed.

'Been interviewed by the police, I mean.'

'Oh, right.' He watched McBride jotting in his notebook. What, he wondered, was the best – the wisest – thing to say. 'Well . . .'

'It's either yes or no,' said Geddes, in what was almost a snarl. 'Surely you can remember.'

'Of course. It's just . . . Well, it depends what you . . .' He smiled deliberately. 'I was interviewed once by the Greek police. A long time ago. It was all a . . . misunderstanding.'

'Rhodes, November 1988.' Ferguson grinned. 'It's amazing what the Europol computer can turn up.'

'Like I said: a long time ago.'

'A missing-person inquiry. Suspected murder.'

'But she didn't stay missing. She hadn't been murdered. There was nothing to it.'

'Luckily for you.'

'Is this relevant?' Miss Sinclair asked sharply. 'I understood you wanted to question Mr Barnett about rather more recent events.'

'We do.' Ferguson acknowledged the rebuke with a faint inclination of the head. 'The death on Friday of Peter Askew. The death on Sunday of Mervyn Lloyd. The death last night of John Dangerfield.'

'You were on the train Mr Askew fell from,' said Geddes. 'Correct?'

'Yes.'

'And you were staying in the Kilveen Castle Hotel when the car rented by Neville Wiseman on arrival at Aberdeen airport suffered unaccountable damage to its steering mechanism,' said Ferguson. 'Correct?'

'I don't know when or how it was damaged. Or even *if* it was damaged.'

'Oh, it was damaged. There's no doubt about that. And the rental company have the maintenance records to prove it left their hands in perfect condition.'

'I'm sure they do.'

'Which means it must have been tampered with while it was at Kilveen Castle. Where you were staying. Is that correct?'

'I was there, yes.'

'And you were also staying at Sweet Gale Lodge when Mr Dangerfield was killed.'

'Yes. I was.'

'Did you kill him, Mr Barnett?'

'What?'

'Did you kill him?'

'No. Of course not. Like I told you, we—'

'Found him dead when you got back there. Yes. We know. But there's a problem. I'm referring to your fortuitous reunion with Mr Chipchase. How did that come about?'

'I spotted Shona – Danger's cleaner – buying Barry's favourite brand of cigar. I suspected he was lying low with her. And I was right. Check with Shona if you need confirmation.'

'Oh, we have.'

'Well?'

'Mrs McMullen confirms he's been staying with her. But she was at home all last night and she saw nothing of you. Or Mr Chipchase.'

'I stopped him as he was going in. We spent the rest of the evening in a pub. Cameron's Bar. Near the docks.'

'Start any fights?' asked Geddes.

'What?'

'It might have made your visit more memorable to the staff.'

'For God's sake, this is—'

'A doubtful story,' Ferguson interrupted. 'That's what it is, Mr Barnett. Look at it from our point of view. We have two murders in which the victim was physically overpowered. It's tempting to conclude a *pair* of murderers were responsible. Mr Askew may not have been capable of putting up much resistance, but Mr Dangerfield was certainly no pushover. We also have a third murder – and an attempted murder – in which the modus operandi requires expert knowledge of

131

motor-car steering mechanisms. And then we have you and Mr Chipchase. A pair. A partnership. Former co-proprietors of a car sales and repair business, no less. With a criminal conviction, in Mr Chipchase's case, relating to a fraudulent enterprise of which the dead men may well all have been victims.'

'Danger didn't invest in Chipchase Sheltered Holdings. He told me so himself. Nor did Peter Askew. You can check that.'

'Can we? I doubt we'll find Mr Chipchase kept meticulous records. Even if he did, they might lack a certain credibility, don't you think?'

'Neither of us has anything to do with this.'

'Well, we'll have to see about that. Mr Dangerfield clearly knew his murderer – or murderers. There was no sign of a break-in. And he certainly knew you two.'

'We weren't there when it happened, Chief Inspector. Find the taxi driver who took us out to the house last night. He can tell you what time we arrived.'

'Can you describe him, sir?' asked McBride. 'Or the taxi itself?'

'He was . . . middle-aged, I suppose. Local. Nothing . . . out of the ordinary.'

'Pity,' said Geddes.

Harry pressed on. 'He was driving . . . an average saloon.'

'Aren't they all?'

'Even if we traced the driver and he remembered you, Mr Barnett,' said Ferguson with a long-suffering air, 'it wouldn't prove you didn't kill Mr Dangerfield, then go into town and return by taxi for the specific purpose of establishing an alibi.'

'In that event, Chief Inspector,' put in Miss Sinclair, 'wouldn't my client have ensured he could give a better description of the taxi and its driver?'

Ferguson smiled coolly. 'Perhaps he might think that . . . too obvious.'

'That's very tortuous reasoning.'

'Goes with the territory, luv,' said Geddes.

132

'Mr Barnett,' said Ferguson, a pursing of his lips hinting at irritation with Geddes, 'I want to put it to you that Mr Chipchase has been the prime mover in all this. You've just . . . tagged along. No doubt you're horrified by what's happened – and your complicity in it. But I'm afraid protestations of innocence aren't going to achieve anything. We need the truth. If you volunteer it to us now . . . it's bound to stand you in good stead later.'

'A man your age,' said Geddes, 'needs to think carefully about how many years he wants to spend banged up.'

'Do yourself a favour,' said Ferguson. 'Nobody else will.'

Miss Sinclair shot her client a cautioning glance. They had come to the crunch.

Harry cleared his throat. 'Let me make this very clear. Neither Barry nor I had any part in these murders – if that's what they all were. We're innocent men. And while you're trying to prove otherwise, Johnny Dangerfield's murderer is out there somewhere, busily covering his tracks – and laughing at you.'

A brief silence fell. Ferguson rolled his eyes. McBride scribbled in his notebook. Then Geddes leaned across the table and fixed Harry with a stare. 'No-one's laughing, Barnett. No-one at all.'

Another silence followed, broken this time by Kylie Sinclair. 'Do you intend to charge my client, Chief Inspector? Your case against him so far seems wholly circumstantial. I note you've made no mention of forensic evidence linking him to any of the killings, presumably because there is none.'

'Not yet, maybe,' said Ferguson. 'We're still awaiting the results of several tests.'

'And while you do?'

'All right.' Ferguson stroked his chin. 'If Mr Barnett's prepared to surrender his passport, we'll release him on bail. To return here . . . one week today . . . for further questioning.'

Miss Sinclair leaned close to Harry's ear. 'The passport

request's not unreasonable in view of your Canadian domicile,' she whispered. 'I suggest you agree.'

'Yes, but . . .' Relinquishing his passport created a practical obstacle to what he most desired: an early return to domestic bliss in Vancouver with Donna and Daisy. It also seemed sickeningly symbolic of the gap opening up between him and the comfortable simplicities of family life. It was an admission of what he most feared: that his circumstances were bound to worsen before they improved – if they were to improve at all. And yet . . . there was nothing else for it. 'OK,' he said, pointedly ignoring Geddes and looking straight at Ferguson. 'I agree.'

TWENTY-FOUR

Kylie Sinclair told Harry before he left the police station that she was confident of securing Chipchase's release on the same terms as his. 'Assuming,' she added, with a narrowing of her gaze, 'he tells the same story.'

'It's the only story either of us *can* tell, Miss Sinclair. It's the truth.'

'Good. Let me know where you'll be staying, won't you? And make an appointment for you both to come in and see me. As soon as possible. We need to talk about next week.'

'OK. How long before they let Barry go, do you reckon?'

'If the questioning proceeds much as yours did . . . an hour or so.'

'Can you tell him I'll wait for him in the Prince of Wales?'

She smiled. 'Feeling in need of a drink, Mr Barnett?'

'Yes. And if I know Barry . . .'

'He will be too.' She nodded. 'I'll tell him.'

Sergeant McBride also expressed an interest in Harry's future whereabouts when he saw him on his way.

'We'll need to have an address for you by the end of the day, sir.'

'You'll know as soon as I know.'

'Fine. But you do appreciate you can't return to Sweet Gale

135

Lodge, don't you? It's sealed off as a crime scene and it'll stay that way for quite a while.'

'What about my belongings?'

'We let Mrs McMullen pack a few things for you. They'll be with her. Bar what we retained as evidence, of course.'

'Such as?'

'A disposable camera found in your room. I'll give you a receipt for it.'

'Half a dozen snaps of the gathering at Kilveen Castle. You call that evidence?'

'Maybe.'

'Of what, exactly?'

'Ah well . . .' McBride smiled. 'That remains to be seen, doesn't it?'

A cold, grey morning greeted Harry on his exit from the station. Tired, hungry and unshaven, his thoughts manoeuvring ineffectually around the many problems he was beset by, he focused as best he could on the one thing he had to do without delay. He bought a high-value phone card at the first newsagent's he came to and rang Donna from the nearest call-box.

It was the middle of the night in Vancouver, but Harry knew Donna would be worried by the lack of a call the previous evening. She answered with the speed of someone who had not been sleeping soundly and was certain who the caller would be. Initially, she was simply relieved to hear his voice. But her relief did not last long.

'Johnny Dangerfield's dead?'

'The police are treating it as murder.'

'My God, Harry, this is serious. There really is a murderer on the loose?'

'Looks like it.'

'I want you on the next plane home.'

'I want that too. But the police have other ideas. They've confiscated my passport.'

'*What?*'

'There's nothing I can do, Donna. I have to stay here until they've ruled out Barry and me as suspects.'

'*Suspects*? They can't be serious.'

'I only wish they weren't.'

'Right. If you can't come to me, I'll come to you. There's nothing else for it.'

'Don't do that. Please. It'd put you in hot water at the University and—'

'You think I value my job above your welfare?'

'Of course not. But it's unnecessary. They *will* rule us out. It's just a question of time.'

'How much time?'

'A week or so.'

'During which I'll be worried sick about you and unable to do a single damn thing to help.'

'You couldn't do anything even if you were here, Donna.'

'That's not the point.'

'It is. Because if you came *I'd* be worried about *you*. And Daisy would be worried about both of us. Whereas this way she needn't know there's any cause for concern. Not that there is, of course. Not really.'

'Oh yeah?'

'Listen. I can't leave the country. But I don't have to stay in Aberdeen. I'll go back to Swindon. Probably tomorrow. Clear the house out, as planned. I'll take Barry with me. We can watch out for each other. Next week, we'll come back up here and sort everything out.'

'You hope.'

'The solicitor's adamant they'll . . . eliminate us from their enquiries.'

'You've hired a solicitor?'

'Reckoned I needed to.'

'And what about Barry? He's not exactly a trustworthy guy, hon, is he? Are you sure he's . . . on the level?'

'He's never been "on the level" in his life. But he's as much

137

in the dark about all this as I am. Until next week we're going to have to stick together. It's the only way.'

The only way amounted to rather more than Harry was letting on. He had no intention of passing his week on police bail clearing out his mother's house, with or without Chipchase's assistance. But what he meant to do instead was not for Donna's ears.

He phoned Shona next, intending to ask if he could come and pick up his bag before booking into a hotel. But she had other ideas.

'You can stay here, Harry. Then you and Barry can tell me what in God's name is going on. Who'd want to kill Mr Dangerfield? He was such a kind and gentle man. How did you work out Barry was staying with me? And what are the two of you going to do now?'

She had, it soon became apparent, many more questions than Harry had answers. He accepted her invitation and said he and Chipchase would see her later.

Several brief calls followed: to the police, leaving a message for McBride to the effect that he could be found at the McMullen house, at least for a day or so; to Legg, Stevenson, MacLean, making an appointment with Kylie Sinclair for five o'clock that afternoon; and to the hospital, confirming that, as expected, Wiseman had been discharged.

Anxious to assure Wiseman of his and Chipchase's innocence, Harry then tried the mobile number listed for him in Dangerfield's letter about the reunion. But he was soon to regret doing so.

'Hello?'

'Magister, this is Harry . . . Ossie. I—'

'What do you mean by phoning me? Are you no longer in custody?'

'No. But listen. Barry and—'

'They've told me Danger was murdered. And that you and

Fission are under suspicion. For that *and* sabotaging my car. I've no idea what the hell's going on or—'

'Neither have we.'

'*Or* what you've been up to. But in the circumstances I'm amazed – *horrified* – that you should try to harass me in this way.'

'I'm not harassing you. I'm just—'

'Phone me again and I'll report it to the police.' Wiseman ended the call there and then. And Harry did not redial.

Instead, he made one further call with what little credit remained on his card: to Erica Rawson. But she was not answering. He could do no more than record a message.

'You said I should get in touch if I needed help. Well, I do. Badly. I expect you've heard about Johnny Dangerfield. There's something I'm hoping you can tell me. It's important. Could we meet up? Soon? I'll call again later. 'Bye.'

That done, he headed for the Prince of Wales.

TWENTY-FIVE

Harry did not have to wait long for Chipchase to join him. He was making inroads into a second pint of Bass when a familiar and disgruntled figure hove into view through the pub's prevailing murk.

'Those bastards,' was all Chipchase managed to say before he made a start on a pint of his own, accompanied by a whisky chaser. Then he grew more eloquent. 'Those sadistic bloody bastards.'

'Did they take your passport?'

'No. But only because I didn't have it on me. I've got to deliver it to Smiley Kylie for onward transmission by the end of the day.'

'That's handy. I've made an appointment for us to see her at five o'clock.'

'For words of good cheer and encouragement, I sincerely bloody hope.'

'I doubt it.'

'Yeah. So do I. We're up the creek without a paddle, Harry old cock. You know that, don't you? They want my passport to stop me dashing off to Zürich and cleaning out that numbered bank account where they've convinced themselves I stashed the Chipchase Sheltered Holdings missing millions. And they want to pin these murders on us by any means it takes, fair or bloody foul.'

'They've certainly convinced Magister we're guilty. I

140

phoned him. He threatened to have me arrested just for doing that.'

'Paranoid prat.'

'At least Shona's standing by us. She's invited me to stay at her house for the duration.'

'The woman has a heart of gold. I've always said it. But is that what the next week holds, Harry? You and me bunked up at Shona's waiting to see if Plod fits us up before the barking bloody madman who's really doing this decides to pay us a call?'

'I wouldn't recommend it.'

'No. Neither would I. So, what *are* we going to do?'

'I've told Donna we'll head for Swindon.'

'Swindon? That's all I need. A stroll down bad memory lane.'

'It's safer than waiting here.'

'Maybe. But—'

'Anyway, waiting isn't exactly what I had in mind.'

'Got a get-out-of-gaol card tucked up your sleeve, Harry? If you have, let me tell you: it's time to play it.'

'Somebody's killed three men, Barry. Three friends of ours. Who did it? And why?'

'Haven't a bloody clue.'

'Do you want to let them get away with it?'

'Of course I don't. Danger was a good bloke. And I wouldn't have wished ill on the other two either. But just at the minute I'm more concerned with getting you and especially me out of the frame rather than putting someone else in it.'

'Same difference.'

'Come again?'

'You said you hadn't a clue. Well, I've got one. Several, in fact. Since the police don't seem to want to follow them up, I—'

'Hold up. I'm not playing Dr Watson to your Sherlock bleeding Holmes.'

'I'm just talking about asking a few questions, Barry. That's all.'

141

'Yeah. And that's all it'd take for friend Ferguson to pull us in for obstructing his enquiries. One night in the cells is more than enough for me.'

'He's not making any enquiries. Not in the right place, anyway.'

Chipchase frowned sceptically. 'Going to tell me where the right place is, are you?'

'What sparked off the killings? The reunion, yes?'

'Well, I . . .'

'The notice about your nursing homes fraud was planted on Askew to—'

'Fraud my left buttock,' Chipchase barked. 'How many times do I have to explain to you that—'

'All right, all right.' Harry raised a placatory hand. 'Your sadly unsuccessful business venture. Call it what you like. I don't mind. The point is that the subject was dragged in to deflect the police's attention from where it should have been focused: on Kilveen Castle fifty years ago.'

'*What?*'

'Something happened there that you and I missed. Something linking the dead men *and* some of the others. Something they were – and are – keeping secret.'

'How do you know that?'

'Because nothing else makes sense. Danger organized the reunion. Now he's dead. So, it's too late to ask him why he *really* organized it. Even supposing he'd have told us. Which I don't. Not for a moment.'

'I thought it was for old times' sake.'

'Think again. There was a hidden agenda from the start, Barry. Askew as good as told me that at Waverley station. I just wasn't listening. Lloyd started behaving oddly as well. Then Stronach—'

'Stronach? Are you telling me the old buzzard's still alive?'

'And kicking. He called the reunion "risky". As if we were tempting providence by getting back together. As if . . .' Harry paused for a reflective slurp of beer. 'I don't know. But we've got to find out what it was really all about.'

142

'How are we going to do that?'

'Like I said: ask questions. And see what answers we get.'

'Starting with who?'

'Erica Rawson. She's as close to a neutral observer as we're going to find. I phoned her earlier and left a message.'

'You're talking about Starkie's research assistant?'

'Yes.'

'Well, any excuse for a chat with a sexy girl, I suppose. Bit of a looker, as I recall.'

'As you recall?' Several seconds passed before the discrepancy assembled itself in Harry's mind. 'When did you meet Erica Rawson?'

'I didn't exactly *meet* her. She was driving out of Sweet Gale Lodge when I got back there . . . Thursday afternoon. Yeah, that's right. Danger told me who she was. He'd already mentioned she was going to be at the reunion. Missing out on a closer encounter with her was the only thing I regretted, to be honest.' A nervous grin suddenly crossed Chipchase's face. 'Well, that and a chinwag with you, of course.'

'Of course. Did Danger say why she'd called round?'

'No. I assumed . . . to confirm she and Starkie were going to turn up. I don't know. I didn't really think much about it. I was too busy putting together my cover story for doing a runner come Friday.'

Chipchase's explanation for Erica's visit to Sweet Gale Lodge was by far the likeliest. Somehow, though, Harry was unconvinced. And troubled. Maybe she was not so neutral after all. 'Is there a payphone here?'

'Think so. Yeah. At the far end of the bar.'

'Wait here. I'm going to give her another call.'

It was a vain effort. There was, once again, no answer. This time, Harry did not bother to leave a message. He did not want her to think he was badgering her. If he had brought his mobile with him – and charged it – he could have left a number for her to call him back on. But he had not. It seemed

143

there truly was a price to pay for resisting the intrusions of technology.

Chipchase had lit a cigar in Harry's absence. He had grabbed a discarded newspaper from a nearby table and was studying the racing page between puffs.

'You're back soon. No joy?'

'She's probably busy.'

'Or giving you the brush-off. If you'd had the benefit of my salutary experiences in life, Harry old cock, you'd know people go right off the idea of answering the phone to you once you've got into a spot of bother.'

'She suggested I call her if I was in trouble,' said Harry stiffly.

'Just busy, then.' Chipchase's expression implied he suspected otherwise. 'Like you say.'

A minute or so of silence followed, while Chipchase continued to scan the odds. Then he sighed heavily.

'It's tragic, really. Even if I won a fortune on a five-hundred-to-one outsider in the three thirty at Kempton Park, I couldn't jet off to the French Riviera to spend the money and forget my troubles, could I? No bloody passport. At any price. Nope. I'd still be stuck here, bulging wallet or no. Or maybe in Swindon. Which isn't exactly a glamorous alternative. With you, though, either way. Waiting, like a pair of turkeys, for Christmas to—'

'All right.' Harry drained his glass. 'Drink up. We're off.'

'Where to?'

'Wait and see. I've had an idea.'

'God help us.'

Harry stood up. 'Are you coming?'

Chipchase polished off his whisky, clamped the cigar between his teeth, grabbed his hat and coat and rose to his feet. 'Apparently,' he mumbled.

TWENTY-SIX

When Chipchase discovered that their destination was the Caledonian Hotel, he expressed the candid view that Harry was mad.

'Ferguson will have given Lloyd's widow and daughter the clear impression we sabotaged Wiseman's motor. How do you think they'll react to us popping in for a cup of tea and a chat?'

'Danger was going to assure them of our innocence.'

'Yeah, but look what happened to him.'

'We have to make them understand how absurd that whole idea is, Barry.'

'Easier said than done.'

'And the daughter can tell us more about what happened during Askew's overnight stay at her house in London.'

'Did anything happen?'

'I don't know. That's what we're going to find out.'

It was, however, as Chipchase had pointed out, easier said than done. The receptionist at the Caledonian informed them that Mrs Lloyd and Mrs Morrison, her daughter, were both out. This was no real surprise, given why the pair had come to Aberdeen in the first place.

Harry retreated to a table in the foyer to record a message for Mrs Morrison on a sheet of hotel writing paper. It was hard to know how to word it and harder still to concentrate on the task with Chipchase craning over his shoulder. But he persevered.

Dear Mrs Morrison,
    I hope you do not feel we are intruding on your grief. Please accept our condolences. Your father was a good man. The police are mishandling their enquiries into his death. We only want to learn the truth. I am sure you do too. Could we meet to discuss what happened? It might be helpful for all of us. You can contact us on—

He broke off to remind himself of Shona's phone number. But, as he was delving into his pocket, Chipchase said, 'You can give her my mobile number, if you like.'

Harry stared at him in amazement. 'You've got a mobile?'

'Certainly.' Chipchase plucked a smart-looking model from inside his coat. 'You should get up to speed with the communications revolution yourself.'

'But . . . you let me troop off to the payphone in the pub. You even directed me to it.'

'A man in my straitened financial circumstances has to watch his budget. This is a strictly pay-as-you-go jobby. I can't have you holding rambling conversaziones on it. You'll be dialling the delectable Donna before I know it. But for *receiving* calls, in an emergency, which I suppose this counts as, well . . .' Infuriatingly, Chipchase smiled. 'Be my guest.'

Harry finished the note and delivered it to the receptionist; then, with a sarcastic excess of politeness, he asked if he might possibly make brief use of Chipchase's mobile. He rang Erica, who was still incommunicado, but this time he was able to leave a message complete with a number to call back on.

After a late and hurried pizza-parlour lunch, they took a taxi out to Torry and kept it waiting while Chipchase fetched his passport. Shona was wherever her Tuesday afternoon

146

cleaning duties took her and Benjy mercifully absent. The house was small and cramped, a Victorian dockworker's dwelling not dissimilar to 37 Falmouth Street, Swindon, but more fashionably furnished. Chipchase spared a moment to draw Harry's attention to the convertible sofa he was destined to spend the night on – 'Looks like a real back-breaker, doesn't it?' – before they left.

Next stop was Legg, Stevenson, MacLean, where Chipchase left Harry to pay the taxi driver, arguing that the fare could be offset against future phone usage. It had not taken long, Harry reflected, for his former partner to revert to freeloading type.

Kylie Sinclair was in clinically efficient mode, relieving Chipchase of his passport and making a note of their address in Torry before giving them an unvarnished assessment of their situation.

'What happens when you return to the police station next week depends entirely on what Chief Inspector Ferguson and his team learn in the interim. If there's anything to your disadvantage you think they *might* learn, you should tell me about it now. Forewarned, gentlemen, *is* forearmed.'

'There's nothing,' said Harry.

'Less than nothing,' added Chipchase. 'Ferguson's barking up the wrong baobab.'

Miss Sinclair puzzled for no more than a fraction of a second over Chipchase's weakness for colourfully customized metaphors. 'I need to know any and all relevant information. You do understand that, don't you?'

'We do,' Harry responded. 'And we're being completely open with you.'

'Good.'

'What really worries me, though, is what I pointed out in my interview. By concentrating on us, the police are giving the real murderer ample opportunity to cover his tracks.'

'Or hers,' Chipchase chimed in unhelpfully.

'Quite,' said Miss Sinclair. 'Well, that really is their problem, isn't—'

'Excuse me,' Chipchase interrupted. 'It's *our* bloody problem if we're next for the chop.'

'Are you genuinely concerned about such a possibility?' The expression on Miss Sinclair's face suggested it had simply not occurred to her until now that they might be.

'Of course we are. Wouldn't you be? Say, if several of the legal eagles who qualified at the same time as you started turning up dead in suspicious circumstances.'

'It's an unlikely scenario.'

'Well, it's the scenario we happen to be in, unlikely or not.'

'Perhaps. But I don't see—'

'We've thought of checking out a few possibilities ourselves,' Harry cut in. 'You know? Ask some of the questions we reckon the police should be asking but aren't.'

'That would be most unwise. Chief Inspector Ferguson could interpret such behaviour as interference in his conduct of the case and hence a breach of your bail conditions.'

'A complete no-no, then?' asked Chipchase.

'Absolutely.'

'Despite—' An electronic travesty of the theme music to *The Great Escape* suddenly started jingling inside Chipchase's coat. 'Sorry,' he said, pulling out his mobile. 'I should have . . . Hello? . . . Ah, yes. Of course. Hi. Er, good of you to . . .' He rolled his eyes meaningfully at Harry. 'Yes. Well, it's, er . . .'

'If we're barred from taking any action ourselves, Miss Sinclair,' Harry said, speaking loudly enough to distract her attention from Chipchase's burblings and improvising as he went, 'are we also barred from taking ourselves off to what we think might be a safer location? My mother's house in Swindon, for instance. We could stay there until next week, couldn't we? We can't flee the country without our passports, so what would be the objection to us getting out of Aberdeen for a few days? I mean, it's not as if—'

Harry broke off as Chipchase ended his conversation with the words, 'See you then,' and sheepishly tucked his phone back into his pocket. 'Sorry,' he said, grinning apologetically.

'Mrs McMullen. Checking up . . . on our whereabouts. Where, er, were we?'

'Discussing the possibility of you spending the period between now and your appointment at the police station next Tuesday in Swindon,' said Miss Sinclair.

'Ah. Right. Excellento. Swindon-by-the-Sea. The Wiltshire Riviera. Can't beat it.'

Once again, Miss Sinclair was only momentarily bemused by Chipchase's badinage. 'Well, I can't see any reason why you shouldn't base yourselves there in the interim. Citing a concern for your safety could even make a favourable impression. Chief Inspector Ferguson might ask you to report to the police in Swindon while you're there, but he has no justification for vetoing the trip. If you give me the address . . . I'll run it past him.'

'Fine,' said Harry.

'Great,' said Chipchase.

There was a pause. Miss Sinclair looked at them expectantly. 'So, do you have any other questions?'

A few minutes later, they were walking away from the practice's imposing Georgian front door.

'That thing we assured Smiley Kylie we wouldn't do,' said Chipchase. 'You remember? Interfering in the case, sticking our noses in where they aren't wanted.'

'I remember,' said Harry.

'We start doing it in half an hour. Helen Morrison's agreed to speak to us.'

TWENTY-SEVEN

Helen Morrison was a pear-shaped, middle-aged woman with frizzed hair and a moon face, the skin around her eyes red and puffy from recent shedding of tears. The dark suit she was wearing looked to have been bought when she was at least one dress size smaller. This, together with the nervous tremor in her hands, made Harry want to comfort her with a hug. But bland words were all that he felt able to offer.

'It's good of you to see us, Mrs Morrison,' he said, as he and Chipchase settled in their chairs round the corner table where they had found her waiting for them in the bar of the Caledonian Hotel. 'Jabber – your father – was a good friend to us back in our National Service days. His death's a real tragedy.'

'But we didn't have anything to do with it,' said Chipchase, his bluntness causing Harry to suppress a wince. 'The police have got it all wrong.'

'I know,' said Mrs Morrison.

'You do?' Harry could hardly disguise his surprise.

'That's why I'm, well, glad you phoned. I haven't told Mum, by the way. Arranging for Dad's body to be flown back to Cardiff is as much as she can cope with at the moment. As for this . . . murder business . . . well, she can't really get her head round it.'

'The police are trying to connect the deaths with a company

I used to run,' said Chipchase, in a tone that implied it could have been ICI.

'So they said. But that doesn't make sense.'

'Delighted you realize that, Mrs Morrison.'

'What makes you so sure it doesn't?' asked Harry, catching but ignoring a glare from Chipchase.

'Well, for a start Dad never invested in . . . whatever it was called.'

'No. But—'

'And then there was the chat I had with him over the phone Saturday evening. Real worried, he was, after what had happened to Peter Askew; Crooked, as he called him. He wanted me to check the room Crooked had slept in Thursday night. See if he'd left anything there. Well, he hadn't, unless you count the contents of the wastepaper basket. I'd emptied it by then, of course, but Dad wanted me to fish through the rubbish to see what there was. I told him not to be so daft, but he sounded that worried I promised to do it. I went through it with a fine-tooth comb. There was nothing there. Nothing at all. I phoned Dad later and told him so.'

'How did he take the news?'

'He seemed . . . disappointed. I asked him what he'd been hoping for. And he said: "Something linking this with the other deaths." Those were his exact words. *"Something linking this with the other deaths."'*

'You repeated that to Chief Inspector Ferguson?'

'Oh yes. And the other thing Dad said. The last thing, before he rang off. The last thing he *ever* said to me, apart from "'Bye, love". *"Ossie doesn't see it. But I do."'*

'"Ossie doesn't see it,"' Harry echoed under this breath. '"But I do."'

'You're Ossie, aren't you?'

'Yes.'

'That's what convinced me you couldn't have . . . well, killed anyone.'

'It doesn't seem to have convinced Ferguson,' said Chipchase.

'No, well, he never stopped going on about that company of yours. Fraudulent, he called it.'

'He would.'

'When I told him what Dad had said about "other deaths", he said to his sergeant, "We'll have to trawl through all the investors." I took him to mean he thought some more of them might have . . . been killed.'

'Bloody hell. Doesn't he ever give up?'

'But I don't think those could have been the deaths Dad meant. I don't think that's what he had in mind at all.'

'No,' said Harry. 'I don't think so either.'

Helen Morrison asked two favours of them as they were leaving. 'Please don't come to the funeral. My brothers are hot-headed and don't think straight at the best of times. I'll have to tell them what the police have said about you two in case they get to hear about it some other way and think I'm holding out on them. There might be trouble. And Mum couldn't take that. But if you find out what really happened – why Dad was killed – you will call me, won't you? I want to know. Whatever it is. Good or bad. *I want to know*.'

They retreated to the Prince of Wales to talk over what they had learned. To Harry's surprise, Chipchase did not dispute which deaths Lloyd must have been referring to, especially after he had heard more about the Welshman's behaviour during the reception on the castle roof.

'It's got to be the Clean Sheeters who have died over the years, hasn't it?'

Harry nodded. 'Reckon so.'

'Have you still got Danger's round-up of who's done what and where?'

'Right here.' Harry pulled out his by now seriously crumpled copy of Dangerfield's letter and smoothed it flat as best he could. 'Four dead'uns and one as good as.' He ran his finger down the names. 'Babcock: stroke; Maynard: AIDS; Nixon: drowned; Smith: heart attack; Yardley: motorbike crash.' The recital of the names stirred a recent memory. 'Askew talked abut Nixon's death on the train. I've just remembered. He asked me if I thought Nixon might have been murdered.'

'And Lloyd heard him ask?'

'He'd have been bound to.'

'Did Askew mention the others?'

'No. There was some . . . joke running. Yardley came into it. I . . . can't quite recall.'

'Pie-eyed by that stage, were you?'

'We all were. Except Askew. He'd drunk a good bit, but he seemed . . . horribly sober, now I look back. I didn't take what he said seriously. Well, why would I? But now . . .'

'Victims of AIDS, a stroke and a heart attack we can forget about. I actually spoke to Maynard's old boyfriend when I called round to try and solicit an investment in Chipchase Sheltered Holdings. He gave me a graphic account of how the poor bugger had died. Not a diddy doubt about the nature of *his* demise, I think we can safely say.'

'Nor Smith's, I imagine.'

'Right. A motorbike crash and a drowning, on the other hand, *could* be iffy.'

'But they're both so long ago. Forty years in Yardley's case. Twenty in Nixon's.'

'Maybe the murderer's operating on a long cycle. You know, like a comet.'

'A *comet*?'

'There was this book on astronomy I read while I was in . . .' Chipchase studied Harry's bemused expression. 'Forget it. You're right. They *are* a long time ago. Too long for us to go ferreting after the facts.'

'Not necessarily. Danger doesn't spell out how he got all his information. But for Nixon – and for Smith, I see – he gives a widow's address, in case we might want to send them our condolences.'

Chipchase sighed. 'One of the best, Danger. Always . . . doing the right thing.'

'So he was.' Harry examined the note about Nixon with heightened concentration. 'This phrase he used to describe Nixon's drowning. "Circumstances unknown." That's odd, isn't it, if he'd spoken to the widow? Surely she must know how her husband came to drown.'

'Perhaps she didn't want to talk about it.'

'Yeah? Well, perhaps it's time she was persuaded to. You know what they say. It's good to talk.'

TWENTY-EIGHT

Shona assured Harry that he would be welcome to stay with her as long as he needed to. But if, on the other hand, he and Chipchase felt safer quitting town . . .

'You lads had better do what you think is best. The polis don't always see past the ends of their noses. That Ferguson fellow struck me as all fast-track management training and no real experience. Somebody murdered Mr Dangerfield and they'll get away with it if it's left to the likes of him.'

'So, tell me,' said Chipchase, after Shona had taken herself off to bed, leaving the lads, as they were charmed to be described, to their late-night whisky. 'When do we leave?'

'I'm not sure. I want to speak to Erica if I can before we go. But she still hasn't phoned back. I've no address for her. Or any phone number other than her mobile. It's odd she hasn't called. I don't understand it.'

'Simple enough, Harry old cock. We've had our collars felt. We're unclean.'

'She wouldn't shun us.'

'Don't you believe it.'

'Well, I do believe it. And there it is.'

'Tried the phone book?'

'Ex-directory.'

'Aren't they always?'

'Hold on, though.' Harry jumped up and hurried out into

155

the hall, where a battered copy of the Aberdeen phone book was stored on a shelf under the telephone. He grabbed it and returned to the sitting room.

'I thought you just said she isn't listed.'

'She isn't. But I'm hoping . . . Yes. Here he is. Starkie, Dr D. At least we can pay him a visit.'

'Starkie? You'll get nothing out of that old Dryasdust.'

'We'll see, won't we? At the very least, he can hardly deny knowing where Erica's to be found.'

'Yeah? Well, I suppose so. But just remember: the answer could be nowhere.'

True to Chipchase's prediction, a night on Shona's sofa-bed was an experience not to be recommended, other than to someone with a keen interest in medieval torture instruments. To add interruption to likely injury, one of Harry's few spells of sleep was ended by the flinging open of the door. The hall light was on, initially blinding him. For a few seconds, he believed he was about to be set upon by the person or persons who had done for Dangerfield. Then, as his eyes adjusted, he saw a tall, spectacularly thin, grungily dressed young man, with long hair sprouting from beneath a condom-tight beanie hat, swaying in the doorway. Benjy he had to be.

'Who the fuck are you?' came the slurred question.

'Harry. A . . . friend of Barry's.'

'Harry and Barry. A regular fucking . . . rhyming couplet.'

'Didn't your mother mention me?'

'Who knows, man? Who cares? She can screw who she likes – and ask his mates round. It's . . . fuck all to me.' Benjy turned and stumbled off up the stairs, mumbling inaudibly as he went and conspicuously failing to turn off the light.

Harry struggled out of the pitiless embrace of the sofa-bed, staggered into the hall and flicked the light switch off, then staggered back into the sitting room, slamming the door shut behind him and savouring the thought that Benjy might meet with an accident on the suddenly darkened stairs. But, though accident there was imminently to be, Benjy was not the victim.

'Why are you limping, Harry old cock?' Chipchase enquired as they left Shona's house next morning and headed for her car, which she had generously said they could borrow. 'All this running around getting to you, is it? Can't say I'm surprised. If they had MOTs for humans, you'd need a lot of work in the body shop even to scrape a pass.'

'Since you ask, I bashed my knee on the TV stand when I got up in the night.'

'Ah. The old bladder can't manage eight hours' kip without a toddle to the lav, hey? It's a bugger, isn't it, living past your prime?'

'You're chirpy, I must say.' Harry could not help wondering if Chipchase's cheery mood had anything to do with Shona, Benjy having succeeded in planting a suspicion in his mind that their relationship might be closer than he had supposed.

'Don't worry,' said Chipchase with eerie ambiguity as he flung the passenger door open for Harry. 'It won't last.'

They started away, heading for the bridge over the Dee. Harry was on the point of describing his nocturnal encounter with Benjy, minus a few conversational details, when Chipchase asked, 'Why didn't you phone Starkie before we left to make sure he'd be in?'

'To be honest, I thought he might make some excuse not to see us.'

'Give us the cold shoulder, like Erica?'

'I just didn't want to give him the chance.'

'But we could find he's simply not at home.'

'He doesn't strike me as the type to stray far.'

'Are you saying we might have to lie in wait for him?'

'It's possible, I suppose.'

'Great. That should make for a really exciting day.'

*　　*　　*

157

Starkie's address was a ground-floor flat in a converted Georgian house in Old Aberdeen, close to the University, where cobbled quadrangles and ancient college buildings preserved an Oxbridgian atmosphere of studious separateness.

There was no response to several rings on Starkie's bell and a squint through his window revealed many signs of him – a disorderly desk, books and magazines piled here and there, a glass on a side-table with what looked like whisky still in it – but not so much as a glimpse of the man himself.

Chipchase was in the midst of a semi-serious suggestion that they try the post office, in case it was the good doc's pension day, when the front door was flung open by a plump, pinch-faced woman of indeterminate age, trussed up in a raincoat and headscarf (though it was neither raining nor blowing a gale), who gave them a thin, cautious smile as she emerged, carefully closing the door behind her.

'Is it Dr Starkie you're after?'

'It is,' said Harry, smiling ingratiatingly.

'He's no in.'

'Apparently not. We, er, met him at the weekend and, er . . .'

'At the Kilveen do?'

'Oh, he mentioned it, did he?'

'Aye. He did.'

'So, where do you, er, think he might . . .'

'You're out of luck, I'm afraid. He had to go away.'

'Away?'

'His sister died. Down south, somewhere. Manchester, I believe. It was awful sudden.'

Harry cast a wide-eyed look of sickened astonishment at Chipchase, who responded in kind.

'Did you know the lady?'

'No. Er . . . We didn't.'

'Only you look upset.'

'You could say we are.'

'Och, well, I'm sorry, but there it is. I must be about my business.'

'Sure.' As she moved past them a thought struck Harry – half hopeful, half despairing. 'Oh, by the way . . .'

'Aye?' She turned back and looked at him.

'I wonder if you know a former pupil of Dr Starkie's. She's probably visited him here. Erica Rawson.'

'No. I canna say I do.'

'She teaches at the University.'

'Rawson, you say?'

'Yes. In the Psychology Department.'

'I don't think so.'

'Sorry?'

'There's no-one of that name on the academic staff.'

This could not be, Harry told himself. *This was not possible.* 'How can you be . . . so sure?'

'I work part-time in the University office. There's definitely no Rawson on the payroll. I can tell you that for a fact.'

'But . . .'

'You're sure you're thinking of *Aberdeen* University? People get confused since they upgraded the old Institute of Technology. Though I doubt that has a psychology department.'

'I'm positive. Aberdeen.'

'Some misunderstanding, then.'

'Some sort. Yes.'

'Sorry I can't be more helpful.'

'That's all right. Actually, you've been very helpful. Thanks.'

'You're welcome. Goodbye now.'

''Bye.'

They watched her walk away along the street. A few moments of reflective silence passed. Then Chipchase cleared his throat. 'Ever been had, Harry old cock?' he enquired lugubriously.

159

TWENTY-NINE

The North Sea was grey and turbid, heaving to a slow, queasy rhythm. Harry stared out through the windscreen of Shona's car at its chill, blurry expanse from a parking bay on Aberdeen's esplanade, with Chipchase alternating heavy sighs and muttered curses beside him.

'Got a fag?' Chipchase asked suddenly.

'I gave up years ago.'

'Bloody hell.'

'Haven't you got your cigars with you?'

'I never smoke cigars before lunch. Lunch*time*, anyway. A man buffeted by the cruel winds of fate as I've been can't be sure of—'

'Put a sock in it, for God's sake.'

'No need to be so tetchy.'

'Really? I'd have said there was every need.'

'The dead sister in Manchester was a low punch, it's true. I'd never have thought old Starkie had a sense of humour, albeit a sadistic one. Just shows how wrong you can be.'

'What are they up to, Barry?'

'Him and the now-you-see-her-now-you-don't Miss Rawson? Christ knows. Something deep and dark would be my guess. Bloody deep. And bloody dark.'

'Danger must have known all along Erica wasn't what she claimed to be.'

'So he takes a header from his own landing. And she

disappears. Along with Starkie. Q. E. bloody D. We're Conference against Premiership here, Harry. Way out of our league.'

'We've got to do something.'

'You could try her mobile again.'

'Very funny.'

'Or we could just . . . head for the hills.'

'Which hills, exactly?'

'I don't know. We could make it to Ireland without passports. Lose ourselves out west. Hope they don't come looking for us.'

'But they would.'

'Not such a bright idea, then. Besides, I hear all the bars there are non-smoking now. Bloody savages.'

'We *should* head for the hills, though. The Aberdeenshire ones. I've just had an idea.'

'Here we go.'

'Start driving, Barry.'

'Where to?'

'Lumphanan.'

The Clean Sheeters were scattered. Starkie and Erica Rawson had fled. But one horse, if Harry was any judge, would still be in his stable.

'Stronach knows something,' he said, as they sped west out of Aberdeen. 'I'm sure of it.'

'He was just the castle handyman, Harry. What *could* he know?'

'He kept his eyes peeled. He missed nothing.'

'If you say so.'

'He called the reunion risky.'

'Anything seems risky to a man like him. He's spent his whole miserable life in that village. Can you imagine how bloody narrow-minded that must make him? He's probably never been to Edinburgh, let alone London.'

'I'm not interested in his take on the zeitgeist, just his pin-sharp memories of Kilveen Castle fifty years ago.'

161

'Sharper than ours, you think?'

'I'm betting on it.'

'Barnett,' said Stronach by way of expressionless greeting when he opened the door of his cottage. 'And Chipchase. A well-matched pair, if ever there was. What can I do for you?'

'You can call this bloody dog off for a start,' shouted Chipchase, who had retreated towards the gate in the face of the Jack Russell's barking proximity to his ankles.

'You canna keep a good ratter down.'

'What the hell's that supposed to mean?'

'Don't make such a fuss, man. He won't bite, and, if he did, it'd only be a wee nip.'

'Can we come in?' Harry asked.

'You're no fugitives, are you?'

'No, we are not.'

'I just wondered. The *P and J* said the polis had taken in a couple of suspects for questioning after Dangerfield's murder. You two came straight into my head.'

'Did we really?'

'I told you you shouldn't have had any truck with a re-union.'

'So you did.'

'Och, well, come in, then, if you want. You'll have to take me as you find me, though, I warn you. I'm not exactly geared up for entertaining.'

The degree of understatement in Stronach's warning was evident as he led them into a kitchen equipped in an antique style the National Trust would be proud to preserve, but not maintained in a fashion they would be pleased with. Most of the metalwork of the range was invisible under a crust of dried spillages and the table looked to be permanently laid for one, with a drift of breadcrumbs, tea leaves, bacon rind and tobacco covering most of its surface. At one end a pipe, pungent even though unlit, was propped in a saucer next to an

162

egg-smeared plate and a grease-stained copy of the *Press and Journal.*

Stronach poured himself a cup of some treacle-coloured liquid from a teapot on the range and sat down at the table. He did not offer his guests any refreshment, for which Harry for one was grateful. The dog followed them into the room, paying close attention to Chipchase but no longer barking at him and not seeming to pose an immediate threat.

'What's brought you out here, then?' Stronach asked, eyeing them hardly less suspiciously than the dog.

'Why was the reunion such a bad idea?' Harry responded bluntly.

'You tell me.'

'We don't know.'

'What makes you think I do?'

'You said it was risky. Why?'

'I sensed it, you might say.'

'How about saying a bit more?'

'I know nothing, man.' Stronach loaded some tobacco into his pipe. 'For a fact.'

'Forget facts. What do you *sense*?'

'I'm not sure. I never have been.' The pipe was lit in what seemed a deliberately protracted procedure. 'But something wasn'a right up at Kilveen. You know that as well as I do. Probably better. Why were you there in the first place, for instance?'

'An experiment in teaching techniques.'

'Aye. Well, that was the story, wasn't it?'

'It was the bloody reality as well,' said Chipchase. 'We should know. We sat through it.'

'Did you? Sure of that, are you now?'

'Of course we're bloody sure.'

'Aye. I'd have said the same. I didn'a see so much of you, but Mrs Stronach cooked for you every day. Regular as clockwork. The whole time.'

'Yeah. I still get indigestion thinking about it.'

163

'What are you driving at, Stronach?' Harry asked, trying not to become impatient.

'Just this. You're not the first of your Clean Sheet band to come here, asking me questions about your spell up at the castle. No, no. Not by a long chalk. Nor by a long time. It must be more than twenty year since the black boy called round to see me.'

'The black boy? You mean Leroy Nixon came here?'

'He did that.'

'When?'

'Like I say. More than twenty year ago.'

'It'd have to be. He died in 1983.'

'And how did that happen?'

'He drowned.'

'Did he now? Do they have that down as suicide, accident – or another murder?'

'We don't know the circumstances.'

'Well, I'm sorry to hear it, anyhow. He was a good lad. Though far from a lad when I last saw him.'

'Do you think that was the year he died? Or earlier?'

'I canna say. He mentioned he was living in Brixton. There'd been race riots reported there. I asked him about them. You could place it from that, I dare say. It was this time of year, though. Spring. I'm sure of that.'

'What did he want to know?'

'It was . . . vague stuff. Like with yourselves. Something niggling at him. Some . . . doubts that wouldn'a go away.'

'He came all the way here from bloody Brixton to share a few *doubts* with you?' snapped Chipchase. 'Pull the other one.'

'It wasn'a just that.' Stronach paused for a puff at his pipe. 'Maybe I shouldn'a tell you. It could get us all into a lot of trouble. It might have got him drowned. And these other men killed. But at my age . . .' He smiled crookedly. 'I'm risking death every night just by going to sleep.'

'What did he want to know?' Harry repeated.

'Whether any of you had ever left the castle. Whether there

164

were times I went up there and some of – or even all of – you were gone.'

'We were stuck there for the bloody duration,' said Chipchase. 'Bar a fortnightly booze-up in Aberdeen.'

'Aye. I know. That's what I told him.'

'How did he react?' Harry asked.

'He seemed pleased at first. Relieved, I suppose you'd say. But I don't know that he wasn'a just . . . acting that way . . . for my sake. It's a strange thing, but, looking back, I don't think he really believed me. I don't think I told him what he wanted to hear.'

THIRTY

'Yes, OK . . . Well, like you say, it's fair enough . . . No, no. It's quite clear . . . Yes, we'll make sure of it . . . Without fail . . . OK . . . See you then . . . Thanks. 'Bye.'

Chipchase ended the call and slipped his mobile into his pocket. He picked up his pint of beer, still three-quarters full, whereas Harry's was nearly empty, and downed several large gulps.

They had been in the front bar of the Boat Inn at Aboyne for an hour or more, hoping food and drink would aid their analysis of what Stronach had told them. So far, little progress had been made, other than in depleting the landlord's stock of Thrappledouser bitter. Even Chipchase's call to Kylie Sinclair had been born of necessity rather than inspiration.

'Well?' prompted Harry.

'Oh yeah.' Chipchase set down his glass. 'It seems Ferguson has no objection to us decamping to Swindon. According to Smiley Kylie, he's actually in no position to stop us. But he does insist on us registering with the local Plod. She wants us to let her know when we plan to leave.'

'The sooner the better.'

'So we can stop en route and quiz Nixon's widow?'

'Don't you think we should?'

'I think Coker was off his head. That's probably why he managed to drown himself. You know, I know, Stronach knows, that none of us left Kilveen during Operation Clean

Sheet. Even if my grandmother really *had* died while I was there, I'm not sure they'd have let me off to go to her funeral. So, all we're likely to accomplish by visiting the widow Nixon is to drag up a lot of sad memories for the poor woman.'

'But remember what Lloyd was looking for? A "connection with the other deaths". Nixon's is one of them. And he was clearly preoccupied with Operation Clean Sheet. It's only logical to follow it up.'

'It's over twenty years ago, Harry. If you're seriously suggesting Nixon was knocked off by the same ruthless bloody killer who did for Askew, Lloyd and Dangerfield – assuming they *were* all murdered – perhaps you'd like to explain to me why he waited a cool couple of decades to tick off some more names on his death list. And, just to be generous, I'll give you time to think about it. A few minutes, anyway. I'm off to splash my boots.'

Harry did his best to apply his mind to the problem during Chipchase's absence, but found himself unable to focus his thoughts, thanks in part to the sudden activation of the Boat Inn's special attraction for children: a model steam train that chugged and whistled its way round the bar on a shelf above the picture rail. Harry watched its progress, knowing Daisy would have called it 'silly' but would have enjoyed the spectacle nonetheless. If he could only climb on a train now that would bear him straight back to her and Donna, he surely—

'Bloody hell,' said Chipchase, returning to the table. 'You look as if you've cooked up some hare-brained theory you think I might actually swallow.'

''Fraid not, I was just . . .'

'Daydreaming?'

'Home thoughts from abroad. You know?'

Chipchase sat down and grimaced. 'If I had a home in this country or any other, I suppose I'd know what you mean.'

'I can't give you the explanation you want, Barry.'

'Thought not.'

'But there is a link between Nixon's death and the others. Not much of one. But it *is* a link. Nixon was asking whether he – or anyone else – had left Kilveen during Operation Clean Sheet. On the train up here, Askew was questioning the purpose of Professor Mac's experiment. Then Lloyd had his fit of déjà vu on the castle roof. They were all, in different ways ... querying the record.'

'What about Danger? What was he querying?'

'Well ... nothing ...'

'Exactly.'

'He must have known Erica Rawson wasn't on the University staff, though. Which means he must have known what she and Starkie were really up to.'

'One up on us, then.'

'Except that he's dead.'

'Too bloody true. Which is not what I want to be in the near future.'

'Nothing ventured ...'

'Nothing lost.'

'Unless you count our passports. And perhaps our liberty, if we leave Ferguson to concoct a case against us.'

'Harry, Harry. Listen to yourself, will you? It's all so ... bloody half-cocked. You seem to have conveniently forgotten, for instance, that Lloyd only died because *Wiseman's* car was sabotaged.'

'Ah.'

'Yes. *Ah.*'

'I have thought about that, actually.'

'Oh, good.'

'Why couldn't it have been sabotaged at Braemar? While they were in the pub, collecting Magister's fancy fountain pen and no doubt toasting its recovery with a drink or two. They could have been followed there from Lumphanan. The steering took a long time to fail if it was tampered with at the castle. Not so long if Braemar is where it was got at. In which case, Lloyd *could* have been the target.'

'OK. Say I give you that. Provisionally. But who targeted him? *Who* was the saboteur?'

'I don't know. The killer isn't one of us. He wasn't at the reunion. He can't be in two places at once: Braemar *and* the pub where we all had lunch. But I suppose he has to be working with one of us. To be tipped off about what Askew said on the train so that he could get on later in the journey and deal with him. To—'

'Who heard what Askew said on the train?'

'Who? Well, me, Lloyd, Fripp, Judd, Tancred. We were all there. Not Gregson, though. He stayed behind when we went to the restaurant car.'

'Right. And we can rule you and Lloyd out as suspects. Which leaves . . .'

'Fripp, Judd and Tancred.'

'Bloody hell.' Chipchase rubbed his eyes. 'I'm getting as bad as you. I have to believe one of those is a party to multiple murder?'

'If my theory's right, then . . .' Harry felt surprised by the unavoidability of the conclusion. 'Yes.'

'But it's a bloody big if. And there's an even bigger hole where their motive should be.'

'There'll be a motive. We just have to find it.'

'Starting with Mrs Leroy Nixon?'

'Well, unless you have a better suggestion . . .' Harry spread his hands. 'Yes.'

He phoned Donna from Shona's house late that afternoon – breakfast-time in Vancouver – to console her with the news that (a) he was all right and (b) he was about to leave Aberdeen.

'We're catching the sleeper. Next time I call we'll be in Swindon.'

'Well, that's something. I'll feel happier knowing you're out of harm's way.'

'Me too.'

169

'If you really will be. There's nothing going on you're not telling me about, is there, Harry?'

'Absolutely not. Come next week the police will have to give up hounding us. We'll be free to go. And I'll be heading straight home.'

'That sounds good.'

'Until then, try not to worry.'

'Are you serious? Of course I'll worry.'

'I only said *try*.'

'You will be careful, won't you, hon?'

'As careful as can be.'

'Don't let Barry talk you into anything . . . stupid.'

'No chance.'

'Really and truly?'

'None at all.'

He had not told Donna the real reason for travelling by sleeper was to speed their arrival in London and give them a day in the capital to pursue the truth about Leroy Nixon's death back in 1983. But nor had he lied by insisting he would not be persuaded by Chipchase to take any risks, simply because it was he who had done the arm-twisting on this occasion. Chipchase had told Kylie Sinclair at his instigation that they would be travelling to Swindon tomorrow. They were thus not expected to register with the local police until Friday. Their stopover in London was a scheduling sleight of hand. The credit for whatever came of it – or the blame – would be solely Harry's.

Shona drove them to the station that evening. She too was concerned for their welfare, though perhaps more for Chipchase's than for Harry's. The farewell kiss she gave Chipchase was certainly more than a friendly peck.

'You'll look after yourselves, won't you?' she called to them as they headed for the train.

'Like cats with only one of their nine lives left,' Chipchase called back. 'Don't worry about us.'

'"Cats with only one of their nine lives left",' Harry said to him under his breath. 'Is that supposed to be reassuring?'

'No. It's supposed to be an all too bloody accurate description of you and me, Harry old cock. I intend to keep a firm grip on that ninth life. And I advise you to do the same.'

THIRTY-ONE

Not having booked sleeping berths in advance, Harry and Barry were banished to the seated coach on the train. Chipchase's response to this hardship was to stock up with enough tins of lager to ensure oblivion, failing genuine slumber, for at least part of the journey. Harry was manoeuvred into paying for them, despite having already been obliged to buy both their tickets, Chipchase pleading an unspecified difficulty with his credit card.

In the circumstances, Harry felt drinking his fair share was a point of principle. The predictable result was a raddled, hung-over arrival in London the following morning. Breakfast at Euston station after the indignity of washing and shaving in the underground loo failed to redeem their start to the day. Nor did a Tube journey at the fag end of the rush hour fill their hearts with glee.

They emerged at Stockwell into a muggy, drizzly morning and headed towards Brixton, navigating by an *A–Z* bought at Euston. Their destination, Colsham House, was one of several drably similar blocks of flats in an area that prompted various chunterings by Chipchase suggestive of a lack of enthusiasm for the concept of a multiracial Britain.

'Can you see any other white faces around here, Harry?' he muttered as they waited at a pelican crossing with a group of local residents. ''Cos I can't. Not a single one.'

'Now you know how Coker felt all the time.'

172

'Yeah. Foreign.'

'We're *from* a foreign country, Barry. Didn't you know? It's called the past.'

Colsham House boasted a ramshackle but evidently functioning entryphone system. Harry pressed the button for number 112 and braced himself for a tortuous, static-fuzzed conversation with Mrs Nixon. But the only response was the decisive buzz of the door release. They went in and made for the lift.

The door of flat 112 was a short step along an open landing on the fifth floor. Somewhat to their surprise, it stood ajar, in readiness for their arrival.

'Hello?' Harry called as he stepped cautiously into the flat, Chipchase lagging even more cautiously behind.

Empty white spaces met Harry's gaze. More accurately, empty primrose-yellow spaces, accompanied by the distinctive smell of fresh paint. 'You're early for once, Chris,' came a lilting, female voice. Then a bustling, sturdily built young woman in blue jeans and a red T-shirt emerged into the passage from an adjoining room. A mass of dreadlocked hair framed her broad, smiling face. But her smile was fading fast. 'Shit,' she said. 'Who are you guys?'

'We're, er . . . looking for Mrs Nixon,' Harry replied. 'Mrs . . . Leroy Nixon.'

'My mom?'

'Well, I suppose . . .'

'Who *are* you?' The woman frowned and placed her hands on her hips. 'What do you want with Mom?'

'We used to, er . . .'

'We were friends of your father, luv,' said Chipchase. 'Leroy. Well, Coker to us, but—'

'It was a long time ago,' Harry cut in.

The frown lifted slightly. 'You mean . . . you're some more of Dad's RAF buddies?'

'Yes,' said Harry with some relief. 'That's right.'

'How do you mean?' asked Chipchase. '*Some more?*'

'If you're part of the group that guy in Aberdeen wrote to Mom about a few months back, you must know she isn't here.'

'Must we?' Harry suspected his expression answered the question succinctly enough.

'You're friends of Gilbert Tancred, aren't you?'

'Tancred? Yes. We are.'

'Oh yeah,' said Chipchase, determined, it seemed, to over-egg the pudding. 'Tapper and us are like that.' He raised his hand, second finger folded around index finger to confirm undying if wholly fictitious amity.

'So, you surely know he paid for the trip.'

'What trip would that be?' asked Harry, as nonchalantly as he could contrive.

'Mom's cruise to the Caribbean. Her first chance to see Antigua again in more than forty years. It was really kind of him. With her fear of flying, she thought she'd never set foot on the island again. We're redecorating the flat while she's—'

'When's she due back?'

'Not for another six weeks.'

'Thanks to . . . Gilbert?'

'Yeah. That's right. It's all down to him. Didn't he tell you?'

'No. He didn't breathe a word.'

'Just like the bloke.' Chipchase grinned broadly. 'Good deeds discreetly done are Tapper's speciality. Isn't that so, Harry?'

'Absolutely. Yes. Hides his light under a bushel.'

'Gold bar for a heart.'

'One of the best.'

'They just don't make them like him any more.'

'More's the pity.'

'They broke the mould after—'

'Will you two cut it out?' The young woman had folded her arms. Her brow was sceptically furrowed. 'Anyone would think he had some sinister motive, the way you're going on.'

174

*   *   *

Joyce – as it transpired Nixon's daughter was called – offered them tea, which they accepted. The absent Chris rang while she was making it to report that, far from being early, he would actually be quite late. With a tranche of spare time suddenly wished upon her, she had no objection to sitting down in the kitchen and talking to Harry and Barry about her late father, her Antigua-bound mother . . . and the uncommonly generous Gilbert Tancred.

'I was only two when Dad died. I don't remember him at all. Mom never used to talk about him. What I know I got mostly from other people. Just mentioning him was seriously taboo when I was growing up. Mom's opened up a bit more about him these last few years, but not a whole lot. He was troubled, though. Even before they got married. That I do know. There were . . . demons inside his head. I think Mom hoped she could heal whatever was hurting him. But it was beyond her. He'd go off, apparently, for weeks at a time. Searching for something. But nobody ever knew what. Then, one day, Mom heard he'd been drowned. Lost overboard from a ferry off the coast of Scotland.'

'Where was the ferry going?' asked Harry.

'I don't know. Nobody ever said. Is it important?'

'Probably not.'

'The letter from your friend Johnny Dangerfield was forwarded from the house where they used to live in Lewisham. Mom wrote back and explained Dad had passed away. Then your other friend Gilbert Tancred showed up, asking how it had happened. I didn't like him at first. He comes across as seriously up himself. But when he offered to pay for this cruise for Mom . . . She was so thrilled there was no way we could turn him down. I had a postcard from her only a couple of days ago. From Bermuda. She's having the time of her life.'

'That's good to know.'

'Honestly, it's the best thing that's ever happened to her.'

'I'm sure it is.'

'So, why do you both still look as if you suspect Gilbert is . . . up to something?'

'It's our twisted personalities, luv,' said Chipchase. 'He's put us to shame and we're finding the idea hard to get used to. That's the pitiful truth. Maybe we should force ourselves to call in on Tapper and congratulate him for what he's done for your mother. What d'you reckon, Harry?'

'Well nigh essential, I'd say.'

'That's it, then. We'll do it.'

'So you'll be seeing him soon, will you?' asked Joyce.

Harry exchanged a glance with Chipchase before replying. 'I should think so.'

'Then, can you tell him how much Mom's enjoying the cruise?'

'No problem.'

'And pass on my thanks, will you?'

'Oh, we'll be sure to.'

'Does anyone know where your father went on his wanderings, Joyce?' Harry asked as they were leaving.

'No. Except that last time. And even then . . . not really.'

'When were the riots here, d'you know?'

'The *Brixton* riots?'

'Yes.'

'The year I was born. 1981. Why?'

'Because Leroy was in Scotland that year as well, luv,' said Chipchase. 'It's probably where he always gravitated to.'

'Why did he go there?'

'We don't know.'

'But we intend to find out,' Harry added. 'You could say we have to.'

THIRTY-TWO

'When were you planning to pay Tapper this little social call, then?' Chipchase asked as they trudged back towards Stockwell Tube station.

'Right now,' Harry replied. 'We've got his address, thanks to Danger.'

'Yeah. Leafy Carshalton. All right for some, hey?'

'Did he ever strike you as the impulsively generous type?'

'Anything but. There were moth holes in his ten-bob notes.'

'So, why would he send Mrs Nixon off on a luxury cruise, all expenses paid?'

'To get her out of the way. To ensure she couldn't let slip anything significant about Coker's long ago, mysterious demise.'

'Good to know we're thinking along the same lines, Barry.'

'We make a good team, Harry. You know we do. The old firm back together. A winning combination.'

'You've said that before.'

'Have I?'

'Quite a few times. And every one of them . . . has been the prelude to disaster.'

Carshalton was a far cry from Brixton. Cherry trees were in blossom round the old village pond, the quacking of ducks audible above the rumble of traffic. They crossed a park where several pedigree Carshaltonians were exercising their pedigree hounds, then walked along a well-spaced row of half-timbered, double-gable-fronted houses with Land Rover Discoveries and E-class Mercedes gleaming on the drive-ways.

Tancred's contribution to the vehicular excess was a sleek, sporty Jaguar. Its owner, dressed for golf in check trousers and bottle-green sweater, was loading a bag of clubs into the capacious boot as Harry, with Chipchase as usual in the rear, turned in from the road.

'Tapper.'

'What?' Tancred whirled round. 'Good God. Ossie. And . . . yes, it's Fission, isn't it?'

'Long time no dirty looks, Tapper,' said Chipchase.

'What brings you two here?'

'You've heard about Danger?' Harry asked.

'Yes. Magister phoned. I should tell you that he didn't . . . speak kindly of you.'

'He's a little overwrought.'

'Forgivably so, I rather think.' Tancred closed the boot and jangled his car key. 'I have no idea what you're mixed up in, of course, but—'

'A triple murder inquiry, Tapper. That's what we're mixed up in. And it's not a pleasant experience, let me tell you. Especially when you consider that we're innocent.'

'I'm sure you are. Nevertheless, someone did murder Danger, didn't they? We can be sure of that, I gather. And you were on the scene, so I also gather. I suppose it's inevitable you'd come under suspicion.'

'Aren't you just an itty-bit worried in case some homicidal bloody maniac's knocking off us Clean Sheeters one by one?' Chipchase asked in a challenging tone.

Tancred smiled nervously. 'I confess I am.'

'You don't look it.'

'Appearances can be deceptive. They also have to be main-tained. I haven't told my wife there's any cause for concern, so . . . I'm obliged to carry on as normal.'

'Is your wife in at the moment?' Harry asked.

'Er, no. She isn't.'

'Perhaps we could step inside for a word, then. If it's convenient.'

'It's not, actually. I'll be late for my round of golf if I don't leave soon.'

'It won't take long.'

'Even so, I—'

'It concerns a Caribbean cruise you recently paid for.'

'What?'

'Coker's widow, Tapper,' said Chipchase. 'You put her out of our reach, didn't you?'

'I certainly did nothing of the—' Tancred broke off, shaped a friendly grin and waved to a neighbour strolling past the end of the drive, leading a Dalmatian. 'Morning, Hugh.'

'Morning, Gilbert.' Hugh waved back.

'All right,' said Tancred reluctantly, once Hugh and the Dalmatian had moved on. 'Come in if you must. But I can't spare you more than a few minutes.'

'Don't worry, Tapper,' said Chipchase as they headed down past the double garage towards the side-door of the house. 'We won't stay any longer than we need to.'

They got no further than the kitchen, Tancred seeming unwilling to let them invade his domain any further. They were there, his frowning, pettish expression made clear, strictly on sufferance.

'One or two nice vintages here, Tapper,' said Chipchase, eyeing the wine rack. 'You're obviously more of a Bordeaux man than a—'

'Shall we cut the small talk? *If* that's what you'd call it. The fact of the matter is that Magister specifically warned me you might be in touch. When I tell him of your visit, he'll take it as confirmation of your complicity in a plot against him. I was inclined to regard that plot, or at any rate your involvement in it, as a figment of his imagination, but I'm beginning to think I may have to . . . reconsider my position.'

'We're under suspicion,' said Harry. 'That much is

179

undeniable. So, we're having to do what the police don't seem prepared to do. Find out what's really going on.'

'Well, you're wasting your time, then. I certainly can't tell you. It's as big a mystery to me as you say it is to you.'

'Not quite. We don't know why you paid for Mrs Nixon to go a-cruising. But you do. So, why not fill us in?'

'It's none of your business.'

'Oh, but it is. We wanted to talk to her about Coker's death. Your . . . generosity . . . has stopped us.'

'Sorry, I'm sure. Naturally, I had no idea it would prove so inconvenient.'

'What would she have told us, Tapper?'

'Nothing of any relevance, I strongly suspect.'

'Why did you do it, then? Why did you send her away?'

'I didn't *send* her. I simply . . . enabled her to go.'

'But *why*?'

'Why shouldn't I?'

'*Why*?'

'All right.' Tancred slapped the flat of his hand irritably on the work top. 'I'll explain. Even though I strongly object to being obliged to. Danger suggested I call on her and pay my respects – *our* respects. The visit . . . stirred my conscience. I used to patronize Coker. You know that. Several of us did. Spectacularly unfunny remarks about bananas and coconuts and so forth. Looking back, I'm . . . pretty ashamed of how I treated him. Paying for Glenys to see Antigua again was . . .' He shrugged. 'My way of making up for it.'

'You expect us to believe that?' snapped Chipchase.

'I do.'

'Why did you keep it such a secret?'

'Isn't that obvious? To avoid having to admit to you and the others why I did it. I dislike . . . showing my feelings. I always have. I strongly disapprove of the current vogue for soul-baring. I believe some things – perhaps even *most* things – are best left unsaid.'

'Can you lend me a hanky, Harry?' Chipchase sarcastically enquired. 'I think I might be about to blub.'

180

'You must have chatted with Glenys at some length before coming up with the cruise idea,' said Harry.

'What if I did?'

'Discuss Coker's death with her, did you?'

'Briefly.'

'What did she say?'

'Nothing of any significance. He was depressed. Unstable. Mentally ill, it seems clear now. The drowning could have been suicide . . . or an accident. Who knows?'

'He fell overboard from a Scottish ferry.'

'So I believe.'

'You never mentioned it when we were talking about him on the train.'

'I didn't want my arrangement with Glenys to be satirized by you lot. I've already told you that. So, I . . . pretended to know as little as everyone else.'

'Where was the ferry sailing to, Tapper? And where was it sailing *from*?'

'I don't believe I asked. To or from one of the islands, probably. Inner Hebrides. Outer Hebrides. I really can't say. Does it matter?'

'Perhaps. What do you think?'

'I think it's probably . . . unimportant.'

'Yeah,' said Chipchase. 'I bet you do.'

'Have we covered the ground?' Tancred fired back. 'I really do need to get on.'

'All right,' said Harry, confronting the dismal certainty that they would get nothing more out of him – and the disturbing thought that there was nothing more to be got. 'We're going.'

'But we're not going *away*.' Chipchase winked at Tancred. 'Know what I mean?'

THIRTY-THREE

Hard by Carshalton Pond stood the Greyhound Inn, a mellow-bricked Georgian watering hole. In its bar, as thinly populated at noon on a Thursday as might be expected, Harry and Barry sat by a window, drinking Young's bitter and debating the credibility of local worthy Gilbert Tancred.

'He might be telling the truth,' said Harry. 'His explanation made a certain amount of sense.'

'Then again,' said Chipchase, 'he might be lying through his teeth.'

'There's no way to tell, is there?'

'Yes there bloody is. He was a merchant banker, wasn't he? So it stands to reason you can't believe a word he says. Besides, you were adamant: one out of him, Fripp and Judd had to be in on the plot.'

'I was, wasn't I? But, thinking about it, Fripp's a non-starter. He didn't know about Chipchase Sheltered Holdings.'

'One out of two, then. And Tancred's the one who's had to cobble together a cover story.'

'But we can't *prove* it's a cover story, Barry. We can't prove a damn thing.'

'What are we going to do, then?'

'I don't know. Any suggestions?'

'Well, we could . . . rattle Judd's cage. See how he responds to some . . . gentle pressure.'

'I can't see him being mixed up in murder.'

'Neither can I. But . . .'

'It's worth a try?'

'Yeah. Particularly when there's nothing else *to* try.'

Epping was at the far eastern end of the Central line. The journey there from Carshalton was long and slow enough to prompt numerous doubts about its wisdom. A walk of a mile and a half from the station to Judd's large mock Tudor house on the edge of Epping Forest converted those doubts into grumblings of outright discontent on the part of Chipchase, who falsely claimed that he had recommended phoning ahead, whereas Harry's recollection of the plan hatched at the Greyhound was quite otherwise.

A short-haired, snub-nosed woman of middle years dressed in a velour tracksuit was power-hosing a behemoth-proportioned Jeep on the driveway as they limped in off the road, Harry still bothered by his injured knee, Chipchase by rank unfitness and thin-soled shoes. The woman switched off the hose as they approached and semi-rural quietude suddenly descended.

'Afternoon,' said Harry. 'Judder about, is he? Er, Bill, I mean.'

'Sorry, no,' she replied. 'What did you, er . . . ?'

'We're a couple of his . . . old RAF chums, luv,' panted Chipchase.

'Oh, right. You must have been at this thing in Scotland, then.'

'We were,' said Harry. 'Reckoned we might drop by and see what he made of it.'

''Fraid you've had a wasted trip. He and Mum flew to Fuerteventura yesterday. They've got an apartment there. They won't be back for a week or so.'

'A *week*?'

'At least. Could be longer. Well, they're free agents. That's the beauty of retirement, isn't it?'

'Oh yeah,' said Chipchase. 'There's just nothing to beat it.'

*   *   *

Their dishevelled, footsore appearance moved Judd's daughter to offer them a lift to the station, which they gratefully accepted. Slumped aboard a lumbering Tube as it bore them back into London, they found nothing to say. Even recriminations were beyond Chipchase now. Somewhere in the vicinity of Snaresbrook, he fell asleep. And somewhere not much further on, so did Harry.

They woke at Ealing Broadway, roused by the sputtering death rattle of the train's motor and the draught from its open doors. Chipchase looked much as Harry felt, which was a long way short of top form. 'Where are we?' he growled as they grabbed their bags and stumbled out onto the platform. And Harry's answer was grimly apt. 'The end of the line.'

It seemed pointless to backtrack to Paddington now they had come this far west, so they caught a stopping train to Reading and carried on from there to Swindon. Their arrival on a grey, chill, drizzly evening was altogether about as miserable as Harry had feared it might be.

Accordingly, he raised no objection when Chipchase suggested stopping off at the Glue Pot en route to Falmouth Street. It had to be more than thirty years since they had last drunk there together. They went in and toasted old times with best bitter.

'Who'd have thought it, hey? The two of us back in the Pot.' Chipchase managed a weary smile. 'We've sunk a good few pints here between us.'

'I've pulled a few too. I had to take a job behind the bar when you and Jackie skipped to Spain.'

'Bloody hell. We're not going to go over that again, are we?'

'Just making an observation, Barry. That's all.'

'Well, try making a bloody cheerier one.'

'None springs to mind.'

'Pity.'

They said no more, but drank on in silence as the pub gradually filled around them.

* * *

The door of 37 Falmouth Street did not open with its normal fluidity when they made the short transit there from the Glue Pot two hours later. Harry had to yank a tangle of letters out from beneath it to complete their entrance.

Most of the letters were junk mail for Mrs Ivy Barnett, the computers that had generated them remaining stubbornly impervious to her death. But one was for Harry, a surprise which registered even through the beery blur that fogged his mind. It was a padded envelope, addressed by hand in large, jagged capitals. He tugged it open and a computer disk slid out into his palm. He peered inside the envelope in search of an accompanying note. But there was none.

'What the bloody hell's that?' asked Chipchase, peering over his shoulder.

'What it looks like.' Harry held the disk up. 'Shame I haven't got a computer to run it on.'

'Is this something . . . you were expecting?'

'No. I wasn't expecting any post at all. Other than a bill from the undertaker. Which somehow I don't think this is.'

'Who sent it?'

'I don't know.' Harry peered at the envelope. 'Posted in . . . Edinburgh . . . last Friday.'

'Know anyone who was in Edinburgh last Friday?'

'Yeah. So do you. Me, Askew, Lloyd, Fripp, Gregson, Judd and Tancred. Our train stopped at Waverley station for about ten minutes.'

'Long enough to post a letter if you looked lively?'

'Probably. But only two of us got off.' Harry replayed his encounter on the platform with Askew in his mind. Askew had been breathing heavily. Had he just run to and from the nearest post box? It was possible. It was definitely possible. 'Only two of us. Me and Peter Askew.'

THIRTY-FOUR

'We're fine. Honestly. Everything's OK. I'll call you tomorrow. There's a kiss coming down the line. And one for Daisy too. 'Bye, Donna. 'Bye.'

Harry put the telephone down and returned to the front parlour, where he had left Chipchase with the Drambuie bottle his mother had made such negligible inroads into since receiving it as a gift on her ninetieth birthday. Chipchase, to his surprise, did not seem to be putting it away with much abandon either. He was, in fact, just concluding a call on his mobile when Harry entered.

'Who was that?' Harry asked.

'Abracadabra Cabs. They'll be here in about ten minutes.'

'You've ordered a taxi?'

'I have. We're off to see the wizard. Or, in this case, the witch.'

'What the hell are you talking about?'

'Ah, well, while you and Donna were billing and cooing, I did some thinking. We need access to a computer to find out what Askew sent you on that disk. Who do we know in Swindon who might let us use theirs? Jackie. That's who.'

'You phoned Jackie?'

'I did. Caught her at a good time. Hubby's away. Out of her life or just out of town I'm not sure, but it doesn't really matter, does it? She's willing to give us the use of her pc, this very night. So, let's high-bloody-tail it over there . . . and see what we've got.'

Jackie had moved house at least once since Harry had last paid her a social call some seventeen years previously. Her new property was smaller but more tasteful, almost Cotswoldian, in fact, as far as he could judge in the exurban depths of a moonless night.

The transition from dolly-bird secretary to mature, elegant businesswoman was one Jackie had managed with greater aplomb than Harry would ever have predicted. Quite why she was dressed in an expensively flattering black trouser-suit for an evening originally destined for domestic solitude was unclear, but her outfit was not the only puzzling aspect of her appearance. Some hints of grey had been permitted to enter her expertly styled blonde hair, but her looks were magically youthful and her figure, as Chipchase eagerly remarked, was a tribute either to her genes or to her gymnasium.

'From what I remember of your mother, darlin', it's got to be the gym that's kept you in such good shape.'

'If your hand slides one millimetre further in the direction it's going, Barry, I'll demonstrate some of my martial arts skills for you. I didn't acquire them from my mother either.'

Chipchase's hand recoiled from her hip. 'Sorry, darlin'. Old habits and all that.'

'How are you, Harry?' Jackie treated him to a more lingering kiss than her ex-husband had received. 'I was sorry to hear about Ivy. She was a lovely lady.'

'Thanks, Jackie. It's, er, good to see you again. And to, er . . . see you looking so good.'

'Divorce has put a spring in my step. I recommend it. Not to you, of course, with . . . Donna, isn't it? . . . waiting for you in Vancouver. But . . .' She smiled. 'Generally.'

'Divorce, Jackie?' queried Chipchase. 'Are we to take it Tony's had the heave-ho?'

'You are. He's history.'

'That must make me *ancient* history.'

187

'Guess so. Do you two want a drink?'

Neither of them objecting to the idea, Jackie lithely led the way into a spacious, modernistically furnished, spotlit lounge. She had opened a bottle of something straw-yellow from New Zealand, which Chipchase happily agreed to join her in a glass of. For Harry, however, a bottle of ale from Swindon's very own brewer, Arkell's, had been provided.

'Correct me if I'm wrong, but this is what you used to drink in the Plough at lunchtimes.'

'Well remembered.'

'Oh, there's nothing wrong with my memory.' She looked darkly at Chipchase. 'Nothing at all.'

'How's hairdressing?' Chipchase asked after coughing down a mouthful of wine.

'Profitable, thanks. I'm opening a salon in Oxford next month. That'll make six.'

'A real entrepreneuse, aren't we? I taught you well, darlin'. No doubt about it.'

'You were an education, Barry. There's no doubt about *that*.' She smiled coolly at him, then more warmly at Harry. 'I must say I never expected to see the pair of you together again.'

'Neither did I,' said Harry.

'I'm one up on both of you there, then,' said Chipchase. 'I always reckoned our paths through life would converge again sooner or later. It was written in the stars.'

'Why *are* you together?' asked Jackie, still looking at Harry.

'Long story.'

'And one you're keeping to yourselves?'

'Safer that way,' Chipchase answered. 'We don't want to get you mixed up in anything dodgy.'

'Or dangerous,' said Harry.

'Shouldn't you be leading quieter lives at your age?'

'Definitely.'

'No bloody choice in the matter, darlin',' said Chipchase. 'We're in a spot of bother. Through no fault of our own.' He grinned. 'Naturally.'

'More than a spot,' added Harry.

'How much more?' Jackie asked.

'You're better off not knowing.'

'But the contents of this . . . disk . . . could get you out of it?'

'It's possible.'

'Either way, we need to know,' said Chipchase. 'A.s.a. bloody p.'

'When I started work with you two,' Jackie remarked as they entered her study-cum-office, 'high tech meant an electric typewriter. Times certainly change.'

'That they do,' mused Chipchase. '1968: the summer of love. And miniskirts. Micro-mini in your case, Jackie. I bet you'd still look great in one.'

'Well, you're not going to find out. Where's the disk?'

Harry handed it over and watched Chipchase trace in the air with an appreciative hand the curve of Jackie's bottom as she stooped to slide the disk into the tower under the desk. Then she slipped into the ergonomically cutting-edge swivel chair in front of the screen and began clicking the mouse.

'What have we got?' Chipchase asked, craning over her right shoulder while Harry craned over her left.

'First up is some kind of message. See for yourselves.'

> Peter: what follows went before us. It is as I clearly
> remember it. It is the truth. I entrust it to you as I
> once entrusted my heart. You knew what to do
> then. You will know what to do now. Tread
> carefully. But do not tread too fearfully. My love
> goes with you. Les.

'You know these people?'

'Yes,' Harry replied. 'It's to Peter Askew. From . . . Lester Maynard?'

'Has to be,' said Chipchase.

'I didn't know they were . . .'

'You do now.'

'But what follows? What . . . "went before us"?'

Jackie clicked the mouse. The next message, however, was less revealing. *Please enter password to proceed.* 'You can only open the attached file if you know the password. And I have this funny feeling you're going to say you don't.'

'We don't.'

'It's nine digits.'

'Might as well be ninety-nine,' growled Chipchase. 'We still bloody don't.'

'You've no idea at all?'

'What about their nicknames?' said Harry. 'Crooked and Piggott.'

'They're both seven letters each,' objected Jackie.

'Alzheimer's setting in, is it, Harry?' snapped Chipchase. 'Didn't you hear what Jackie said? Nine bloody digits.'

'Well, if you can supply them, Barry, be my guest.'

But Chipchase could not. His own surname was one of only two associated with Operation Clean Sheet that fulfilled the nine-digit quota and neither it nor MacIntyre did the trick. This was no surprise to Harry, who pointed out that Professor Mac's name was actually spelt McIntyre and thus contained only eight letters. Combinations and permutations of other names fared no better. Nor did hopeful stabs in the dark. Askew's address in Cardiff and Maynard's in Henley-on-Thames were mined for the answer, to no avail. Altogether, Jackie must have typed in several dozen words, many of them no better than anagrammish gibberish, before, with a heartfelt sigh, she called a halt.

'We're not getting anywhere here, are we, boys?'

Harry shook his head despondently. 'No.'

'Bloody hell,' said Chipchase.

Jackie closed the computer down and removed the disk. 'Find the magic password and you're in business,' she said, handing it to Harry. 'Otherwise . . .'

'We're sunk.'

'That bad?'

'Could be, Jackie.' Harry nodded. 'Could very well be.'

THIRTY-FIVE

Jackie drove them back into Swindon that night in her top-of-the-range BMW. Chipchase, banished to the rear, rapidly fell asleep. But Harry, sitting alongside Jackie in the front, remained wide awake.

'You should have gone straight back to Canada after your mum's funeral, Harry,' she said as they cruised through a sprawl of neon-lit suburbia entirely unknown to him.

'You're right. I should've.'

'Why not go now?'

'It's too late.'

'Because of him?' She flicked her head in the direction from which Chipchase's snores were emanating.

'Not really. For once, this isn't Barry's fault.'

'He looks as if he's had a rough few years since I last saw him.'

'He has.'

'Poor old sod.'

'Feeling sorry for him, Jackie?'

'On a scale of one to ten, it clocks in at two and a half. I've got the sentiment well under control. I hope you have too. Want some advice?'

'Why not?'

'Go it alone. Whatever the problem, the solution isn't teaming up with Barry. I learned that the hard way.'

'If you remember, so did I.'

'So you did.' She gave him a rueful smile. 'Well, then?'

'I've no choice in the matter, Jackie. Barry and I are in this together now. For good or bad.'

It seemed clear to Harry that there was really only one course to follow if they were to stand any chance of learning the secret Maynard had entrusted to Askew. The following morning, over a spartan breakfast, he put it to Chipchase.

'You said you'd spoken to Maynard's old boyfriend. That's right, isn't it?'

'Yeah. Pernickety little blighter. Clifford . . . something.'

'Why don't we renew your acquaintance? Henley's not far. We can go there after registering at the police station. He might be able to tell us the password straight off.'

'Able isn't necessarily willing. News of Maynard's pash for Askew could knock him sideways.'

'We'll have to do what Maynard recommended in that message, then. Tread carefully.' Harry grinned gamely. 'But not too fearfully.'

The formalities at the police station were brief and painless, though disagreeable nonetheless. Harry resented having to notify the local constabulary of his presence in his home town, while Chipchase was plunged into sour-faced gloom by every aspect of their visit. His mood picked up quickly when they left, however, and by the time they had reached the railway station he had become, if not cheerful, at least less taciturn.

'Tell me, Harry old cock,' he said as their train pulled out, 'did you have any inkling back when we were all together . . . about Askew . . . and Maynard?'

'Not the remotest,' Harry replied, accurately enough. 'You?'

'The same. Despite sharing a Nissen hut with the pair of them. They hid it well. I'll say that.'

'You had to in those days.'

'Even so, I'd have thought we might have . . . sensed something.'

'Would you? It seems to me, Barry, that there was an awful lot going on then we didn't notice. And most of it we still haven't come close to uncovering.'

'Funny, ain't it? The whole kit and caboodle could be on that tape. The answer to every question, nestling in your inside bloody pocket. But we can't get at it.'

'I've been thinking about that. Why would Askew send it to me unless he thought I could access the information?'

'Maybe he did it on the spur of the moment.'

'Exactly. He must have realized he was in danger. And that means he must have been in danger *because* of the disk. He was killed for it, Barry. I'm sure of it. But his killer went away empty-handed.'

'What's on it must be dynamite, then.'

'Reckon so.' Harry thought for a moment. 'Let's just hope it doesn't blow up in our faces.'

Henley-on-Thames was the end of the branch line from Twyford. The house Lester Maynard had owned until his death was a short walk from the station. His partner Clifford had been living there at the time of Chipchase's futile fund-raising visit. The route took Harry and Barry along the riverside and the finishing stretch of the regatta course. They had attended the regatta once, during Barnchase Motors' sadly brief heyday, as guests of tyre-trade titan Brian Cosway. They had both drunk far too much of the free-flowing Pimm's, of course, and the memory of a stripe-blazered Chipchase falling into the river at a late stage of the proceedings was graphically clear in Harry's mind. Charitably, he refrained from mentioning it. Then Chipchase did it for him.

'Maynard was probably watching the regatta himself that day we were here, Harry. His pad actually overlooks the river. We might have passed him on the towpath without knowing it. He might even have seen me being fished out of the bloody river. Strange, isn't it? The past. And the dead people in it. So near and yet so bloody far.'

'Steady, Barry. That sounds almost philosophical.'

'Don't worry. I'll soon snap out of it.'

Belle Rive was an elegant, gabled, brick-and-render villa, boasting, like several of its neighbours, a boathouse and a lawn running down to the river. The Thameside life of Lester Maynard, comedy writer, had clearly been a pleasant one. Belle Rive had been divided into flats since his death. Chipchase identified the bell labelled *C. Enslow* as the one they wanted and gave it a good long press.

'Remember,' Harry whispered. 'The disk's hot stuff. We can't risk telling him about it directly.'

'We just ask him the password without explaining what it's the password *to*. Yeah. Should be a piece of cake.'

The practicality or otherwise of this tactic was to go untested in the immediate future, however. There was no response from Clifford Enslow to the repeated ringing of his bell. Eventually, one of the windows in the ground-floor bay opened and a clearly irritated woman leaned out.

'Can I help you?' she enquired snappishly.

'Sorry to disturb you,' said Harry, reprising his multi-purpose ingratiating smile. 'We're looking for Clifford Enslow. It's a matter of, well, some importance. I don't suppose you . . .'

'I believe this is one of his charity-shop mornings. You should find him sifting through holey jumpers and dog-eared paperbacks at Age Concern in Duke Street.'

Enslow was in fact sifting through nothing when Harry and Barry entered the Henley branch of Age Concern ten minutes later. A tall, thin, gaunt-featured man with a dusting of white hair on his half-bald, half-shaven head, he was dressed in what might once have been donations to the shop and was standing listlessly behind the counter, sipping from a mug and staring into space. It appeared that they had caught him at a quiet time.

'Remember me, Cliff?' Chipchase launched in. 'Barry Chipchase. Old friend of Lester's. This is Harry Barnett, ditto.'

'Chipchase?' Enslow frowned. 'Ah yes. I *do* remember. Two or three years ago.'

'Any chance of a word in private? There are a couple of things we, er . . .'

'Were you at the reunion in Scotland?'

'Sorry?'

'At Kilveen Castle.' Enslow looked sharply at them. 'I had a letter from a Mr Dangerfield a couple of months ago. Well, it was addressed to Les, but I dealt with it. Then, earlier this week, I saw a small piece in the paper reporting that two people attending the event had died in mysterious circumstances.'

'It's three now,' said Harry.

'*What?*'

'Johnny Dangerfield's dead too.'

'Good God.'

'We're trying to get to the bottom of it. Making what enquiries we can. We'd really like to talk to you about Lester.'

'What's Les got to do with this? It's eighteen years since . . .' A shadow of half-buried grief crossed Enslow's face. 'He's been gone a long time.'

'We know, but even so . . .'

'Well, I can't talk to you now. And frankly I fail to see what I could tell you that would be of the slightest value.'

'Let us be the judge of that, Cliff,' said Chipchase.

'Why don't you allow us to buy you lunch?' Harry suggested, eager to take the edge off Chipchase's faintly threatening tone. 'It's the least we can do. In return for a little information.'

'Lunch?' Enslow's expression brightened. 'Well, I suppose . . .'

'Excellent. Where and when would suit?'

THIRTY-SIX

Enslow's choice for lunch alighted upon Henley's very own Café Rouge. Harry and Barry would naturally have preferred to be tucking into pie-and-pint pub fare. Chipchase had ample opportunity to complain about the salad-oriented menu while they waited for Enslow to join them. But he was all smiles when their guest arrived promptly at 12.30, ordering a bottle from the expensive end of the wine list with an alacrity that suggested he intended Harry to pay for it.

'I was sorry to hear Lester had died,' Harry said after they had started on the wine. 'You and he . . . were together a long time?'

'Twelve years.' Enslow sighed. 'Looking back, it seems hardly any time at all.'

'Did he ever mention any of us? Peter Askew, for example.'

'Wasn't he one of the two who died last weekend?'

'Yes. He was.'

'Well, I don't remember the name cropping up.'

'They might have been close,' said Chipchase. 'At some point, you know. Before you and Les . . .'

'They might,' Enslow coolly agreed. 'I wasn't in the habit of interrogating him about . . . earlier attachments. Nor he me.'

'So,' said Harry, 'he never talked about the RAF – or Operation Clean Sheet?'

'I didn't say that. As a matter of fact . . .'

'What?'

'It's all so long ago. It can't have any bearing on . . .' Enslow shook his head. 'I'm sure there's no connection.'

'Why don't you run it past us?' said Chipchase. 'Then we'll *see* whether there's a connection.'

'Oh, very well.' Enslow took a healthy swallow of wine. Harry topped up his glass. 'Les told me about Operation Clean Sheet after hearing of the death of someone who'd been involved in it with him. This would have been in . . . 1983.'

'Leroy Nixon,' said Harry.

'That's correct. Nixon. Drowned, evidently. Lost overboard from a ferry off the coast of Scotland.'

'Any idea what route the ferry was on?'

'None. I'm not sure I ever knew. I wasn't particularly interested and frankly I couldn't understand why Les was. But it became for him . . . something of an obsession. He went up to Scotland that autumn. And again the following year. I offered to go with him, but he insisted on travelling alone. And he refused to tell me where exactly he was going. But I know he met the old professor at Aberdeen who'd set up the experiment.'

'Professor Mac? Les visited McIntyre?'

'Yes. He did. Les was ill by then. Further travelling became impossible. And McIntyre died, of course. Of old age. Unlike poor Les. When I think of what he went through . . .' Enslow looked away. 'I'm sorry. It still upsets me. They could save him now, you know. They could give him back a normal life. But not then. Then he was doomed. He used to spend hours on his computer – all day sometimes, all *night* – searching for a cure. At least, I suppose that's what he was searching for. When I looked through the material he'd stored – after his death, I mean – I couldn't make any sense of what he was working on. It didn't seem to have any relevance to his illness at all. He was researching a drug I've never heard of before or since called MRQS.'

'What does that stand for?'

'I don't know. It was never spelt out. Even if it had been, I doubt it would have meant anything to me. He was in touch with a laboratory in Reading about preparing a sample of the stuff when he . . . went into his final decline.'

'Have you still got this . . . material, Cliff?' asked Chipchase.

'No. There was so much. I got rid of it. Well, I had to, really, with Belle Rive passing into other hands. Oh, here's lunch, I think.'

Their meals had indeed arrived. A hiatus ensued, while the waitress served them and Chipchase blithely ordered a second bottle of wine. An oddity remained lodged in Harry's mind during this period, which he raised as soon as he was free to.

'Who inherited the house, Cliff?'

'Ailsa Redpath. She's been very kind to me. I pay much less rent than the other tenants.'

'How was she related to Les?'

'She wasn't, as far as I know. Not as such.'

'Really?' Harry judged from the frown on Chipchase's face that he too had counted the letters in Ailsa Redpath's name without arriving at the magical figure of nine. 'What was their connection, then?'

Enslow gave a sheepish little half-smile. 'I don't really know.'

'Come again?' Chipchase stared quizzically at him.

'It's true. In fact, I've never actually met her. The whole thing was handled through solicitors. And an agent deals with everything concerning the house. Mrs Redpath never comes down here.'

'Down from where?' asked Harry.

'Did I say down?' Enslow looked briefly discomposed, as if caught out, not necessarily in a lie, but certainly in a misrepresentation. 'Over would be more accurate. She lives abroad.'

'Whereabouts?'

'Er, Italy. Why do you—'

Suddenly, *The Great Escape* was under way – at least musically. Chipchase plucked out his phone. 'Hello? . . .

Yes . . . Sorry? . . . Oh, *hello* . . . Yes. Just hold on.' He looked across at Harry and Enslow. 'Sorry. I'll have to take this call. You carry on without me.' The sidelong grimace he gave Harry as he rose from the table failed to convey whatever meaning was intended. He headed for the exit, phone clamped to ear.

'I hate mobiles,' said Enslow, watching Chipchase go. 'I hate the false urgency they confer on mind-numbingly insignificant exchanges.'

'Me too,' said Harry, sensing Enslow was keen to deflect him from the subject of Ailsa Redpath. The name sounded Scottish to him; distinctly so. 'You don't think Les met Mrs Redpath during his trips to Scotland, do you?'

'It's possible. I really couldn't say.'

'You must have been curious, though. About how they knew each other.'

'I was. I still am. But the lady values her privacy. And I'm her tenant. On very favourable terms. I'm sure you can understand why I'm disinclined to rock the boat.'

'Of course.'

'It's as I warned you. There's nothing I can tell you that will shed any light on these recent deaths.'

'Lester's, er . . . researches . . .'

'Yes?'

'Did he . . . safeguard them in any way?'

'How do you mean?'

'Well, with a . . . password or somesuch?'

'Password?'

'On his computer.'

'Oh, I see what you mean. Mmm.' Enslow considered the point while assembling a forkful of Caesar salad, which then remained poised between plate and mouth as he continued. 'Well, yes, he did. But I knew what it was, of course.'

'And, er . . . what was that?'

'It hardly matters now.' Enslow swallowed his forkful of salad. 'You should be able to guess, anyway.'

'Should I?'

'Sorry about that, chaps,' Chipchase announced, startling both of them with his uncharacteristically soft-footed return to the table. 'Irritating bloody things, aren't they, these mobile jobbies? But handy in emergencies.' He flopped down onto his chair. 'Where were we?'

'Cliff was just about to tell us the password Les used in his computer.'

'Oh yeah?' Chipchase stiffened alertly.

'Apparently we should be able to work it out ourselves.'

'You might be overestimating us there, Cliff. Brain teasers aren't our Trust House. Know what I mean?'

The blank look on Enslow's face suggested he did not. 'Forte,' Harry explained.

'Word play evidently *is* your speciality,' said Enslow drily. 'Les's password was his RAF nickname.'

'Piggott.'

'Exactly. Conferred by your good selves, perhaps. Or some other rapier wit you served with. But, as I explained, the files are long gone. Along with the computer. And Les too, of course.' Enslow sighed. 'A long time gone. So, the password is utterly unimportant.' He looked narrowly at them. 'Which makes your disappointment all the harder to fathom.'

'Disappointed?' Chipchase prodded himself in the chest. 'Us?'

'I'd say so, yes.' Enslow gave them a thin, faintly puzzled smile. 'Palpably.'

THIRTY-SEVEN

'Do you want the good news or the bad news?' Chipchase whispered to Harry as Enslow took himself off to the loo straight after placing an order for dessert and coffee.

'Are they both connected with that phone call you took?'

'Yeah.'

'Give me the good, then. I could do with some after drawing a blank on the password.'

'Helen Morrison is more than ever convinced we're innocent and Plod's barking up the wrong tree.'

'That was her on the phone?'

'It was.'

'She didn't call just to say that?'

'No. That's where we get onto the bad news.'

'OK. Spit it out.'

'She's in Cardiff with her mother. When she heard about it on the local news this morning, she double-checked, so there's no—'

'Heard about *what*?'

'*I'm trying to tell you.* There was a fire at Askew's flat last night. The place was gutted. Everything destroyed.'

'Good God.'

'The Fire Brigade suspect arson. So do I, come to that. The question is—'

'Who did it? And why?'

'We shook Tancred's tree yesterday. Cause and effect, do you reckon?'

'Could be. Then again—'

'Hold up. Cliff's back. Smile, Harry. You're on Enslow-vision.'

Harry and Barry said little as lunch drifted to a close. Enslow took up the conversational slack with his less than riveting observations on the changes he had seen in Henley over the years. Eventually, even these petered out. Harry paid. Enslow thanked them. They left.

Harry walked out with Chipchase onto Henley Bridge. They gazed up the regatta course and watched Enslow's beetling progress along the riverside in the direction of Belle Rive. The sun was out, making a pretty scene of the lawns and the weeping willows and the graceful sweep of the Thames. But gloom had settled on Harry. Every question they asked either went unanswered or raised more questions. With every step they took, they slipped back at least as far.

'Well, he got a free lunch out of that,' growled Chipchase, pointing with his thumb at Enslow's receding figure. 'What did we get?'

'You got a free lunch as well, Barry. Since you ask. I got . . . precious little.'

There was a pause, during which Chipchase apparently decided to ignore the reference to his freeloading. 'Nixon and Maynard were both after the same thing in Scotland, weren't they?' he asked.

'Probably.'

'But we haven't a clue what that was.'

'Oh, we've got a clue. On disk. We just can't get at it.'

'Do you think Askew's flat was searched before it was torched?'

'Who knows? Maybe that's *why* it was torched. To destroy the evidence of a break-in.'

'But the disk is what they were after?'

'Has to be.'

'Then we've got to find out what's on it.'

'If you know how to do that without the password, Barry, now's the time to say.'

'I don't.'

'Somehow, I thought you didn't.'

'But I know a man who might.'

Chipchase's 'man who might' was Andy Norrington, former fellow inmate of Channings Wood Prison. A bank clerk who had siphoned money from clients' accounts to fund his cocaine habit, his credentials as a manipulator of computer technology were undeniable. Released several months before Chipchase, he had written to his old cell-block neighbour urging him to make contact when he got out. 'But that was the last thing I wanted to do. He'd only have reminded me of the whole ghastly bloody experience just when I was trying to forget it.' So, Norrington had gone uncontacted. Until now.

Four trains and three hours later, they arrived at the Beckenham bungalow of Norrington's parents, fervently hoping he had not moved on to a place of his own. The mobile-phone number he had given in his letter was no longer active and his e-mail address was of little use to the low-tech pairing of Harry and Barry. Tracking him down was more than a little hit or miss.

The door was answered by an elderly, gentle-voiced lady who confirmed that she was Mrs Norrington. When Chipchase mentioned Andy, however, her face froze. All she managed to say was, 'Oh dear, oh dear. Oh Lord.' Chipchase was halfway through a stumbling explanation of how he knew her son when Mr Norrington, a stooped and shuffling old man with vast, greasy-lensed spectacles as thick as milk bottles, appeared in the hall.

'You're a friend . . . of Andy's?' he wheezed.

'That's right. From . . . Well, er, we met . . . inside, if

you know what I mean. He may have mentioned me. Barry Chipchase.'

Norrington looked blankly at his wife and she looked blankly back at him. 'I . . . don't think so,' he said.

'Oh dear, oh dear. Oh Lord. You tell them, Perce. I can't . . .' With that Mrs Norrington turned and tottered away out of sight.

'Tell us what?' Harry prompted.

'Well . . .' Norrington swayed slightly and placed one hand against the door to steady himself. 'Thing is . . . Andy's no longer . . . with us.'

'He's moved away?' Chipchase responded.

'No, no. I mean . . . he's . . .'

'No longer with us,' Harry whispered into Chipchase's ear, having already grasped what the old man meant. 'Passed away. Gone to a better place. *Dead*.'

'It was the drugs,' said Norrington. 'He went back on them . . . when he couldn't . . . get on as he'd hoped. Only it . . . was worse than before and . . . one day he . . .'

The exact circumstances of Andy Norrington's fatal overdose were never spelt out. They hardly needed to be. He would not be cracking codes for anyone. Harry and Barry made their way back to the station with nothing to show for their visit.

'A waste of time, I'm afraid,' said Harry, for no very good reason beyond breaking the silence that had settled glumly upon them.

'And bloody depressing too,' said Chipchase. 'I'd have backed Andy to make it on the outside. I thought he had what it took. I thought I had what it took. I'm not so sure any more, Harry. I've got the skids under me. Maybe the bastard who did for Danger would be doing me a favour if—'

'For God's sake, Barry, it's not that bad.'

'Isn't it?'

'While there's life, there's hope.'

'Yeah. Trouble is, it's false hope every bloody time.'

*　　*　　*

The journey back to Swindon did nothing to boost Chipchase's spirits. The rush hour's encroachment into early evening made it sweatily crowded as well as agonizingly slow. Conversation was ruled out by the seats they managed to find being widely separated and none was stimulated by their weary trudge from the station to Falmouth Street. Chipchase stopped short at the Glue Pot, where Harry undertook to join him after phoning Donna.

He caught her on her mobile at the University, as he had banked on doing.

'Do you think your colleagues in the chemistry department will have heard of a drug called MRQS, Donna?'

'What does it stand for and what does it do?'

'No idea on both counts.'

'It's going to be a tough call, then. I'd have to persuade one of them to spend a chunk of time checking their databases.'

'What about that guy Samuels? Isn't he a chemist? The way he was looking at you at the Christmas party, I'd say he was eminently persuadable.'

'I don't actually want to encourage Marvin, Harry. How important is this?'

'Could be very.'

There was a lengthy pause before Donna said: 'Oh God. All right, then. I'll see what I can do. On one condition.'

'Which is?'

'Take extra care, OK? Just for me, hon. I'm still worried about you, you know. If not more so.'

Taking extra care, as Harry had promised to do, was easy in one way. There were no other avenues left to explore. All they could do now was sit tight in Swindon. And tight he and Chipchase certainly were after an evening in the Glue Pot imbibing a beer with the ominous name Monkey's Revenge. When they returned home, Harry found a message from Donna waiting for him on the telephone. 'Marvin's on the case. Speak to you tomorrow. Lots of love from me and Daisy.'

Harry slept poorly, disturbed by vivid dreams and Chipchase's snoring in the next bedroom. His brain began grinding its way through possible nine-letter passwords to no avail. Then the past closed around him, as it was always likely to do in that bed and that room and that house, where he had slept both as child and adult and where virtually nothing had changed in all the years of his life.

When he heard the noise he thought at first he was dreaming, even though he believed himself to be awake. There was a crash from below, a whoomph of ignition, a slowly growing roar. His senses responded sluggishly, his brain wrestling stiffly with what it could not assimilate. The night grew lighter, bewilderingly so. There was a crackling now, buried within the roar. He sat up. And saw, through the half-open door, the source of the sound and the sallow, flickering glow.

Fire was climbing the stairs.

THIRTY-EIGHT

By the time Harry reached the landing, the stairwell was engulfed in flame. There was no escape that way. All he had on was pyjama bottoms and a T-shirt, but he could not turn back to fetch any of his clothes. He had been caught in a house fire once before. He knew how quickly he might be overwhelmed. Thick, dark smoke was billowing up to the ceiling. His chest was already tightening.

He rushed into the next bedroom, where Chipchase was still asleep, snoring for Britain. Harry jostled him awake, shouting his name in his ear.

'Wha . . . What . . . What the bloody hell?' Chipchase opened his eyes and instantly broke into a cough. There was a haze of smoke thickening around them. The speed with which the blaze was taking hold was frightening.

'Get up, Barry. Quick. The house is on fire. We've got to get out of here.'

Amid woozy blinks and phlegmy coughs, Chipchase put his feet to the floor and sat up. He stared transfixed at the plume of flame beyond the door, roaring up from the hall as if from the mouth of a furnace. 'Bloody hellfire,' was all he found to say. But it was apt enough.

Harry slammed the door shut. 'We'll go this way,' he shouted, pointing to the window. It overlooked the sloping roof of the kitchen. Never had it mattered so much to him that the houses of the Railway Village were originally built without separate kitchens, which were added later as single-storey extensions. That one detail of obscure architectural history was suddenly a lifeline. Harry ripped the curtain aside and yanked up the sash. 'Come on. Hurry.'

Chipchase loomed at his shoulder, in the act of pulling on his threadbare bathrobe. 'Bugger me, Harry. Is this safe?'

'A lot safer than staying put. You go first. *Move.*'

Coughing and spluttering, Chipchase hoisted one hastily shod foot over the sill. He clambered out onto the slates, one of which instantly slid from under him. 'Bloody hell,' he cried, grasping the window frame and grimacing back at Harry.

'Move over to the chimney.'

In a lurching slither that loosed another couple of slates, Chipchase made it to the stack of the chimney that had once served the range. Harry climbed out onto the roof, regretting as he did so that he had not stopped to put on shoes himself. Then a glance behind reminded him that it might have proved fatal if he had. The landing was evidently ablaze now. Flames were licking and snapping round the bedroom door.

He moved towards where Chipchase was clinging to the brickwork of the chimney and tried to reassure him. 'It's OK, Barry. We're going to be all right.'

'How do we get down without breaking our bloody necks?'

'Follow me out over the privy. We can climb down from there.'

'I can't see where I'm bloody going.'

'*Just follow me.*'

The roof of the old outdoor loo, set at right angles to the kitchen, took them further from the fire, whose flames lit their path across the slates. The heat at their backs was growing with every second. The contents of the house were being consumed in a crackling inferno. A petrol bomb or something of the kind must have been pushed through the letterbox. Nothing else, it seemed to Harry, could explain the swiftness of the destruction.

He reached the edge of the roof, crouched down and lowered himself gingerly into the gulf of shadow below, where he eventually set his foot on the dustbin. He let go of the gutter and shouted up to Chipchase. 'It's easy. Come on.'

It had not been easy, of course. As Chipchase's awkward, scrambling descent made apparent. 'We're both too old . . . for this kind of thing,' he panted. And Harry could only agree.

They stood together, in the backyard, gulping air and coughing, shaking from what they had done as well as the mental buffeting it had given them. The chill of the flagstones seeped up through Harry's bare feet. He was shivering from the cold, but at his face beat the full heat of the blaze, which had spread now to the kitchen. The house where he was born and where his mother had lived through all the years of her marriage and the many more of her long widowhood had become an inferno.

'Bloody hell,' said Chipchase. 'We're lucky . . . to have got out of that alive.'

'We'd better call the Fire Brigade. If the neighbours haven't already.'

'We'll have to go to one to do it. My mobile's in there. Along with my clothes. Everything.'

'Same here.'

Chipchase looked round at him. 'Including . . . the disk?'

Harry nodded. 'Melted by now, I should think.'

'Bloody hell.'

'Yeah. Like you say, Barry. Bloody hell.'

The neighbours had indeed already called the Fire Brigade. The first engine arrived within minutes. Several more soon followed. Once they had put their hoses and extinguishers to work, the fire was rapidly brought under control and prevented from spreading. But the conflagration at number 37 was strong and stubborn. Harry and Barry watched the firemen's struggle with it from the shelter of the house opposite, where Mrs Jenkins gave them tea, as well as blankets to wrap themselves in. And the loan, in Harry's case, of a pair of her late husband's slippers.

By the time the police arrived, they had already told the fire officer in charge that they had no idea what had started the blaze. 'We were woken by the smoke and got the hell out.' It was true as far as it went. The evidence of arson would eventually be uncovered and Harry sensed the less they said for the moment the better. The police settled for that and left. But they would be back. It was inevitable. Especially when they realized the two occupants of 37 Falmouth Street were the same two the Grampian force had asked them to keep an eye on.

As the fire abated, Harry walked across for a closer look, hobbling as he went, his climb to safety having aggravated the injury to his knee he had suffered in Aberdeen. The neighbouring houses had escaped largely unscathed, he saw, but his old home had been reduced to a burnt-out skeleton. Hoses were still being played on the smouldering interior. The walls between rooms were just about the only features that remained recognizable. The rest – doors, windows, stairs, furniture and all – had been reduced to heaps of ash and blackened wreckage.

'You the tenant?' a fireman asked, approaching from one of the engines.

'Er, yes. Yes, I am.'

'I picked this up.' He handed Harry a framed photograph. 'It's a pity not to save something.'

He walked away, leaving Harry to squint in the lamplight at the Commonweal School group photograph of September 1948, which had hung on his bedroom wall from then until this last night of the Barnetts' presence in Falmouth Street, Swindon. It was over now. It was finished. Not much sooner but a lot more brutally than he had anticipated, the end had come.

Back in 1948, Harry had mischievously run round behind the group after the camera had begun shooting, in order to appear at both the left- and right-hand extremities of the picture, grinning triumphantly. As he looked at it now, however, he saw the heat of the fire had not only cracked the glass

210

but had singed the edges of the paper. A dark brown scorch mark obscured all but the middle third of the group. There was Dr Jones, the headmaster, flanked by his staff. And there, behind them, were the central ranks of boys and girls. But of Harry, at either end, no trace remained. His grin had disappeared in both places. He had been erased twice over.

'What's that?' Chipchase asked, materializing at his elbow.

'Nothing worth keeping,' Harry replied, tossing the picture down among the broken glass and other debris in front of them. 'That's for sure.'

'Bloody hell,' said Chipchase, looking up at the house. 'What a mess.' He wrapped a consoling arm round Harry's shoulder, which had to amount to the warmest gesture of friendship he had ever displayed. 'It's a facer and no mistake.'

'You could say that, Barry. Yes, I think you could.'

'But look on the bright side.'

'Is there one?'

'Certainly. You don't have to clear the place out now, do you?'

THIRTY-NINE

The Fire Brigade were still on the scene, albeit at a reduced level, when a new day dawned, preposterously bright and vernal. Sunlight glinted on the puddles of water in Falmouth Street, limned with rainbow slicks of diesel, and shafted through the smoke drifting up from the hollow, blackened walls of number 37.

Harry surveyed the dismal scene through the window of Mrs Jenkins' front parlour. It was a small mercy for which he was duly grateful that his mother had not lived to witness the destruction of her home. But he was aware that it was really no mercy at all. If she had still been alive, he would be safe in Vancouver with Donna and Daisy, blissfully unaware that an Operation Clean Sheet reunion had even been held, let alone disrupted by murder. And the house he had been born in would be as he remembered it, not the gutted, smouldering ruin he saw now.

The door opened behind him and Harry turned to see Chipchase, wearing one of Mrs Jenkins' home-knitted cardigans and a pair of her late husband's capacious bowls trousers under his bathrobe, looking as a result like a be-wildered fugitive from a down-market nursing home. Harry might have laughed, but for the knowledge that his own outfit was not one he would wish to be seen in on the streets of Swindon.

As far as that was concerned if no farther, Chipchase was

the bearer of good news. 'Jackie's going to buy us some clothes as soon as Marks and Sparks opens and bring them round. She knows my size and you're about the same. It's the spring '05 leisure look for you and me, Harry old cock. She said she'd pop into Boots, as well, and kit us out with a toothbrush and razor each. She never took such good care of me when we were married, I can tell you. I'm seeing a whole new side of her.'

'I hope she's not expecting us to pay her for all this stuff.'

'She knows we got out with nothing but our hides. Play our cards right and she might even . . . extend us a loan.'

'We'll need one.'

'At least until Donna wires us some cash, right?'

'Ah. Donna.'

'You'll be telling her about this, won't you?'

'Actually . . . I'm not sure.'

'*Not sure?*'

'I'm worried how she'll react. Until we decide what to do next . . .'

'What can we do without the disk?'

'I don't know, Barry.' Harry looked back through the window at the remains of number 37. 'I just don't know.'

Jackie arrived shortly after 9.30 with two large M&S carrier bags bulging with clothes and an offer of emergency accommodation at her house. Chipchase was all for accepting, but Harry felt obliged to object.

'Somebody tried to kill us last night, Jackie. They might try again. We'd only be endangering you by staying at your place.'

'You really think it's as bad as that?'

'Every bloody bit,' Chipchase reluctantly agreed.

'Then you should tell the police.'

'They'll realize it was arson soon enough. But as for catching the arsonist . . . they're more likely to conclude we did it ourselves to get us off the hook with Grampian CID.'

'Surely not.'

'I'm afraid so.'

'Yeah,' said Chipchase gloomily. 'They very well bloody might.'

'Give them the disk. They'll have the resources to—' Jackie broke off and looked at each of them in turn. 'You don't have it any more, do you?'

'It's just a lump of goo under a scorched floorboard now. I should have grabbed it as I left the bedroom. But . . .' Harry shrugged. 'I didn't.'

There was a brief silence. Then Jackie asked, almost plaintively, 'What are you going to do?'

'I asked him that myself earlier,' said Chipchase.

'And I still don't have an answer,' said Harry.

An answer of sorts, though hardly a reliable one, had emerged by the time they checked in at the police station. The duty sergeant gave no hint that he had any knowledge of the previous night's fire – or their connection with it. Nor did he react much at all to Harry's announcement that they were planning to return to Aberdeen the following day.

'Very good, sir. We'll let them know.'

'We're not going back to Aberdeen tomorrow, are we?' Chipchase asked as they threaded their way through the Saturday morning crowds in the Brunel Centre.

'We have to go back there sooner or later.'

'Yeah? Well, in the meantime you and I need to conduct what you might call a strategic overview. I get the distinct impression we're in a canoe heading for the rapids without a paddle between us.'

'OK. Where do you want to go for this . . . tactical talk?'

'Well, the Pot should just have opened.'

'Good idea. But they'll expect us to pay for our drinks. So, first things first.'

*   *   *

214

The hairdresser whose eye they caught upon entering Jacaranda Styling's Swindon New Town salon waved them through to the back office, where Jackie was waiting.

'There you are, Harry,' she said, handing him a bulging wallet. 'I guess I'm settling a debt that's been outstanding ever since I let Barry talk me into running out on you all those years ago. So, I added some interest to what you asked for. I even bought you something to keep the money in. If I were you, I'd dole it out to Barry in single note instalments, strictly as the need arises.'

'Thanks for the vote of confidence, darlin',' said Chipchase, smiling ruefully.

'I still think you should tell the police everything.'

'Maybe we will,' said Harry.

'And maybe we won't,' said Chipchase.

'I suppose it's pointless urging you to be careful.'

'No,' said Harry. 'It isn't. We will be careful. Believe it or not, we have been. All along.'

'Yeah,' said Chipchase. 'And look where that's got us.'

'You know,' Chipchase announced after a first swallow of the first pint of Monkey's Revenge pulled at the Glue Pot that morning, 'I was pretty sure last night I'd drunk enough of this stuff to guarantee a steam-hammer hangover. Instead, my head's clear as a bell. Must be down to all that night air I got the benefit of. How are you feeling?'

'Great,' Harry replied. 'Just great.'

'You don't look it.'

'That's because I'm aware somebody wants us dead and may be determined to finish the job they started last night.'

'Plus of course beige isn't your colour. Or would you call that taupe?'

'Maybe we *should* go back to Aberdeen. Today rather than tomorrow. Protective custody could be our safest bet.'

'You're obviously not feeling at your most sparklingly optimistic.'

'Nor should you be. Someone's after our blood, Barry. You do understand that, don't you?'

'Of course I do. But old Chipchase doesn't turn tail and run at the first whiff of grapeshot. Counter-attack. That's what we've got to do.'

'But counter-attack *who*? We still haven't a clue who's doing this. Or why.'

'My money's on Tancred.'

'What's his motive?'

'Beyond a twisted personality? Well, I don't actually . . .' Chipchase's boldly launched analysis of their options trickled away, like water into desert sand. He grimaced and gulped down some more beer.

'Exactly. No plausible motive. And not a shred of evidence. We've got—'

'*Harry*,' the barman called.

'Yeah?' Harry looked round.

'Woman on the phone for you.' He held up the receiver.

Harry was vaguely aware that he had heard the telephone ringing a few minutes before. It would never have occurred to him, however, that it had been ringing for him. He advanced cautiously to the bar and took the receiver.

'Hello?'

'Harry, this is Erica Rawson.'

'*Erica*?'

'Yes. Returning your call. The mobile number you left is out of order. Something to do with last night's fire, perhaps.'

'You know about that?'

'Certainly. We've been doing our best to keep tabs on you ever since you left Aberdeen.'

'*We*?'

'Well, as you know, I don't work for Aberdeen University. But I do work for another organization. So, *we* is appropriate, I think.'

'What organization is that?'

'Not something I can discuss over the telephone, I'm afraid. Which is why I suggest we meet face to face. If you and Barry leave the pub now, you'll be at the station in ample time for the next London train. Get off at Didcot. I'll meet you in the long-stay car park.'

'Hold on. I—'

But the line was dead. Harry had been summoned. And the possibility that he might refuse to answer the summons was simply not allowed for.

FORTY

Chipchase devoted most of the short journey to Didcot to an unconvincing explanation of how he would have extracted more in the way of solid information from Erica before agreeing to meet her. 'You've danced to her tune a sight too long, Harry. She's going to be disappointed if she expects old Chipchase to be as meek and mild as you've been.'

It was futile to point out that Chipchase was in no position to say how meek or mild Harry had been. It was futile, indeed, to speculate what Erica wanted with them – what for that matter she had wanted all along. They would find out soon enough. Shaken by their experiences of the night before, Harry for one was content to wait until they did.

It was 12.30 when the train reached Didcot. Harry and Barry got off, trailed through the subway and followed a knot of people obviously bound for the car park as they headed along the main platform, then took a path that led to a footbridge over the lines, beyond which serried ranks of commuter cars filled the tarmacked expanse of what had once been a goods yard.

'How are we going to find her in the middle of that lot?' Chipchase demanded as they crossed the bridge.

'Maybe she'll find us.'

'She could have found us at the Glue Pot. Why we've had to come to this godforsaken hole for the privilege of a chat with Miss High and Bloody Mighty I don't—'

'Neither do I, Barry. OK? Ask her, not me.'

'I will. If I get the chance.'

The people ahead of them peeled off to their vehicles. Doors slammed. Engines started. Cars nosed out of parking bays. Harry and Barry wandered towards the farthest, emptiest corner of the car park, drawing ever closer as they did so to the huge, squat, gently steaming chimneys of the nearby power station.

A black four-by-four with reflective windows stood conspicuously alone near the distant boundary fence. Its headlamps flashed once as they approached. The passenger door opened and a tall, barrel-chested, broad-shouldered, dark-haired man dressed in jeans and windcheater climbed out. He lit a cigarette, then wandered slowly away from the car, leaving the door open behind him.

'Who the bloody hell's that?' muttered Chipchase.

'Never seen him before.'

'Looks like a bloody bouncer.'

'Well, just as long as he's not planning to bounce us.'

'Think he'd give me a fag? I could just do with one.'

'You really want to find out?'

Chipchase thought for a moment. 'Maybe not,' he said with a sigh. 'The poor sod's probably only lit up now because Her Nibs told him he couldn't inside the car.'

They covered a few more yards towards the four-by-four in silence. Harry caught sight of Erica, seated behind the wheel, dressed casually in jeans and fleece. She glanced coolly at him, her face expressionless.

'That definitely her?' whispered Chipchase.

'Yup.'

'You really know how to pick 'em, don't you?'

Harry let the remark pass, despite the fact that he had in no sense picked Erica. If anything, *she* had picked *him*. He stopped by the open passenger door and looked in at her. 'Hello, Erica,' he said quietly.

'Hello, Harry.' Her reply was neutrally pitched, giving away no more than her calm, unflinching gaze. 'And Barry, I presume.'

'That's right,' growled Chipchase.

'Get in. Please.'

Harry climbed into the seat beside her. Chipchase opened the rear door and clambered in behind him.

'Something wrong with your knee, Harry? You seem to be limping.'

'It's nothing.'

'What he means,' said Chipchase, 'is that it's the least of his problems.'

'Yes. I suppose it must be.'

'Who's your chum?'

'A colleague.'

'What sort of business do you have to be in to get a colleague like him?'

'I'm sorry I had to . . . misrepresent myself . . . in Aberdeen. And I'm sorry I can't be specific about what I do for a living. Or the nature of my interest in your . . . old airmen's reunion. But there it is. Those are the ground rules.'

'A bit bloody limiting, aren't they?'

'Yes. But they are what I'm obliged to operate within. Why don't you shut the doors? It's a little draughty in here.'

The doors closed in a single synchronized clunk. Marlboro Man came into view, prowling the empty parking bays in a slow arc, drawing on his cigarette while never taking his eyes off the four-by-four and its three occupants.

'You didn't need to bring a bodyguard, Erica,' said Harry.

'I know. But he insisted.'

'You're not a psychologist, are you?'

'An amateur one, maybe. But no. For your purposes, I'm not.'

'And you're not with the police.'

'No.'

'Some other branch of the forces of law and order, then?'

'Not exactly.'

'Secret bloody Service,' put in Chipchase. 'That's what it is, isn't it? MI bleeding five.'

'You're jumping to conclusions, Barry.'

'Yeah? Well, it beats jumping for your life from a burning house, I can tell you. From personal bloody experience.'

'You had a lucky escape.'

'Too true we did, darlin'. So, how about making our day and laying on a lucky escape for us from all our recent troubles?'

'What exactly did you have in mind?'

'Who's been killing our old comrades, Erica?' Harry asked. 'And trying to kill us?'

'I don't know.'

'Why would anyone want to?'

'I don't know.'

'What makes Operation Clean Sheet so important all these years after the event?'

'I can't say.'

'Significant change of tone there, Harry old cock. Did you notice?' Chipchase leaned forward between the seats. 'Some things she doesn't know. Others she can't say.'

'Exactly,' said Erica softly.

'You invited me to call you if I needed help, Erica,' said Harry. 'Well, I called. Because I do need help. We both do. Badly.'

'I know. But my freedom of movement's become . . . limited.'

'What the bloody hell's that supposed to mean?' snapped Chipchase.

'It means I can't help you as much as I'd like to.' She glanced round at Harry and he held her gaze.

'How about at all?'

'That depends.'

'On what?'

'How much you know. How much you've learned. How much you've . . . deduced.'

'That's easily answered,' said Chipchase. 'Sweet FA.'

'For your sakes, I hope not.'

'We've figured out a few things,' said Harry. 'But not enough to understand what's going on.'

'The fire at Askew's flat in Cardiff suggests the murderer feared there might be evidence to be found there pointing to his identity. Could the fire at your house in Swindon have been started for the same reason?'

'Maybe.'

'Do you mean you have such evidence?'

'Sort of.'

'If you can lead us to the killer, I can do something for you. Get the police off your backs. Arrange safe passage . . . wherever you want to go. We looked after Starkie. We can look after you.'

'What did Starkie do for you?'

'What we asked him to.'

'And Dangerfield?'

'What have you got for me, Harry? What's the evidence? It has to be *quid pro quo*. I'm not authorized to operate any other way. Tell me you have something to trade.' She looked intently at him, eager, it seemed, to be told a deal could be done. 'Please.'

'Askew sent me a computer disk. We've been trying to decrypt it. Without success.'

'Where is it?'

Harry shook his head.

'It wasn't . . . destroyed in the fire?'

He nodded.

'Oh dear.' She sighed. 'How sad.'

'Is that sad for you, darlin'?' Chipchase asked. 'Or us?'

'Principally you, I'm afraid. There's nothing I can do without it. Or something like it. My hands are tied.'

'No chance you could *untie* them?'

'None.'

'So, where does that leave us?'

She did not answer directly. Her gaze shifted. She pursed her lips and stared into the middle distance. Harry exchanged a helpless glance with Chipchase. A silent minute slowly elapsed. Then, at last, she spoke. But all she said was: 'I'm sorry. I really am.' Then she started the engine.

'Are we going for a spin, darlin'?' asked Chipchase.

'No, Barry. I'm afraid it's time to say goodbye. Would you mind getting out? I need to be on my way.'

'Tell us what's going on, Erica,' said Harry, no longer trying to conceal his desperation. 'Please. I'm begging you.'

'I can't.'

'Rules were made to be broken,' said Chipchase.

'Not these rules.'

'Our lives could be on the line,' said Harry, the pitch of his voice rising. 'You realize that, don't you?'

'Yes.' She closed her eyes briefly. 'I do.'

'Then—'

'It's no good, Harry.' She raised her hand. It was a pre-arranged signal to Marlboro Man. He tossed away his cigarette and started towards them. 'You're on your own.'

FORTY-ONE

As a venue for what amounted to a council of war, the buffet at Didcot railway station left something to be desired. But since neither Harry nor Barry had felt able to suggest a smart move in any direction after watching Erica's four-by-four roar out of the car park, destination unknown, the buffet it had to be. It catered for people in transit, after all: those who had set off on a journey but not yet reached its end; and that was Harry and Barry to a tee.

'Fat lot of bleeding good coming here did us,' Chipchase complained, slurping McEwan's Export between drags on the first cigarette in a newly purchased pack.

'It was impressive the way you controlled the discussion from start to finish, certainly,' Harry observed, his tolerance of Chipchase's reproachful tone wearing thin.

'What did you expect me to do? She's some kind of spook. *And* she had a minder. She said her freedom of movement was limited. Well, it's better than no bloody freedom at all.'

'It's not as bad as that, Barry. Here we are, with money in our pocket and the run of the rail network. Where d'you want to go? Penzance? Pembroke? Pwllheli?'

'The money's in *your* pocket, since you mention it. And, without passports, making a run of it's a waste of what little time we have to play with before Plod starts twitching on our leash.'

'True enough.'

'So?'

Harry leaned back in his comfortless chair and rubbed his eyes, which were still smarting from the smoke they had had to contend with the night before. 'Meeting Erica wasn't the total washout you seem to think, Barry.'

'No?'

'Well, like you said, she turns out to be a spook. MI5. MI6. One or the other – or similar. The point is, there's some kind of overlap between Operation Clean Sheet and the Secret Service. God knows what it is. But no-one who does know is going to tell us. We're on our own. She said so, didn't she? She made that very clear.'

'If you're trying to cheer me up, you're—'

'*I'm trying to tell it like it is.* Listen. Erica doesn't know who the murderer is. Or what their motive is. So, the murders can't be directly connected with the spy angle to Operation Clean Sheet, whatever *that* is. They're about something else. Which means we're as well placed to figure out the answer as anyone.'

'Go on, then. Figure it out.'

'Back at the Pot, you were all for counter-attacking. Was that just the beer talking?'

'It might have been the humming the chorus. Indecision's the real bugbear. I can't decide whether I'm angrier than I am frightened. But on balance . . .' Chipchase took a long draw on his cigarette. 'Probably more frightened. Come to think of it . . . a lot more. And that makes me angry. That and being left in the lurch by Miss Four-by-Four. It all makes me bloody livid, as a matter of fact.'

'Me too.'

'So, I guess I still favour counter-attack.'

'Good.'

'But what – or who – do we go after?'

'Well, I'll phone Donna as soon as it's a civilized hour in Vancouver. See if she's turned up anything on Maynard's mystery drug – MRQS.'

'What if she hasn't?'

225

'Then we'll go back to Enslow. He lied to us about Ailsa Redpath. I'm sure of that. She doesn't live in Italy. He didn't want to tell us her real address in case we decided to pay her a visit. Now, why d'you think that might be?'

'Dunno.' Chipchase stubbed out his cigarette and smiled manfully. 'But I'd be willing to try and find out if it involved giving the fragrant Clifford a hard time.'

Thanks to the vagaries of Great Western's Saturday afternoon connections at Reading and Twyford, it was nearly four o'clock when they reached Henley. The sole advantage of their late arrival was that it was now breakfast-time in Vancouver. Armed with an international phonecard bought before leaving Swindon and a cover story fine-tuned along the way, Harry called Donna from a payphone at Henley station, while Chipchase paced up and down outside and made further inroads into his cigarette supply.

There was something subtly wrong in Donna's tone even before Harry embarked on his explanation of why he was not ringing from his mother's. He tried to tell himself he was imagining it, that his guilt about lying to her was getting to him. But he remained, on some level, unconvinced.

'They've disconnected Mother's phone. God knows why. Some misunderstanding, obviously, but I can't sort it out over the weekend. My mobile doesn't seem to be charging either and Barry's has been cut off. No need to ask why that might be. So, I'm reduced to call-boxes. Any news on MRQS?'

'None at all, Harry. Marvin drew a blank. But he's volunteered to follow a few more hunches, so he might turn up something yet. He's horribly eager to oblige. You can count on him doing his best. It might help if you told me how you came to hear of the drug in the first place.'

'It's a long story. And these payphones fairly gobble credit. MRQS could be an anti-AIDS drug from a while back. Or it could be for something else altogether. I just don't know. I don't even know if it's important.'

226

'But it may be?'

'Maybes are all I have to go on at the moment.'

'And you're being careful? Like you promised you would.'

'Yes. I'm being careful. I'm practically following the Green Cross Code every time I reach the kerbside. There's nothing for you to worry about.'

'I wish I could believe that.'

'You can. I'll phone again later. I've got to go now. Have a nice day. Love you. And Daisy. 'Bye.'

Still troubled by an inflexion in Donna's voice that he was not sure had really been there at all and unable to recall anything in her actual words to substantiate his concern, he rejoined Chipchase outside the station.

'No joy on MRQS,' he tersely reported.

Chipchase shrugged. 'Can't say I'm surprised. Whatever this is about, I don't see how the battle against AIDS comes into it. In the days of Operation Clean Sheet, there was nothing worse than a dose of the clap to worry about, which-ever way you hung your flag.'

'All right. Let's go and see Enslow.'

'That's more like it. Old crocks we may be, Harry, but I reckon we can put the squeeze on Cliff. And it'll be interest-ing to see what oozes out when we do.'

They took a cautious peer into the Age Concern shop, but there was no sign of Enslow behind the counter. Chipchase popped in for a flirtatious word with the lady in attendance and was rewarded with the information that he had just left.

They agreed it was likely he would go straight home, so made a bee-line for Belle Rive. Their route took them past Café Rouge, where they had entertained him to lunch only the day before, though to Harry it felt far longer ago. Every-thing prior to the destruction of his old home in Swindon had a distant, sepia-tinged quality to it now, as if most of his life had gone up in smoke along with his mother's bric-à-brac and mementoes of the family's past.

'There he is,' said Chipchase, interrupting Harry's gloomy train of thoughts with a grab at his elbow.

Enslow was ambling along a footpath through an old grave-yard that was clearly a short-cut to the next street and the lane serving Belle Rive and neighbouring properties. Harry and Barry overhauled him in half a dozen strides.

'Afternoon, Cliff.'

Enslow started at Chipchase's words and whisked round. 'What? Oh. Good God. You two.'

'Yeah. We just can't stay away from heavenly Henley.'

'Really? I—'

'Actually, it's you we can't stay away from.'

'Sorry?'

'Got what you might call a supplementary question for you. Arising from our little chat yesterday.'

'Surely we . . . covered everything.'

'Not everything.' Chipchase grinned. 'There's one tiny point we somehow overlooked.'

Harry summoned a grin of his own to match Chipchase's. 'You know what they say. There's no such thing as a free lunch.'

'We need you to tell us where Ailsa Redpath lives,' Harry explained after they had piloted Enslow to a nearby bench and settled beside him. 'But before you do that, I ought to make a few things clear. Firstly, we know she doesn't live in Italy, so don't waste your breath on the Tuscan villa cover story. Secondly, you ought to be aware the Grampian police have us in the frame for those murders in Aberdeenshire you've read about. We're due to be grilled by them on Tues-day. We're not guilty, by the way, in case you wondered. But someone is. And they're after all of us. If we tell enough people you're the keeper of Lester Maynard's secrets, it's my bet you'll be added to the hit list. Co-operate with us, how-ever, and we'll keep your name out of it. All you have to do is point us in your landlady's direction and stifle any temptation you might feel to warn her we're looking for her. It really is as simple as that. So, how about it?'

'I . . .'

'We'll make it easy for you, Cliff,' put in Chipchase. 'You can omit the post code.'

Enslow sighed heavily. He thought for a protracted moment, then said, 'All right.'

FORTY-TWO

Not Italy. Not even Scotland. Ailsa Redpath lived in London. Harry and Barry left Enslow to make his way home and hurried back to the station, arriving short of breath but in ample time for the 5.20 train.

At Paddington, Harry bought his second *London A–Z* in as many days and traced Ailsa Redpath's address to a chunk of Chelsea between King's Road and Fulham Road. They could be there within the hour.

Enslow had maintained his attempt to mislead them had been motivated by nothing more than a desire to avoid causing his landlady any trouble for fear she might review his rent. Harry was not so sure. He thought it distinctly possible that Mrs Redpath had asked Enslow to divert any enquiries concerning her. He also thought Enslow might already have reported their visit of the day before to her, even though he had denied doing so. But the real question was not whether she had taken active steps to guard her privacy. It was why she might have done. And there was only one way to find out.

It was gone seven o'clock on a cool, grey evening when they emerged from the Underground at South Kensington. A stiffish march through quietly affluent residential streets took them within half an hour to Elm Park Road – and a white-stuccoed, black-railinged Victorian terrace of well-worn gentility.

'How are we going to play this, then?' Chipchase asked, pausing before the steps leading to the gleaming blood-red front door of number 27.

'By ear,' Harry replied, striding up the steps and pressing the bell. 'Just follow my lead.'

Harry had time for a second, longer press before the door opened. A tall, grey-haired man of middle years, with a fine-boned face, piercing eyes and the dashing looks of an ageing film star, regarded them unsmilingly, almost challengingly. He was dressed casually but expensively, with a glittering chunk of Rolex lolling from the wrist of the hand he had wrapped round the edge of the door.

'Yes?' A faint upward twitch of the eyebrows accompanied the peremptory greeting.

'We're, er . . . looking for Ailsa Redpath,' said Harry.

'Who are you?' There was the hint of a Scottish accent buried deep in the man's clipped, cosmopolitan voice.

'My name's Harry Barnett. This is my friend, Barry Chipchase.'

'Never heard of you.'

'There's no reason—'

'I'm Iain Redpath. Ailsa's my wife. I know all her friends . . . and acquaintances. I don't know you.'

'We've never actually met your wife, Mr Redpath. We are old friends of the late Lester Maynard, however. He bequeathed her a house in Henley, as you'll be aware. It's in connection with Lester that—'

'Ailsa isn't here.'

'No?'

'She's gone away.'

'Really? Where to?'

Redpath's grip on the door tightened. His gaze narrowed. 'None of your business.'

'Are you always this hostile to visitors, squire?' put in Chipchase.

'*What?*'

231

'It's not as if Harry's stepped out of line. We're only making a few polite enquiries.'

'This is very important, Mr Redpath,' said Harry, emolliently. 'To your wife as well as us. We need to get in touch with her. Urgently. If you could just tell us—'

'I'll tell her you called. OK? Barnett and Chipchase. Old friends of Lester Maynard. I've got that right, haven't I?'

'Yes. But—'

'Want to leave your number in case she decides to call you?' His tone implied this was so unlikely as to be inconceivable.

'We don't actually . . . have a number.'

Redpath looked them both up and down. 'Why am I not surprised?'

'But we could . . . come back.' Harry ventured a smile. 'When you've had a chance to talk to your wife.'

'Yes. I suppose you could. But I can save you the bother. There's nothing Ailsa will want to discuss with you. I can guarantee it.'

'If you could just see your way to—'

'Goodbye.' With that – and the faintest of smiles – Redpath closed the door in their faces.

'That went well, I thought,' said Chipchase as they wandered away along the street, retracing their steps in the vaguest of default modes.

'He's hiding something,' grumbled Harry.

'His wife, you mean?'

'We'll go back.'

'He's already told us what answer we'll get if we do.'

'*We'll go back.*'

'OK, OK. We'll go back. For all the bloody good it'll do us. How about a drink in the meantime? I could murder a—'

'Hi.' The door of a rust-pocked Ford Fiesta parked at the kerbside a few yards ahead of them had swung open and the driver had climbed out into their path. He was a podgy, round-faced young man with short, greasy hair, John Lennon glasses and several days' growth of beard. His leather jacket, T-shirt and trousers were a uniform shade of matt black. There was a sheen of sweat on his high forehead and a skittering look of nervousness in his eyes. This last feature Harry found strangely endearing after Redpath's glacial show of contempt. 'You're looking for Ailsa, right?'

'We might be,' Chipchase replied.

'We are,' said Harry definitively.

'Me too,' said the young man. He wiped his mouth with the back of his hand. 'Her husband's a tight-lipped bastard, isn't he?'

'To put it mildly.'

'What d'you want with Ailsa?'

'We could ask you the same.'

'Yeah.' Another wipe of the mouth. 'I suppose you could.'

'How about we trade answers?'

'Well . . .'

'Over a drink,' said Chipchase.

FORTY-THREE

During the short drive to a nearby pub, little more than introductions were exchanged. The young man's name was Mark Howlett. He lived over the river in Bermondsey. Chelsea was not his normal stamping ground, something the contrast between his car and most of those parked in and around Elm Park Road had already made obvious. He said no more for the moment, but a stack of posters which Harry found himself sharing the back seat with hinted at the cause of the stress he was clearly under.

HAVE YOU SEEN HER? was printed above a head-and-shoulders photograph of a woman about Howlett's own age, with short fair hair, delicate features and a calm, almost studious expression. Beneath was the imploring message HELP ME FIND KAREN SNOW – PHONE MARK 07698 442810. There looked to be at least fifty copies. Discreetly, Harry folded one up and slipped it into his pocket.

The Anglesea Arms was full without being overcrowded. Harry bought the drinks while Chipchase navigated a path through the ruck to a table by the window, Howlett trailing distractedly behind him. The lad's hangdog air seemed of a piece with the pitiful note struck by the poster. It was possible to believe, despite all evidence to the contrary, that he was more parlously placed than they were.

He took a large gulp from the lager Harry delivered to him

and accepted the offer of a cigarette from Chipchase. Then his gaze swivelled to and fro between them and he asked, 'Who are you guys, then?'

'We already told you,' said Chipchase. 'He's Harry. I'm Barry.'

'Yeah, but . . . who are you *really*?'

'Old National Service chums of Ailsa Redpath's late benefactor, Lester Maynard,' said Harry.

'*Who*?'

'Lester Maynard.'

'The name doesn't mean a thing to me.'

'What about . . . Peter Askew?'

'Askew?' Howlett's eyes lit up. 'You know Askew?'

'We used to,' said Chipchase, before theatrically running his forefinger across his throat.

'He's dead?'

'Got off a train while it was still moving up in Scotland last week. Moving at top bloody speed, actually. *Very* bloody, for poor old Askew.'

'Askew's *dead*?'

'It was in the papers,' said Harry.

'I haven't . . . been following the news. I . . .' Howlett rubbed his eyes. 'When was this?'

'A week ago yesterday. He was on his way to an RAF reunion in Aberdeenshire. I was on the train myself. Barry and I both served with him. Back in the fifties.'

'In the RAF?'

'Strange as it may seem,' said Chipchase, rolling his eyes.

'*Friday*?'

'How did you know him, Mark?' Harry asked mildly.

'I didn't. It's just . . . the name. Karen, my girlfriend, knew him. Well, met him.' A frown of uncertainty formed on Howlett's face. 'I think.'

'Where's Karen now?'

'I don't . . .' He licked his lips. 'I don't know.'

'Hence this?' Harry took the poster out of his pocket and unfolded it.

Howlett's mouth sagged open. He nodded. 'Yeah. She's been missing more than a week now. Since the day before your friend died, actually. No-one seems bothered about it. Except me. If Askew's dead . . .' He raised a hand to his face. 'Christ, what does that mean for her?'

'When did they meet?'

'The evening she went missing. Thursday. Well, I don't know for a *fact* that they met, but . . .' He sighed. 'We were supposed to be going to the cinema that night. She phoned and cancelled. Said she had to meet a guy who might be able to give her some information about the Haskurlay mystery. She didn't actually name him, mind. I got that from the jotter beside the phone at her flat. *Askew, 7.30, Lamb.* The Lamb's a pub she sometimes goes to after work. She's a palaeontologist at the British Museum. Anyway, she—'

'Hold on,' Harry interrupted, backtracking furiously in his head. 'What's the . . . Haskurlay mystery?'

'Oh right. Yeah. I suppose you don't know. Though that was in the papers as well. Four years ago this month.'

'You'll have to fill us in, Mark.'

'OK. Right. Well, Karen was at Leeds University then. So was I. That's where we met. Anyway, she went off during the Easter vac with some other archaeology and palaeontology students to do a dig on Haskurlay. It's an island in the Outer Hebrides. Uninhabited now, but there are remains of ancient settlements, including a burial mound. So, they got digging . . . and turned up something . . . they didn't expect.' Howlett paused to slurp some lager.

'Which was?'

'A couple of skeletons . . . from the recent past . . . buried in the mound along with the prehistoric bones.' Howlett took another gulp of lager. 'Recent . . . as in about fifty years old.'

FORTY-FOUR

Howlett peered at Harry and Barry in turn, studying the
bafflement and disbelief that must have been written on their
faces. 'You sure you don't remember this?' he asked. 'There
was quite a bit of media interest at the time.'

'I was out of the country,' said Harry.

'And I guess the *Racing Post* didn't send a correspondent,'
said Chipchase. 'Assume we know zilcho, Marky.'

'OK. Right. Well, there were holes in the skulls of these
skeletons. Like they'd been shot. I mean, like murdered,
y'know? They were dated to . . . forty or fifty years ago. The
last of the island's population left closer to a hundred years
ago. So, the police had a double murder on their hands.
Nothing to do with Karen, really, except . . . she was the one
who actually found the bodies . . . and got her face on the telly
. . . and . . . always hankered for an explanation.'

'Did she get one?' Harry asked.

'Not exactly. The police identified the bodies eventually.
They belonged to a crofter and his son from Vatersay – the
nearest inhabited island – who'd gone missing on a boat
trip. Everyone thought they'd drowned, but . . . it seems
they hadn't. Several crofters from Vatersay and its larger
neighbour, Barra, grazed sheep on Haskurlay at the time,
apparently, so—'

'What time *was* that?'

'Oh, didn't I say? The spring of 1955.'

''Fifty-five?'

'Yeah.'

Chipchase's gaze met Harry's. 'Busy around then north of the border, wasn't it?'

'There can't be any connection with Operation Clean Sheet, Barry. We were on the opposite coast, for God's sake.'

'I know. But there *is* a connection. I feel it in my bones. So do you.'

'What's Operation Clean Sheet?' asked Howlett.

'We'll tell you later,' Chipchase replied. 'Meanwhile, spell Haskurlay for us.'

'*Spell it?*'

'Just humour a dyslexic old man, son. How do you spell Haskurlay?'

'H-A-S-K-U-R-L-A-Y.'

'H-A-S-K-U-R-L-A-Y,' Chipchase repeated after him. 'I make that nine letters. Harry?'

'It can't be.'

'It bloody can.'

'But—'

'What are you two going on about?' asked Howlett, sounding increasingly exasperated.

'Finish *your* story first, Marky,' Chipchase replied. '*Then* we'll tell you ours.'

'What were the crofter and his son called?' Harry prompted.

'Munro. Hamish and Andrew Munro. There were surviving relatives, so the police were able to use DNA tests to identify them. As to who shot them . . . they hadn't a clue. There were rumours, but . . .'

'What sort of rumours?'

'Oh, that there was some kind of . . . military presence on Haskurlay. Secret stuff . . . that the Munros blundered into. The MoD said no way, absolutely not. And the police went along with that. I guess they had no choice. There's actually no sign anything even vaguely military took place there, according to Karen. So, it's a . . . total mystery.'

'Where does Ailsa Redpath come into it?'

'Hamish Munro was her father. Andrew was her older brother.'

'Bloody hell,' said Chipchase. He looked round at Harry. 'That has to be the reason Maynard left her his house.'

'Yes,' said Harry. 'It does. But . . . I still don't get it.'

'Karen's never given up trying to figure it all out,' said Howlett. 'She went up to Stornoway last autumn to address a conference on Pictish culture. Well, that was her excuse. But I know for a fact she stopped off in Barra. There's a causeway linking Barra to Vatersay now. They're basically one island. So, I reckon she asked around about the murders while she was there. Maybe she visited Haskurlay again. Maybe she spoke to Ailsa's younger brother, Murdo. He still lives on Vatersay. Maybe, one way or another, she did enough . . . to attract the attention of your friend Askew.'

'Maybe. Though the truth is, Mark, we have no idea why Peter Askew should have contacted her – or what he might have told her.'

'It has to have been something to do with the murders. She said so.'

'Really?'

'See for yourself.' Howlett pulled a piece of paper from his wallet, unfolded it and held it out in front of them. It was a sheet from Karen Snow's phoneside jotter. *Askew 7.30 Lamb* was not the only thing she had written on it. *HASKURLAY* was written at the top in deeply scored capitals and, beneath that, *Check with Ailsa*.

'It was *all* to do with the murders,' said Howlett. 'Askew had the answer she was looking for.'

'We can't be sure of that.'

'*I'm* sure.'

'So what are you doing about it?' put in Chipchase.

'I've told the police, but they don't want to know. They reckon Karen's taken off somewhere without telling me, so it's none of their business. I've asked around. All her friends. Colleagues at work. They're baffled, but they don't know

239

what to do. I've stuck the poster up in as many shops, bars, clubs and pubs near her flat as'll let me. No response. No news at all, good or bad.'

'Have you contacted her family?' Harry asked.

'She's an only child. Parents separated. Mother's seriously loopy. Suggested Karen had gone to ground to get away from me. Fucking bitch. No idea where her father is. So, the family's a write-off.'

'Which leaves you with Ailsa.'

'Yeah. I found her listed in Karen's address book. That and the wording of the note – *Check with Ailsa* – made me think they'd been in touch more often than Karen had ever let on. So, I went round there. Got the brush-off from her husband. He said Ailsa was away. Wouldn't say where. Offered to let her know I'd called. But you could tell he didn't mean it.'

'We got the same spiel.'

'The way I see it, she's gone into hiding. I thought it was just Karen's disappearance that had spooked her. But if we add Askew's death to the mix . . .'

'Where do you think she's gone?'

'I wondered if she was just lying low at the house. But I've kept watch there for hours every day. No sign. No trace. I reckon she must have gone away. Somewhere she feels safe.'

'Any idea where?'

'Vatersay. The family croft. I phoned the brother, y'see. Spoke to his wife. Well, she *said* she was his wife. And she was adamant Ailsa wasn't there. But he might not *have* a wife. That could have been Ailsa I spoke to, covering her own tracks. See what I mean?'

'Thought of going there to find out?'

''Course I have. But it's a long way to go if it's actually a wild-goose chase. I might miss her here in London while I was away. Or I might miss a lead on Karen's whereabouts. It's too long a shot.' Howlett's shoulders slumped. 'On the other hand . . .'

'You're running out of alternatives.'

'I think I *have* run out.'

'Look, Mark, we know of nothing linking Peter Askew to the Outer Hebrides fifty years ago. He was in Aberdeenshire, with us. But so were Lester Maynard and another bloke we all served with, Leroy Nixon. Yet Maynard left his house in Henley to Ailsa when he died – a woman he had no known connection with. And Nixon, like Maynard, took numerous trips to Scotland over the years. On one of them, Nixon drowned. Lost overboard from a ferry. We don't know what route the ferry was on, but my guess is that if we checked . . . we'd find it was going to or from Vatersay. And Askew? Maynard entrusted him with a secret before he died, encrypted on a computer disk under a nine-letter code. The disk's lost, but I think we just cracked the code, don't you? Haskurlay.'

'You've come over to my side on that, have you, Harry?' put in Chipchase.

Harry pointed to Karen's note, still clutched in Howlett's hand. 'Askew, Ailsa and Haskurlay. All on the same piece of paper. I think that clinches it. I haven't a clue what it means. But it means something.'

'Our necks, quite bloody likely. If I catch your drift correctly.'

'What . . .' Howlett gaped at each of them in turn. 'What drift?'

'Harry's planning a little Hebridean jaunt for us, Marky.' Chipchase smiled grimly. 'Aren't you, Harry?'

Harry shrugged and smiled back at Chipchase. 'I might be.'

FORTY-FIVE

'You guys are serious about this?' Howlett still seemed to doubt, despite several repetitions, that they meant what they had said – what Harry had said, at any rate, with Chipchase's less than wholehearted support.

'We're going to Vatersay, Mark. With or without you. We mean to find out what this is really all about. And that's where all the clues lead. Vatersay – and Haskurlay.'

'Yeah. I guess they do. OK.' A widening of Howlett's eyes signalled the decision he had reached. 'I'm in.'

'Good.'

'When d'you want to leave?'

'Sooner the better.'

'I checked up on how to get there a few days ago.' Howlett pulled a crumpled piece of paper out of his hip pocket. 'It's ... quite a drag.' He squinted at his notes. 'There's a car ferry to Barra from Oban most days. It's a five-hour trip. Or you can fly ... via Glasgow. But that could be pricey.'

'And tricky,' observed Chipchase. 'Airlines have a habit of insisting on ID.'

'So?'

'We're a little short of ... documentation.'

'Oh yeah?'

'Does the ferry run on Sundays?' Harry asked, eager to rein in Howlett's curiosity.

'Er, let's see ...' More squinting. 'Yeah. It does.'

'What time?'

'Er . . . fifteen ten.'

'And how long would it take to drive to Oban?'

'It's about five hundred miles. I guess . . . ten hours.'

'In your rust-wagon that'd feel like ten days,' Chipchase remarked.

'Hey, I'm not forcing you to take a ride with me. If you've a smarter motor to—'

'We haven't,' said Harry, glaring at Chipchase. 'The point is, Mark, if we leave tonight . . . we can be on that ferry tomorrow afternoon.'

'Yeah. I suppose.'

'You said you were in. And time's pressing.'

'Pressing hard,' muttered Chipchase. 'Take our word for it.'

'All right, all right.' Howlett rubbed his face. 'OK. Let's do it. Let's go.'

'Great,' said Harry.

'You know it makes sense,' Chipchase added through gritted teeth.

'We'll have to swing past my place so I can pack a bag,' said Howlett. 'What about you two?'

'No baggage beyond this,' said Harry, pointing to the small rucksack Jackie had bought to hold toiletries and a change of clothes.

'Except the mental kind, of course,' muttered Chipchase.

'No car. No ID. No baggage to collect.' Howlett pondered their suspicious lack of trappings. 'You two really do travel light, don't you?'

'You have to at our age, Marky,' said Chipchase. 'Otherwise you'd never travel at all. And then where would you be? Tucked up in bed at home with a mug of cocoa and not a care in the world.' He drained his glass. 'Can't have that, can we?'

Howlett did not invite them in when they reached his flat, to the rear of a row of shops near Bermondsey Tube station. He said he would be gone only a few minutes, then vanished through a gate next to the dented, graffiti-blotched door of a seemingly abandoned garage. It was the first chance Chipchase had been presented with to give Harry his uncensored opinion of the journey they were about to embark on. And he did not waste the chance.

'The Outer bloody Hebrides, Harry? Ends of the bloody Earth, more like. Is taking off there really such a smart move?'

'Maybe not. But it's the least futile. It's odds on Ailsa's hiding out with her brother on Vatersay. Howlett's girlfriend could well be with her. He hasn't said so, but that's really why he's agreed to go. Because he hopes they're hiding *together*.'

'From what?'

'We'll ask them.'

'Great idea, Harry. A hum-bloody-dinger, if you don't mind me saying so.'

'They already know what we'd have learned if we'd been able to decrypt that disk, Barry. We have to speak to them.'

'Fine. So, let's suppose we track them down. And they agree to share the secret with us. Has it occurred to you – has the thought flitted across the farther horizons of your see-a-windmill-let's-take-a-bloody-tilt-at-it mind – that knowing what the secret is could be a whole sight more dangerous than *not* knowing?'

'Yes,' Harry replied, surprised by how calm he felt. 'Of course it has.'

'Oh, good.' Chipchase fell silent for a moment, then added, 'That's reassuring.'

Harry's calmness, as it turned out, was not destined to last the night. Several hours later, during a stop at Sandbach services on the M6, he called Donna. She did not answer the phone. But it *was* answered. By someone whose voice he recognized very well: their old friend, Makepeace Steiner.

'Hi, Harry.'

'Makepeace? What are you doing there? Donna never mentioned you were paying a visit.'

'Kind of a last-minute arrangement. Donna asked if I could

244

look after Daisy for a few days. And I don't need to remind you of all people how many favours I owe Donna, so—'

'She's not there?'

'No, Harry, she surely isn't.'

'Then . . . where is she?'

'Somewhere over the Rockies. On a plane heading your way.'

'*What*?'

'She wouldn't tell me what's going on any more than I expect you will, but it was pretty clear she was worried. About you. With good cause, I take it.'

'Oh God.'

'Thought so.'

'I asked her to stay there. Pleaded with her.'

'She's a stand-by-your-man kinda gal, Harry. You should know that.'

'I do. Worse luck.'

'Are you OK?'

'Don't I sound it?'

'Since you ask . . . Not really.'

'It must be a bad line.'

'Yeah. Sure thing.'

'Before she left . . . did Donna say anything about a bloke called Marvin Samuels? He was . . . looking into something for her. Well, for *me*, actually.'

'She never mentioned him.'

'Or about a drug called . . . MRQS?'

'Nope. Not a word. But she can give you an update herself tomorrow. Her flight's due into Heathrow at two p.m. your time. She said she'd go straight from the airport to Swindon. And that's where you are, right?'

Harry steeled himself. 'Yes. I'm in Swindon.'

'So, what's the problem?'

'No problem.' Harry suppressed a groan. 'None at all.'

FORTY-SIX

They were nearing the Scottish border as dawn broke, a windless, mizzly morning revealing itself in ever paler shades of grey. Harry had still not decided what to say to Donna when he phoned her, as phone her he must, before she reached Swindon and found 37 Falmouth Street a burnt-out ruin. She was somewhere over the Atlantic now, her mobile switched off, decisively out of contact, asleep perhaps – or more likely wide awake and thinking of him, even as *he* was thinking of *her*. What had she learned from Samuels? What had prompted her to fly to Harry's rescue? What did she know that he did not?

'Want something to read now it's light?' Howlett asked suddenly. He was hunched beside Harry at the wheel of the Fiesta, gazing ahead along the unwinding ribbon of road. Chipchase lay asleep behind them, sprawled across the back seat, his snores drowned by the noise of the engine and the babble of the latest radio station Howlett had tuned to. 'I brought with me the report on Haskurlay Karen wrote as part of her dissertation at Leeds. It'll give you most of the known facts about the island. Interested?'

'You bet.'

'OK. It's in my bag in the boot. I'll dig it out when we stop for breakfast.'

*   *   *

The breakfast stop was not long in coming. A wash, a shave, a fry-up and several strong coffees were had in virtual silence at Gretna services, then Howlett went outside to phone in sick to the trade magazine he worked for. This offered Harry the chance he had been waiting for to give Chipchase the news from Vancouver.

'She's on her way?' Chipchase spluttered through the fumes of his post-bacon-and-eggs cigarette.

'Even as we speak.'

'Bloody hell.'

'Yeah. Which there'll be to pay when she reaches Swindon.'

'You need to head her off at the pass, Harry old cock.'

'How do you suggest I do that?'

'Well . . .' Chipchase applied his mind to the problem. 'There's Jackie, I suppose. We could ask her to meet Donna at Heathrow and explain you only kept her in the dark about the fire so as not to put the wind up her and that . . . you and me have had to . . .'

'Yes? What exactly have we had to do, Barry?'

'OK. Let's regroup. Jackie meets her, fills her in on the fire but assures her you're fine – *we're* fine, in case she's two bits bloody bothered about how old Chipchase is faring – and invites her to stay at her place, pending word from us, which we've promised there'll be . . . as soon as . . . possible.'

'She'll think I'm trying to avoid speaking to her.'

'Aren't you?'

'No. Of course not. It's just . . .'

'If you do, I bet you'll end up telling her where we're going and why. She won't let you get away with anything less than the truth and once your over-developed husbandly conscience kicks in . . .'

'I don't want her coming after us, Barry. It's too . . .'

'Dangerous is the word you're groping for, Harry.'

'Let's just say . . . risky.'

'Whatever we say, the only way you can be sure she won't follow us is by staying incommunicado.'

'It's not as simple as that. She might have found out something about MRQS. Something *we* need to know.'

'Or she might not have.' Chipchase took a drag on his cigarette and studied Harry through a slowly exhaled lungful of smoke. 'It's your call.'

It was indeed Harry's call. He made it a few minutes later, from one of the service area's payphones. Jackie responded surprisingly well to being woken from her beauty sleep early on a Sunday morning with a thinly reasoned request to cancel whatever else she had planned for the afternoon and drive to Heathrow to collect an unexpected house guest off the two o'clock flight from Vancouver. But she had a warning to give as well.

'Donna will realize why you're staying out of touch soon enough, Harry. You have to give me something more to tell her.'

'Tell her I'll phone . . . tomorrow.'

'What time tomorrow?'

'I don't know. It depends.'

'What on?'

'I don't know that either. But tomorrow . . . without fail.'

They drove on north. Harry started reading Karen Snow's Haskurlay report, grateful for anything that might distract him from the subterfuge he had been forced to resort to. There was not much he could be sure of. But the overriding need to keep Donna out of whatever was waiting for them at the end of their journey constituted one certainty he could cling to. He tried to concentrate.

HASKURLAY

Summary Report of Study Party Visit (Department of Archaeology & Prehistory, University of Leeds), April 2001, by Karen Snow.

248

Haskurlay lies 13km SSW of Barra, in the Outer Hebrides. It covers an area of 415 ha and has a maximum height of 238m. It is composed mostly of gneiss, with some granite. Its last human inhabitants left in 1910. It is owned by the National Trust for Scotland, who acquired it in 2000 from a syndicate of Barra crofters, who grazed sheep there.

The cliffs on the western side of the island are 150m high in places and are an active breeding site for various sea-birds, including guillemots, kittiwakes and skuas. There is also a colony of puffins on the island. There are two inland summits of more than 200m. Between them, grouped around an east-facing bay, are the heavily over-grown ruined cottages of the deserted village.

The purpose of the study party visit was to examine the remains of ancient human occupation to be found on the island, in particular a 7m high burial mound located on the northern side of the bay. It is unclear whether this is a neolithic structure or of later origin. Tradition has it that a large stone circle stood at the opposite end of the bay until it was demolished by the villagers in the 18th century, the stones being incorporated in the walls of their cottages and bothies. This suggests active neolithic occupation. Unfortunately, no trace of the circle now remains. Several stones near the ruined chapel bear Pictish carvings, however. The mound might therefore date from the Pictish period. The island was presumably also occupied at different stages by Celts and Vikings, though there is little or no visible evidence of this. The chapel itself is a 19th century structure.

The remit of the study party was to excavate a portion of the burial mound and to recover sufficient ossified human remains to facilitate a more definite dating of its origin. Unfortunately, for reasons outside the study party's control, this project had to be abandoned shortly after initial excavation had begun in what appeared to be a disturbed area of the mound. As a result, no ancient material was removed for analysis and dating of the mound remains speculative.

It was decided, in the interests of making best use of the study party's time, to leave Haskurlay following the abandonment of the excavation and to carry out a survey of known burial cairns on the neighbouring islands of Mingulay and Berneray. These have, of course, been adequately surveyed in the past and no new findings were therefore anticipated. (See separate report for details.) It is to be hoped that a future study party can return to Haskurlay and implement a definitive dating of the mound. When that might be possible is presently unknown.

Harry read the report through again to be sure he had not missed something, then handed it to Chipchase with a warning that he should not hope to learn anything valuable from it.

'You wouldn't even know why the dig was abandoned if Karen's account was all you had to go on.'

'It's a piece of academic writing,' said Howlett, snappishly enough to suggest he did not like anyone to criticize his girlfriend, however mildly. 'What do you expect?'

'You promised me "most of the known facts about Haskurlay", as I recall.'

'And that's what you've got.' Howlett shot Harry a grim little smile. 'There just aren't many of them.'

FORTY-SEVEN

The hump-backed hills of Barra and Vatersay came into view as the *Clansman* car ferry sailed into the setting sun that evening. It was, in its way, a beautiful sight, the last land before Labrador silhouetted against a golden, cloud-barred sky. Chipchase for one, however, was in neither mood nor condition to appreciate it, having complained of seasickness ever since the ship had cleared the Sound of Mull and misgivings about the trip for rather longer.

Harry shared many of those misgivings, but did his best to stifle them. Tracking down Ailsa Redpath was their best if not only chance of unravelling the mystery they were caught up in. They were due to return to Police HQ in Aberdeen on Tuesday. If they did not, they would be officially on the run. There was, accordingly, no time to be lost. And the possibility that they were wasting what little remained of it was not to be contemplated.

The *Clansman* performed a slow, elegant turn as it entered the harbour of Castlebay. This gave Harry and Barry a panoptical view of the hills of Barra; of the modest, mostly modern houses of the island's capital strung out around the shore; of the fortress built on an islet in the bay that supplied the town's name; and of the lower hills and inlets of Vatersay away to the south. The landscape was starkly treeless and ruggedly green, largely untouched by man. It was not the sort

251

of place either of them was familiar with. Harry's one spell of island living, on Rhodes, was far removed from the cutting wind and limitless ocean of the Outer Hebrides. And Chipchase, by his own admission, was a town rat by birth, breeding *and* inclination.

The same, they assumed, applied to Howlett, but they were in no position to check the point. He was still below, afflicted by a migraine, induced, to hear him tell it, by long hours of driving, though probably not helped by the quantity of lager he had drunk during the voyage. With Chipchase's sea-sickness only slowly abating, Harry was left to co-ordinate their disembarkation. Fortunately, the drive to the hotel they had booked themselves into by phone from Oban could hardly have been shorter.

The Castlebay Hotel, standing four-square and grey-stoned on the hill above the harbour, was warm and comfortable. Chipchase's spirits lifted slightly once he was on dry land. As he watched the *Clansman* cast off for its onward voyage to South Uist from the window of the twin-bedded room he and Harry were sharing, his summary of their situation was marginally less bleak than it might have been.

'We're stuck here now, Harry old cock. For better or worse. So, do we get wrecked in the bar – or ask Marky if he wants to head straight for Vatersay?'

A walk along the corridor to Howlett's room supplied the answer. They found him prostrate on his bed, curtains firmly closed against the persistent evening light.

'There's no way I'm moving from here tonight, guys. Just driving up from the pier has made the migraine worse. I'll have to sleep it off. Don't worry. Sleep always cures it. I'll be fine in the morning.'

The bar it was, then, though only after a diversion to the hotel's restaurant, Chipchase's sudden hunger testifying to his recovery. It was dark by the time they stepped out into the cold, clear silence of Barra by night and strolled round to the cosily lit Castlebay Bar, their stomachs well filled with fresh island fish.

There were only a dozen or so locals inside, two of them engaged in a largely wordless game of pool. The atmosphere was far from uproarious. The amiable barman told them Sunday evenings were always quiet. 'You should have been in last night. We had a grand ceilidh. The Vatersay Boys played.' He nodded at a dais in the corner, adorned with a drum-set, and explained that the folksily Gaelic music rumbling in the background was from the Boys' latest album – *The Road to Vatersay*.

'We'll be taking that tomorrow,' said Chipchase as he lit a cigar.

'Buying their CD?'

'No, no. Taking the road to Vatersay. Visiting the island.'

'Are you over on holiday, then?'

'We certainly are.' Chipchase took a deep and evidently inspiring swallow of whisky. 'Birdwatching. Hill-climbing. Deep-sea diving. We can't get enough of that sort of thing, can we, Harry? We're a pair of genuine wilderness lovers. The Outer Hebrides is our idea of paradise.'

'We're just looking round,' said Harry. 'There are quite a few uninhabited islands south of here, aren't there?'

'That there are.'

'Wasn't one of them in the news a few years back? Haltersay? Haskurlay? Some . . . mystery or other.'

'Haskurlay,' replied the barman, frowning as if doubting whether Harry's uncertainty about the name was genuine. 'You'll be thinking of when they found the bodies there.' He sighed. 'Aye, that was a dismal business.'

'What was it all about?' enquired Chipchase.

'Och, nobody rightly knows. Though you'll meet a few who claim to. Take Dougie over there.'

The barman had pointed to a wizened old man seated near the door, nursing a glass of whisky and a noxious-looking pipe. He was grim-faced, lantern-jawed and sharp-nosed, dressed in a frayed grey suit and black polo-neck sweater, with a still blacker beret perched at an incongruously rakish angle on his apparently pebble-bald head. He was watching the languid manoeuvrings of the pool players with the unfocused gaze of someone waiting for something more interesting to enter his field of vision. As Harry and Barry were about to.

'Looks a testy old bugger,' murmured Chipchase.

'That he is,' agreed the barman. 'But talkative as well if you give him the right encouragement.'

'And what might that be?' asked Harry.

'Well, he's awful fond of the Talisker. A dram or two of that . . . and you'll have your work cut out to shut him up.'

Talisker malt whisky proved to be as effective a tongue-loosener with the initially taciturn Dougie McLeish as the barman had promised. The old boy was eighty-seven, a fact he mentioned more than once, proud as he was of the distant reach of his supposedly flawless memory. The construction of a bridge linking Barra to Vatersay was a recent and to his mind lamentable development. 'What God has set asunder let no man join together.' When Chipchase greeted this observation with a muttered 'Bloody hell,' he was rebuked for profanation. He seemed tempted to retaliate by snatching the tumbler of barely diluted Talisker from McLeish's thin, faintly smiling lips, until reminded by a kick under the table from Harry that the only reward they needed for their generosity was solid information.

'Why would the pair of you be interested in the Haskurlay mystery, then?' McLeish asked when Harry none too subtly raised the subject.

'No reason,' said Harry, unconvincingly. 'Just . . . idle curiosity.'

'Aye, well, curiosity killed the cat, don't they say?'

Chipchase stifled another curse and grinned stiffly. 'You could give us the real story before we get our heads filled with all kinds of nonsense, Dougie. I'll bet no-one would tell it as accurately as you.'

'You have that right.'

'So . . .' Harry prompted.

'Where were you two in the spring of 1955, I wonder.'

'Us?'

'Aye. I'm not talking to the bench-backs behind you.'

'Well, we . . . were doing our National Service together, as a matter of fact. In the RAF.'

'Were you, though? Where were you based?'

'Dyce. Near Aberdeen.'

'Aberdeen, was it?'

'Does it matter?'

'I wouldn'a know. But you were in the Forces, weren't you? That's my point.'

'Point . . . taken, then,' said Chipchase, still grinning fixedly.

'You're sure it was Aberdeen where you were based?'

'We're sure,' said Harry.

McLeish sighed. 'That's a shame.'

'Why?'

'Well, for a moment there I thought you might know more than you were letting on. There's a military strand to this tale, you see.' He had pronounced *military* as four distinct and elongated syllables. 'So they say.'

'But what do *you* say, Dougie?' asked Chipchase.

'I say the word was put round among the crofters here and on Vatersay in May 1955 that they shouldn'a consider landing on Haskurlay for a couple of weeks. No reason given. *Advice*, they called it. From the Crofters' Commission in Inverness, would you believe. Whose tune they were dancing to you must judge for yourself. But some of the fishermen claimed a Royal Navy frigate was out by night to the south of here, off Haskurlay. The rumour was the island was used for some kind of military exercise. All very hush-hush. Well, who was to complain about that? The Cold War was on, after all. Whatever was done, it caused no harm. So we thought, anyway. Even when Hamish Munro and his son went missing. The weather was bad enough for it to be no difficult thing to believe they'd been drowned while fishing. Their boat was washed up on the coast of Skye. No sign of them, though. They were lost. Taken by the sea, it was to be supposed.'

'Not true, though,' said Harry. 'As it turned out.'

'No. Not true at all. You have to understand that Hamish Munro was a hard man to warn off. He was born on Haskurlay, a couple of years before the last crofters moved from there to plots on Vatersay. So, he had stronger links with the island than most. Knowing the man, I'm no so very surprised he decided to break the ban and take a peek at what was going on there. *If* that's what he did. We canna be sure, can we?'

'What can we be sure of?'

'That he died there. Him and his son Andrew. Thanks to those archaeologists and their diggings and delvings four years since, we know now the pair of them . . . were murdered . . . and buried in the ancient mound north of the deserted village on Haskurlay.'

'Did you meet any of the archaeologists?'

'Och, they were in and out of here. I spoke to several of them. Told them what I knew. Which was a sight more than they did.'

'Have any of them been back since?'

'Off and on. But no lately. They've put it all behind them, I dare say. Like a good few people would prefer to.' Oddly, then, it seemed Karen Snow had failed to bend McLeish's ear during her visit the previous autumn. 'The polis set a fine example on that score. They didn'a exactly strain every sinew to crack the case.'

'At least they identified the bodies.'

'Hard not to, with plenty of us old'uns on hand to remind them of the Munros' disappearance and relatives still living to settle the matter whether the powers that be wanted to or no.'

'Relatives . . . here on Barra?'

'On Vatersay. Murdo Munro is Hamish's second son. He lives where he was born, as men are wise to. If you look out of yon window, you'll see a few lights in the distance, beyond the bay.'

McLeish paused, apparently expecting them to look as directed. Harry obediently rose, steered an evasive course round the backside and jutting cue-end of a stooping pool player and peered through the window. There were indeed a few twinkling lights visible on the far side of the bay. 'Highly bloody illuminating,' muttered Chipchase, who had tagged along. They turned and retreated to their table.

'That's the coast of Vatersay, isn't it, Dougie?' Harry asked.

'Aye. One of those lights'll likely be the Munro house. Not the same house Hamish left for the last time one morning fifty year ago, mind. Murdo's built himself a smart new bungalow with the money from Brussels they throw around here to no good purpose. He's turned the old place into his garage, would you believe. Still keeps the name, though. The house is called Haskurlay. After the old times.'

'Were there other children of Hamish's? You mentioned relatives plural.'

'There's a daughter. Ailsa. But she moved to Glasgow years back. Married some . . . financier.' The word was given similar treatment to *military* and came out closer to *feenancieer*. 'Moved to London since, I hear. Money, money, money. You have to chase it to keep it. And then where's the time for contemplation, I should like to know.'

'Bags of time for that round here, I expect,' said Chipchase glumly.

'Aye. So there is. You could do worse than try to get the knack for it yourself.' McLeish squinted at Chipchase. 'Though you don't look a naturally contemplative man to me.'

'Is Murdo carrying on the family line?' Harry asked, eager to keep McLeish to his subject.

'Murdo's a bachelor. Like too many men of his generation.'

'Are you a bachelor, Dougie?' Chipchase enquired, seemingly heedless of Harry's agenda.

'Widower. With sons and grandsons to my name.'

'Does Ailsa ever visit the island?' Harry asked, glancing reprovingly at Chipchase.

'Now and then. As it happens, I—' McLeish broke off. His mouth tightened. Caution had suddenly overtaken him. He sipped his Talisker and treated Harry to a long, narrow look of scrutiny. 'Now and then,' he repeated, in a lower, gravelly tone. 'But no very often.'

FORTY-EIGHT

'Exactly how much dosh did Jackie give you?' Chipchase asked when Harry returned from the bar with another around of drinks.

'Never you mind,' Harry replied, taking a slurp of beer.

'I only ask because pouring Talisker down Dougie's throat could be regarded as flagrantly wasteful given how little we learned from the crabby old bugger.'

McLeish had just left, claiming it was way past his bedtime, though looking alert enough to suggest that may not have been the literal truth. He had relapsed into taciturnity once Harry's interest in Ailsa Redpath's whereabouts had become apparent and had shown no inclination to expound further on the Haskurlay mystery.

'I wouldn't mind a drop of Talisker myself. While we're up here, we may as well sample the—'

'You'll have Bell's and be grateful. You won't be able to taste the difference through that cigar anyway.' Harry was beginning to regret buying Chipchase a replacement pack of Villiger's during their stop in Oban. 'And we learned more from Dougie than you seem to think.'

'Did we?' Chipchase blew a defiant ring of cigar smoke towards the ceiling. 'You'd better remind me what exactly.'

'Ailsa's here. On Vatersay. With her brother. The man's a bachelor. Dougie said so. There's no Mrs Munro. So, the woman Mark spoke to must have been Ailsa.'

'Bachelors have been known to entertain women other than their sisters. I'm glad to say.'

'Ailsa's here. Dougie knows that. She's been seen. He only went coy on us when his loyalty to a fellow islander kicked in.'

'OK. Have it your way. She's here. *We're* here. Though God knows why. We never have been before. You know that as well as I do, Harry. Whatever went on on some unin-bloody-habited lump of rock out there fifty years ago' – Chipchase gestured towards the night-blanked window – 'has sod all to do with us.'

'It shouldn't have, I agree. But it does, Barry. You know *that* as well as I do. You just don't want to admit it.'

Chipchase puffed out his cheeks. 'Bloody hell,' he growled.

'We're linked to the Haskurlay mystery in some way or other. Everyone in Operation Clean Sheet is. Tomorrow . . . we'll find out how.'

'Is that a promise?'

'I suppose it is.'

'Funny. It sounded more like a threat to me.'

There were no more rounds. With midnight fast approaching, they decided to head back to the hotel. Close by though it was, Chipchase opted to visit the bar's loo before leaving. Harry said he would wait for him outside. As a reformed smoker, he had no wish to linger in the fug created by Chipchase's cigars and the locals' cigarettes.

The air that enveloped him as he left was certainly fresh. It was also on the wintry side of cool. But the wind had dropped. A pallid serpent-tail of moonlight stretched out across the bay towards Vatersay. Harry stared towards the distant peninsula where Murdo Munro lived – and where, he strongly suspected, Ailsa Redpath had taken refuge.

Then someone whistled to him, softly but distinctly, from the bottom of the path leading up from the road. Harry looked down and saw a figure standing there, gazing up at him. An aromatic drift of pipesmoke clinched his identity.

'I thought you said it was past your bedtime,' Harry remarked, strolling down to join McLeish at the roadside.

'Decided on a walk before turning in. Pure chance I should be coming back this way as you stepped out of the bar.'

'That a fact?'

'Where's your uncontemplative friend?'

'Getting rid of some of the beer he's drunk.'

'Is he the only one of the men you served with you're still in touch with?'

'Not the only one, no.'

'Have regular reunions, do you?'

'I wouldn't say that.'

'And you were definitely based in Aberdeen?'

'Definitely.'

'Not Benbecula, say, or somewhere . . . closer to hand?'

'No. Not Benbecula. What are you driving at, Dougie?'

'Was there a black fellow in your unit?'

'What?'

'Name of Nixon.'

'*What?*'

'I'd judge from your reaction there was.'

'OK. Yes. There was. Leroy Nixon. Dead and gone now, I'm afraid.'

'Aye. As you say. Dead and gone.'

'What do you know about Leroy?'

'Take a turn down to the quay with me and I'll tell you. You can leave your friend to make his own way back to the hotel. I wouldn'a want to be . . . interrupted.'

They descended a short hill and turned onto the quayside road, where Castlebay's few shops formed an orderly row facing the bay. McLeish crossed the street and gazed out at the stark black outline of the offshore castle.

'Kisimul was nought but a ruin when I was a boy,' he said, pitching his voice so low Harry had to strain to catch his words. 'The Forty-Fifth MacNeil came back from America just before the war and set about restoring it to its former

261

glory. You can take a tour. Most of the holidaymakers do. The boat leaves from the jetty in front of the post office. Well worth it, I'm sure. If you have the time and the inclination. But you have neither, do you? Because you're not here for a holiday, are you?'

'What makes you think that?'

'The use of my faculties. The polis never connected the murders on Haskurlay with the Nixon drowning back in 1983, but I did. You can be sure of that.'

'Leroy died here?'

'Lost overboard from a ferry on the way to Oban. The body was washed up on the coast of Skye. Like the Munros' boat all those years before. 'Twas only the CalMac ticket they found on the poor fellow that accounted for what had happened to him. He was remembered at the guesthouse he'd stayed in here, of course. And he was remembered by me.'

'Why particularly by you?'

'I kept a sea-going boat in those days. Took visitors out on trips round the islands. To see the seals and puffins and such. Landed them on Mingulay if the weather was fair, which it was the day your friend Nixon was one of the party. But he never got as far as Mingulay. When we passed close to Haskurlay, he seemed to . . . recognize it. I don't know how else to put it. He'd never been there before, he said. And yet . . . He asked me to land him on the island. Paid me well enough too. So, I put him ashore – which was no easy matter – and took the others on to Mingulay. We picked him up on the way back. That was no easy matter either. He'd had four or five hours alone there by then.'

'How did he seem?'

'Stunned, I should say. Aye, stunned is the word. And a word is more than I had from him all the way back here. He walked off up the pier like man in a trance. I never saw him again. He took the ferry next morning. In more ways than one.'

'He had . . . mental problems, I'm told.'

'I wouldn'a disagree with that. The question is: what caused them?'

'I don't know.'

'Do you not? Do you really not?'

'No, Dougie, I really don't.'

'Why are you here, then?'

'It's . . . too complicated to explain.'

'Oh, I don't doubt it's complicated. Facts are facts, though, however few they may be where the Munro murders are concerned. You and your friend are awful interested in the Haskurlay mystery. It goes a lot deeper than curiosity. Does it not?'

'Yes. It does.'

'Have either of you ever been to Haskurlay?'

'No. Absolutely not.'

'But that's what your late National Service chum Mr Nixon said, of course. And the fellow who turned up a few months after his death . . . enquiring about the circumstances. He'd be about your age too. Name of—'

'Lester Maynard.' Pretence on the point seemed suddenly futile. 'He's dead as well. Natural causes, though.'

'Aye, well, they claim us all in the end. Serve with him too, did you?'

'Yes.'

'In Aberdeen?'

'Yes.'

'Of course. In Aberdeen.'

'Did you take Maynard to Haskurlay too?'

'No. But some other skipper might have. It wouldn'a surprise me. Nor you, I suspect.'

'None of us came here in 1955, Dougie.'

'If you say so.' McLeish drew on his pipe, the tobacco glowing amber-red in the bowl. 'But it's no me you have to convince, is it? It's yourselves.'

263

FORTY-NINE

The weather changed overnight. When Harry tugged back the curtains of their room next morning, he was met by a vista of blanketing grey. Low cloud had bonneted the hills and pulled in the horizon. The coast of Vatersay was barely distinguishable in the murk. The hummocked shapes of Vatersay's other hills and the uninhabited islands beyond, which Harry had seen the previous evening, were just a memory.

He washed and shaved, then made coffee, using the sachets and kettle provided. Chipchase stirred at the sound of the kettle boiling, but uttered no words until several gulps of black coffee had passed his lips.

'Are migraines contagious? I think I might have caught young Marky's.'

'I expect you'll find it's just a standard hangover.'

'Yeah, well, thanks for the sympathy. I didn't sleep well, you know.'

'That snoring was just for show, was it?'

'I mean I had some disturbing dreams. In one of them you came back from a midnight stroll with Dougie McLeish and claimed he'd told you Nixon and Maynard had been ferreting around here twenty odd years ago – and Nixon had gone drownabout after a day trip to Haskurlay.'

'That's what the man said.'

'I don't like the way this is shaping up, Harry old cock.

You'd agree with me we've never been to the Outer bleeding Hebrides before, wouldn't you?'

'I haven't, certainly.'

'Well, neither have I.'

'I believe you. At any rate, I believe you believe it.'

'Don't start talking in riddles, Harry, for God's sake.'

'But it is a riddle, Barry, isn't it? That's the problem.'

They knocked at Howlett's door on their way down to breakfast, but got no reply. Nor was there any sign of him in the restaurant. They reckoned he must be taking a shower and assumed he would join them before they had finished munching their way through porridge, bacon and eggs and several slices of toast. But he did not.

Harry gave his absence little thought, preoccupied as he was by what sort of a breakfast Donna would be having with Jackie in Swindon. As distracted a one as his, if not more so, seemed likely to be the answer. He longed to call her and set her mind at rest, but sensed that if he did she would start for Barra as soon as he put the phone down. Until he had spoken to Ailsa Redpath and knew what and who they were up against, it was safer to leave Donna in ignorance of his plans and whereabouts. But safe was not easy. Far from it.

Chipchase popped out of the hotel for a cigarette after breakfast, leaving Harry to try Howlett's room again. When he reached it, he found the door held half-open by a rubbish bag. He stepped in to be greeted by a cleaning lady, who was busy making the bed.

'Good morning.'

'Good morning. I, er . . . was looking for . . . Mr Howlett.'

'An early riser, I'm glad to say. Maybe he's looking round the town.'

'Yeah. Right. Thanks.'

Chipchase was coming back into the hotel, frowning in puzzlement, as Harry reached the foot of the stairs.

265

'Marky's Fiasco doesn't seem to be in the car park, Harry. What d'you make of that?'

'He must have driven over to Vatersay.'

'Without us?'

'Looks like it.'

'But . . . why?'

'God knows. We'll ask him – if we get the chance.'

'What are we going to do?'

'Follow him. What else?'

Following was easier said than done. Taxis were not a Barra speciality and the landlady's recommendation of the bus came with a caveat: the service to Vatersay was infrequent and the next one was not due until 10.35. Harry was reduced to looking at the framed Ordnance Survey map in the entrance hall and wondering if they could walk it. But he reckoned they would be overtaken en route by the bus even if they set off straight away. And that assumed Chipchase's questionable stamina got him to the top of the first hill. Besides, there was no way to tell how much of a start Howlett had on them. In that sense, haste was pointless. The 10.35 bus would have to suffice.

Harry's eye drifted down the map beyond Vatersay's southern coast to the uninhabited islands strung out like a giant's stepping-stones across the broad blue expanse of the featureless ocean. There, among them, was Haskurlay, its contours and crenellations minutely represented. But no roads were marked, no place names, no settlements. The island had freed itself of man. It stood alone and apart. It meant nothing to him. Nothing at all.

Yet it seemed Harry meant something to Haskurlay. And it also seemed he was bound to find out what.

The bus – more accurately, minibus – pulled away punctually from Castlebay post office at 10.35 on what the driver aptly described as 'a dull, dreich morning' and bore its two passengers – Harry and Barry – away towards Vatersay.

'Sparky Marky was planning to cut us adrift all along, wasn't he?' said Chipchase as the bus climbed into the cloudbank west of the town. 'Migraine my left buttock. He probably drove over to the Munro place last night, while we were in the bar pouring malt whisky down Dougie bloody McLeish.'

'More likely he waited until we were tucked up in bed. But, yes, the migraine does seem to have been a ploy. What I don't understand is—'

'We could draw up a bloody long list of things you and I don't understand about this, Harry, so I suggest you save your breath.'

'All I'm saying is: why wouldn't he want us with him when he confronted Ailsa Redpath?'

'Because there was something he wasn't telling us. That's why.'

'But what?'

'Dunno. But I'll bet Ailsa does. And Karen the comely archaeologist, who's probably skulking over there with her. And the stay-at-home brother too. McLeish as well, I shouldn't wonder. They all know. Everyone knows.' Chipchase fixed Harry with a look of uncharacteristic seriousness. 'Everyone except you and me.'

FIFTY

The road to the causeway was wide and well maintained. On the Vatersay side, however, it became narrow and winding, clinging to the shore for the most part as it looped round bleak hills of rock and scrub en route to the island's main settlement.

A still narrower side-road served the houses whose lights they had seen from the Castlebay Bar the previous night, dotted along the spine of an exposed peninsula. The bus driver offered to take them down it, but Harry opted to be dropped at the junction, despite Chipchase's muttered protests. He preferred to approach the Munro croft on foot, judging that in such a bare landscape they would then see the house before they were seen from it. It was hard to say exactly why he felt such a precaution necessary, but Howlett's un-announced departure had worried him more than he was prepared to admit. Chipchase was right. Everyone, even the hapless Howlett, was a step ahead of them.

The few habitations lining the road were widely separated – modern, pebble-dash, tile-roofed bungalows for the most part, usually with the ruin of an old stone cottage alongside. Castle-bay, across the sound, looked positively metropolitan from this stark and empty vantage point. A flock of sheep scattered as the two of them rounded a bend by a deserted jetty. Otherwise, there was no sign of life.

'Bloody hell, Harry, I don't know about you, but this place

gives me the creeps,' Chipchase complained. 'I never thought I was prone to agoraphobia, but I'm beginning to feel a bad bloody case of it coming on. Does anybody really live out here?'

'Murdo Munro does for one.'

'But there's nothing here except . . . more nothing.'

'Some people prefer a quiet life.'

'There's a difference between quiet . . . and silent as the bloody grave. It's enough to give an urbanite like me the heebie-jeebies.'

'Pull yourself together. We're not here on holiday, you know.'

'Thank Christ for that. I'd be asking for my—'

'Hold on.' Harry cut Chipchase short with a raised hand and stopped. A house had come into view ahead as they crested a gentle rise. It was another modern bungalow. But the old stone habitation it had replaced was not a ruin. It stood next to the bungalow, roofed in green corrugated iron, with a garage door installed in the gable end facing the road. 'That must be the Munro place.'

'There's no sign of Marky's motor.'

'It might be parked out of sight round the side.'

'Or this might *not* be the Munros' ancestral dwelling. McLeish could have sold us a dummy.'

'Why would he have done that?'

'Christ knows. But if you ask me, we were seen coming before we even got off the bloody ferry. Everything since . . . has smelt like a set-up to me.'

'What do you want to do, then? Slink back to the main road and wait for the bus? It'll be on its way back to Castlebay soon.'

Chipchase gazed ahead, then around at their featureless surroundings. 'Might not be such a bad move. The Castlebay Bar probably opens at eleven. It must be gone that now.'

'Leaving here empty-handed isn't an option, Barry. Unless you want to give Ferguson and Geddes a helping hand in fitting us up for triple murder.'

269

Chipchase winced. 'Ferguson and Geddes. Bloody hell. For a blissful moment, I'd forgotten those evil-minded bastards even existed.'

'Well, try to bear them in mind. And step lively. We have a house call to pay.'

Nothing stirred at the Munro residence as they approached. The windows were closed and net-curtained. The garage door was shut. And Howlett's car was nowhere to be seen. If anyone was at home, they were lying low. And if they simply declined to answer the bell, there was little Harry or Barry could do about it. The absence of the Fiesta was particularly puzzling – and disturbing. If Howlett had not come here, where in God's name had he gone? And why?

'Didn't McLeish say the house was called Haskurlay?' Chipchase whispered as they neared the porched front door.

'Yes.'

'Then we've come to the wrong place.' Chipchase pointed to a hand-painted sign attached to a post at the edge of the road. It bore the mysterious name THASGARLAIGH.

'Probably Haskurlay in Gaelic.'

'You've got an answer for everything, haven't you?'

'If I had, we wouldn't be here.'

'I suppose you think that's—'

'Shut up, Barry. Just shut up.'

'Pardon me for bloody breathing. I only . . .'

Harry strode decisively forward and rang the doorbell. And at that Chipchase did indeed shut up.

A general, all-enveloping silence followed. No sound emanated from the house. Squinting through the lozenge of frosted glass set in the door, Harry could discern no movement within. He rang again, more lengthily. A current of air stirred a wind-chime suspended from one of the porch struts into a passable representation of a Swiss cowbell, causing both of them to start violently. A distant sheep bleat reached their ears, faint and mocking. Then the silence reasserted itself. And they exchanged baffled, despairing looks.

'Told you,' whispered Chipchase. 'No-one at home.'

'No-one answering, at all events.'

'Same bloody difference. Unless you're planning on a spot of breaking and entering.'

'Of course not. But we could take a look round the back. There might be a ... window open.'

'Yeah? Well, if there is, it'll need to be a decent size and at a low level if either of us is going to climb through it. Cat burglars retire young if they've any sense.'

'Just follow me.'

Harry set off round the corner of the bungalow, peering in the windows as he went, to no avail thanks to the net curtains hung at each of them. He walked along between the house and the blank stone wall of the garage and stepped round to the rear.

'Well, well, well.'

'Bloody hell,' said Chipchase, looming at his shoulder. 'That's careless.'

The back door of the house stood open, held on a stout, hooked stay. It was, in its way, as clear an invitation as could be imagined.

The door led to a cluttered kitchen. It was clean and tidy, though. Either Murdo Munro was a houseproud bachelor or his sister had been on hand recently to maintain standards.

'Hello?' Harry called. 'Anyone at home?'

There was no response.

'Two mugs and a couple of plates on the drainer,' said Chipchase, pointing to the sink. 'Murdo's obviously not alone.'

'Where are they? That's what I want to know.'

'Fishing. Shopping in Castlebay. They could be anywhere.'

'With the door left like that?'

'Maybe it's always like that. Vatersay's hardly a crime hot spot, is it?'

'Unlocked, maybe. But wide open? Come off it. *Hello*?'

Harry pressed on into the short hall that led to the front

door. There was a lounge to his right, simply but comfortably furnished, a bathroom and two bedrooms to his left. The doors all stood open. One bedroom was neater than the other, but both looked as if they were in use. After glancing into each of them, Harry went into the lounge.

Murdo Munro's domestic life was not overburdened with possessions, to judge by the bareness of the room. Beyond the furniture and a surprisingly large television set, there was nothing in the way of books, ornaments or pictures. The walls were virgin expanses of magnolia paint. A clock of some age stood on the mantelpiece, however. Next to it was propped a letter in a buff window envelope.

Harry walked over and picked up the letter to check the addressee's name. Mr M. H. Munro. Not much doubt that they were in the right house, then. The letter was from the Inland Revenue. Maybe that was why Murdo had not opened it.

Then Harry noticed the silver-framed photograph the letter had been propped against. It was a black-and-white snap of three children, wearing clothes dating from the post-war years, standing in a smiling group by a ruined stone wall, a grassy slope visible behind them. Two boys and a girl, the eldest boy in his early teens, the younger scarcely more than a toddler, the girl aged somewhere between. Andrew, Murdo and Ailsa Munro, circa 1950? It had to be. And was the wall all that remained of Hamish Munro's birthplace on Haskurlay? Was that the double significance of the photograph – a lost brother *and* a lost home?

'*Harry*,' called Chipchase from another room, his voice intruding between Harry and the grainy images of distant childhood.

'What is it?' Harry shouted back.

'*Come here. I've found something.*'

Harry went back into the hall. Chipchase was standing in one of the bedrooms, beckoning to him.

Behind the door, out of sight until Harry entered the room, was a desk, supporting a computer screen, keyboard and printer. Lying across the keyboard was a sheaf of printed pages, the topmost page bearing a single paragraph, its wording instantly familiar.

Peter: what follows went before us. It is as I clearly remember it. It is the truth. I—

Harry snatched the page aside and saw the next one beneath, filled with print. And then he saw the single capitalized word at its head.

HASKURLAY.

FIFTY-ONE

Peter: what follows went before us. It is as I clearly
remember it. It is the truth. I entrust it to you as I once
entrusted my heart. You knew what to do then.
You will know what to do now. Tread carefully.
But do not tread too fearfully. My love goes
with you. Les.

HASKURLAY

My recollections of the three months in 1955 that I spent at
Kilveen Castle in Aberdeenshire as a participant in Operation
Tabula Rasa (better known as Clean Sheet) became ever
more confusing as the years passed. Recently, thanks to
the dubious wonders of regressive hypnosis and a greater
clarity of thought and memory that seems to be just about
the only beneficial side-effect of my illness, I have been able
to sift the real from the imagined and the forgotten from
the superimposed. The truth that has become known to me is
a disturbing one. But the researches and enquiries I have
carried out leave me in no position to deny, even if I wished
to, that it *is* the truth.

I have not long to live. I am setting down the facts of
this sombre matter so that an accurate record of what
actually took place will survive me. The use others will make
of it after my death is not for me to decide. The future is
not something I need care about. That is one blessing of my

condition. The past, however, I cannot escape. Nor do I wish to.

The avowed purpose of Operation Clean Sheet, as devised by Professor Alexander McIntyre of Aberdeen University, was to test the receptiveness of fifteen recalcitrant National Servicemen to academic teaching methods under experimental conditions in an isolated setting, the RAF generously supplying Professor McIntyre with his suitably unpromising students. The circumstances that led to my selection – it was an irresistibly attractive alternative to serving 56 days' detention for a second offence of falling asleep on guard duty – were typical. I think we all viewed our spell of intense tuition in the depths of Deeside as a soft option. And that, we believed, is precisely what it turned out to be. The time passed painlessly, with little in the way of learning imparted. Then we went our separate ways.

The experiment, it seemed, was a failure. So we all supposed. But I now know that Operation Clean Sheet had a hidden agenda and that improving our minds was never the object of the exercise. We were taken to Kilveen Castle for quite another and far more sinister purpose.

During our months there, we were given regular injections of a drug known in today's nomenclature as MRQS (modified re-entrant qualianized serotonaze). The effect of MRQS is to disrupt short-term memory, rendering the subject highly suggestible where recent experiences are concerned. The purpose of the experiment was to determine the exact dosages necessary to achieve complete erasure of memory. The value of such a drug in a Cold War world of state secrets and spying missions is obvious and can hardly have diminished since. No wonder the RAF was willing to supply fifteen guinea pigs at short notice to test its effectiveness.

What the experiment swiftly established was that we could be induced to forget certain specified events and activities, including the administration of the drug itself, and to extrapolate other memories to fill the resulting gap. The featureless weeks we spent failing to learn most of what

275

Professor McIntyre's colleagues tried to teach us comprised in fact many more varied events and activities, all of which we obediently and obligingly forgot. MRQS was also administered surreptitiously to most of the academic and support staff, to prevent them giving the game away. Only a few key personnel knew what was really going on.

The need was felt as the experiment proceeded to establish whether the drug could wipe from our minds even the most highly memorable of experiences. An exercise was duly devised for the purpose. Ten of us were to be deposited on an uninhabited island in the Outer Hebrides, with provisions for a week and orders not to attract the attention of passing boats. No indication was to be given of precisely when the group was to be collected. The other five would remain at Kilveen, with no information supplied about the fate or whereabouts of their comrades. When the two groups were reunited after twelve days, it was expected that we would talk of little else but what had happened on the island. The results of the next injection of MRQS would therefore clinch the issue of its reliability under extreme circumstances. I understand it passed the test with flying colours. Once again, we all forgot. And, shortly afterwards, Operation Clean Sheet was wound up.

Professor McIntyre's paymasters in British Intelligence naturally paid no attention to the obscure case of a crofter and his son from the island of Vatersay who went missing during the time ten members of Operation Clean Sheet spent on the nearby island of Haskurlay. I have established that Professor McIntyre did become concerned about it, but took no action, feeling there was no action he safely *could* take.

I was one of the ten men marooned on Haskurlay. The others were Aircraftmen Askew, Babcock, Barnett, Chipchase, Dangerfield, Lloyd, Nixon, Smith and Yardley. The five left behind at Kilveen were Aircraftmen Fripp, Gregson, Judd, Tancred and Wiseman. Those of us bound for Haskurlay were flown from Dyce to Benbecula, then shipped down to the island.

Haskurlay was not a congenial place for an open-ended stay. The ruins of a village and the presence of an ancient burial mound testified to former human occupation and I for one was not surprised the island had been abandoned. The weather was unpredictable and often harsh, spring turning back to winter with depressing frequency. The landscape was devoid of vegetation higher than grass or heather and the west coast was unapproachable due to the hostility of nesting seabirds. We pitched our tents near the deserted village on the relatively sheltered east coast and could do little but stay there in hope and expectation of early removal.

The uncertainty of when we would be taken off preyed on all our minds, some more than others. We had been supplied with one pistol and one rifle between us and had been in-structed to use them only in an emergency. We had also been supplied with a radio on the same basis. We soon put the rifle to use, however, bagging rabbits for the pot. The island teemed with them. Sheep were also numerous, but we left them alone, knowing they were the property of crofters from the populated islands. The days passed, slowly and disagree-ably, boredom alternating with the irrational fear that the ship would never return for us. There were several arguments, leading on one occasion to a fight between two of us. We were scarcely a credit to our uniform.

After a week had elapsed, we decided to radio for rescue, emergency or not. But there was no response to our message. I established later that this was a deliberate ploy to alarm us. It worked. Stuck on the island as we were, cut off from the world, often confined to our tents by ferociously stormy weather, we fell prey to paranoid fears and delusions. Perhaps an outbreak of nuclear war explained the radio silence. Perhaps the mainland had been laid waste. Absurd, of course, but it was what our anxieties reduced us to. We were not the strongest-willed of groups. But, then, we were not intended to be.

I was increasingly troubled in the decades after Clean Sheet by disturbing dreams and fragments of memory that did not fit with what I thought I knew of my past. MRQS is not an absolute guarantee of forgetfulness, it seems. Time slowly undoes its work, at least in some cases. I realized I was not alone in this when I learned of Leroy Nixon's death in Hebridean waters in the spring of 1983. It seemed clear he had committed suicide. The question was: what had driven him to it? The scattered pieces of my suppressed recollections fell into place – and that question was answered – when I travelled to Barra later in the year, visited Vatersay and Haskurlay and learned as much as I could of the disappearance of Hamish and Andrew Munro in 1955. Later discussions with Professor McIntyre, who in old age had come to regret conducting Operation Clean Sheet, and his recommendation of sessions with a hypnotist, enabled me to assemble an accurate picture of the real course of events during our stay at Kilveen and, in particular, during our stay on Haskurlay. It is not a complete picture, far from it, but it does mean I can state definitively how Hamish and Andrew Munro met their deaths.

It was our tenth day on the island. Only another two were to pass before the ship came for us, but we had no way of knowing that. We were running short of provisions of all kinds. Our spirits were low, despite a spell of fair weather. There was much bickering between us. We were not in a happy state.

Two of the party had gone out to shoot rabbits at the northern end of the island, where the warrens were most extensive. There was a landing-place in a cove nearby, of which we were unaware. Munro and his son came ashore there. Climbing up from the cove, they may well have heard a rifle report. Hamish Munro had a shotgun with him. Perhaps he feared for the safety of his sheep. They topped a rise and surprised the pair from our party. The man with the rifle reacted in the panic of the moment, shocked by the sudden appearance of two strangers, one of them armed. He fired at Hamish Munro, killing him. Then, realizing what he had done and knowing the son had just witnessed his father's murder, he shot and killed Andrew Munro as well.

The deed was done. It could not be undone. The pair returned to the main party and confessed to the killings. The rest of us were appalled and horrified. There was much anguished debate about what to do. Slowly, the realization dawned on us that we might all be condemned for the killings and very possibly accused of complicity in them. The pair who were actually responsible – and who steadfastly refused to say which of them had carried out the shootings – played on this fear to argue that we should bury the bodies and say nothing of what had occurred when we were eventually taken off the island. They had, they only then admitted, cast the boat the strangers had arrived in adrift. The falling tide had already carried it far out to sea. Without it, there was no proof anyone had come ashore. Additionally, of course, though they did not mention this, none of us could use the boat to leave the island. We were bound to remain there, cut off from the world, for as long as our superiors decreed. And we still had no way of determining *how* long that might turn out to be.

The isolation we had endured for ten days had led to many a spat. But it had also, without our being aware of it, drawn us together. Group loyalty had evolved, unsuspected and undetected, until this crisis forced it into the open. The decision we eventually took, reluctantly but unanimously, was in part the product of this unity of purpose, a unity which, speaking for myself, seemed both surprising and overwhelming. Emotional revelations of a more personal nature complicated my own feelings about what we should or should not do, but that is no excuse. I consented. I agreed. I aided and abetted. We all did.

We dug a hole in the lower slope of the ancient burial mound at the northern end of the bay and buried the bodies there. We thought they were probably father and son and took some small comfort from knowing they would lie together. Prayers were said. A form of ceremony was observed. There was nothing hugger-mugger about it. We did our best by them in the circumstances.

But we also swore to keep the fact and manner of their

deaths secret. Morally – and criminally – our actions were and are indefensible. They did not seem so at the time, but I believe that is a testament to the enervated and irrational state of mind we had been reduced to. I have little doubt some of us would eventually have broken our pledge of secrecy after we had been restored to the wider world and had had the chance to view events on the island in undistorted hindsight.

Thanks to our unwitting participation in Professor McIntyre's memory-wiping experiment, however, that chance was to be denied us. The secret was safer than any of us could ever have imagined. It became the secret we did not even know we shared. Until, years later, in the baffled minds of a few of us, the wall of amnesia built around it began, little by little, to fall away.

I have said almost all I can about the murders of Hamish and Andrew Munro, to which I was undeniably an accessory, albeit after the fact. There remains only the issue of the identities of the two men who went hunting rabbits that day. I have searched my heart on this score and have concluded that I should make a clean breast of it. The truth must be entire or it is not the truth. I must name them.

Aircraftmen Barnett and Chipchase.

FIFTY-TWO

'We didn't do this, Harry,' said Chipchase, looking up as he finished reading the last page of Maynard's account a few seconds after Harry. 'We didn't bloody do this.'

'I know.'

'It's a stitch-up. That's what it is.'

'*I know*.'

'What can have possessed Maynard to . . . to . . .'

'He didn't, Barry. This has to be a doctored version of what he actually wrote. If it was true, I'm the last person Askew would have sent it to.'

'You think . . . it's a pack of lies from beginning to end?'

'No. I imagine most of it's genuine. But our names have been substituted for the names of the two who really killed the Munros. It wasn't us, though. I can be sure of that.'

'The disk isn't here.' Chipchase pointed to the computer tower. 'I've checked.'

'It wouldn't be. The original was probably destroyed in the fire at Askew's flat. The copy he sent me went the same way. That leaves the altered copy *this* was printed from . . . as the only game in town.'

'And the others it says were on the island are all dead.'

'Exactly. Murdered, in several cases. The doctored disk gives us a motive to have carried out those murders. The police are meant to conclude we've been eliminating the remaining witnesses to what happened. And I'd bet that's what they *will* conclude. Unless we can give them some good reason not to.'

'What about McIntyre's records? He must have kept some. Maybe we weren't even in the group sent to Haskurlay.'

'And maybe we were. I can't remember. Can you?'

'Of course not.' Chipchase jumped up, grabbed the sheaf of papers and tore it angrily in half. 'Bloody Professor Mac. Meddling with our memories. If we get out of this, I swear I'll sue the MoD for a small fortune. No, make that a big one.'

'They'll deny they ever used MRQS on us, Barry. It's a can of worms they can't afford to have opened. That's what Erica Rawson has been doing. Keeping the can firmly closed.'

'You think so?' Chipchase looked suddenly hopeful.

'I do.'

'Then it's not so bad after all. They could never let us be tried, could they? Not if *this*' – he held up the two halves of Maynard's account – 'was the evidence against us.'

'No. But that makes it worse, not better.'

'How d'you mean?'

'I'm not exactly sure. But whoever's setting us up will have worked out all the angles. Every if. Every but. Every therefore.'

'They wanted us to come here, didn't they?'

'Yes.'

'Why?'

'I don't know. But—'

The ringing of the telephone in another room struck Harry silent. He and Chipchase stared at each other, listening to its insistent brr-brr, brr-brr. They waited for the answering machine to cut in, but Murdo Munro evidently did not have one. The telephone went on ringing. And did not stop.

'Why don't they hang up?' asked Chipchase, mournfully enough to suggest he had already guessed the answer.

'Because they want to speak to us. And they know we're here.'

'What are we going to do?'

'Get it over with.'

Harry marched out into the hall. The telephone was mounted on the wall in the kitchen. It went on ringing as he approached. He did not hurry. He knew it would not stop – until he picked up the receiver.

'Hello?'

'Thank God.' It was Howlett's voice. He sounded breathless and anxious. 'It's Mark, Harry. Is Barry with you?'

'Yes. Where are you?'

'I can't— Listen. Tell Barry to pick up the extension in the lounge.'

'All right. But—'

'Please. Just do it. OK?'

'OK.' Harry mimed the request to Chipchase, who headed for the lounge. A few seconds later, the line clicked.

'I'm here,' said Chipchase, his voice echoing hollowly.

'Thanks,' said Howlett, sounding as if he meant it. 'Now, Harry, I'm going to . . . hand you over . . . to the guy who's holding us.'

'*Holding? Us?*'

'Just do as he says. For God's sake. It's—'

'Harry.' Another voice had suddenly supplanted Howlett's: low-pitched and precisely enunciated. 'Frank here. Don't worry about my surname. You don't need to know it. What you *do* need to know is that your friend Mark, along with Karen Snow and Ailsa Redpath, are relying on you to do what I tell you. Have you read the printout?'

'Yes.'

'I have the disk. I also have three hostages, whose lives will be forfeit if you fail to co-operate. Is that clear?'

Harry tried to answer, but for a second was unable to speak.

'*Is that clear?*'

'Yes,' said Chipchase.

'Yes,' Harry hoarsely confirmed.

'Good. Listen carefully. I won't repeat myself again. You should know I'm armed with a Browning nine-millimetre automatic pistol. Standard issue to RAF officers and air crew during your days in uniform. The very weapon either one of you might have misappropriated fifty years ago . . . and kept ever since. This one's in perfect working order. With me so far?'

'Yes,' Chipchase and Harry replied in reverberating unison.

'Excellent. Now, I want you to leave the house and walk back along the road to the jetty you passed on your way there. There'll be a boat waiting for you. I also want you to open the garage as you leave and look inside. Then you'll have no doubt of the gravity of the situation. Clear?'

'Yes.'

'One more thing. If you're not at the jetty within ten minutes, I'll kill the hostages, then come looking for you. And I'll find you long before the police get here – should you decide to phone them. But I wouldn't, if I were you. I really wouldn't.'

The line went dead in that instant. The one-sided conversation was over.

Chipchase reached the kitchen while Harry was still holding the telephone. He looked as shocked and irresolute as Harry felt himself.

'What do we do?'

'You mean apart from what he's told us to do?'

'Yeah. Apart from that.'

'Do you believe he meant what he said?'

'Every word.'

'So do I.'

'In that case . . .'

'We don't have much choice, do we? And we don't have much time either.'

Harry led the way out of the house and round to the front of the garage. He took a deep breath, turned the handle of the up-and-over door and gave it a tug.

The mechanism was well lubricated. It rose smoothly and silently into position. Grey light spread into the garage, over and round the rear of a red pick-up truck.

A sheepdog lay huddled and motionless near the driver's door to the truck, blood pooled beneath it on the concrete floor of the garage. A few feet further on the boiler-suited lower half of a man was visible. He was slumped across the wing of the truck, head down in the engine cavity, partly shielded from them by the raised bonnet.

'Bloody hell,' murmured Chipchase. 'It's Murdo, isn't it?'

'Reckon so.'

'I'll take a look.'

Chipchase moved apprehensively along the narrow corridor between the truck and the garage wall, grasping one of the struts supporting a shelf loaded with paint pots as he stepped gingerly over the dead dog. He peered down into the shadowy recesses of the bonnet, then turned, grimaced at Harry and shook his head.

A few seconds later, he was back outside. 'Bullet through the temple,' he said, his eyes reflecting the horror that his matter-of-fact tone did not express. 'Must have been tinkering with the engine when Frank arrived. Probably never knew a thing. Lucky sod. Then Fido came to see what the noise was. Bang. We're looking at the work of a cold-blooded killer here, Harry. You know that, don't you?'

'Yes. I do.'

'And we're going to walk calmly down the road and go for a cruise round the bay with him, are we?'

'Apparently.'

'Bloody hell.'

'Unless you've got an alternative to suggest.'

'No. I haven't.'

Harry sighed. 'Thought not.'

FIFTY-THREE

They saw the boat standing offshore as they rounded a bend in the road and headed down towards the jetty. It was a smartly painted, newish-looking launch. A figure was visible on deck – a tall, broad-shouldered, darkly clad man, his head in shadow. He moved out of sight as they approached. Then the launch nudged in towards the jetty.

'You want to know what I think?' Chipchase enquired in a gloomy undertone.

'No,' replied Harry.

'This is suicide.'

'I said I didn't want to know.'

'But you already knew.'

'True enough.'

'As a betting man, I've got to tell you—'

'Don't tell me, Barry. Please. *Don't tell me.*'

They reached the jetty. The launch was bobbing in the gentle swell of the rising tide at its far end. The man they had glimpsed earlier stepped into view and nodded faintly in greeting. He was dressed in black jeans and sweatshirt, his clothes filled out by a muscular frame. His face was gaunt and raw-boned, his hair a close-cropped thatch of grey-flecked black. He studied them with chilling impassivity as they walked slowly down the ramp of the jetty.

'Frank?' Harry called.

'You're a little late.' Frank remained expressionless. But he moved his right arm, which had been folded behind his back, so they could see the pistol clasped in his leather-gloved hand. 'I'll overlook it, though. Seen Murdo, have you?'

'Yes. We've seen him.'

'So, you know I'm serious.'

'Oh yes.'

'Good. Come aboard.'

'Where are the others?'

'Just come aboard, Harry.' Frank raised the gun. 'Or I'll shoot you where you stand.'

'Bloody hell,' said Chipchase under his breath. And, silently, Harry echoed him.

It was an awkward step from the jetty down into the launch. Harry managed it in a stumbling stride. As he looked round, he was astonished to see Howlett sitting calmly at the wheel, smiling over his shoulder at him, without the least sign of duress. Indeed, he was in control of the vessel, a fact that loosed a cascade of sickening thoughts in Harry's mind.

The slack-jawed look of amazement on his face had caused Chipchase to hesitate. But Frank was having none of that. 'Get down here, Barry. Now.'

Chipchase cannoned into Harry as he scrambled aboard. Then he too saw Howlett, screened from him until then by the cockpit roof. 'Bloody hell. Marky. You're—'

'Not Marky. And not a hostage. You've got it, Barry.'

'Where are the hostages?' Harry demanded, anger simmering beneath his fear.

'There's just the one actually,' Howlett replied. 'Ailsa Redpath. She's in the cabin.' He nodded towards a pair of closed doors sealing off the fo'c'sle.

'What about Karen?'

'Probably cataloguing a mummy in the British Museum even as we speak. All that crap I served you about her going missing was just a come-on. And you fell for it big time, I have to say. I put on a pretty good show, didn't I?'

'You lured us all the way up here?'

'Correcto.'

287

'Why?'

'Never mind,' snapped Frank. 'Unbolt the cabin doors and go through.' His gaze flicked up to the shore, then back to them. '*Move.*' He gestured with the gun.

Harry edged past Howlett, slipped the bolts holding the doors shut and pulled them open. A cramped triangular cabin revealed itself, a narrow bench running round either side to meet at the end, with a table in the middle. A slim, grey-haired woman dressed in jeans, trainers and fleece was seated awkwardly on the bench, her hands tied with rope behind her back, the rope fastened in turn to one of the table legs. A strip of brown tape had been placed across her mouth. She flinched at the sudden invasion of light, closing her eyes for a second, then turning to blink at Harry in obvious alarm.

'Keep moving,' barked Frank. And Harry did, stepping down into the cabin and making room for Chipchase, who stumbled in after him.

'What are you—' Harry's question was cut off by the slamming of the doors behind them. Darkness descended on him like a hood. He heard the bolts slide back into place. Then the woman moaned. 'Don't worry, Ailsa,' he said, to raise his own spirits as much as hers. 'You're not alone now.'

'I spotted a switch here somewhere,' said Chipchase, fumbling around the door frame. 'Yeah. Here we are.'

An overhead light flickered into life. As it did so, the engine revved throatily and the launch reversed away from the jetty. Then the sound altered again to a smooth, surging rumble. The boat changed direction and accelerated forward.

'Snug quarters we've got here,' said Chipchase. 'Snug as a bloody tomb.'

'For God's sake, Barry,' said Harry, shooting him a glare before moving round the table to where Ailsa was trapped. Gingerly, he removed the tape.

'Thank you,' she gasped, grimacing at the taste the tape had left on her lips. She was, Harry saw, a good-looking woman who had once been beautiful, with high cheekbones, a heart-shaped face, gentle features and grey-blue, far-seeing eyes. 'Who are you?'

'I'm Harry Barnett. And this is—'

'Barry Chipchase.' Chipchase moved round the other side of the table. 'I'll untie you.'

'Ah. Of course.' Ailsa sighed, as if some dismal expectation had only now been fulfilled. 'Barnett and Chipchase. The scapegoats.'

'Too bloody true that's what we are,' said Chipchase, his voice muffled by the tabletop beneath which he was crouching.

'Have you read Maynard's statement?' Harry asked.

'Their version of it, yes,' Ailsa replied.

'You realize we didn't kill your father and brother?'

'Of course I do. This entire exercise is designed to conceal the identity of the real killer. He's who these people work for. And now he's responsible—' She broke off, squeezing her eyes briefly shut. When she opened them again, they were moist with tears. 'Now he's responsible for killing *both* my brothers.'

'Do you know who he is?'

'No. And I doubt I'm going to get the chance to find out. I doubt any of us is.'

'Where are they taking us?'

'I'm not sure. But . . .'

'Haskurlay?'

'That's my guess.'

'What are they planning?'

'Our deaths,' said Chipchase, still struggling with the tightly knotted rope. 'That's what they're planning.'

'Yes,' said Ailsa. 'I fear they are.'

FIFTY-FOUR

The southerly turn the launch took after they had headed east for long enough to clear the Vatersay coast made Haskurlay an ever likelier destination. The ride became rougher as they entered the open sea, forcing Howlett to slow slightly. Ailsa reckoned it would take an hour or so to reach the island. For that hour, at least, they were probably safe.

There was time enough, then, for them to discuss what had brought them to such a desperate plight. Ailsa sat hunched on the bench, massaging her chafed wrists, as Harry told her of the Operation Clean Sheet reunion; of the crop of mysterious deaths it had sparked off; of the house fires in Cardiff and Swindon; of the attempts he and Chipchase had made to discover the truth; and of their ill-fated journey to Vatersay.

Much of this Ailsa already knew. 'I moved to Glasgow long ago, thinking I could put the mystery of Father and Andrew's disappearance behind me. But I never quite succeeded. The ache of not knowing ruined Mother's life. Murdo's too, I think. When Lester Maynard, a total stranger, left me a house in Henley and a good bit of money besides, I tried to tell myself it had nothing to do with what had happened to Father and Andrew. But I knew in my heart it had to be connected. Then Dougie McLeish told Murdo that Maynard had been to Barra a few years before, enquiring about the drowning of a man called Nixon. And Murdo told me. There was no doubt in my mind at that point. The rumours of some sort of military exercise on Haskurlay were true. But still I couldn't be sure Father and Andrew had fallen foul of it. Not till four years ago, too late for Mother sadly, when their bodies were found at last, buried on the island. And even then certainty wasn't proof. The authorities did as little as they could get away with doing. The case was filed and forgotten. It's what I tried to do with it myself. It's certainly what my husband *wanted* me to do with it.

'Then, two weeks ago, Peter Askew contacted me. He said he was an old friend of Lester Maynard's and was in possession of information he felt he ought to pass on to me. He wondered if I'd agree to meet him. Naturally, I did. He came to London the following day. This would have been a couple of days *before* he turned up on your doorstep in Swindon. We met at a café near South Kensington Tube station. He was nervous, hesitant, unsure, it seemed to me, of what he should or shouldn't tell me, how much of the truth he could afford to reveal. The upshot was this. The discovery of the bodies on Haskurlay had confirmed the accuracy of a statement Maynard had arranged to be sent to him after his death. They'd been very close at one point, he said. I didn't pry into exactly what that meant. I had the impression that if I put any pressure on him he might clam up completely. He knew who was responsible for the deaths of my father and brother. He wanted to give that person a chance to come to terms with his responsibility, which, bafflingly, he said he might well be unaware of. An RAF reunion they were both to attend the following weekend would give him the opportunity to broach the subject. Then he'd feel free to show me the statement and explain everything.

'He was never able to do that, of course. It wasn't me *or* Karen Snow he met on his way up to Scotland later that week. I believe it must have been the man who killed Father and Andrew. But he didn't react as Askew had hoped. He decided to suppress the evidence of his guilt by eliminating Askew and anyone else he had reason to believe might know what he'd done.'

'Lloyd was beginning to remember things,' Harry observed. 'That made him a target. And our man probably suspected Dangerfield had an ulterior motive for arranging the reunion in the first place. But three killings were never going to be written off as accidents or suicides. Someone had to take the rap.'

'And by going to ground I effectively volunteered for the role,' grumbled Chipchase. 'Bloody hell.'

'With me lined up as your accomplice,' said Harry. 'Askew must have seen or heard something on the train that alarmed him. He must have realized our man was planning to move against him. So, he tried to ensure the truth would come out whatever happened to him by posting the disk containing Maynard's statement to me during the stopover in Edinburgh. But why send it to *me*?'

'He must have trusted you to bring the truth out in the open,' said Ailsa. 'Perhaps you were never on Haskurlay and therefore had no reason to conceal what happened there. Perhaps neither of you were. If so, our man may be punishing you for having no share in his guilt.'

'It has to be Tancred,' said Chipchase. 'He could easily have met Askew in London on the q.t.'

'So could Judd,' Harry pointed out.

'But he's in Fuerte-bloody-ventura.'

'That proves nothing. He—'

'For the moment, it doesn't matter who it is,' Ailsa cut in. 'What matters is what he's arranged for us.'

'A nasty end,' muttered Chipchase. 'That's what.'

'These men he's hired are utterly ruthless. They kill without hesitation. I came up here when I heard of Askew's death and the two deaths that followed it because I thought I'd be safe so far away from everything. I dare say I would have been but for our man's uncertainty over whether Askew might have sent me a copy of the disk. But all I actually achieved by taking refuge with Murdo was to put him in the line of fire.' Ailsa's voice faltered. She blinked away some tears. 'It was all so sudden. I thought the gunshots were backfires from the engine of the truck. Then that man . . . Frank . . . burst into the house and clapped a gun to my head. I thought he meant to kill me there and then. In some ways, I wish he had.'

'He needed us on the scene,' said Harry. 'He's putting together a set of circumstances and a sequence of events that will persuade the police *we* killed your father and brother fifty years ago, then Askew, Lloyd and Dangerfield last week, then Murdo and . . .'

'Me.'

'Yes. Hence the old RAF pistol he's using. Hence the statement left on display. He said he had the doctored disk, but he's more likely to have hidden it in the house, where the police will eventually find it. They'll conclude you were in possession of it all along and we came up here to destroy it and . . . to eliminate you and Murdo.'

'Why take us to Haskurlay?' asked Chipchase.

'I'm not sure. But they don't intend any of us to come back. That's clear. This case has to be closed down. Because of the security angle, the police will be happy to do that. *If* there's no-one around to be charged or tried. So, what's the story they're setting up? We're losing it. We're no longer in control. We steal this boat, kill Murdo, kidnap Ailsa, take her to Haskurlay. And then . . . your guess is as good as mine.'

'Or as bad. For our long-term, medium-term or even bloody short-term health.'

'Yes. They mean to end this on Haskurlay.'

'To end *us*.'

''Fraid so.'

'How do we stop them, Harry? Tell me you have an idea.'

'I can't tell you that.'

'Great. Just great.'

'But maybe . . . in however long we have left . . .'

'We can come up with one?'

'Yes. Maybe.'

'Or maybe not.'

Harry nodded in reluctant agreement. 'Exactly.'

FIFTY-FIVE

A despairing silence settled over them. There was no more to be said. The launch surged on towards Haskurlay, its bow bucking through the waves. Chipchase smoked a cigarette, the vibration of the hull masking the tremor in his hand, while Harry's thoughts turned to Donna, waiting for news of him in Swindon, and to Daisy, asleep in her bedroom in Vancouver, unaware that her silly old daddy had been sillier than usual today – and was shortly to pay for it with his life.

They would be landed on the island where this whole tragic, tangled tale had begun and executed one by one. Harry no longer hoped for any other outcome. There was no point. That was how it was going to be. He was sure of it.

How were Frank and Mark going to make it look? He turned the matter over in his mind, almost as if it were a mental exercise unrelated to his own imminent demise. What exactly were the police intended to suppose? That he and Chipchase had taken Ailsa to Haskurlay and killed her, obviously. What then? A falling out among murderers, perhaps. The killing of one, followed by the suicide of the other? That would fit neatly into the fiction. Yes. That was probably—

'Hold on,' he said.

'What is it?' asked Ailsa, looking at him with sudden animation.

'You've had an idea, haven't you?' spluttered Chipchase,

294

spilling ash on the table in his excitement. 'You've bloody had an idea.'

'Sort of.'

'Well? What sort?'

'It's just . . .'

'There isn't another episode next week, Harry. You can spare us the suspense.'

'*What is it?*' pressed Ailsa.

'This boat,' said Harry, smiling at them in spite of himself.

'What about it?' snapped Chipchase.

'Don't you see? If we're to be found – dead – on Haskurlay, there has to be a boat we got there in. Moored, or adrift. But there has to be one. And our friends on deck have to have one to make their getaway in.'

'So?'

'So, there must be a boat waiting for us at Haskurlay. Smaller than this, probably. One they can easily land us in. And they have to transfer us to it. Alive. Because ordering people around is much harder when they're dead.'

'Flawless bloody logic, Harry. Ten out of bleeding ten. Now, tell us what your bright idea is. I'm ready to be dazzled.'

'The transfer is our chance. We outnumber them. And there's only one gun.'

'That you know of.'

'The Browning has to account for everyone, Barry. Otherwise the police will smell a rat.'

'So what this so-called chance amounts to is . . .'

'Somewhere between leaving this cabin and boarding the other boat . . . we rush them.'

'*Rush them?*'

'Which one d'you want? Frank or Mark? Mark's the safer choice. He's unarmed.'

'You're crazy. Does Frank look like a pushover to you? He has a gun, Harry. And it isn't loaded with blanks. Ask Murdo. He didn't—' Chipchase broke off, regretting the reference to Ailsa's dead brother. 'Sorry,' he said. 'I didn't mean to . . .'

'Never mind,' said Ailsa. 'Harry's right. It's our only chance, however slim. We have to take it.'

'*Try* to take it.'

'Yes.' She looked at them solemnly. 'We have to try. And I do mean *we*. We only outnumber them if we all play a part. And that includes me.'

The plan of action they devised in the next few minutes was riddled with optimistic assumptions. It relied on Ailsa's ability to distract their captors by staging a collapse as she left the cabin; on Chipchase's dexterity in removing the fire extinguisher from its bracket in the cockpit where he claimed to have noticed it earlier and deploying it as a weapon; on Harry's momentum at the charge being sufficient to propel Frank overboard; above all, on fortune favouring the underdogs in this looming contest to an improbable degree.

The odds against them were even longer in Harry's own, unspoken estimation. True, Frank's use of a gun other than the Browning would taint the trail of evidence he was laying. But a knife posed no such problems and Mark could easily be carrying one. There was also the distinct possibility that a third man was waiting in the second boat, in which case their slim chances of success faded to zero.

But their chances of survival, if they allowed themselves to be shepherded meekly ashore, were also zero. He knew that. So did Ailsa. So did Chipchase. Harry could read the knowledge in their tight, anguished, determined expressions. And he could feel it, hard as iron, locked within himself. It truly was do or die.

The launch slowed and veered to the right – the west, if Ailsa's judgement of their direction was correct. She looked at her watch. 'Long enough,' she said quietly. 'This is the turn for Haskurlay.'

'Small change of plan, Harry old cock,' said Chipchase, leaning across the table towards him. 'You go for the extinguisher. It's clipped above the doorway leading to the cockpit. You can't miss it. Clobber Marky good and hard. I'll deal with Frank.'

'Why switch targets at this stage?'

'Because you're a husband and a father. And I'm neither. So, if anyone's going to take a bullet . . .'

'Don't turn heroic on me, Barry. Please.'

'Heroic? No bloody way. That pistol's an antique. Overdue to jam, I'd say. Or blow up in the bastard's physog.'

'You reckon?'

'I'd bet on it.'

'But—'

'Not another word, Harry, hey?' Chipchase winked. 'You know it makes sense.'

FIFTY-SIX

The launch hove to. There was movement on deck as it wallowed in the swell, but the cabin doors stayed shut. No-one dared say a word now the engine's roar had faded to a gentle tick-over. Then they heard the squeak of a fender and knew Harry had been right: there was a second boat. A moment later came a sound that made them jump even though they had been waiting for it: the sharp snapping back of a bolt.

One, but only one, of the cabin doors swung open. Daylight flooded in, drowning the sallow glow of the overhead lamp. They saw Frank crouched in the companionway, gazing down at them, the gun cradled in his hand. 'I see you two Boy Scouts let the lady go. But that's fine. Just fine.'

'What's going on?' Harry asked, injecting as much firmness into his voice as he could.

'You'll find out soon enough. Let's have you on deck. One by one. We'll start with you, Harry, since you're so curious. Step this way.'

The glance Harry exchanged with his two fellow captives was laced with despair. Their plan, such as it was, seemed to be falling apart around them. Perhaps Frank had taken account of their numerical advantage. If so, he would give them no chance to exploit it.

'Get moving, Harry. Now.'

Reluctantly, Harry obeyed. Frank retreated onto the deck

as he struggled out of the cabin through the narrow single doorway. He could see Mark towards the stern, pulling in a rope. The fire extinguisher should be within reach if Chipchase was right about its location, though whether—

Harry froze in mid-stride. The bracket above the cockpit entrance was exactly where Chipchase had said it was. But it was empty.

'Looking for this?' Frank stretched down to his left and lifted an object into view: the extinguisher. 'We noticed Barry eyeballing it when you came aboard. I don't know what he thought you could do with it, but . . .' He tossed it over the side without taking his eye off Harry. 'Back to business. Close the cabin door behind you and bolt it.'

'But—'

'*Just do it.*'

Harry sighed. The game was up before it had begun. He turned and saw Chipchase mouthing a silent obscenity. With a shrug, he closed the door in his friend's face. He jerked the bolt into place with a clunk, then, hoping his body was blocking Frank's view, eased it back until it was barely holding. Frank said nothing. Harry took what encouragement he could from the success of the manoeuvre. He turned back to Frank.

'Step out here.'

Harry moved slowly out onto the deck. Away to his left was a broad bay of white sand enclosed by rolling green hills: the island of Haskurlay, it had to be. Given long enough, he could probably have made out the ruins of the village beyond the dunes rimming the beach, maybe even the infamous burial mound on the lower slope of the hill at the northern end of the bay. But he had no time for sightseeing. He had very little time of any kind.

The second boat was smaller than the launch – an open-decked inflatable with an outboard motor. Mark was tying it fast against the starboard side, ready, it seemed clear, for the transfer to shore. As Harry watched, he tightened the rope, turned to Frank and nodded. 'We're all set.'

'Good.' Frank leaned back against the stern rail and smiled at Harry. 'Sit down.'

Harry lowered himself onto the bench behind him. 'Why have you brought us here?' he asked, as if for all the world he did not know the answer.

'Thought you ought to see the island . . . at least once, as you and Barry have never been here before. Though that, of course, will have to be our secret. Actually, you aren't going to Haskurlay even today. This is as close as we get.'

'What?'

'Banking on a landing, were you? No, no. That would be far too risky. From our point of view, I mean. A little too . . . unpredictable. So, the trip ends here. For you and Barry. And Ailsa.'

'Who are you working for?'

'That would be telling.'

'Whatever you intend to do to us, you won't get away with it, you know.'

'Oh, I think we will. We've been lucky with the weather. And you played along beautifully. But now it's going to become messy. And I have to consider how it is going to look. That's why I have to do this . . . out of sequence.'

'Sequence?'

'I mean the order of the killings.' Frank pushed himself away from the rail and advanced slowly towards him. 'We'll make it look like you killed Ailsa first, then Barry, because you couldn't trust him to keep his mouth shut, then . . . yourself, because you were suddenly overwhelmed by the horror of your actions, or . . . whatever. Anyway, the other killings are straightforward, but suicide needs precision. You can't shoot yourself from six feet away, can you?'

'We should move him first,' cut in Mark.

'Should we?' Frank responded, his gaze still fixed on Harry.

'They have to be found in the inflatable. I can be linked to hiring this boat.'

'You don't need to worry about that.'

The next second, and the few seconds that followed,

billowed into minutes in Harry's mind. Frank swung round, raising the pistol as he did so. Harry guessed what he was going to do before the possibility of treachery even entered Mark's thoughts. Mark was just another fall guy. He had been seen with Harry and Barry in Castlebay and on the way there. He had been seen altogether too often. His place in Frank's plan for how things were going to look was pre-ordained.

The gun went off with a loud crack. Mark's head jerked back. His mouth fell open, shaping an unspoken 'Oh' of futile surprise as blood trickled from a neat round hole between his eyebrows. He staggered back against the gunwale, then slowly toppled over. Harry did not see him hit the water. But he heard the splash. And sprang up at the sound.

It was his only chance. That thought – that instinct – overrode everything else. He threw himself at Frank, head lowered, arms outstretched. If rugby had been played at Commonweal School in his day, he might have made a better job of it. As it was, he was aided by a sudden pitching of the launch caused by Mark's fall. His charge caught Frank off-balance. They tumbled to the deck. The gun was jolted from Frank's hand. It slid away out of his reach. Harry tried to pin him down and for a moment they were staring into each other's eyes, their faces no more than a few inches apart. Then Frank's relative youth and fitness told. He pushed Harry off, kneeing him violently in the groin as he did so.

Harry rolled to one side, pain sucking what strength he had clean out of him. He heard, as if from a great distance, several thumps, followed by a splintering of wood. Chipchase must have broken out of the cabin, alarmed by the gunshot on deck. There came a shout. '*Harry!*' Then another noise he could not identify.

Chipchase had called his name. But he was nowhere to be seen. Only Frank appeared in Harry's sky-dominated field of vision, looming above him, the gun retrieved and pointing directly at him, the barrel rock-steady and drawing closer as Frank stooped towards him. *You can't shoot yourself from six feet away, can you?* The question drifted into Harry's mind.

He aimed a kick at Frank's leading foot. But Frank dodged it with ease, smiling in satisfaction at his own nimbleness. He crunched his knee into the crook of Harry's left elbow and closed a crushing hand round his right forearm, flattening him against the deck.

Frank brought the gun down in a slow, careful arc, judging to a nicety the ballistics of the suicide Harry's death was meant to be. Harry swivelled his head to either side, but could not escape. When he looked up, the black hole of the gun barrel was waiting and growing, ready to swallow his world.

There was a roar. For a fraction of a second Harry assumed the sudden noise and heat were the last sensations of his life. But no. The gun was gone. Frank was screaming. He had let go of Harry and raised his hands to his face, his features obscured by a searing plume of flame. Ailsa was beside him. She had hold of something. It was wedged in Frank's jaws. His screams were sculpted by a mouthful of fire. He fell on his side, some sparking, sputtering object separating itself from him as he did so. But his screams did not cease.

Harry saw Ailsa bending to grab something from the deck: the gun. Then she was above Frank, standing over him, aiming the weapon. Harry propped himself up on one elbow. He knew what Ailsa was about to do. There was a moment when he could have shouted at her to stop. But he did not.

She fired three times. Bang; bang; bang. Neither fast nor slow. Deliberate. Conclusive. Without margin for error.

The screaming stopped. Dead.

FIFTY-SEVEN

Harry struggled to his feet and sat down on the starboard
bench. He looked across at Ailsa, who was sitting on the other
side of the boat. The gun was still in her hands. Between them
Frank lay sprawled across the deck like some great black fish
they had just landed, blood oozing from beneath him and
lapping first towards Ailsa, then towards Harry, with the pitch
of the vessel.

'What did you . . . attack him with?' Harry asked numbly.

'A safety flare,' Ailsa replied, pointing to a scorched red
and yellow metal tube lying in the stern. 'I found it in a locker
under the wheel. It was . . . the obvious place to look and . . .
the only thing I could think of.'

'Thank God you knew how to set it off.'

'Thank growing up on a small island for that and all the
messing about in boats that goes with it.' She glanced down at
the gun. 'Do you know . . . how to unload this?'

'The magazine's in the handle, I think. There'll be a catch
somewhere to release it. Barry might—' Harry broke off,
bemused by Chipchase's absence – and the fact that it had not
yet occurred to him to question it. 'Where *is* Barry?'

'He knocked himself out on the lintel of the cabin doorway.'

'He did *what*?'

'I'm sorry. We should . . . see how he is. But . . . I think he's
all right.'

Harry hurried into the wheelhouse and down into the cabin. Chipchase was slumped on the floor, with his back against one of the table legs and his feet spread out before him. He was blinking like a man hoping his vision would soon clear and rubbing a nasty-looking wound on his forehead that was already forming a lump with a livid bruise purpling around it.

'He was so worried about you he forgot to stoop,' Ailsa called from the deck. 'He's going to have quite a headache.'

'Barry?' Harry crouched beside his friend and grasped him by the shoulders. 'Barry?'

'There you are, Harry.' Chipchase opened his eyes wide, which seemed to bring his vision into focus. 'What's . . . going on?'

'Don't worry. We've, er, dealt with Frank and Mark.'

'You have?'

'Terminally.'

'Bloody hell.'

'Not pretty. That's a fact.'

'So . . .'

'Everything's OK.'

'Really?'

'Really.'

'Well . . . didn't I tell you it would be?' Chipchase grinned. 'With me in charge.'

Chipchase did not ask for any details of what had occurred during his brief period of unconsciousness. His lack of curiosity might have worried Harry had he not been so grateful for it. He had no wish to relive the events any time soon. Nor, clearly, had Ailsa. The shock of what had happened and the almost greater shock of surviving it had reduced their range of thought and action to the needs of the moment.

Chipchase turned out to be no more familiar with the design of a Browning pistol than Harry was. In the event, it was Harry who removed the ammunition, rendering the weapon safe. He also found a tarpaulin folded away under one of the benches, which he draped over Frank's body. Mark's was a dark shape in the water, drifting slowly in towards the shore of Haskurlay. There was no way they could retrieve it. Someone else would have to do that. The police, presumably.

The launch had a VHF radio, which they could have used to summon help there and then. But Ailsa was confident she could handle the controls and favoured heading for Castlebay to raise the alarm. 'If we radio from here, they'll tell us to stay put,' she reasoned. 'I don't want to sit out here waiting for them. Do you?'

Harry did not. And Chipchase expressed no preference, much of his initial chirpiness on regaining consciousness having deserted him. Ailsa washed his wound as best she could and dressed it with a bandage she found in the first-aid kit. Barry decided a cigarette would aid his recovery and sat out on deck smoking it as they accelerated away from Haskurlay, towing the inflatable behind them.

Harry watched the island recede slowly into the distance, doubting he would ever set foot there now. Ailsa did not look back. She stayed at the wheel, gaze fixed on the northern horizon. Harry wondered if she too had seen her last of the island. It was easy to believe she might never want to return.

But the future was as difficult to predict as the past was to fence off. The one was always infecting the other. And the past that had lured them to Haskurlay was not finished with them yet.

'The police will find out who hired Frank,' Harry said to Ailsa, standing beside her in the cockpit as the launch sped towards Barra.

'I don't care if they do or not,' she said, so quietly he had to strain to hear her above the roar of the engine. 'I only ever wanted to know the truth about how Father and Andrew died. Well, we know now, don't we?'

'We do, Ailsa, yes. But I'm not sure the powers that be will want the public to learn what Operation Clean Sheet was all about. They'll organize some kind of cover-up.'

'Let them. I don't care about that either. I have a husband and children I love. The kids have no idea what's been happening. I want to go back to my life with them. I want to bury Murdo next to his mother and father and brother and then . . .' She looked away, dabbing at her eyes with a tissue. 'I'm sorry. I can't seem to stop crying.'

'Don't worry about it. What were you going to say? "And then . . ."?'

'Oh.' Ailsa sighed. 'I was going to say: forget all this.'

'That won't be easy.'

'No. But it may be possible. In time.'

'The police will ask a lot of questions.'

'I'm sure they will.'

'I'll make it very clear you had no choice about shooting Frank. It was kill or be killed.'

'Just tell them everything, Harry.' She smiled grimly at him. 'That's all we can do.'

'Yes. I suppose it is.'

'I'm all right. Really. Go and talk to Barry. I . . . can't say any more. Not just now.'

Harry nodded. 'Fair enough.'

Chipchase was bending over the side of the vessel, spitting out the last of a mouthful of vomit, when Harry reached him. He was white-faced, breathing fast but shallowly. What with that and the bandage round his head, through which blood was still seeping, he looked far from well.

'Maybe you should go below, Barry,' Harry suggested. 'You didn't seem to feel seasick down in the cabin.'

'I didn't . . . did I?' Chipchase swivelled round on the bench to face Harry. 'You . . . could be right.'

'Want a hand?'

'No, no. I can still . . . walk down a flight of steps, y'know.' Chipchase struggled to his feet. 'I'm not a . . . bloody inva—' He winced and bowed his head. 'Jesus. That—'

He fell like a toppling tree. Fortunately, Harry was in his path of descent. He caught Chipchase and lowered him gently the last few feet to the deck, kneeling with him as he went.

'Barry? Are you all right?' There was no answer. Harry repeated the question. But still there was no answer.

FIFTY-EIGHT

The air ambulance rose deafeningly into the sky above Castle-bay and turned for its high-speed run to the mainland. Harry stood at the edge of the playing field that doubled as a helipad, watching it go and wishing the patient it was carrying well. The hours that had elapsed since Chipchase's collapse were a blur in his memory. Anxiety about his old friend's condition overshadowed his attempts to explain to the police what had happened earlier in the day and to reassure Donna over a crackly phone line to Swindon that all was well with him – if not, alas, with Chipchase, who had undergone an emergency craniotomy at Barra Hospital to drain a blood clot on the brain prior to being transferred to a specialist neuro-surgical unit in Glasgow.

It seemed absurd and unfair that Chipchase might have inflicted a fatal injury on himself in the process of cheating death at the hands of a pair of hired killers. But Harry knew enough of the absurdity and unfairness of human existence to realize that it was only too possible. And the doctor who had operated on Chipchase had made no bones about the serious-ness of his condition. 'The next twenty-four hours will be critical; it could go either way.'

So it was that a comatose Chipchase was borne away to fight for his life in a distant hospital ward, while Harry remained on Barra to answer any questions that might be put to him by the small team of detectives helicoptered down from Stornoway to investigate three violent deaths at the normally uneventful southern extremity of their command area.

Ailsa, after making a statement to the Stornoway team, had retreated to the house of a family friend. Harry had barely spoken to her since their arrival in Castlebay aboard the launch. They had radioed ahead and been met halfway by the lifeboat, so that Chipchase could be rushed to the hospital. Only the resident officer at Barra police station had been waiting for them at the pier, in a strangely low-key start to what was to become a multiple homicide inquiry.

One of those homicides had been an act of self-defence, of course. Harry had stressed that at every opportunity. The detectives, however, led by a dour and inscrutable chief inspector called Knox, had given the circumstances of Murdo Munro's death far more attention than those of his killers'. There was an unspoken implication that they had got no less than they deserved for descending on such a peaceful little island set on mayhem and murder. The scenes of crime – the launch, the Munro croft on Vatersay and the inshore waters of Haskurlay, where there was a body still to be recovered – had become the focus of their activities. The tangled connections between what had occurred that day and the deaths of two other members of the Munro family fifty years before had barely been addressed.

They would be eventually, though. Harry was well aware of that. There would be a combing of old files. There would be consultations with the Grampian and Tayside forces. There would be a lot of assimilating of information and assessing of evidence. And it would all take time. Nothing would be concluded quickly.

The intelligence dimension to the case would be a further complication. With the original version of Maynard's disk lost, the true purpose of Operation Clean Sheet remained unprovable. And Harry felt sure it would be officially denied. The role of MRQS as a memory-wiping drug was no better than a rumour in the pharmacological world anyway, according to what Samuels had told Donna – something the US Army might or might not have tried out on some of its own men back in the fifties. This had nevertheless been sufficient to convince Donna she could no longer sit idly by in Vancouver. Her discovery upon arrival in Swindon that Harry had omitted to mention to her the small matter of the destruction of his old home had only heightened her alarm. And the cryptic message he had left for her with Jackie had done nothing to lessen it.

At least she now knew he was safe and well. Harry walked slowly up from the playing field to the Castlebay Hotel rehearsing in his mind various ways to explain to her why he had misled her and reckoning that an abject apology would probably serve him best. A blue and white police launch was heading in fast across the bay towards the pier, perhaps bearing some of the investigating team back from Haskurlay. If so, they might have more questions for him. But they knew where to find him. He was going nowhere without their consent. He had given them his word on the point and meant to stick to it. It was the best demonstration of his innocence he could devise. And there remained the possibility that his innocence might still be questioned in some quarters. Ailsa had said she did not care who among the Clean Sheeters had killed her father and brother and hired Frank and Mark. But Harry cared. And so would a good few others when they heard what had happened.

Harry's earlier call to Donna had been from the police station. Now, in the privacy of his hotel room, he was able to speak to her more freely.

'I'm sorry I didn't tell you everything that was going on. I knew you'd be tempted to do what you did in the end anyway – fly over. And I didn't want to expose you to the danger I was already in. It really was as simple as that.'

'We're man and wife, Harry. We're supposed to be a team.'

'I know. But it's a team of three. Someone had to look after Daisy.'

'While you looked after yourself?'

'Well, I didn't do such a bad job, did I?'

'You've been lucky. That's what it amounts to.'

'Unlike Barry.'

'Yeah. Sorry, hon. How is he?'

'Not good. The doc muttered about his unhealthy lifestyle catching up with him.'

'How long will the police want you to stay on Barra?'

'No idea. There's a lot for them to get their heads round. It could be a few days. More, even. I just don't know.'

'I reckoned not. So, I'll join you there tomorrow.'

'You will?'

'I'm booked on an early flight to Glasgow. Jackie's going to drive me up to Heathrow at the crack of dawn. The connecting flight to Barra gets in at ten.'

Harry had not expected to be reunited with Donna so soon. The prospect of seeing her again in a matter of hours rather than days suddenly reminded him how much he had missed her. 'Ten tomorrow morning? That's great.'

'You're not going to try and put me off again?'

'Absolutely not. It'll be—' A sharp rap at the door sounded in his other ear. 'Hold on.' He covered the receiver and called out: 'Yes?'

'Chief Inspector Knox, Mr Barnett. I need a word. Urgently.'

'Just a minute.' Swearing under his breath, Harry went back to Donna. 'I'm going to have to ring off. The police want to speak to me. I'll call you again as soon as they've gone.'

'Make sure you do. I'm *still* worried about you.'

'Don't be. 'Bye for now.' Harry put the phone down. 'Come in.'

Knox entered quietly, closing the door behind him. He was a short, squat, sandy-haired man in his forties or early fifties, with a guardedly polite manner and an unreadable demeanour. 'Sorry to interrupt,' he said, though it was impossible to tell whether he genuinely was or not.

'My wife,' Harry explained.

'Relieved you're in one piece, no doubt.'

'Yes. Naturally. She'll be joining me here tomorrow, as a matter of fact.'

'Tomorrow?' Knox frowned.

'Is that a problem?'

'I'd have to say it is.'

'Why?'

'Because . . . I'm hoping you'll agree to do something for us, Mr Barnett. And if you do . . . you won't be here when she arrives.'

FIFTY-NINE

Knox prowled briefly around the room before settling in its only armchair, facing Harry, who was sitting on the bed nearest the telephone.

'You were sharing this room with Mr Chipchase, I think you said,' Knox remarked, apropos of nothing as far as Harry was concerned.

'That's right.'

'How is he?'

'No-one seems too sure. He's on his way to Glasgow for specialist treatment. But . . . he hasn't regained consciousness since he passed out on the launch, so . . .' Harry shrugged helplessly. 'It's touch and go.'

'I expect you'd like to follow him to Glasgow. Be on hand for, er . . . any changes in his condition.'

'Of course I would. Are you saying I can?'

'I'd better explain, hadn't I? To be honest, I'd rather have got more of a grip on the case before considering any moves like this, but . . . the timing leaves us little choice. I've spoken to Chief Inspector Ferguson in Aberdeen and Inspector Geddes in Dundee. They've filled me in on the background and I've brought them up to speed with what's happened here. They agree with what I'm proposing.'

'Which is?'

'I'll come to that in a moment. Let me start by saying I've

no doubt of Mrs Redpath's truthfulness or the accuracy of her statement.'

'What about mine?'

'In effect, she's your guarantor, Mr Barnett. She's why we now also regard you as a truthful witness.'

'Thanks very much,' said Harry levelly.

'We had to take account of your status as a suspect in a parallel inquiry. I'm sure you understand that.'

'I . . . suppose so.'

'Good. Now, I propose to leave the whole matter of the deaths of Hamish and Andrew Munro on Haskurlay fifty years ago and the alleged military exercise there—'

'It's a bit more than alleged, isn't it?'

'I don't know. And neither do you, according to your own statement.' Knox's gaze hardened briefly before he continued. 'At all events, I propose to leave that matter till another day. My priority *this* day is finding out who hired the two men who killed Murdo Munro and attempted to kill you, Mrs Redpath and Mr Chipchase. As it happens, we've made some progress on that score, which is what brings me here. Frank was obviously the one in charge. Yes?'

'Yes.'

'And obviously intended from the outset to eliminate Mark at some point.'

'Yes.'

'After killing you all aboard the launch, he must have planned to make his escape in the inflatable. He could hardly have crossed to the mainland in such a craft, but it would have done him for a return trip to Barra. We found the Ford Fiesta parked on the verge further along the road from the Munro house. That's presumably where he meant us to find it. So, the question is: how did he plan to leave Barra? The next ferry to Oban's not till tomorrow morning. Nor is the next flight to Glasgow. You came over by ferry yourself, so you may not know the airport here on Barra is simply a beach, albeit a grand wide one, away on the north coast. It's an afternoon high tide just now, so it's a morning

314

service only. That's why we had to come down by helicopter ourselves.'

'So he would have been trapped here?'

'Ah no. We've good reason to think not. Our theory is that he actually planned to take the inflatable a little further, to Eriskay, the next island north of here. That's linked by causeway to South Uist and Benbecula. If he had a car waiting for him on Eriskay, he could have driven to the proper tarmac airport at Benbecula and caught the five-thirty flight to Glasgow from there. There are several single male passengers booked on it. We expect one of them to be a no-show.'

'Frank.'

'It makes sense. The inflatable would have been a safe distance from the scene of the crime. And with Mark identifi-able as the man who hired the launch here on Barra this morning, he'd be in the clear. Not to mention Glasgow, where we're certain he planned to be tomorrow morning.'

'What makes you so certain of that?'

'You didn't search the body, did you, Mr Barnett?'

'No.'

'If you had, you'd have come across nothing to put a name or address to him. Maybe he left his credit cards and so forth in the car on Eriskay, if our theory about his method of escape is correct. But it might take us a few days to find the car. And we can't wait till then. Because what he did have in his pocket was a mobile phone, on which he'd recently recorded – but not yet sent – a text message. Did he strike you as a vain man?'

'Vain?' It was not something Harry had considered before. Frank's capacity for murderous violence had been of more immediate interest than whether he habitually admired his reflection in shop windows. But, now the question had been posed . . . 'Well, he was certainly no shrinking violet.'

'Only there's a hint of vanity to my mind in drafting the message *before* the event.'

'What was the message?'

'"Contract executed. Confirm Blythswood Square for settlement, 8 a.m. tomorrow."'

'Where's Blythswood Square?'

'Central Glasgow.'

'I see.'

'A pay-off in Glasgow fits our theory rather neatly.'

'Do you know who he was going to send the message to?'

'No. But we have the mobile number it was destined for. We've traced it, naturally. A phone bought in the West End of London – O2 in Oxford Street, to be precise – twelve days ago. Pay as you go. And a cash sale. So, we've no idea who made the purchase.'

'Twelve days?' That took it to the period between Askew's meeting with Ailsa in South Kensington and his departure for Kilveen with Harry and assorted other Clean Sheeters later in the week. 'It has to be whoever Askew was threatening to expose as the Munros' murderer.'

'But who was that, Mr Barnett? According to your statement, several of those still in the frame live in London. And those who don't could have gone there for the day. Well, there's really only one way to find out which of them it is, don't you think?'

'Send the message.'

'Just so.' Knox paused and gave Harry a long, scrutinizing look. 'As we already have.'

'You've sent it?'

'The media only know about a murder on Vatersay. Nothing about two dead hit men. We'll keep it that way for the next twenty-four hours. So, the recipient of the message has no reason not to present himself in Blythswood Square tomorrow morning at eight o'clock to pay Frank whatever he's due. But Frank won't be there. We will.'

'A trap?'

'One our man may slip through, unfortunately. Given that we don't know who we're looking for. What we need is someone able to recognize the person who turns up.'

'Ah,' said Harry. 'You mean me.'

'I do, Mr Barnett, yes. We'd have you under surveillance throughout. And miked up into the bargain. You'd be running no risks. Anything you drew out of him could be valuable.' A hint of a smile quivered at the edges of Knox's mouth. 'A full confession would be ideal.'

'What if he just legs it as soon as he spots me?'

'We grab him. At least we'll know who to grab. So, will you do it? We have to get you to Glasgow and set everything up. It can be done, but we're sorely pressed for time. I'd like to be able to give you a while to think it over, but . . .'

'You can't.'

'I'm afraid not. I need your answer . . . here and now.'

SIXTY

Even Donna agreed Harry had to do it. This was a chance to end the uncertainty: to nail the one among the original fifteen members of Operation Clean Sheet guilty of murder – in the past *and* the present; to look him in the face and to know he would pay for what he had done – then *and* now. This was a chance Harry had realized at once he was bound to take.

So it was that Tuesday morning found him sharing the cramped rear of an unmarked white Transit van parked on the western side of Blythswood Square, Glasgow, with a battery of electronic surveillance equipment and an overweight, shaven-headed technical expert overly fond of Danish pastries called Dylan.

'Sure you don't want one?' Dylan enquired, wafting a cinnamon-scented bagful in Harry's direction.

'Sure, thanks.'

'Have you had any breakfast?'

'Just coffee. It was, er . . . an early start.'

That was something of an understatement. Accommodated overnight in the Milngavie Travel Inn on the northern outskirts of the city, Harry had been woken at dawn by one of Knox's junior officers and transported to Strathclyde Police HQ for final briefing and microphone-fitting. Handily, Blythswood Square lay close by. In the quadrangle at its centre, trees and bushes shaded a circular path round a flower-bedded lawn, with benches spaced at intervals. The square was overlooked by elegant Georgian buildings mostly occupied by the offices of solicitors, recruitment consultants and financial advisers. One of those offices had been temporarily converted into Knox's observation post. Police-men in white-collar-worker disguise were on patrol around the square as eight o'clock approached, while Dylan shuffled a pack of CCTV images on his monitor screen and chomped remorselessly through his supply of Danishes. 'You should still have had breakfast,' he said, inadvertently spitting a pastry flake onto Harry's shoulder. 'It's the most important meal of the day.'

'I had a fry-up yesterday morning. Plus porridge.'

'I bet your day went all the better for it.'

'Oh, definitely. Found some poor bloke shot dead in his garage. Got taken prisoner by his killer. Narrowly avoided a similar fate myself. Witnessed a couple more fatal shootings. Assisted the local constabulary with their enquiries. Hung around hospital corridors waiting for news of a critically ill friend. Volunteered to take part in a police stake-out. Then . . . I got an early night. It was a breeze.'

'You're a dry one, aren't you?' Dylan grinned, which was not a pretty sight. 'How's the friend?'

'Still critical.'

'Not so bad, then.'

'As what?'

'As dead.' Dylan swallowed the final mouthful of his latest Danish and squinted at the screen with sudden intensity. 'Hold up . . . No, I don't think so. Too young. And . . . he's moving on.'

'What time is it?'

'Seven to eight. Won't be long now. Where are they treat-ing him, then?'

'Who?'

'Your friend.'

'Western General. Here in Glasgow.'

'Oh dear. *Western General.*'

'What's the matter?'

'My uncle went in there a few months back for a hip replacement. Caught some super-bug the minute his bum touched the mattress. He's in the cemetery now. A real waste.'

'Sorry to hear that.'

'Don't be. He was a miserable old sod.'

'I thought you just said what a waste it was.'

'Aye. Of a brand-new artificial hip.' Dylan squinted at the screen again. 'Hold up. I think . . . we might be in business. Take a look.' He made as much room for Harry as his bulk allowed, which in the confines of the van was not a lot.

A blurred and flickering black-and-white picture of the centre of the square, captured from a camera mounted on one of the surrounding buildings, presented itself to Harry's view. A couple of people were moving across the square, using it as a short-cut to their places of work, but there were two stationary figures, one seated on a bench, reading a newspaper, the other bending over something at the side of the path. The picture was far too fuzzy for any details of clothing or appearance to emerge. But it was only a few minutes short of eight o'clock. Harry supposed they both had to be candidates.

Not so, according to Dylan. 'Forget the stooper. He's a down-and-out doing the rounds of the bins. See?' The bending man straightened up and shuffled away, revealing the bin that had been the object of his attentions. 'Clock the guy on the bench.'

'He's just reading a paper.'

'Maybe.'

'Plus I don't recognize him.'

'You'd be hard put to recognize your own mother on one of these. I've told 'em we need to upgrade the technology for this kind of work, but the only upgrades they're interested in are to Chief Super and beyond. Cheapskates, the lot of them.'

'Can't you try some of the other cameras?'

'It won't help.' Views of the same scene from several

different but equally distant and unilluminating angles flashed across the screen. 'See what I mean?'

Harry peered more closely at the blurred figure on the bench. He had lain awake for an hour or more in his Travel Inn bed the night before, trying to decide who Frank's paymaster was. The process of elimination led in only one direction every time. Of those still alive, Babcock was as good as dead in an Australian nursing home and had never been capable of killing anything larger than a wasp anyway. Nor had Fripp and Gregson. That left Judd, Tancred and Wiseman. But Judd was out of the country and Wiseman had nearly died in the car crash that had killed Lloyd. Logically, it *had* to be Tancred.

But was it Tancred he could see on the screen, sitting idly on the bench, newspaper open before him, clothes a smear of pale grey, head a smudge of a darker shade? It might be. It could be. It should be. But *was* it?

'It's eight on the button,' said Dylan. 'And he's not moving. QED, he's waiting.'

'I can't say for sure if I know him.'

'No choice, then. You'd better take a closer look.'

'Yes. I suppose so.'

Dylan switched on the van's link to the observation post and spoke into a microphone. 'No ID on Bench Man from here, people, so our boy's going for a stroll in the park. Pin back your ears and prise open your eyelids. It's movie time.'

It was nearly over, Harry told himself as he clambered from the van and Dylan pulled the doors gently shut behind him. The end was close. Donna's flight would be landing at Glasgow Airport in a quarter of an hour or so. They would soon be together again. When they had parted twelve days ago, Operation Clean Sheet had been no more than an obscure and forgotten episode in Harry's misspent and undistinguished youth. In many ways, he wished it still was. But wishing was not the same as forgetting. It lacked the power to deceive. Reality was the chill, bright, gusty morning through which he walked, waiting for the traffic to thin, before he crossed the road and entered the park.

Ahead he saw the figure on the bench. Knox had insisted he wear a baseball cap to strengthen his chances of reaching the subject before being recognized. As it was, the man he was heading towards was not looking in his direction at all, but was studying his newspaper with apparent concentration, his face masked by its open pages, the crown of a trilby or the like visible above them. He was dressed in a light mac, dark suit and gleamingly polished black shoes. There was a brief-case beside him, propped against his thigh. The newspaper's pinkish colour revealed it to be the *Financial Times*. All in all, the man looked like a dapper, slightly old-fashioned banker or stockbroker.

Then, when Harry was about halfway along the path towards him, the man turned to another page, folding the paper briefly shut as he did so. Still he did not notice Harry, but in that instant there could be no mistaking who he was.

'My God,' Harry murmured, wondering if the hidden microphone would catch his words. 'It's you.'

SIXTY-ONE

'Hello, Magister,' said Harry, stopping in front of Wiseman and pulling off the cap. 'Fancy meeting you here.'

Wiseman looked up. His eyes widened. His face lost most of its colour. For a moment, he seemed wholly incapable of assimilating the message his senses were transmitting to his brain: that Harry Barnett was not lying dead, apparently by his own hand, on a launch off the coast of Haskurlay in the farther reaches of the Outer Hebrides, but was standing a few feet from him in the genteel surroundings of Blythswood Square, Glasgow.

'How are your shares doing?'

'Wha . . . What?'

'Thanks. Don't mind if I do.' Harry sat down on the bench next to Wiseman, the briefcase between them. 'The pay-off's in the case, is it? Cash only in this line of business, I assume. How much, as a matter of interest? How much does it cost to have your old buddies knocked off one by one?'

'I . . .'

'Don't know what I'm talking about? Can't imagine what I mean? You'll be adding insult to injury if you try denying everything, Magister. And it won't get you off the hook anyway. You're here because you got a message from Frank telling you to be. Only the message wasn't from Frank. It was from the police. They have the square surrounded. You'll be arrested if you try to leave.' Harry had agreed with Knox that,

323

just in case the subject was armed, which both of them were confident he would not be, the hopelessness of his situation should be made clear to him at the outset. 'So, stay awhile and tell me . . . why in God's name you did it.'

Wiseman closed his newspaper with exaggerated care and flattened it across his knees. 'Who's . . . Frank?' he asked.

'Your hired hit man. Maybe you knew him by another name. I don't suppose either of them was genuine.'

'*Was?*'

'He's dead. Like I'd be, if the plan he cooked up on your behalf hadn't gone pear-shaped.'

Wiseman glanced about him, as if expecting to see a policeman behind every bush. Then he turned and stared at Harry, fear of retribution and a conceited man's rage struggling almost visibly for mastery of his thoughts. 'You can't . . . prove anything,' he said through gritted teeth.

'I'm not going to try. But the police will. And I reckon they'll succeed. You being here is the crunch. How do you account for that if it's not in response to Frank's message? And if the briefcase is full of money, what's it for if not to pay off him and his accomplice? Who's also dead, in case you're interested.'

'Accomplice?'

'Mark Howlett. Obviously an alias, but—'

'*Mark?*'

'Yes. Mark.'

'He's dead?'

'Very dead.'

'What . . . did he look like?'

'Look like? What the hell does that matter?'

'*What did he look like?*'

Wiseman seemed determined to have an answer, so Harry gave him one. 'Young. Shortish. Fattish. Brown hair overdue for a wash. Bit of a beard. John Lennon specs. Sweated a lot.'

In the same instant that horror gripped Wiseman's features, Harry saw the resemblance for the first time: the shape of the nose, the set of the jaw, the cold gleam of the eyes. He saw it, but for the moment could not bring himself to believe it. 'Was he . . .'

'My son. Marcus. No wonder he hasn't responded to my messages.' Wiseman lowered his head. 'Who killed him?'

'Frank. You got yourself a double-crosser there, I'm afraid.'

'And who killed Frank?'

'Ailsa Redpath fired the actual shots. But it could just as easily have been me. It was him or us.'

'Dear God.' Wiseman raised a hand to his face. 'Oh dear God.'

'It's your fault, though. *All* your fault. For hiring a man like Frank. For letting your son work with him. What were you—'

'*I didn't hire him.*' Wiseman lowered his hand and stared bleakly at Harry. The news of his son's death had shocked him out of his earlier defiance. 'And I had no idea Marcus was involved in the actual . . .' He made a fist of the hand he had lowered and tightened it until the knuckles were white, then slowly relaxed it. 'I'm sorry.'

'You're *sorry*?'

'It was never meant to come to this. And now . . . I've lost more than was originally at stake. A lot more. Everything, in fact. Everything that matters.'

'What do you want? My condolences?'

'You don't understand. It was . . .' Wiseman sighed. 'Askew forced my hand.'

'How? By showing you Maynard's statement and asking you to admit what you'd done fifty years ago?'

'Yes. All right. That *is* what happened. Though now . . . it hardly seems to matter.' A shake of the head; a long blink; a shudder. 'My poor boy.' Wiseman looked away, gazing past Harry into the middle distance, his focus blurring. 'What do you want to know?'

'Askew showed you the statement and gave you a few days to reconcile yourself to being identified as the Munros' murderer. Yes?'

'Yes. Maynard had named me as the one who killed them. Askew insisted their relatives had a right to know the truth.

He wanted me to make a clean breast of it. He wanted *all* of us to make a clean breast of it. But especially me.'

'Do you remember shooting them?'

'Not exactly. But it fits with . . . flashbacks I've suffered from for years.'

'And you decided you weren't willing to let the truth come out?'

'There was no reason why it had to. It wasn't as if it was really my fault. God knows what the side-effects were of that drug they used on us. I wasn't responsible for my actions. None of us were. I tried to make Askew understand that. But I was wasting my breath. He was on some born-again ethical high: we had to acknowledge what we'd done, etcetera, etcetera. Even if it meant, in my case, pleading guilty to double murder.'

'So you hired Frank to take Askew out?'

'I told you: I didn't hire Frank. What I did was warn Marcus I was about to be publicly disgraced – and worse. It was he who . . . suggested a solution to the problem. He used to be a roadie for a rock band. They took a couple of bodyguards round with them. Marcus reckoned one of the bodyguards could . . . put him on to somebody. I've had to help the boy out of a lot of trouble over the years. He saw this as his chance to . . . repay me.'

'You let *him* hire Frank?'

'Yes. And when I met Askew for the second time, the night before he travelled up to Kilveen, I told him I'd do what he wanted. We agreed to put it to the rest of you at the end of the reunion. But Frank had already assured me Askew would never make it to Kilveen, let alone the end of the reunion.'

'What about the auction in Geneva you were supposed to be attending?'

'I flew to Aberdeen from London, not Geneva. There *was* an auction. But I didn't go. I knew Frank intended to make his move against Askew on the train and I didn't want to be there when he did. I also knew Askew couldn't put the lie to my cover story without admitting we'd met the night before, which he'd promised to keep secret until the time came for us all to face the truth. My absence must have worried him, though. He must have guessed somehow what we had in mind for him. That's why he sent you the disk with Maynard's statement on it. I was certain he'd have it on him when Frank struck. But he didn't. It wasn't in his bag either. If only we'd got hold of the disk then, I'd have been completely in the clear.'

'Leaving Barry and me to carry the can.'

'Chipchase was the obvious fall guy. Dodging the reunion only made it look worse for him. You were inevitably suspect as his former partner. But there was never likely to be enough to pin Askew's murder on either of you, assuming it was even officially recognized as a murder. You'd never have been charged, let alone convicted. It would all have . . . fizzled out. Still, the missing disk was a loose end I couldn't afford to leave dangling. Worse, once we'd all got together at Kilveen, Lloyd started to . . . remember things. I began to wonder if Askew had turned the disk over to him.'

'So you took him out too.'

'It was Marcus's idea. I think by then . . . he was beginning to enjoy himself. I lured Lloyd out to Braemar. Frank searched his room after the rest of you had gone, but drew a blank. On the way back from Braemar, I pulled off the road into a deserted picnic area in the woods. Frank was waiting. He knocked Lloyd out. We searched him, but there was still no sign of the disk. Then Frank tampered with the car's steering, helped me stage the crash in the river and made sure Lloyd was dead. He also posed as the passing motorist who gave me a hand. We made it look like I could easily have died as well, so no-one was ever going to think I was party to sabotaging the car. But . . . we still didn't have the disk.'

'Is that why you had Dangerfield killed? Because you thought Askew might have sent it to him?'

'I know nothing about Dangerfield's death.'

'Pull the other one.'

'It's true. My guess is that the Secret Service used him to

arrange the reunion as a check on the long-term effectiveness of MRQS. When the police started a murder inquiry that could have led them close to the truth about Operation Clean Sheet, it must have been decided he was a liability.'

There was no reason left for Wiseman to lie. Harry sensed, indeed, that his 'guess' was all too accurate. But he had no intention of saying so with Knox and his crew listening in. 'When did you realize Askew had sent the disk to me?'

'When I considered who he was most likely to trust out of those lucky enough to be left behind at Kilveen while the rest of us went slowly mad on Haskurlay.'

'And who were they?'

'You, Chipchase, Fripp, Gregson and Judd. We swapped you and Chipchase for Tancred and me in the doctored version of Maynard's statement. Well, Marcus did the swapping, actually. And the rest of the doctoring. He knows – *knew* – his way round a computer far better than I do.'

'Why you and Tancred?'

'Because he's the only other member of the Haskurlay party still alive, unless you count Babcock. With Tancred off the list, it made it look as if you'd been rubbing them out one by one. I went out shooting rabbits alone that morning, according to Maynard. So, I was obviously in no position to deny shooting Hamish and Andrew Munro. There never was a pact of silence with anyone.'

'Why did you set fire to Askew's flat?'

'Frank broke in and found the disk. The fire was to destroy any hidden copies or other incriminating evidence. But there still remained the copy I felt more and more certain *you* had.'

'So then we got the arson treatment too.'

'The disk was more of a target than you or Chipchase. But we couldn't be sure it was destroyed in the fire. Besides, if you'd already read the statement . . .' Wiseman gave a heavy, regretful sigh. 'All you had to do was tolerate the police breathing down your necks for a while. They'd have given up eventually. Or the Secret Service would have called them off. But that was too easy, wasn't it? That was just too sensible. Instead, you decided to go after the truth in your own particular bull-headed, bloody-minded way. No wonder you and Chipchase used to be business partners. You're a well-matched pair – of fools.'

'Perhaps you should have explained it all to us, Magister. Then we'd have known the parts we were supposed to play. Simple, really. I'll make sure Barry appreciates that. If he ever regains consciousness.'

'So Frank got one of you, did he?'

'You could say so.'

'Good.'

Harry's instinct was to land a punch on Wiseman's grimly smiling face at that moment. He had turned on the bench and raised his arm to strike before the thinking portion of his brain intervened. There was more to be told yet. Wiseman would have to be humoured. For just a little longer.

'What a forbearing fellow you are, Ossie.' The smile faded.

'How much did you know about the plan to kill us along with Ailsa Redpath and Murdo Munro?'

'Everything. Except Marcus's active involvement. He told me Frank had brought in a man he'd worked with before to help him manage the thing. But the plan was Marcus's. I can only suppose he wanted to see it carried out . . . in the flesh. Then he'd have been able to . . . surprise me with his versatility.'

'Four more murders, Magister. Didn't that trouble your conscience?'

'It should trouble yours, not mine. It was a fall-back in case you contacted Ailsa Redpath. If you did, we reckoned that meant you'd read the statement and were determined to root out the truth. Leaving us no choice.'

'Bullshit. You had the *choice* of facing up to what you'd done. Or at least of not making it any worse.'

'Easy for you to say.'

'You'd never have gone to prison for what you did on Haskurlay. There were extenuating circumstances galore.'

'Not for killing Askew, there weren't.'

'No. Not for that.'

'And one thing does tend to lead to another. I like to finish what I start.'

'Well, congratulations. It's finished now.'

'Is it?'

'Even if we'd all been killed as planned, you'd still have lost Marcus. Frank shot him in cold blood. He had his *own* plan. And your wellbeing wasn't part of it. He'd have come here today and taken your money and walked away and let you learn later that he'd murdered your son along with us.'

'Yes. He would have. I suppose that's the kind of risk you run when you deal with such people. Marcus wasn't . . . a good judge of others. He wasn't . . . a lot of things. But he *was* my son. Do you have children, Ossie?'

'A daughter.'

'No son?'

'I *had* a son. He died.'

'You know how I feel, then.'

'No. I don't. I don't have the remotest clue how you feel. I'm not sure you have feelings that the rest of us would recognize as normal at all.'

'I'm a respected man. Widely admired. Envied, even. Why should I have to give all that up at the say-so of a pipsqueak like Askew? Do you seriously think any of you spineless bastards would have stood by me if he'd had his way and—' Wiseman broke off and looked up at the sky. Grief had sapped his anger. It was a frail and transitory thing now. The sigh that followed was almost a moan. 'You're right. It's finished. More conclusively than you seem to imagine.'

'What do you mean?'

'I mean: what happens now?'

'They arrest you.'

'And then? Will I be charged? Tried? Convicted? Imprisoned?'

'Of course. As you should be.'

'"As I should be."' Wiseman chuckled mirthlessly. 'Naïvety

330

in a young man is excusable. In one of your age it's pitiful. I take it this conversation is being recorded?'

Harry nodded. It was pointless to deny it. 'Yes,' he said. 'It is.'

'For use in evidence against me. Naturally. Well, I think they have more than enough now, don't you? So, this last . . . observation . . . can remain strictly between ourselves.' Wiseman raised a cautionary finger to his lips, then leant close to Harry's ear and whispered a few words to him.

'*What*?'

'You heard.' Wiseman stood up, tossed the newspaper down on the bench and grabbed the briefcase. 'Let's go. It's time you turned me in.'

SIXTY-TWO

After Wiseman's arrest Harry was taken to the ground-floor office on the southern side of the square which had served as Knox's observation post. Wiseman was en route to Strathclyde Police HQ for questioning by then, having cast Harry an enigmatic glance of farewell through the window of the squad car as he was driven away. The operation had ended in the smooth success Knox had confidently anticipated. He shook Harry by the hand in a congratulatory fashion. An air of quiet satisfaction hung over the comings and goings of the junior members of his team. All had ended well.

'Thank you for your assistance, Mr Barnett. It's been invaluable.'

'Am I free to go now?'

'Certainly. But it'd be appreciated if you could remain close at hand for a little longer. We might need to check a few things with you. This is a complicated case and no mistake.'

'How close?'

'I was thinking . . . here in Glasgow. We've booked you and your wife into a city-centre hotel for a couple of nights. Well, we don't need to hide you out at Milngavie now there's no danger of you bumping into our chief suspect before we're ready for him, do we? Your wife's already on her way to the hotel, as a matter of fact. A couple of Strathclyde WPCs met her off her flight. So, why don't you relax there? Visit your

332

friend in hospital. Maybe take in a few sights. We'll be in touch as soon as we need to be.'

'All right.'

'One thing, though. We couldn't pick up something Wiseman said to you. Just before you vacated the bench. From what I could see on the monitor, he seemed to be whispering into your ear.'

'He was.'

'And what did he whisper?'

'"I don't regret a thing,"' Harry lied. 'That's all.'

Harry phoned the hospital before leaving Blythswood Square to find out if there had been any change in Chipchase's condition. Why he expected to hear bad news he could not afterwards have explained; he was not pessimistic by nature. Whatever the reason, though, his expectation was confounded. 'There's been a big improvement overnight,' the sister informed him. 'Mr Chipchase is sitting up and taking notice. He'll probably be on a general ward before the end of the day. The doctor's very pleased with him.'

So it was that Harry was able to greet Donna at the Millennium Hotel with the broadest smile he had worn in many weeks, though not as broad as the one with which *she* greeted *him*.

'Hi, hon,' she said, hugging him close. 'Is it good to see you! There have been times this last couple of weeks—'

Harry silenced her with a kiss and gazed warmly into her eyes. 'Don't say it. I'm sorry for all the worry I've put you through. Let's leave it at that.'

'Leave it? You must be kidding. I want to hear every last detail.'

'And you will. But remember: it's over now. However hair-raising some of it may sound, it *is* over.'

'Thank the good Lord for that.'

Harry nodded. 'Amen.'

*   *   *

Two hours later, they were seated at Chipchase's hospital bedside. He had been moved from intensive care to a private room. A large bandage covered his head, which had been shaved prior to the craniotomy, and a drip was attached to a cannula in his right arm. In the circumstances, he had no right to look as well as, strangely, he did.

His memory of recent events, however, was patchy. 'A spot of amnesia's only to be expected, according to the doc.'

'There's a lot of it about,' said Harry with a smile. 'I'll fill you in on the ins and outs of our latest exploits next time I come in.'

'But we *are* in the clear, right?'

'Absolutely.'

'Great. Now, what do you mean by "next time *I* come in"? Won't Donna be with you?'

'Do you want me to be?' Donna asked.

'Too bloody right I do, darlin'. I want you to see me a good bit closer to my normal irresistible self. Then Harry will really have something to worry about.' Chipchase winked. 'Know what I mean?'

'According to Marvin's researches, some of the US troops they *allegedly* experimented on with MRQS in the fifties tried to sue the Defense Department,' said Donna over an early lunch in a café back in the city centre. 'The action failed for lack of evidence, of course, but . . .'

'You think I should sue the MoD?'

'No. But there's bound to be hard evidence now for *some-one* to act on. Or there will be when Wiseman stands trial.'

'*If* he stands trial.'

'Why shouldn't he?'

'No reason. Except he doesn't expect to.'

'Pardon me?'

'It was almost the last thing he said to me before they arrested him. In a whisper, so they didn't pick it up on the microphone. "I'll never make it to court."'

'What made him say that?'

334

'I don't know. But if it's true he wasn't responsible for Dangerfield's death . . .'

'My God. They wouldn't do that, would they?'

'I'm not sure. But I'll tell you what I *am* sure of. Whatever happens to Wiseman – if anything does – I won't be challenging it. And I won't be suing anyone. It was difficult enough to get off this particular hook. I don't intend to do anything that might get me back on it.'

Relieved that Chipchase was on the mend and their shared troubles – bar a lot of no doubt time-consuming police paperwork – were over, Harry managed for the rest of the day to do just what Knox had recommended: he relaxed. Ordinarily, he would have pulled a face at Donna's suggestion of a visit to the Kelvingrove Art Gallery, such places tending to leave him weak at the ankles and yawning uncontrollably. But the prospect of strolling around anywhere with his wife was deliriously appealing after all he had been through. And she promised him they could go to a pub afterwards.

As fate would have it, the Kelvingrove was closed for refurbishment and they ended up in the Transport Museum on the other side of the road, where the vintage cars and venerable steam engines were actually of more interest to Harry than to Donna. As he explained to her later over a pint, it only confirmed what he was slowly coming to believe: his luck had changed at last.

Dinner at a good restaurant rounded off their day of unlooked-for contentment, marred only slightly by the knowledge that another parting was not far off. Donna would have to return to Vancouver as soon as possible to appease her ireful head of department. A week or so at least seemed likely to pass before Harry could join her. But this time, he promised, he would be accepting no out-of-the-blue invitations to far-flung get-togethers. This time, he would be caution personified.

'It's the quiet life for me after this, Donna. For *us*.'

'Not *too* quiet, I hope.'

'Unlikely, with Daisy around.'

'She's missed you.'

'And *I've* missed *her*. But we'll all be together soon.'

'I'll drink to that.' Donna raised her glass.

And Harry raised his. 'Cheers.'

The bedside telephone roused Harry shortly before eight o'clock the following morning. It had been a late night – and a delightfully energetic one. A long lie-in was what Harry's sluggish thought processes told him he needed. But the telephone did not stop ringing. A glance at Donna revealed her to be out for the count. He grabbed the receiver.

'Hello?' he said in a sandpapery *sotto voce.*

'Gretchen at the front desk here, Mr Barnett,' trilled a birdsong-bright female voice. 'Sorry to disturb you, but there's a lady in reception who wants to speak to you. She says it's very important.'

'Who is she?'

'Her name's Rawson. Erica Rawson.'

Ah, Erica. Of course. Why had he not anticipated this? He rubbed his eyes and tried to concentrate, wondering whether his change of luck might not be as wholesale as he had fondly imagined.

'Mr Barnett?'

'Tell Miss Rawson I'll be right down.'

SIXTY-THREE

There was no sign of Erica in reception. Gretchen pointed helpfully towards the main entrance. 'She said she'd wait outside, Mr Barnett.'

'Thanks.' Harry plodded out apprehensively into a cool, leaden-skied morning. The Millennium Hotel fronted onto George Square, focal point of the city, round which rush-hour traffic was currently roaring. Erica was standing on the opposite side of the street from Harry, near the pelican crossing adjacent to the hotel. She was dressed in tracksuit and trainers, had her hands on her hips and was gazing expectantly in his direction.

She continued to study him as he waited for the crossing light to change in his favour. Harry struggled to put the brief interval this gave him for tactical deliberation to good use, but found his thoughts still fogged by the rudeness of his awakening. He had left a note for Donna: *Gone for a stroll. Back soon. Order breakfast.* That had sounded good to him and still did. But breakfast was already beginning to seem a distant and uncertain prospect. Yet Erica was alone. And George Square was as public a place as Harry could wish for. There was surely no threat to him. He felt marginally less anxious than when he left his room.

The traffic slowed to a halt. The green man lit up. Harry crossed. 'Good morning,' he said neutrally. 'Come a long way?'

'Haven't we both?' Erica nodded towards the hotel. 'Does Donna know you're meeting me?'

'Not yet. She's still asleep.'

'Jet lag?'

'It's just early, Erica. Unless you're a working girl.'

'Which I am. But you're right. It *is* early. As you can see, I was caught on the hop myself.'

'Caught by what?'

'Let's get away from this din.'

The light had changed back in favour of the traffic by then and a retreat from the noise was welcome. They headed into the centre of the square, dominated by Glasgow's answer to Nelson's Column – a statue of Sir Walter Scott perched on a lofty pillar – and commenced a slow circuit round the plinth at its base.

'I thought we should have a word before the police contacted you. They've told me what happened yesterday.'

'I'm sure they have.'

'But this morning . . . there was an unexpected development.'

'Oh yes?'

'Wiseman was found dead in his cell a couple of hours ago.'

Harry said nothing. There was nothing he *could* say.

'You don't seem very surprised.'

'I've had lot of surprises lately. Maybe I'm developing an immunity.'

'They think it was a heart attack. There'll have to be a post mortem, obviously.'

'Obviously.'

'He may have had an ongoing heart condition, of course. But then a man of his age would be under a lot of stress in such a situation even if he was in perfect health.'

'Oh yes. Men of his age can find all sorts of situation stressful.'

'You seem to have coped pretty well with recent events. But then you've had more experience than most of such things.'

'Have I?'

'There's a file on you, Harry. Not such a slim one either. I've taken a look at it. Interesting reading. Very interesting.'

'Perhaps I should ask to see it myself. Under the Freedom of Information Act.'

'I wouldn't if I were you.'

'No?'

'How's Barry?'

'Getting better, thanks.'

'Good.'

There was a momentary silence between them. Then Harry said, 'Well, it was . . . kind of you to bring me the news . . . about Wiseman.'

'Not really. But I have been kind to you. Kinder than you know. Let me explain how things stand. With Wiseman dead, there'll be no trial. No trial, no publicity. Operation Clean Sheet stays forgotten. That's how we'd like it to be. That's how it can be. If you behave sensibly. And Barry too, of course. I'll assume you speak for him in this. I can guarantee all the police investigations involving you will be dropped. You'll be able to go back to Canada and your life with Donna and Daisy. And Barry will be able to go back to . . . whatever he does best. Provided you agree to accept the *status quo*, that is. Provided you undertake not to rock the boat. Make waves and there's a danger you may drown in them. Which would be regrettable. And unnecessary. When you have so much to live for.'

'I have, yes.'

'I've read the transcript of your conversation with Wiseman. My interpretation of your comments immediately following his denial of responsibility for Dangerfield's death is that you didn't believe him. Is that correct?'

'Absolutely.' It was the lie that had to be told. Dangerfield, fair-minded fellow that he was, would have understood why. But, still, it was a hard thing to have to do. Harry silently tendered his old comrade a heartfelt apology.

'Good. And Chief Inspector Knox tells me the unrecorded remark Wiseman made to you towards the end of the conversation was actually "I don't regret a thing". Is that also correct?'

'It is.'

'You're never likely to present some other version?'

'I'll stick to what I told Knox. There'll be no other version. Ever.'

'Good.'

'Mind if *I* ask a few questions?'

'Please do.'

'Has Dr Starkie gone home yet?'

'No. But he will soon. Very soon.'

'And Ailsa Redpath? What's going to happen to her?'

'Nothing. The Procurator Fiscal will conclude she killed the man calling himself Frank in a legitimate act of self-defence. He'll also conclude, in the light of this morning's development, that no purpose would be served by a continuing investigation of the circumstances surrounding the events of two days ago.'

'That's neat.'

'I'm glad you approve.'

'And the others. Fripp, Gregson, Judd and Tancred. They'll be . . . left to get on with their lives?'

'Everyone will, Harry. As long as you let them.'

'Me? You've nothing to worry about there. I've always been a live-and-let-live sort of bloke.'

'That's what I thought.'

They halted, facing the hotel. Pedestrians passed them en route across the square. The traffic continued to surge round it. A flight of pigeons lifted off from the war memorial away to their right. The world went on moving. 'Tell me, Erica,' Harry said slowly, 'is MRQS still being used?'

'Not as such.'

'What does that mean?'

'I think you should be getting back now. But before you do . . .' She unzipped a pocket in her tracksuit top and took out two passports, held together by a rubber band. 'Returned by the Grampian police. Your passport – and Barry's.'

Harry took them from her outstretched hand. And waited for the answer to his question that he suspected he was never going to get.

Erica smiled. '*That* means you're free to go.'

SIXTY-FOUR

The funeral of Murdo Munro took place on Vatersay a week later. Harry was the only mourner who was neither a relative nor an islander. Ailsa had asked him to attend if he could, though her husband's demeanour suggested he would have preferred him to stay away. Others may have felt the same. Dougie McLeish for one shot him several disapproving glances as the coffin was lowered into the ground. Nothing was actually said, though. Even by McLeish.

Much would be said later, of course. The rumour mill would grind on, probably for years. Harry knew that. He also knew that attending the gathering held afterwards in Vatersay's community hall would not be the smartest of moves. Murdo's friends were aware that a great deal was being kept from them about the circumstances of his death. They did not need Harry's company to remind them of the fact.

Ailsa was to some degree in the same position as Harry, though granted special consideration as the sister of the deceased and only surviving child of the late lamented Hamish. This, she explained when she drove Harry up to the airport in good time for his flight back to Glasgow, was the real reason why she had pressed him to come in the first place.

'You're the only person who experienced it all with me,' she said, as they crossed the causeway to Barra. 'I'm holding out on people to greater or lesser degrees and they know it.

342

Aunts, uncles, cousins, old friends of the family. Even my own children. I tell them so much and no more. It's in their own interests, of course, but . . .'

'It rankles.'

'It does. With them *and* me. There's no alternative. I realize that. And Iain agrees. I've told *him* everything. As I assume you have your wife. Does she feel the same way?'

'Yes. Let sleeping dogs lie seems to be the general consensus.'

'Sleeping dogs – or dead ones.'

'What has Knox told you about Wiseman's death?'

'Heart failure. A congenital weakness, apparently.'

'Congenital – and convenient.'

'Quite.'

Wiseman's death was of course even more convenient than Ailsa knew, since it ensured no-one would need to ask awkward questions about who else might have killed Dangerfield – and why. But Harry had no intention of mentioning that aspect of the affair, so it seemed safer to change the subject. 'Will you keep the croft in the family?' he asked.

'No, no. We'll let it go. There'll be nothing to bring me back here now. And in the circumstances . . .'

'That may be best.'

'Yes. It may.'

Harry had spent the previous night at the Heathbank Hotel, close to the airport and diplomatically distant from Castlebay. They stopped there to collect his bag. The cycle of the tides had shifted flights to and from Barra into the afternoon since his last visit. The plane was not due to depart for Glasgow until 4.15, leaving him with time on his hands. Ailsa was in no hurry to return to Vatersay. It was clear to Harry, indeed, that she was glad of any excuse not to. She drove him out past the airport to a beach at the far northern end of the island, where they strolled across an empty expanse of white sand beneath a wide blue sky mirrored in the glassy plane of the ocean.

'Good weather for a landing on Haskurlay,' said Ailsa, after they had walked in silence for several minutes.

'Will you ever go there again?'

'I'm not sure.'

'I saw a photograph at the house of the three of you as children on a trip to the island with your father. You all looked . . . very happy.'

'That photograph is how I'd like to remember it. And them. And maybe I can. If I stay away. Ironically, of course, *you've* never been there.'

'No. Though if Wiseman had had his way . . .'

'Why did he do it? Killing Father and Andrew in a panic was . . . almost pardonable. But cold-bloodedly commissioning the murder of several of his old comrades fifty years later . . . How could he bring himself to do *that*?'

'As far as he made any sense on the subject to me, it came down to pride and vanity. He couldn't stomach the shame of admitting what he'd done. And it seems he never thought of us as his comrades in any true sense. We were just . . . problems he hired Frank to solve for him.'

'But in the process . . . he lost his own son. Poetic justice, I suppose. Blood for blood.'

'Is that how it seems to you?'

'No, Harry. It just seems like a madness that's run its course. And for that at least . . . I'm grateful.'

Half an hour later, they were standing in the airport car park next to the terminal building, watching the small Twin Otter touch down on the broad, flat sands of Traigh Mhor. Soon, Harry would be on his way. Soon, very soon, he would be leaving this tranche of his past far behind.

'Has your wife gone home yet?' Ailsa asked as the plane taxied across the beach towards them.

'Last weekend. Duty called, I'm afraid.'

'When will you join her?'

'Tomorrow.'

'Will you see Barry before you leave?'

'Oh yes. We're meeting for a farewell drink before I fly out.'

'Is he up to that?'

'Apparently. He's been convalescing with his ex-wife in Swindon. I think he's feeling better than he's letting on, actually, for fear she'll turf him out. Which she will do, of course. Eventually.'

'What will he do then?'

'I don't know. I don't suppose he knows either.'

'Insecurity at his age can be difficult to cope with.'

'True. But like he said to me before he left hospital, it's better than oblivion. He could easily have died on that boat. We all could have. So . . .'

'We'd better enjoy everything life has to offer.' Ailsa beamed at Harry. 'Hadn't we?'

SIXTY-FIVE

While Chipchase had been recuperating at Jackie's house in Swindon, Harry had visited his own ex-wife, Zohra, and her growing family, in Newcastle. He had also spent a few days with his – and Zohra's – former landlady, Mrs Tandy, in Kensal Green. He was, quite consciously, taking his leave of those he was fondest of in the land of his birth. With his mother dead and his old home destroyed, there was no telling when – or even if – he would be back.

The final farewell promised in its way to be the most poignant, manfully though both he and Chipchase would strive to disguise the fact. Harry stayed overnight with Mrs Tandy following his late return to London from Barra and took the train to Swindon the following morning. It had been arranged that he and Chipchase would fit in a couple of hours in the Glue Pot before Jackie drove Harry to Heathrow for his 4.30 flight to Vancouver.

This, then, was the end of many things. It could not be helped. It was bound to be. Harry belonged elsewhere now, happily so. Yet still his heart was heavy as he left Swindon station and headed west past the boundary wall of the GWR engineering works that were no more towards the Railway Village – and 37 Falmouth Street, that was also no more.

An inspection of the fenced-off gap between numbers 35 and 39 was an experience he intended for the moment to spare himself. Instead, he retraced his steps of three weeks before, across the park and up past his old primary school to Radnor Street Cemetery.

One happy consequence of the misadventures that had come his way during those weeks was that his return to Vancouver had been delayed long enough for him to be able to admire the re-erected and additionally inscribed headstone on the grave where his mother had so recently been buried, all of sixty-seven years after his father.

STANLEY REGINALD BARNETT
1905–1938
ALSO HIS LOVING WIFE
IVY ELIZABETH BARNETT, NÉE TIMMS
1912–2005
REUNITED

'I hope your reunion up there went better than the one I got talked into attending down here, Mother,' Harry murmured as he stood at the foot of the grave. 'It can't have gone worse and that's a fact. But I'm OK. Which you'd probably say is the main thing.'

Harry's route from the cemetery enabled him to reach the Glue Pot without traversing Falmouth Street or even glancing along it. Later, after a suitable infusion of Dutch courage, he reckoned he might be up to taking a look at the burnt-out remains of the house he had been born in. He might even ask Jackie to drive round that way. Then again, he might not. He would have to see how he felt when the time came.

Chipchase was already installed in the pub and had been for a little while to judge by the inroads he had made into a pint of beer, not to mention the amount of cigarette smoke hanging in the air. It was barely past noon and there were only a few other customers. A tranquil atmosphere prevailed, sunlight shafting hazily through the windows, the past readily conjurable in surroundings that were for Harry instantly and intimately familiar.

'They've still got the Monkey's Revenge on,' said Chipchase, who looked less like an invalid now his head was unbandaged, but rather more like an escapee from a chain gang thanks to the partial regrowth of his hair. 'I've put one in for you.'

'I thought you said you were feeling fine.'

'I am.'

'You can't be if you're paying for the first round.'

'Ha-bloody-ha.' The freshly pulled pint was plonked in front of Harry by the barman. 'Get that down your neck and stop being so sarky.'

'Cheers.' Harry smiled and savoured a first swallow of beer. 'That's good.'

'Let's park ourselves over there.' Chipchase slid off his bar stool and led the way to a settle just inside the door.

'You're sure you *are* fine, aren't you?' Harry asked after they had sat down. 'Joking apart.'

'Not according to the doc. He says I'm killing myself with booze and fags. But apparently they're likely to be the culprits when I snuff it, not that bash on the bonce I gave myself. So, yeah, old Chipchase is officially as close to tip-top as he's ever going to get.'

'Delighted to hear it.'

'There have been times when you might have preferred to hear I was sinking fast.'

'There have been times when I had every right to feel that way. But after all we've been through together these last few weeks . . .'

'Don't tell me I'm back in your good books at long bloody last.'

'I wouldn't go that far. But I'm definitely willing to let bygones be bygones.'

'Is that all I get for laying my life on the line for you? Bloody hell, Barnett, you're a hard man.'

'I'm a pushover and you know it.'

'*Bygones.*' Chipchase stubbed out his cigarette, quaffed some beer and glanced around the bar. He grew suddenly thoughtful. 'Well, there are more than a few of ours linked to this place.'

'That there are.'

A minute or so of reflective silence passed. Memories, remote as well as recent, crowded in around them. Then Chipchase said, 'But let's not start wallowing in nostalgia. Look ahead, not behind. That's always been my motto. Even if just lately the view in either direction hasn't been exactly mouth-watering.'

'Made any plans?'

'For the future, you mean?'

'Well . . .'

'I applied the old brainbox to the problem while I was laid up, since you ask.'

'And?'

'Drew a total bloody blank.'

'Oh.'

'Then . . .'

'What?'

'I had a stroke of luck.' Chipchase grinned. 'Yes, Harry old cock. Looks like I might not be a complete bloody write-off after all.'

'How come?'

'You might at least have the decency to look less surprised. My losing streak was bound to end sooner or later.'

'OK. But *how* did it end?'

'Well, while you were in Barra, Shona came down to see me. Wanted to check I was all right. She'd been worried about me, apparently, which was good to hear.'

'I was meaning to ask. Did you and she ever . . .' Harry's raised eyebrows supplied their own question mark.

'Mind your own and stop interrupting. The point is that Shona's suddenly able to afford things like a spur-of-the-bloody-moment trip from Aberdeen to darkest Wilts because Danger left her a little something in his will, soft-hearted old bugger that he was.'

'He did?'

349

'Maybe more than a little. She was a bit coy about the exact number of noughts. Anyway, she's decided to use the spondulicks to start her own business. She talked the idea over with Jackie. Evidently sees her as some kind of role model. They got on like a house on fire.' Chipchase grimaced. 'Bloody hell. Sorry, Harry. I could have put that better, couldn't I?'

'Never mind. What is this business?'

'A guesthouse – well, small hotel, really – in St Andrews. She wants to get out of Aberdeen and reckons Fife is the area to aim for. Probably hopes that shiftless git of a son will refuse to go with her. *I* certainly hope so.'

'Why should it matter to you?' Harry asked innocently.

'Because Shona will need someone to help her run the place. Someone . . . mature, far-sighted, adaptable—'

'*You*?'

Chipchase smirked. 'I'm on a shortlist of one.'

'Bloody hell.'

'Not bad, hey? Not bloody bad at all.'

'I don't know what to say.'

'Congratulations would fit the bill. Well played, old sport. Something along those lines.'

'But . . . St Andrews? Isn't that the mecca of golf?'

'So?'

'You hate golf. And golfers.'

'True. But taking money *off* golfers is a different bunch of bananas altogether. I could get seriously used to that. And just think of the scope I'll have for dangling juicy investment opportunities in front of our golf-crazy, cash-laden guests.' Chipchase finished his beer in a single gulp. 'Let the good times roll. Again.'

Harry laughed. He could not help himself. It was a laugh of genuine pleasure.

'What's so funny?'

'Life, Barry. Just life.'

'Full of ups and bloody downs in my experience. *And* yours. It's best to enjoy the ups while you can, Harry old cock.'

'I'll drink to that.' Harry drained his glass. 'My round, I think.'

'Same again for me.'

'Maybe we should switch to something weaker.' Harry stood up, empty glasses in hand. 'This stuff isn't exactly a session ale, is it?'

'Depends what kind of session you want.' Chipchase clamped a celebratory cigar between his teeth and winked. 'It's up to you.'

ACKNOWLEDGEMENT

I am very grateful to John Brooks for sharing with me his memories of life in the Royal Air Force. Needless to say, his experiences bore no resemblance whatsoever to those of Aircraftmen Barnett and Chipchase.